Passion
in gla...

Three complete no...
be...

MIRANDA LEE

*B*illionaire
Bachelors

'Miranda Lee's *A Rich Man's Revenge* delivers
hot, hot sex scenes, volatile characters and a
good blend of emotions.'
—*Romantic Times*

'Fans of Miranda Lee will be delighted with her
latest, with its very hot and sexy characters.'
—*Romantic Times* on *Mistress for a Month*

'Miranda Lee once again pens a scorcher.
Underneath the sexy tale and sizzling scenes is a
tender romance with emotional characters.'
—*Romantic Times* on *Sold to the Sheikh*

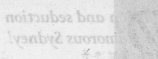

Billionaire Bachelors

MIRANDA LEE

featuring

A RICH MAN'S REVENGE
MISTRESS FOR A MONTH
SOLD TO THE SHEIKH

*M&B™ and M&B™ with the Rose Device
are trademarks of the publisher.
Harlequin Mills & Boon Limited, Eton House,
18-24 Paradise Road, Richmond, Surrey TW9 1SR*

BILLIONAIRE BACHELORS © by Harlequin Books SA 2007

A Rich Man's Revenge, Mistress for a Month and *Sold to the Sheikh*
were first published in Great Britain in separate, single volumes.

A Rich Man's Revenge © Miranda Lee 2003
Mistress for a Month © Miranda Lee 2003
Sold to the Sheikh © Miranda Lee 2003

ISBN: 978 0 263 85845 7

024-0707

*Printed and bound in Spain
by Litografia Rosés S.A., Barcelona*

A RICH MAN'S REVENGE

MIRANDA LEE

Miranda Lee is Australian, living near Sydney. Born and raised in the bush, she was boarding-school educated and briefly pursued a career in classical music, before moving to Sydney and embracing the world of computers. Happily married, with three daughters, she began writing when family commitments kept her at home. She likes to create stories that are believable, modern, fast-paced and sexy. Her interests include meaty sagas, doing word puzzles, gambling and going to the movies.

CHAPTER ONE

"Do you have to play poker *every* Friday night, come rain, hail or shine?"

Charles glanced in the mirror at the reflection of the very beautiful blonde lying face down across his bed, her glorious golden hair spread out over her slender shoulders, her delicately pointed chin propped up in her hands. Her eyes, which were as big and blue as the sky, locked on to his, their expression beseeching.

Charles hesitated only slightly before continuing to button up his grey silk shirt. As much as the idea of joining her back on that bed was very tempting, his Friday-night poker game was non-negotiable.

"My poker buddies and I made a pact some time back," he explained. "If we're in Sydney on a Friday night, we have to show up. Actually, if we're in *Australia*, we have to show up. We can only cancel if we're overseas or in hospital. Although when Rico was in hospital after a skiing accident last winter, he insisted we all come and play in his room."

Charles smiled wryly to himself as he thought of his best friend and his mad passion for the game. "I suspect on the unlikely event of Rico marrying again he'd ask us to accompany him on the honeymoon, just to get his weekly fix. I, however, was more than happy to give up poker during the entire month of *my* honeymoon,'' he pointed out rather smugly.

"Your wife would have been seriously displeased if you hadn't."

"Would she?" He turned and smiled down at her. "How displeased?"

"*Very* displeased."

"And are you displeased tonight, Mrs Brandon?"

She shrugged, then rolled over onto her back, stretching languorously against the ivory satin sheets, her hands lifting up over her head to flop against the side of the king-sized bed. Charles tried not to look at her simply perfect body. But it was difficult not to wallow in her physical beauty. Dominique was every man's fantasy come true. And she was all his.

Charles still could not believe his luck in winning the hand—and the love—of such a glorious creature.

And Dominique *did* love him. He'd dated enough fortune hunters in the past to know the real thing when he found it.

Dominique sighed as she glanced up at him through her long lashes. "I suppose I can spare you for a few hours. I'm going to have to get used to being by myself, anyway, since you're going back to work next Monday."

Back to work…

Charles groaned at the thought, which was a first. For the past twenty years he'd devoted his life to the family brewery business after it had been brought to the brink of bankruptcy by his profligate father. And he'd loved every difficult, challenging, frustrating moment.

From the age of twenty to forty he'd lived and breathed Brandon Beer. Marriage and a family had been relegated to the back-burner as he'd gone from being a near penniless undergraduate to one of Australia's most successful businessmen, putting Brandon Beer back on the world map and buying half a dozen Sydney hotels along the way, each of which now earned him a sizeable fortune from the recent addition of poker machines.

Since meeting and marrying Dominique, however, business had taken a back seat in Charles's life. His mind had been focused on things other than investment opportunities, market projections and expansion programmes. Even now, with the honeymoon over, his focus remained on things other than work.

The prospect of starting a family in the near future excited him almost as much as did the woman he planned having that family with. Dominique wanted at least two children and had decided to stop taking the Pill next month, which pleased him no end, as did her decision not to go back to work herself after their honeymoon. She'd quit her job in the PR department at Brandon Beer's head office shortly after she'd said yes to his proposal, saying she didn't feel right, working there any more.

Charles was well aware, however, that with her looks and personality Dominique could secure another PR or PA job in Sydney at the drop of a hat. And he'd said as much, not wanting her to think he was the kind of chauvinistic husband who expected his wife not to work.

But she'd said no to that suggestion, stating that for the next few years her career was being his wife, and the mother of his children. Maybe, when their last child went off to school, she would consider returning to the workforce.

Whilst not believing himself an old-fashioned man in any way, Charles had to confess he liked the thought of his wife always being there for him when he got home from work, ready to accommodate his every wish and whim, something which didn't seem to be any hardship for her.

"I'm going to miss you terribly," she said somewhat plaintively. "Are you quite sure you have to go back to work on Monday?" she asked, then gave him one of the best come-hither looks since Eve flashed that apple at Adam.

Charles's flesh responded accordingly. He didn't doubt he could survive being away from Dominique for a few hours this evening, but the prospect of not being able to make love to her during the day whenever he felt like it in future was not to his liking. Honeymoons were obviously very corrupting, as were beautiful brides who never said no to whatever their husbands wanted to do.

"I suppose I could take another week off," he said, thinking to himself that the office would survive another five days without his making a personal appearance. He could keep in touch by phone and email. "It would give us some time to look for our new house together." He'd told Dominique to look around for a real home to replace his present penthouse pad, something substantial and stylish in one of the Eastern suburbs. He didn't want to negotiate the harbour bridge on his way to the office every day.

Dominique beamed at him. "What a wonderful idea! But would you really? Take another week off work, I mean? I know your reputation for being a workaholic."

His eyes were rueful as they met Dominique's in the mirror. "You know I'd do just about anything you asked me to." Anything except give up any more of his Friday-night poker games.

His shirt safely buttoned, he turned and braced himself on the mattress on either side of her upside down face. "But you already know that, don't you?" he murmured, his mouth hovering just above hers. "You've bewitched me good and proper."

"Have I?" Her voice went all soft and smoky in that way which always turned him on. Charles groaned. It was incredible, really, given he was nearly forty-one years old, not some young buck in his prime. His desire for Dominique sometimes bordered on insatiable. Charles had never known a woman like her. Or a love like the love he felt for her. It was all-consuming. Possessive. Obsessive, even.

Her hands lifted to touch him, her eyebrows arching. ''Mmm. Charles darling, I can't see you concentrating on cards in such a deplorable condition. Surely your poker buddies wouldn't mind if you were just a teensie weensie bit late…''

He ached to give in to her. But feared that once she started on him, he wouldn't want to stop. If he didn't show up at poker tonight, Rico would have his hide.

No. He'd have to be strong and not let Dominique have her wicked way with him this once.

Which perhaps was just as well. Always getting your own way was never good for anyone, but especially a wife, he imagined. He'd already spoiled Dominique shockingly since she'd become Mrs Charles Brandon. He'd spent a small fortune on designer fashion during their fortnight in Paris. And quite a bit on Italian handmade shoes and other accessories during their stopover in Rome.

But enough was enough. Now that their honeymoon was technically over, he really had to start the day-to-day routine of his marriage as he meant to go on. And he meant to go on playing poker every Friday night.

''On the contrary, my sweet,'' Charles said with a wry smile as he pulled back out of her reach. ''Redirected sexual energies can be very effective. Frustration gives a man an edge. That's why boxers abstain the night before they fight. I guarantee I'll win at the table tonight, and when I finally get home so will you, my love. Now, do stop trying to seduce me, wench. Cover yourself up with a sheet or something till I can get myself out of here. That body of yours should be registered as a lethal weapon.''

She laughed, and rolled over onto her front again. ''Will that do?''

''Better, I guess.'' Though goodness knew her rear view was almost as tantalising as her front. He loved the way her spine curved down her long, slender back, dipping in at her tiny waist before rising to disappear between her peach-shaped behind. Like the rest of her, there was nothing even remotely boyish about Dominique's bottom. It was lush and pouty and perfect. A temptation of the most devilish kind.

Charles knew he wasn't the sort of man most women lusted after on sight. Never had been. As a teenager, girls hadn't looked at him twice. He hadn't fared much better as a young man. Of course, once he became seriously rich it was amazing how many gorgeous girls suddenly found him irresistible. But whilst his looks had improved considerably with age, one could still never call him handsome. Not in the way his father had been handsome. Or Rico. They were both movie-star material. So, Charles had often suspected some of his lady-friends had an eye on his money, rather than being genuinely attached or attracted to him.

Yes, the mirror told Charles the truth when he shaved every morning. He was now a passably attractive man, his main physical assets being his height, his fitness and that inherited gene which meant he'd never lose his full head of thick dark brown hair.

Baldness did not run in the Brandon family.

Of course, Charles had to concede that his successes in life had leant a certain air to the way he conducted himself nowadays. Some financial journalists described him as impressive and imposing. Others inclined towards ruthless and arrogant.

He didn't care what they wrote and said about him, really. Or even what the mirror told him. All that mattered was what Dominique saw when she looked at him.

Clearly, she found him attractive enough. *Very* attractive, actually. She'd confessed to him on their wedding night that her first emotion on meeting him was worry over how incredibly sexy she found him.

Charles could still remember the intense emotion which consumed *him* when he had first come face to face with his future wife. Rico had insisted it was just lust, but Charles knew differently. He knew he'd fallen in love at first sight.

The occasion was the company Christmas party last year, barely five months ago. Dominique had just started work at Brandon Beer that week after moving to Sydney from Melbourne. They hadn't met prior to the party, though he'd been aware of her appointment to their PR division. He'd seen—and approved—her CV.

He knew she was twenty-eight years old, a Tasmanian by birth, with no fancy education or degree to her credit, but a string of night-school diplomas which showed the sort of hard work and drive he admired. Her previous position in Melbourne had been with a sports and entertainment management company, her first job as a personal PA. To the boss of the place, no less. She'd been with him over two years and the reference he'd supplied was glowing. Prior to that she'd worked in reception and guest relations at some quality Melbourne hotels, a step up from her first job of being a housemaid.

Charles had been informed by the man who'd hired her that she was a very good-looking blonde, but seeing Ms Dominique Cooper in the flesh had literally taken his breath away.

She'd been wearing white, he recalled. A calf-length dress with a deep V-neckline which displayed her fabulous figure. Her hair had been up, tiny tendrils kissing her elegantly long neck. Her full lips had been shiny and pink. Pearl drops had dangled from her ears. When he drew closer, his nostrils had been filled with her perfume, an exotic and provocative scent which he now knew was called Casablanca.

He'd asked her out within minutes of being introduced, his desire already at fever pitch. Charles was used to getting his own way with women by then, so he'd been shocked by her refusal, especially when she admitted on further questioning that she wasn't seeing anyone else at the time. She'd told him politely but firmly that she would never date her boss, no matter how attractive she thought he was.

''So you do think I'm attractive,'' he countered, flattered yet frustrated at the same time.

She gave him an oddly nervous look, whirled on her high heels and fled the party.

Smitten and intrigued, he pursued her doggedly over the Christmas and New Year break, ringing her at home every evening and sending flowers to her flat every day—her number and address were in the personnel files at work—till she finally agreed to a dinner date. She still insisted he meet her at the restaurant rather than pick her up. She did not want him taking her home afterwards, which intrigued him further. Clearly, she was afraid to be alone with him. Why?

He didn't find out why till dessert, when she'd explained with quite touching agitation that she'd been foolish enough to date her last boss, then been even more foolish in becoming his secret mistress. He'd promised her the world, but in the end had dumped her and married some society girl with the right connections. That was why she'd moved to Sydney, to get right away from the awful memories, at the same time deciding that she would never again date her boss. Such men could not be trusted. They used silly girls like her because they were pretty and easily impressed. But they didn't love them, or marry them. They just screwed them, and screwed up their lives.

Charles set out to prove her wrong, but she was very difficult to convince. She did accept further invitations to dinner with him and showed him in many incredibly sweet ways that she liked him a lot, but she continued to spurn any advances. Charles became even more enamoured, and vowed to show her that his feelings for her were above board.

He could still remember the look on her face when he told her over dinner one night in early March that he loved her more than words could say. But when he asked her to marry him, producing the most beautiful—and the most expensive—diamond ring he'd been able to buy, her shock quickly turned to disgust.

"You don't mean that," she retorted. "You're just saying it to get me into bed. You think you can buy my love, but you've wasted your money on that rock because the pathetic truth is I've *already* fallen in love with you. I was going to go to bed with you tonight, anyway."

He wasn't able to contain his delight at this announcement. *Or* his desire. He'd never been so hard.

"Oh, just put the rotten thing on my finger if it makes you feel better," she swept on irritably. "Then take me to wherever it is you have in mind to take me. But you and I both know you won't go through with any wedding. After you've had what you want, you'll dump me like my last boss."

"You're wrong," he insisted passionately as he slipped the sparkling rock on her engagement finger.

And he proved her wrong by marrying her a month later without having so much as laid a finger on her. The kiss he gave her after their very small and unostentatious ceremony was their first proper kiss. It had been sheer and utter hell to control himself for so long but he'd managed by focusing on the big picture.

Rico called him insane, marrying a woman he hadn't been intimate with before. A strange sentiment for a man of Italian heritage. Weren't they into virgin brides? Not that Dominique was a virgin. She'd never pretended to be.

But there was a touchingly virginal air about her when she came to him on their wedding night, trembling in her white satin nightgown. Clearly, she was nervous, afraid perhaps that she'd made a big mistake herself, marrying a man *she'd* never been intimate with. For all she knew he could have been the worst lover in the world!

But their wedding night was magic for both of them. Sheer magic. When he witnessed his new bride's awed joy, his own pleasure and satisfaction was boundless.

"I didn't know what real love was till this moment," Dominique had told him as she lay still snuggled up to him somewhere close to dawn. "I love you so much, Charles. I'd die if you ever stopped loving me back."

Impossible, he'd thought at the time. And he still thought the same. If anything, he was more in love with her than ever. *He'd* be the one who'd die if *she* ever stopped loving *him.*

"I have to go," he told her gently, feeling slightly guilty for leaving her alone now. "I'll try not to stay too late, but—"

"Yes, I know," she broke in with a sigh. "I understand. Rico will try to keep you there till all hours."

Dominique clenched her teeth at the thought of Charles's best man doing just that. And it had nothing to do with Rico being a poker addict.

Enrico Mandretti's scepticism over her love for Charles had been evident from their first meeting. Clearly, he thought her a devious fortune hunter. He didn't have to spell out his suspicions. They were there in his dark, cynical eyes.

The trouble was...he was right. Yet oh, so wrong.

She *did* love Charles. More than she'd ever thought herself capable of loving any man. But before she'd met her future husband she'd been exactly what Rico believed she was. A gold-digger. A good-looking girl using her looks and her body to achieve her main goal in life: to acquire a wealthy husband, a gold-plated insurance policy that she would never have to suffer what her mother had suffered.

Dominique was sure that rich men's wives didn't go through what her mother had gone through. They were protected from such ignominies. They could at least die with dignity. That was, if they had to die at *all*.

After her mother's lingering and very painful death, Dominique had vowed that she would marry money, if it was the last thing she did. Becoming a rich man's wife, however, proved not such an easy task, not even for a girl with *her* looks. Rich men married women who moved in their own social circles. Or girls who worked with them; sophisticated, educated creatures with university degrees.

Unfortunately, Dominique's education had been sadly lacking during her teenage years, her schooling constantly interrupted then totally terminated so that she could stay home and nurse her mother till she passed away. By the time she was eighteen, Dominique knew it would take years before she had the skills which would put her into the immediate vicinity of wealthy businessmen.

But she had youth on her side, and tenacity, and she'd finally achieved her aim a couple of years back, that of being in the right place, working alongside the right kind of boss. Single. Good-looking. And rich.

Unfortunately, her target had been even more ruthless than she was. *His* life's plan did not include getting hitched to some no-account girl from the backwoods of Tasmania, no matter how hard she'd worked to educate herself, or how much he fancied her.

Sleeping with her was fine. Lying to her perfectly OK. Marrying her? Never in a million years!

After her mission to become Mrs Jonathon Hall had failed, a distressed and a slightly bitter Dominique had taken her over-generous severance pay along with Jonathon's guilt-ridden, glowing reference and headed for the bigger fish pond of Sydney. Once there, she'd plotted out her strategy for becoming Mrs

Charles Brandon with cold-blooded resolve. More cold-blooded than ever.

But there had been nothing cold-blooded about the feelings Charles had evoked in her during their first meeting. She'd already seen photographs of him and thought him quite attractive—Dominique knew she couldn't bear to marry a man who was physically repulsive to her—but she'd found Charles in the flesh so intensely sexy she'd been totally thrown.

Those icy grey eyes of his had cut right through her defences to that part of her which she'd kept locked tightly away all her life. Dominique had never fallen in love before. Or even into lust. She had felt varying degrees of attraction to members of the opposite sex over the years. She'd even slept with a few. Jonathon, she'd been *very* attracted to. Sex with him had been quite pleasurable, but she'd never been carried away by it, or really needed it. Oh, no. All her responses with Jonathon had been totally faked.

Yet when Charles had stared at her body none too subtly that first day, she'd found herself staring right back at his own tall, lean body and wanting it so very badly.

Panic best described her reaction to this alien craving. It was no wonder she had fled, totally abandoning her plan to seduce Charles Brandon. She wanted to *marry* a rich man, not fall in love with one. Love made a woman weak and foolish and vulnerable. Love brought misery, not happiness.

But Charles wouldn't leave it at that, would he?

And here she was, his wife; his adoring and besotted wife.

Now she knew what her mother had meant when Dominique had once asked her why she'd married a man like her wretched father.

"Because I loved him to death," had been her mother's reply.

Words of considerable irony.

As Dominique watched her husband put on his jacket, she tried not to worry about loving him so deeply. She supposed that with Charles she could afford to be a little weak and foolish and vulnerable. Because he loved her back. And he wasn't anything like Jonathon.

How perverse, she thought, that she'd targeted Charles for that very reason. Because he wasn't as young or as handsome as Jonathon. She'd thought that would make Charles more susceptible to seduction. She'd thought that would give her more power over him.

But just the opposite had happened. He'd been the one who'd exercised all the power over her, coercing her to go out with him, despite her fear of falling for him.

Yet she *was* happy, wasn't she? Deliriously so. There was nothing to be afraid of. Charles was a wonderful husband and lover. And he'd make a wonderful father.

That was another thing which constantly surprised Dominique. Her desire now for children. She'd never thought of herself as maternal before. Never wanted to be the little woman at home. Now she simply couldn't wait to have a baby with Charles. Not just one, either. Suddenly, her idea of Utopia was being his little woman at home with the patter of little feet around her.

Of course, her home would be nothing like her mother's home. Not a shack, but a mansion. *Her* husband was a man of substance who could provide in abundance for his wife and any number of children, not some pathetic failure of a man who couldn't even look after himself, let alone anyone else.

"I'm off now," Charles said as he swept up his cellphone and car keys from the bedside chest. "You know my number if you need me. Be good, now..." And he threw her a wry smile.

A premonition-type panic gripped her heart as she watched him walk towards the bedroom door.

"Charles!" she called out, and he turned, frowning.

"What is it?"

"Nothing. I...I love you."

"I know," he said, smiling again, a little smugly this time. "Keep it warm for me." And he left.

CHAPTER TWO

THE distance between Charles's inner-city apartment block and the Regency Hotel was only a couple of blocks, but Charles still drove. Walking was not his favourite form of exercise. Within five minutes of leaving Dominique, Charles was handing the keys of his silver Jaguar car to the parking attendant at the Regency and striding inside the five-star hotel.

Hurrying across the marble floor, he was passing the row of trendy and exclusive boutiques which lined the spacious arcade-style foyer when his eyes landed on a spectacular piece of jewelry, displayed under a spotlight in the window of Whitmores Opals. Charles ground to a halt and stared at the magnificent choker necklace which was made of two rows of oval-shaped milk opals surrounded by diamonds and linked together with finely filigreed gold.

How marvellous it would look on Dominique with her long, elegant neck and fair hair!

A glance at his watch showed it wasn't yet eight. He had twelve minutes before he was officially late. The shop was still open. These shops remained open till nine every Friday night.

The price was steep, of course. Quality jewels didn't come cheap. He tried telling himself that he really had to stop spoiling Dominique like this, but it was too late. He could already see her wearing it.

The decision made, Charles strode inside and five minutes later he had the necklace in his jacket pocket, nestled in a classy black leather box lined with thick black velvet. By the time he'd collected his visitor's pass-key from Reception and ridden the private lift up to the top floor, it was two minutes to eight. He still had a minute to spare as the lift doors whooshed back and the door to the presidential suite lay straight ahead.

When he'd first told Dominique where he played poker on a Friday night, she'd queried the choice of such an expensive venue. Why didn't they just go to each other's homes? So much cheaper.

He'd explained that it was of no cost to him. One of his poker buddies was an Arab sheikh who stayed in the Regency's top suite every weekend, flying in by helicopter every Friday afternoon from his Hunter Valley property.

Naturally, Dominique had been agog at this news and wanted to know more about this mysterious sheikh who played poker with her husband. Charles had told her the scant details he knew, which was that Prince Ali was thirty-three years old, sinfully handsome and the youngest son of King Khaled of Dubar, one of the wealthiest Emirate states. With four older brothers, Ali was unlikely to ever ascend the throne and had been despatched to Australia several years ago, ostensibly to take care of the royal family's race-horse interests here.

And he'd certainly done a good job of that. The royal thoroughbred stud boasted some of the top-priced yearlings at the Easter sales every year. Rumour had it, however, that Ali's skills as a horseman and businessman had nothing to do with his selection for his present position as manager of the royal stud. Apparently, he'd been exiled from Dubar for his own personal safety after some scandal involving a married woman.

Probably true, in Charles's opinion. Ali had gathered a reputation for being a ladies' man in Australia as well, though not in any obvious man-about-town way. He was never seen out in public alone with a woman, or photographed with one. Word was when he met a good-looking girl who took his eye during his weekly visits to the races in Sydney, private arrangements were made, and if the object of his desire was willing she was whisked up to his country property.

None of Ali's so-called girlfriends had ever sold their story to the media, so, really, talk of these liaisons was all speculation and gossip. Ali never personally revealed anything about his love life, being a very private man.

Charles suspected, however, that this gossip was probably true, too. A man of Ali's extraordinary wealth and looks would find it almost impossible not to become a playboy in the bedroom department.

He'd been a bit of a one himself before he'd met Dominique. Yet he wasn't in Ali's league. The man was a prince, for heaven's sake.

Ali's royal status was the reason they played in his suite here every Friday night, rather than have him visit them. Everything was more secure and more relaxed that way. On the occasion they'd gone to Rico's hospital room last year, Ali had been accompanied by two hired bodyguards. One had stood outside the hospital-room door all night whilst the other had sat in a corner of the room, *after* he'd drawn the shades on the window.

A bit unsettling.

In the hotel suite, there was no need for that. Hotel security was always on high alert when Prince Ali was in residence and no one could access the presidential suite without a pass-key for the lift. Even then, their identity was fully checked out a second time via camera during the ride up in the private lift, and again at the door to the presidential suite.

Charles lifted his hand to ring the doorbell, the door being whisked open within seconds. Clearly, his arrival had been anticipated.

"Good evening, Mr Brandon," the butler greeted.

"It certainly is, James," Charles replied as he walked in. "Very good."

"I trust you had an enjoyable honeymoon, sir," the butler went on in his usual formal manner. Charles suspected he'd been to a school for butlers in England.

Somewhere in his late thirties, tall and dignified-looking with a patrician nose and close-cut sandy blond hair, James was the house butler assigned to the presidential suite at the Regency every Friday night. He was always polite and respectful, and his attention to detail was incredible, as was his memory for names and faces and facts.

"It was marvellous," Charles replied. "Paris in the spring is always superb."

"And Mrs Brandon?"

Charles grinned. "She's superb, too."

James allowed himself a small smile. "If I may say so, sir, you're looking extra well."

"I'm feeling extra well."

"I can't say the same for Mr Mandretti," he murmured, his voice dropping to a low, conspiratorial tone.

"Oh? Has Rico been ill whilst I've been away?" Charles knew that the trio would have still continued to play poker here every Friday night, calling up a substitute player.

"No, not physically ill. I think he has something on his mind. He's been quite short with me tonight, and that's not like Mr Mandretti at all."

No, it wasn't. A self-made success story, Rico was inclined to treat the workers in this world much more politely than the privileged people he now mixed with. He liked and admired Charles because he'd earned his money through hard work and not just inheritance. Rico had little respect for the silver-spooned species.

An exception was their host every Friday night.

Prince Ali might have had his fortune bestowed on him through birth, being one of the pampered sons of an oil-rich Arab sheikh. But he was no sloth. Apparently, he worked his royal backside off at that stud farm he ran, very much a hands-on man when it came to his beloved horses.

Rico had stayed at Ali's property a few times, and seen the man in action for himself. He thought Ali an OK guy, despite his billions, and treated him accordingly.

On the other hand, the fourth and last member of their private poker club wasn't the recipient of Rico's total respect. Rico obviously had ambivalent feelings towards Mrs Renée Selinsky. Although Renée had been very working class before making it big, first as a model, then as the owner of a highly successful modelling agency, Rico had difficulty overlooking the fact she'd subsequently married a banker old enough to be her grandfather.

In his eyes, marrying for money—Rico couldn't conceive that she might have actually *loved* a man in his sixties—was just as bad as inheriting it.

By thirty, Renée had become an extremely rich widow, and had started buying shares in racehorse syndicates. That was how the four of them had met, because they'd all bought shares in one of Ali's beautifully bred yearlings.

On the day their colt had run in and won the Silver Slipper Stakes, the three celebrating owners—and one very proud breeder—had discovered a mutual love of poker. The four of them had played their first game that Saturday night in this very suite.

That had been around five years ago. Now the merry widow, as Rico sometimes called Renée, was thirty-five, still a looker, and still possessing that cool, self-contained air which seemed to get under Rico's skin.

But it was her brilliant brain which niggled Rico the most. He hated it when she beat him at poker. But Renée's bluffing was sometimes simply superb and totally unpredictable. None of them could match her when she was on her game.

Charles accepted her superiority on those occasions with pragmatic logic and played conservatively, hating to waste his money. Ali often tried to force her to fold by raising the stakes outrageously high, and was sometimes successful. Renée was rich, but not in Ali's league. Rico, however, would become testy and rude, sniping at her in a vain attempt to break her nerve, then inevitably making the wrong call, folding when he should have stayed in, and raising when she had an unbeatable hand.

Privately, Charles suspected that Rico fancied the merry widow but wouldn't admit it, even to himself. There was something decidedly sexual in his eyes when he delivered his barbs on these occasions.

There again, Rico was an extremely sexual animal.

At thirty-four, he was still in his prime, a Latin-lover type brimming with testosterone and over-the-top passions.

Charles wondered if Rico's rudeness to the butler tonight had something to do with an overload of male hormones. He'd been divorced over a year now and there wasn't any permanent replacement in his bed as yet. Which was not right for Rico. He was a man who needed to make love, often!

Some warm womanly love wouldn't go astray, either.

Charles believed Rico needed a wife, someone who loved him this time, someone like his Dominique who wanted children. But Rico wasn't about to go down the aisle again in a hurry. Once bitten, he wasn't shy so much as angry, angry that he'd been taken in by a gold-digger.

The appearance of the man himself in the archway which led into the main sitting room showed Charles that James had the situation spot-on. Rico wasn't in any way ill. He looked his usual swashbuckling self in black trousers and a black crewnecked top, his thick, wavy black hair as lustrous as ever, his flashing black eyes as clear as a bell. But he was definitely out of sorts, scowling as he quaffed back the last of the drink he was holding. It looked like Chianti. Rico loved his Italian wines, despite having been born here, in Sydney.

"About bloody time you got here," he snapped without a trace of the Italian accent he adopted for his popular *A Passion for Pasta* TV show. His parents had migrated to Sydney over half a century earlier, not long after the Second World War; all their eight children had been born here—three boys and five girls—and Rico was the youngest.

Charles couldn't get his head around the idea of so many siblings. He didn't have any.

"I'm right on time," Charles countered calmly, in far too good a mood to be riled by Rico's burst of Latin temper.

"No, you're not. The game is supposed to be underway by eight. It's already five minutes past, courtesy of your gasbagging and gossiping out here with the hired help. Here, James, fill this up again, will you?" Rico said curtly and handed the butler his empty glass.

Charles wondered what was eating at Rico but he decided not to ask. Best to just get in there and start playing poker.

The others were already sitting at the card table where it was always set up, next to the bullet-proof plate-glass window which overlooked the city below. Renée, looking softer than usual in a pale pink cashmere sweater, lifted her glass of white wine in Charles's direction in acknowledgement of his arrival.

Ali, dressed in blue jeans and a shirt, managed a polite nod as he sipped his usual glass of mineral water. Ali never touched alcohol himself but always supplied the best in spirits and wine for his guests.

"See, Rico?" Renée said in that silky voice of hers

as the two men sat down at the table. "I told you he'd show up. Though he'd be forgiven if he didn't. After all, he's only been married to that stunner of a wife of his for a month."

Renée was still a stunner herself, Charles appreciated. Just not his type. Too tall and too thin. And a brunette. Charles preferred blondes, and a softer more feminine kind of beauty.

There was nothing soft about Renée. But she was very striking, with those high cheekbones and unusual eyes. Pale green they were, with rather heavy lids which she emphasised by plucking her eyebrows to the finest of arches. The set of her eyebrows gave her face a range of expressions, none of which were soft or sweet. When smiling, she looked either drily amused or downright sardonic. Unsmiling, Renée carried an air about her which could be interpreted as snobbishness, or at the very least belief in her own superiority. Possibly this had been an asset on the catwalk, where models specialised in looking aloof these days. But not such an asset in one's social life.

Charles had not liked her to begin with. But first impressions were not always correct, he'd found. He still could not claim to know her all that well, even now after five years' acquaintance. But he'd warmed to her after a while. Impossible to totally dislike a woman who could play poker as well as she did, and who had what he called strength of character. Renée was always her own person, and he admired that.

It didn't matter to him if she'd married the banker

for his money or not. No doubt she had her reasons. Still, Renée was far too cool and controlled for him. Not like Dominique, who was a wonderful mixture of sweet surrender and wildly impassioned demands.

"Again, Charles," she'd beg him, even after he thought he was done. But he was rarely ever done with Dominique.

Damn. He shouldn't have started thinking about Dominique.

After they had cut cards for the deal—which Renée won, much to Rico's irritation—Charles tried to settle back to enjoy the game. But it was no use. His concentration was shot to pieces. By the time they broke off for supper at ten-thirty, he was losing more than he liked.

"Your mind's not on your game tonight, Charles," Ali remarked over coffee and cake.

"I'm just a bit rusty," he replied.

"Maybe he's setting us all up for a sting later on in the evening," Renée suggested.

Charles smiled what he hoped was an enigmatic smile.

"Trust you to think that," Rico snapped. "That's just the sort of thing a devious female like you would do. But Charles is a straight shooter. The reason he's not playing well tonight is because he can't keep his thoughts above his waist."

"And who could blame him?" Ali said in that rich Eton-educated voice of his. "Renée is right. You are a very lucky man, Charles, to have found a woman so beautiful for your bed."

Charles bristled at the inference that Dominique's role in his life was nothing more than sexual.

"Dominique has a beautiful mind as well as a beautiful body, Ali," he said with a hint of reproach in his voice. "We are friends as well as lovers. Equals, in every way."

Rico laughed. "Who do you think you're kidding, Charles? That girl has you by the short and curlies."

"Must you be so crude?" Renée said with a withering glance Rico's way. "Take no notice of him, Charles. He's just jealous because he can't find anyone to love, or who truly loves him in return."

Rico laughed again, yet it had a hard, hollow ring to it. "I wish I were jealous. Oh, yes. That would be much better."

"Better than what?" Charles asked, not quite following Rico's train of thought.

Rico looked remorseful for opening his mouth. "Nothing. I'm rambling. I've had too much to drink. I think I'll stick to coffee for the rest of the night."

"An excellent idea, Enrico," Ali said. "Alcohol is the root of all evil."

"I thought that was money," Rico retorted.

"No. It's sex," Renée surprised them all by saying. "Sex is the root of all evil. We would all be much better off without it."

"But then there wouldn't be any children," Charles pointed out.

"Exactly," she returned.

"Trust you not to like children," came Rico's cutting comment.

Renée stiffened. "I didn't say that. But the world is overpopulated as it is. And so many children are suffering. I would rather there be no more children than to see such suffering."

"Sorry, but I can't oblige you there, Renée," Charles piped up. "Dominique and I are planning to have children. And soon."

Rico's eyes jerked his way. "I thought you'd put that off for a while," he said with a frown. "Hell, Charles, you've only been married a month!"

"I'm forty-one next birthday, Rico. I haven't got time to waste. Besides, Dominique's keen to have a baby."

"Is she, now?" he said, and Charles heard the cynical note which always flavoured Rico's voice when he spoke about Dominique.

Rico didn't like Dominique. Charles could no longer ignore that fact. Why Rico didn't like her was just as obvious. He thought Dominique was a gold-digger, like his own ex.

Charles could have been insulted by his friend's opinion—didn't he think any woman could love him for himself?—but he understood Rico was still going through a bitter phase after his own wretched marital experience. In time, he'd realise Dominique wasn't anything like Jasmine. When that happened he might even decide to give marriage another go himself.

"I think we should cease to discuss personal issues and get back to the game," Ali suggested wisely. "That is why we meet here each Friday night. To play poker and to escape life's little stresses and strains for a while. Let us leave such matters at the door in future."

Rico and Renée both gave Ali a look which implied a man of his massive power and privilege wasn't subjected to too many of life's little stresses and strains.

Till Charles had met Dominique, he might have agreed with them. Money and success had certainly smoothed his path in life. But he knew now that it didn't bring real happiness. Love did.

Without love, having all the money in the world could become very empty indeed. Charles suspected Ali was no more happy in his private life than was Rico, or the merry widow. You only had to look into that woman's eyes to know *she* wasn't happy. Not where it mattered. Not in her heart.

Earlier, she'd made it sound as if she didn't want children. But was that the truth? Or was it a rationalisation of where her life was heading, fast past that age where it was easy for a woman to conceive, especially without a partner?

Charles was only guessing, of course. Renée was like Ali, never revealing much about her private life. Presumably she did have a love life, but what kind and with whom Charles had no idea. All he knew was that she always showed up at the races alone. And she never cancelled on a Friday night. Unusual for a woman.

There again, Renée was an unusual woman. An enigma. A rather intimidating enigma. Charles pitied any man who ever fell in love with her. No man wanted to be intimidated by his woman. They wanted a woman who could make a man feel good about himself, the way Dominique did.

Aah…Dominique. She was very much on his mind tonight. Ali could command they leave their personal lives at the door but Charles couldn't do that just yet. His love for his lovely wife was all too new, and all too consuming.

He patted the jewelry box in his jacket pocket before he sat back down again, his stomach tightening in pleasurable anticipation of that moment when she opened the lid and saw the necklace. He couldn't wait to put it on her, to see how it looked.

The next two hours dragged, his play deteriorating further. Ali shook his head at his many mistakes. Renée smiled wryly and Rico scowled.

"What am I going to do with you, Charles?" Rico said when the night's poker was over and the two men rode the lift together down to the ground floor. Renée had already gone ahead, always the first to leave after play was halted, usually around midnight. Tonight it had been twelve-thirty, due to their late start.

Charles laughed. "I'll do better next week," he said, thinking that by then he might have the worst of his lust out of his system.

Not that he said that to Rico. Rico would pounce on the word lust, and claim he'd been right all along; it was just the promise of sex which had bewitched and entrapped him.

But Charles knew that wasn't the case. It was only natural that he and Dominique were still going through that phase when they couldn't keep their hands off each other. Unlike most newlyweds these days, they hadn't been living together before their wedding. Hell, they hadn't even kissed!

"Did you mean it when you said you and Dominique weren't waiting to have children?"

Rico's question surprised Charles. "Why would I lie about something like that?"

"But you haven't actually gotten her pregnant yet."

"No. She's on the Pill for now. But she's coming off it next month."

"I honestly don't think that's a good idea, Charles. You should wait at least a year before you take such a big step. Get to know your wife a bit better first. You hardly know the girl, after all."

Charles's forbearance over Rico's negative attitude towards Dominique began to wane. "I know all I need to know," he replied tautly. "Look, Rico, I realise you don't like Dominique. You probably think she's a fortune hunter, but—"

"You're wrong," Rico interrupted, his expression grim. "I don't *think* she's a fortune hunter, my friend. I *know* she's a fortune hunter."

CHAPTER THREE

CHARLES whirled, his fists balling by his sides. "Now, look here, Rico, I'm warning you. Stop this once and for all. Just because Jasmine took you for a ride, doesn't mean that Dominique's doing the same to me. My wife loves me. Renée's right. You're jealous."

The lift doors opened on the ground floor and Charles gave Rico one last uncompromising glare. "I suggest you apologise before we leave this lift or you can consider our friendship over," he pronounced angrily.

Rico looked more concerned than apologetic. "I'm sorry. More sorry, Charles, than you can ever imagine. But I can't let you be taken for a fool. And I can't let you go ahead and blindly have a baby with that woman. I have proof of what I'm saying. Hard and fast proof."

Charles's head jerked back in shock before more anger rushed in. "*Proof?* What kind of proof?" he challenged heatedly.

"Irrefutable proof."

"Such as?"

"The kind supplied by a very reputable private investigator. Facts and figures. Taped conversations with her ex-flatmates in Melbourne, people she's worked with, men she's slept with. You're welcome to hear them for yourself whenever you like. And to see the written report. Your wife *is* a fortune hunter, Charles. Make no bones about that. She openly admitted to her flatmates during her years in Melbourne that her aim in life was to marry money. You became her target after things with her previous marital candidate fell through and she made the move to Sydney.''

Charles tried to swallow the huge lump which had filled his throat but it was stuck there.

''He was her last boss,'' Rico swept on mercilessly. ''Jonathon Hall, a reasonably successful celebrity sports manager. Though not as rich as his lifestyle indicates, which is why he ended up marrying money himself. Apparently, Dominique was livid when he dumped her. She told one of her girlfriends that the next time she wouldn't go for a guy with Hall's looks and charm. She'd try for someone older who didn't think he was God's gift to women, someone who'd be oh, so grateful to have a girl like her even look at him twice.''

Charles wanted to cry out, to scream that none of this was true. Dominique loved him.

But Rico was ruthless in his exposé of his beautiful bride's true nature. ''Dominique isn't even her real name. It's something plain like Joan or Jane. I can't remember which. She changed it to Dominique when she first came to Melbourne from Tasmania when she was nineteen. Which reminds me. Her parents weren't both killed in a car accident, either, like she told you. Her mother died of cancer when Dominique was eighteen, but her father is still very much alive. Lives in a small town on the West Coast, works as a manager in one of the local mines. She's a liar and a fake, Charles, in every way."

The blood began to drain from Charles's face. He vaguely saw horror in Rico's eyes and realised he must look as shattered as he felt.

"Gee, Charles. Don't go collapsing on me. Hey, man, I didn't realise how much you loved her till this moment. I thought it was just infatuation. Man, you look terrible. What you need is a stiff drink. Come on, let's go get you one."

Charles let Rico propel him into a nearby bar, prop him up on one of the stools there and order him a brandy. He downed the drink in two quick gulps and let Rico order him another.

The brandy soon did its work and blood began slowly seeping back into his brain, his inner despair momentarily overlaid by a confused curiosity. He swivelled on the stool to face Rico once more.

"When did you find out all this?" he asked shakily. "Not before the wedding, surely."

"No. I hired the PI whilst you were on your honeymoon. The full report only came in yesterday."

"But why, Rico? Why would it even occur to you to do such a thing?"

"One of the flatmates Dominique confided in is a

cousin of mine. Claudia. She'd gone to Melbourne a couple of years ago for a change of scene after her marriage broke up. Recently, she came back to live in Sydney and was staying with one of my sisters. I was at a family get-together a few days after your wedding and was showing everyone some of the casual snapshots I'd taken when Claudia recognised Dominique. She said Dominique had this fixation about becoming really rich. Apparently, she told Claudia she could never earn enough herself in a lifetime of working for a salary, so the only solution was to marry money. Everything she did had that single aim. To catch herself a rich husband.''

Charles expressed his despair with a colourful four-letter word.

''Absolutely. I agree with you. But at least now you can see why, after what Claudia told me, I thought it was my duty as your best man to find out everything I could.''

''Which you obviously couldn't wait to pass on to me,'' Charles said bitterly. ''But for what purpose, I wonder. Do you think you've done me a favour, Rico, disenchanting me like this? You could have left me in blissful ignorance. That would have been kinder.''

''I was going to for a while, believe me. But not after what you said tonight about starting a family straight away. I just couldn't stay silent and let you do that, Charles.''

''I don't see why not,'' Charles muttered bleakly.

''Fortune hunters fall into two categories,'' Rico

elaborated. "Firstly, there are the Jasmines of this world who marry you for the high life, and never have any intention of spoiling their figures having babies. Their plan is to have a ball for a while at your expense, till you start asking for a kid, like I stupidly did. Then they divorce you and take you for every penny they can in alimony. The second kind—into which your Dominique obviously falls—have a baby as soon as possible to cement their position, guaranteeing them of an even bigger settlement when they also eventually file for divorce. The child is a pawn, not the precious gift it should be. Just another little money-spinner."

Charles wanted to weep at the death of all the joyful anticipation he'd been experiencing over having a baby with Dominique.

"That's why I had to speak up, Charles," Rico said with a sympathetic hand on his shoulder. "Not just for you, but for that baby. No child deserves to be brought into this world as a bargaining chip."

Charles slowly nodded his agreement, although there was a part of him which still wished Rico had stayed silent. Now he'd probably *never* have a child.

"Get rid of her, Charles. Dump her. Divorce her. She'll be lucky to get a cent after the family law court sees all the evidence I've amassed against her."

Rico was right in his advice. But Charles knew he wouldn't do that just yet. Or was the word *couldn't*?

His hand went to his pocket to pat the box which lay there and his heart suddenly stopped breaking apart, cemented back to survival mode by an emotion far stronger than his earlier despair. Love turned to hate was an amazingly powerful motivator.

No, he wouldn't be getting rid of his beautiful new wife just yet. She had to pay for what this necklace had cost him, what *she* had cost him. His male pride demanded it. His hate insisted upon it.

Charles seethed inside when he thought of what a fool she'd made of him. A silly, blind, arrogant fool. Right from the start, she'd played him like a fiddle. Fleeing last year's Christmas party had obviously been a ploy, as had appearing reluctant to date him at first, but her spurning his advances after she finally agreed to date him had been her *coup de grâce*!

He cringed when he thought of how triumphant he'd felt when she'd said yes to his proposal of marriage. But the triumph had been all hers, not his!

How she must have chuckled behind his back when he'd decided not to sleep with her till their wedding night. Her trembling as she'd come to him that night had probably been suppressed laughter. And as for the response she'd showed to his lovemaking…

Well, he'd be having the last laugh. Let's see how good her faking ability was during the next month.

Because he was going to give himself—and her— one month. One month of vengeance.

His mouth pulled back into the travesty of a smile just thinking about some of things he planned for them. She'd probably even pretend to enjoy herself, like the mercenary manipulator she was.

"You're not going to divorce her, are you?" Rico said with a degree of stunned surprise in his voice.

Charles abandoned the rest of his second brandy—being drunk was not on tonight's agenda—then turned to his friend.

"No," he said, his voice menacingly calm. "Not just yet. But don't worry. There won't be any baby." Dominique wasn't the only one who could lie, and deceive.

Rico frowned at him. "I don't know now whether to feel sorry for you, or Dominique."

"I wouldn't waste your sympathy on her, if I were you."

"You won't do anything stupid, will you, Charles?"

"Stupid?"

"Like strangling her when you're making love?"

Charles laughed a cold laugh. "Do you honestly think I'd go to jail because of that little tramp? Rest assured my revenge, such as it is, won't ever take that path, or be allowed to get out of hand." As he slid off the bar stool he clamped a hand over his friend's shoulder, partly to support his own leaden legs and partly in a reassuring gesture. "Don't worry about me, Rico. I'll survive. What are you doing tomorrow?"

"Tomorrow? I'm—er—going to the races."

Charles frowned. "But none of our horses are running, are they? They're all out on spells till the spring.'' Charles and Rico usually only went to the races when they had a runner.

''Yes, but Ali has a couple of horses in with a good chance. And it's something to do,'' Rico added a bit bleakly. ''Why?''

''I was going to come over and pick up that report, and those tapes. Look, could you possibly drop them in at my place on your way to the races?''

''I'm not so sure that's such a good idea till you calm down a bit.''

''I'm perfectly calm,'' Charles bit out. ''Just bring them, will you?''

Rico sighed his reluctant resignation to his friend's request. ''Very well.''

''If you happen to speak to Dominique when you drop by, try to pretend you like her. Use some of that Latino charm you're famous for.''

''If you insist.''

''I insist. Now I must go. Dominique is probably waiting up for me, like a good little mercenary. I wouldn't like to think she'd made the effort for nothing.''

Rico's frown deepened. ''Charles, I don't like the way you're acting. It's not you. You can be a bit pompous at times, but basically you're one of the good guys, which is saying something, considering you're a billionaire *and* a businessman. Look, I know you're upset, and you have every right to be. But you're not thinking straight.''

Charles laughed, his heart like stone in his chest. "I'm thinking straighter than I have in months."

"Perhaps. But your plan of action is all wrong. Revenge never achieves anything constructive. It's a very self-destructive emotion. Trust me. I know. Just get *rid* of her!"

"Oh, I intend to. Eventually. See you tomorrow."

Rico watched his friend stalk from the bar. What had he done? He should never have opened his big mouth. He should have let sleeping dogs lie. Instead, he'd unleashed the dogs of war and who knew where it would all end?

Not happily, that was for sure.

He groaned, turned back to the bar and downed the rest of Charles's brandy.

"Get me another drink, would you?" he asked the bland-faced barman. "Not brandy this time. Bourbon. Straight. No ice."

He could afford to get drunk. He always took a taxi home on a Friday night, home to his empty apartment with its empty bed.

Still, perhaps that was better than going home to a wife like Dominique.

Or was it?

Rico glanced around the bar and saw a stunning-looking blonde of around thirty sitting at the end of the bar. When he smiled at her, she smiled back in the way women had been smiling at men for centuries. She wasn't a hooker—she looked a tad too expensive—but definitely a good-time girl.

Rico knew there was no need for him to go home to an empty bed tonight. The blonde wouldn't say no. They wouldn't even have to go far. The Regency was sure to have lots of lovely vacant rooms. May was hardly peak tourist season in Sydney and Friday night saw most of the interstate businessmen already flying home.

Only one thing stopped him. The surety that taking the blonde to bed wouldn't ease his frustration at all. Only one woman could do that at the moment. And she wasn't likely to say yes to being his bed-mate.

Renée despised him almost as much as he despised her. Why he wanted her this badly Rico could not fathom. It was perverse. And it was becoming increasingly painful.

Maybe...

He cast another look at the blonde at the end of the bar. No, she was far too much like Dominique for his liking. A man in his position couldn't afford to jump into bed with just anyone. He'd been a bit stupid in the past in this regard, and wasn't about to repeat his mistakes.

Women who were *too* beautiful were invariably trouble. He'd known Dominique was trouble the moment he clapped eyes on her. Charles had been stupid to marry her. But then, men in love were often stupid.

Rico's hand tightened around his glass. He didn't want to think about love. He didn't want to think at all!

Damn and blast. There was only one solution for

this problem, even if it was only temporary, and stupid, and futile.

Taking his bourbon with him, Rico rose and sauntered down to the end of the bar, where he slipped up onto the empty stool next to the blonde.

"You alone, honey?" he said with the slow, slightly cocky smile which captivated a worldwide female audience every week on cable television.

Her blue eyes glittered boldly up at him. "Not any more," she purred.

CHAPTER FOUR

DOMINIQUE woke with a start, followed by the swift realisation that Charles was home. She could hear him moving around the penthouse.

Immediately she sat up in the bed, plumping the pillows behind her and picking up the book which had slipped from her hand when she'd fallen asleep. She'd tried to stay awake for him, watching two movies on television and then reading one of those thrillers which claimed would keep you awake till the very last of its four-hundred pages. But this one hadn't lived up to its hype and she'd nodded off before she hit page twenty.

A glance at the bedside clock showed it was ten past one.

Not too late, she supposed. A lot of men played poker all night. Or so she'd heard.

Not that all of Charles's poker buddies were men. One of them was the very beautiful Mrs Renée Selinsky, a wealthy widow and the owner of one of Sydney's top modelling agencies called simply "Renée's".

Dominique had first met Mrs Selinsky at the races, a week before their wedding, and had been more than a little perturbed over the thought that Charles would be spending several hours in her company every Friday night once their honeymoon was over. The woman was not only striking to look at but obviously very clever and conspicuously unattached. She hadn't brought a partner to the races, or their wedding, making Dominique very conscious of the fact that she was footloose and fancy-free.

Dominique's first foray into real jealousy had come when she'd seen Charles and Renée talking together at their reception, which had been held here, in Charles's penthouse. The two of them had been out on the terrace, chatting intimately away and looking more than friends to Dominique's suddenly green eyes.

When she'd questioned him about this later—trying oh so hard to sound interested and not jealous—he'd told her more about his relationship with the striking Renée. The news that they'd been friends for five long years and she'd been a widow all that time did not please Dominique. Neither did her husband's joking remark that Rico called her the *merry* widow.

The nickname implied that she'd led a racy lifestyle since the death of her rich but elderly husband. Despite Renée's rather aloof manner, Dominique reckoned that the merry widow probably had had as many different lovers over those five years as she had shares in racehorses. Not having a public or permanent partner was no guarantee of celibacy these days. Dominique started thinking that maybe Charles had taken her to bed at some time. It seemed not only likely but logical, given they played cards together every week. Moving on to playing games in bed afterwards in one of those very convenient hotel rooms wasn't much of a leap of the imagination.

It had been this thought which had bothered Dominique the most about Charles going to his poker game tonight. She'd be much happier if his card cronies were all male.

Not that she'd said as much to her husband. Dominique was determined not to surrender to jealousy, which was not only new to her nature, but also highly disturbing to her psyche. Jealous women and wives loved too much, and loving anyone too much was dangerous and sometimes deadly. Dominique wanted no part of such excessive emotions.

She couldn't stop herself from loving Charles. She'd tried hard enough and failed miserably. She rigidly refused to let jealousy overtake her as well.

Nevertheless, when Charles still didn't come to bed, Dominique found herself gripping the paperback novel in her hands with white-knuckled intensity and wondering why. What was keeping him? Surely he'd seen her light under the door. Surely he'd know she was waiting up for him.

When she heard water running through the pipes, revealing that he'd turned on a tap somewhere, her heart started thudding behind her ribs, her mind tormented with black thoughts. Was he washing himself clean of that woman's scent? Wiping off all traces of her lipstick from her kisses?

Like a flash, her jealousy erupted, then raced to even greater flights of fancy. Had he even gone to play poker at all? Maybe that story was just a ruse. Maybe he spent every Friday night in bed with the merry widow, enjoying the sort of sophisticated erotic games that such a woman would be well versed in.

Rico would cover for his friend, if asked. But would Prince Ali? Dominique didn't think so. Prince Ali was not a close friend of Charles's. More of a gambling acquaintance.

Still, Dominique was hardly going to call up and cross-question such a man over his activities on a Friday night. She'd only met the prince once—the same day at the races that she'd first met Renée—and had found the Arab sheikh overwhelmingly intimidating. He had not come to their wedding, for which she was grateful. It had been difficult enough, enduring the best man's disapproval and the merry widow's disturbing presence.

The tap was turned off—wherever it was—but Charles still did not make an appearance in the master bedroom. All was suddenly silent out there. Five minutes ticked away. Then ten. Dominique was tempted to get up and go to see where Charles was and what he was doing, but something—some probably irrational fear—prevented her from leaving the bed.

I'm being ridiculous, she lectured himself. Doing what I vowed I'd never do. Screwing myself up with jealousy. Charles loves me. I know he does. He probably walked straight from the front door into the living room when he first came in, without looking down the hallway on his left, so he wouldn't have seen the bedroom light under the door. He probably thinks I'm asleep and is being considerate, using the main bathroom instead of the *en suite*. He's a very considerate man.

Dominique had one of two options. Stay where she was till he finally came to bed. Or get up and go and find him, showing him that she was wide awake and wanting him. Not for him to make love to her necessarily, if he was too tired. But his company. His conversation. His cuddles. That would do for now.

Throwing back the cream satin sheets, she slipped from the bed and hurried over to the his-and-hers walk-in wardrobes which flanked the entrance to their *en suite* bathroom. Despite never wearing anything to bed any more, she had two lovely negligée sets which she'd personally purchased with her honeymoon in mind. The nightgown she'd worn on her wedding night was long and made of pearly white satin. The one she reached for now was also long, but was made of semi-transparent black lace.

Dominique slipped it on over her nakedness, then drew on the matching robe, telling herself that she wasn't trying to seduce Charles. But the sight of herself in the full-length mirror on the back of the door mocked this thought. Seduction was the sole purpose of this kind of nightwear. It was why she'd bought it in the first place.

"Be honest," she muttered to herself. "You want Charles to make love to you. No, you *need* him to make love to you. Now. Tonight."

Sleep would be impossible if she didn't have the reassurance of his ongoing desire. A kiss and a cuddle would not be enough. She had to *know* that he hadn't been with that woman. She had to be sure.

Time was of the essence in that case. She had to hurry. Slipping her feet into the high-heeled black satin mules which complemented the elegantly sexy negligée, she hurried back to her dressing table, where she applied some lipstick and perfume, then went in search of her husband.

Charles was slumped back on the large black leather sofa which dominated the huge living room, nursing the dregs of a very large brandy and staring blankly through the picture window out at the tops of the city skyline when he realised he was no longer alone.

His head turned just far enough to view Dominique fully as she stood for a few moments in the archway that led from the main living area to the foyer.

So the gold-digger was awake again, was she? came the bitter thought even as his insides crunched down hard at the way she looked in that incredibly sexy black lace outfit.

Charles had actually gone straight to their bedroom as soon as he arrived home, eager to start exacting his revenge. But the sight of her curled up asleep had shaken his resolve. She'd looked so sweet lying there under the cream satin sheets. So soft. So...innocent.

He couldn't help it. He'd almost broken down at that juncture, staggering back out of the room to go and wash away the threatening tears. After that, he'd gone and poured himself a mind-numbing tumbler of brandy, searching for solace in its anaesthetic effect.

But there was no solace to be had when you lived with treachery; when your love was false. There was nothing but this terrible emptiness inside.

His gaze swept over her as she started floating towards him, the black lace robe flapping back to reveal a matching nightgown which was not for the faint-hearted. It was semi-transparent, the neckline cut to her navel with just a tiny satin tie keeping the lace anchored across her magnificent breasts.

A few minutes before she'd looked like an innocent young girl, lying naked and asleep in his bed. Now, with this outfit on, she looked every inch the seductress she really was.

Despite knowing her true character, Charles still felt his flesh leap to attention. Amazing, he thought. Deplorable. But exactly what he expected.

"You don't have to tell me," she purred as she came to a halt in front of him, then sank down onto the plush cream carpet at his feet. "You lost."

He stared down at her, struggling to keep the hate—and the desire—out of his face. He certainly had lost. Everything. Everything except what he could still see and touch before him. Her lips. Her breasts.

Her body, which would be ready for him. It always was.

Even as his own rapidly swelling flesh tortured him, he wondered how she managed that. What trick did she use?

"Poor darling," she crooned, leaning her cheek against his thigh and glancing up at him at the same time.

"No matter," he muttered. "It's only money." He reached down with his free hand and ran his fingers through her hair, shocked that he could still find pleasure in touching her. Why wasn't his skin crawling with revulsion?

"I haven't seen that outfit before," he remarked as he continued to sip the brandy and play with her hair. "How long have you had it?" The thought that she might have worn it to seduce the man before him made him want to rip it asunder.

She smiled up at him. Such a lovely smile. Such lovely lips.

"I bought it to wear on our honeymoon," she said, "but after our wedding night you told me you didn't want me to wear anything to bed in future. *Ever*," she added with a saucy little smile.

"So I did."

Charles toyed with the idea of demanding she never wear clothes at all when they were alone here. The penthouse was air-conditioned, after all. She wouldn't be uncomfortable provided she didn't go outside, although the lap pool *was* heated. He would definitely insist she never wear a costume when they went swimming together, in spite of the fact that the pool was in full view of several floors of nearby office buildings. If strangers could see her naked then it would test the level of her greed.

Would she comply? he speculated.

His face darkened with the surety that of course she would.

"Don't you like it?" she asked, a frown gathering on her high forehead.

Charles cleared away his own frown, replacing it with a rueful smile. "It's very sexy," he complimented. "Stand up again and let me get a better look at it."

Her instant obedience thrilled him in a highly corruptive fashion. He could get used to this, having a wife who was his own private love slave. Knowledge was power all right. He'd never have dared demand the kind of things he was going to demand, if he hadn't known what she really was.

Rico's warning that revenge was self-destructive momentarily came back to haunt him. Do you really want to take this course of action? Charles asked himself one last time. Use her beautiful body to satisfy every dark desire you can think of in your quest for vengeance?

As he stared up at her, standing there and looking down at him with pretend love in her eyes, his answer was undeniably...*yes*!

Till now he'd been such a sap, making love to her

so tenderly, so lovingly. He'd been more concerned with her pleasure than his own. He'd thought himself her perfect sexual partner during all the days and nights they'd shared. What a fool he'd been. All faked, all of it. She'd been playing a game with him; a rotten, wicked, manipulative, mercenary game.

Well, the game was his now, not hers. *She* had become the prey, not him. What a satisfying thought.

Revenge isn't destructive, Rico. It's delicious and very, very exciting.

"Take off the robe," he ordered. "Just let it fall to the floor."

She did.

Dear God...no wonder he was captivated by her. She had the most incredible body.

"Now undo the tie," he said coolly, although inside he was hot. White hot.

She complied after a moment's hesitation, her fingers shaking slightly, he noted. Clever witch. She had that move down pat. He recalled her using it on their wedding night.

"Now pull the ends back. No, further. I want to see you."

Her eyes flared wide, her fingers trembling once again as she tentatively obliged.

Her ongoing *ingénue* act began to annoy him.

"Come here," he said brusquely. "Kneel between my legs.'''

Again, that brilliant hesitation. But she obeyed, as

he knew she would. She was even breathing quickly. Nice touch that.

After reaching to put his glass down on a side-table, he leant forward and took her bared nipples between his thumbs and forefingers, then squeezed and tugged them at the same time.

The sound which escaped her lips was half-gasp, half-moan.

"Did you like that?" How cool he sounded. Almost detached.

"Yes," she whispered hoarsely.

Liar!

He did it again. And again. And again.

When she started whimpering he stopped, lifting his hands to take the thin straps of the nightgown and slide them off her shoulders. Then, with one sweeping downwards motion, he stripped her of the garment, leaving her kneeling there nude before him.

Her nipples looked red against the paleness of her skin, almost as red as her lips, which were a deep scarlet. Yet they hadn't been that colour when she'd been asleep in bed, he remembered. She'd been free of make-up. Free of every artifice.

She'd certainly remedied that once she'd woken up and reverted to type.

He had to admire her tactics, however. And her acting. Anyone who didn't know the truth would think she was hopelessly turned on at this moment. Her eyes carried a slightly glazed expression and her lips had fallen temptingly apart as her breathing quickened ever further in pretend arousal.

Charles reached forward with his right hand to touch her hips, to trace their lush oval shape.

He held her eyes with his as he inserted a single finger into her mouth. Then two.

"Suck them," he whispered thickly, and began to move the two fingers in and out of her mouth.

She blinked and swayed slightly on her knees before closing her eyes and doing what he asked.

Charles's gut crunched down hard at the feel of her sucking on his fingers. It was more than a turn-on, which was the last thing he needed if he was going to remain in command of this situation.

It was then that he remembered the necklace and the scenario he'd envisaged earlier that evening.

"Charles," she moaned when he withdrew his hand to reach for his jacket, which was lying across the back of the sofa.

He almost smiled at the genuine-sounding frustration in her voice. What an actress!

"I just remembered," he said. "I bought something for you tonight." And he pulled out the long black jewelry box, flipping open the lid to show her the contents.

She gasped on cue. "Oh, Charles! You…you shouldn't have!"

She couldn't have said truer words. But he would get his money's worth in the next month, he vowed.

"But…but when did you find the time?" she asked

as she stared, first at the opals and then up at him. "I mean...I thought you were playing poker all night."

Charles was taken aback by the suspicion in her voice. Was she thinking this might be a guilt gift, that he'd been up to some kind of shenanigans instead of playing cards?

With whom, for pity's sake? He frowned as he recalled her questioning him about Renée quite closely the day of their wedding and wondered if she thought he was having an affair with the merry widow. Charles supposed duplicitous people always thought the worst of others. Dominique had no concept of what genuine love and loyalty were like. People like her lived for nothing but the acquiring of money, and material things like this necklace. If she was worried about Renée, it would only be because she didn't want to fall off the gravy train and lose her husband to another woman.

Still, Charles slotted away this weakness in Dominique, to be perhaps used at a later date.

Meanwhile, he would continue to play the besotted husband. In a fashion...

"There's a branch of Whitmore Opals in the foyer of the Regency," he reassured her as he drew the glittering and gleaming necklace from its velvet bed. "It's open till nine on a Friday night. I saw this in the window as I walked past and couldn't resist buying it for my lovely wife. Lift up your hair, darling. I want to see what it looks like on you."

This time she complied without any hesitation.

Very co-operative, Charles thought caustically.

He slid the necklace around her throat, the irony of it being a choker not lost on him. Rico had been afraid that that was what his friend would do. Choke her.

But Charles had no use for Dominique dead. He wanted her very much alive for the next month. *And* when he finally told her how long he'd known *exactly* what she was. He wanted to see the look on her face when he revealed how he'd used that knowledge, knowing that she would surrender to whatever he wanted. Like now, for instance. And shortly.

A savage satisfaction buzzed through his brain as he clipped the necklace together, then sat back to stare at her wearing his gift, and nothing else.

The sight was exquisitely decadent. And oh so erotic.

His flesh swelled even further.

''You can drop your hair back now,'' he said as he slowly but deliberately unzipped his trousers.

She took a moment to obey. Was she about to resist? Or to protest? She did neither, despite the fact that he had never treated her like this before. Amazing what a forty-thousand-dollar necklace could achieve.

He watched her take him into her mouth with seeming eagerness, hating her yet craving her at the same time. She was a wicked witch all right, but he was under her spell. He might always be under her sexual spell.

That was the truth of it, the awful truth. He tried to recapture his earlier vengeful anger, but it quickly became lost in his escalating need for release. With a tortured groan, he sagged back on the sofa, surrendering himself to this woman he'd foolishly married.

The feelings she engendered in him were incredibly strong, yet appallingly weak at the same time. Physically there was ecstasy, whilst mentally he was in agony. But soon Charles's emotional pain became blotted out by pleasure, the hard edge of his hate melted by the heat of her mouth and the gentle touch of her hands.

How could she *not* love him when she could make love to him like this?

He groaned and reached out to slide a caressing hand down her right arm. Her head lifted and he stared at her, at her luminescent eyes and her soft, wet lips.

"Do you want me to stop?" she said, her voice low and shaky.

Did he? Could he bear for her to continue? Could he bear for her not to?

It was then that he saw the necklace again, glittering and gleaming at him like some exotic dog collar. Suddenly, everything came back to him in a rush. All the pain of tonight's discovery. The humiliation and the hurt.

His desperation for physical release eased with the return of another need. The need for vengeance.

"No," he said, a calming wave of bitter resolve rippling through him. "No, I don't want you to stop."

Her head bent again, as he knew it would.

Obediently. Beautifully. This time he coolly played with her hair, keeping control of himself for an impressive length of time. Inevitably, however, his control began to slip, and once it did the rush towards release was swift.

But even as Charles knew he could not hold back his climax any longer, he vowed that this would not be the end of it tonight.

There would be no sleep for the wicked just yet.

And no sleep for the vengeful. Or was it the bewitched? No matter. The end result would be the same. She was going to pay for the weakness of his flesh with the weakness of hers. He would push her faking abilities to the limit. He would think of nothing but his own pleasure. He would be demanding, the male animal at his most selfish.

It would be interesting to see if she ever dared say no to him.

He doubted it.

Then tomorrow, after he'd recovered from tonight's excesses, his vengeful game would start all over again, with the stakes raised another notch.

CHAPTER FIVE

DOMINIQUE hummed happily as she stepped under a hot shower the next morning and lifted her face to the spray. It was almost ten o'clock and Charles was still asleep in their bed, out like a light.

And no wonder.

Last night had been incredible!

Although initially startled by her husband's unexpected transformation from a gentle lover to one she'd never known before, Dominique had soon found herself more turned on than ever before. She'd been with him all the way, from the episode in the living room, to the imaginative one in this shower afterwards, and finally a torrid session back in the bedroom.

She couldn't help hoping Charles would lose at poker every Friday night if that was what it did to him! Only sheer physical exhaustion had stopped him in the end and they'd both fallen asleep with their bodies still fused together, spoon fashion, Charles's lips buried in her hair.

And her breasts…

Dominique stopped humming and glanced downwards. She flinched a little as she ever so gently touched her breasts. They were very tender indeed.

Still, they'd recover! She would rub some soothing lotion on them later.

Charles had just got a bit carried away, well, more than a bit, actually. As wildly exciting as the experience had been, Dominique wasn't sure if she could cope with that level of raw passion every night of the week!

Whatever, last night had at least put paid to any silly notion she'd been harbouring that her husband was having an affair with the merry widow on a Friday night. No man could have done what he'd done for as long as he did it after being with another woman beforehand. Not unless he'd sold his soul to the devil.

No, she had nothing to worry about in that regard. And nothing to be jealous over when he played poker on a Friday night any more.

Dominique began to hum again as she started washing.

Charles woke groggily to a hangover and the sound of a hair-dryer in the bathroom. Rolling over with a groan, he saw that it was going on eleven. Another groan escaped his parched lips. He had to get up. Rico could be here shortly.

But he just didn't have the energy to rise. Last night had totally flattened him.

Last night...

It hadn't quite worked out as he'd planned. What had begun as an act of vengeance had eventually changed to the most exciting sexual encounter of his life!

That woman was more than a witch. She was the devil incarnate.

The sudden silence in the bathroom was soon followed by the door opening. And there she was, wrapped neck to knee in a cream towelling bathrobe, her cheeks glowing, her golden hair sleekly blow-dried and falling halfway down her back.

"So you're awake at last," she threw at him with a saucy smile as she padded, barefoot, across the plush cream carpet.

Everything in the master bedroom and *en suite* bathroom was cream, with gold trim, the penthouse having come fully furnished when Charles had bought it. He'd always thought the overall décor a bit bland, especially in here. But Dominique loved it. She thought it elegant.

He watched her sit down on the cream and gold brocade-covered stool which faced the curved cream dressing-table in the corner then pick up a jar from amongst the wide selection of jars and bottles lined up underneath the three-sided mirror.

Charles had realised soon after they were married that Dominique took skin care and make-up very seriously. As she did keeping her body fit and toned. The exercise routine she put herself through every other day in the gym of whatever hotel they were staying at during their honeymoon was gruelling. Charles's choice of exercise was swimming, which he found both energising and relaxing. He wasn't interested in big muscles, just staying lean and healthy.

Charles hadn't seen anything wrong with his new bride's passion with physical perfection before last night's revelations. Now he realised she worked as hard as she did because she viewed her body as a weapon to get what she wanted in life. Looking fabulous had been a necessity in her quest for marriage to a rich man.

Charles had to concede that the first thing which had attracted him to Dominique was her face and figure. Did that make him as shallow as she was? Or just a typical male, more susceptible to visual attractiveness than the female of the human species?

"I was just thinking in the shower," she said as she began unscrewing the lid of the jar, "that if losing at cards always turns you into a primitive beast, I should hope for you to lose every Friday night. Though perhaps not," she added with a rueful laugh as she scooped some cream out with her fingertips. "I don't think my poor nipples could take it. They're terribly sore this morning. You won't be able to touch them for at least a few…hours," she finished, flashing him a wickedly sexy smile in the mirror.

Charles gritted his teeth and watched, his head thudding dreadfully and his mouth as dry as a desert, whilst she slid her hand into the front of the towelling robe and started rubbing the lotion over her right breast and nipple.

"So what are we going to do today?" she asked

as her tormenting hand went round and round. "After I've cooked you breakfast, of course. But can you manage breakfast, darling? You're looking a little peaked over there."

"I'm wrecked," he admitted curtly. "You've wrecked me."

She laughed. "*I've* wrecked *you*! Might I remind you it was *you* who started that whole episode last night? All I came out for was a kiss and a cuddle."

"In that black lace outfit?" he mocked. "Come, now, Dominique, you got exactly what you wanted. Or are you saying you didn't enjoy yourself?"

He watched her reaction to this but she just laughed again. He actually wanted to strangle her then, which reminded him of Rico.

"I have to get up," he muttered. "Rico's due here shortly."

The dismay on her face at this news didn't elude him. She *knows* Rico knows what she is, Charles realised.

"What on earth for?" she said. "And why didn't you tell me before this? You could have mentioned it last night."

His smile was on the cold side. "I hardly had time to talk to you last night. We were busy doing other things. Still, it's nothing for you to worry about." Not yet, anyway. "It isn't a social call. He's just dropping off a report."

"What kind of report?"

"A report from a private investigator."

Did she grow pale at this pronouncement? Or was he just imagining it?

"Rico hired one for me whilst we were away on our honeymoon," he elaborated. "To check up on one of my employees." Again, he watched her closely.

"Really? What's the poor fellow done to make you do something as drastic as that?"

"You've assumed it was a man."

She shrugged, her attitude seemingly nonchalant. He must have imagined her reacting guiltily before. Clearly, she had no idea he was talking about her.

"Most of your employees are men," she said. "Especially in the higher-up positions."

True. She'd been one of the few female executives he'd ever hired. It wasn't a chauvinist decision, just the way it had worked out. Most of the applicants for executive positions were men, and most were more qualified than the women. He'd made an exception in Dominique's case because when he'd read her CV he'd admired her drive and ambition. He hadn't realised at the time just how driven and ambitious she was!

God, but he wished she'd stop rubbing that stuff into her nipples! It was killing him. But be damned if he was going to touch her again this morning.

So much for his vengeful ideas of having her parade around naked for him all the time. He'd end up wanting her all the time. Him, having to listen to her fake moans, whilst his own flesh responded just the same. Blindly. Helplessly. Stupidly!

His so-called vengeance had to have a rest for a few hours at least, which meant he had to get out of here for a while. Out in public her body would be well covered and the opportunities to surrender to temptation were limited. As much as Charles had fantasised about having sex with her out in the pool with lots of office workers looking on, he knew now he would never do anything like that, because the humiliation would again be his more than hers. Dominique was his wife, for pity's sake, and whilst she was his wife he would treat her with respect under the gaze of others, or risk having no respect for himself.

"What did he do?"

For a few confusing seconds, Charles had no idea what she was talking about. And then he remembered.

He looked into her curious and seemingly innocent blue eyes and tried to imagine how she'd react when he finally told her *she'd* been the subject of the investigation. Would she deny everything, then try to persuade him of her love with her body?

Oh, yes. That was exactly what she'd do. Charles had to confess he was looking forward to that moment. He'd save up the darkest of his desires for when she was at her most desperate. That kind of encounter would be real vengeance.

"Nothing strictly illegal," he replied. "But when you discover that an employee whom you promoted to a position of absolute trust has lied to you, more than once, you start to wonder, and to worry.''

''Lied about what?''

''I don't think I can reveal that. There might be a court case at some time in the future.'' Dominique was sure to sue for alimony when he finally asked for a divorce.

''But I thought you said he did nothing illegal,'' she argued. ''Besides, I'm your wife. Surely you can tell me.''

''I will,'' he hedged. ''After I've read the report myself. At the moment, I only know generalities, not details. Suffice to say that it all sounds very damning indeed. Meanwhile, I must get myself into that shower and get dressed. You too, darling. Once Rico has gone I think we'll go somewhere for brunch then out for some serious house-hunting.''

Her face understandably lit up at this news. It was probably one of her goals, being the mistress of a multimillion-dollar harbourside mansion where she could give extravagant parties dressed in her designer gowns. After all, what was the point in marrying money if you couldn't display the fruits of your labours?

And, by God, she had worked hard to catch him and even harder since the wedding. He had to give her credit for that. It couldn't be easy having to pretend she loved him twenty-four hours a day, and now to smile at him with sore nipples...

Charles threw back the bedclothes and headed for the bathroom.

Dominique sighed as she watched Charles hurry into the *en suite*. The last person she wanted to see this morning was Enrico Mandretti. She couldn't stand the way that man looked at her when Charles wasn't looking, as if she was some sort of nasty creature who'd just crept out from under a rock.

Judging by Charles's speed, Rico must be due here shortly. She would have to hurry and get dressed herself. No way did she want to answer the door in nothing but a bathrobe. She knew exactly what kind of look *that* would get!

Rising from the dressing-table, she hurried into her walk-in wardrobe, swiftly selecting a camel-coloured trouser suit which had a thigh-length jacket which minimised rather than emphasised her curvy figure. What was fine for Charles's eyes wasn't for his sneering best man's.

Back at her dressing-table five minutes later, she swept her hair up into a loose twist and applied the lightest and most natural of make-ups. Even her lipstick echoed the natural colour of her lips. Just a touch of mascara. No eye-shadow or eye-liner. She was slipping simple gold studs into her ears when the doorbell rang.

''Oh, damn,'' she said, hearing the water in the shower still running. Charles must have shaved first.

She had no option but to go and answer the door herself. Steeling herself for some even more overt disapproval than usual, Dominique walked reluctantly from the bedroom and along the hallway to the penthouse's elegant foyer. The heels of her Italian leather ankle boots clacked on the foyer tiles as she crossed to the front door. But she didn't whisk it open straight away. First, she gave a final check to her appearance in one of the wall-mounted mirrors which flanked the front door, after which she peered through the built-in security peep-hole to make sure it *was* Rico.

It was.

Unfortunately.

Dominique unlocked, then opened the door, by which time she'd dredged up a polite smile.

"Hello, Rico," she said. "Come on in."

He strode in, his broad-shouldered six-foot-two frame made even more menacing—or attractive, depending on your point of view—by a suave black suit and a matching black crew-necked top. His longish and incorrigibly wavy black hair was slicked back from his slightly large but broodily handsome face and he was sporting what was these days called designer stubble on his chin.

He was one of the most famous Italian cooks on TV in the world today. Which was perverse, since he wasn't a trained chef at all, according to Charles. Or even born in Italy. The two men had discovered a mutual love of gambling and soon became firm friends.

"Charles is in the shower, I'm sorry," was her first

remark. She sounded defensive and not at all apologetic.

"At *this* hour?" he returned, glancing at his watch.

Dominique couldn't help it. She crossed her arms and glared at him. She didn't like Rico any more than he liked her and she was not going to pretend any different.

"It's Saturday," she said coolly. "Charles can stay in bed all day if he likes. What's it to you, anyway?"

Rico's teeth clamped down hard in his jaw. Charles had asked him to be polite today. But it was going to be impossible. Best he just drop off the damned report and get the hell out of here before he said something he shouldn't.

There was nothing more he could do for his friend, anyway. He'd warned him to cut his losses and get rid of this conniving little con-artist. But no, the besotted fool had to keep hanging in there for a while longer, didn't he, all the time kidding himself that he was having some kind of pathetic revenge?

Maybe, when Charles read this report for himself and heard the damning evidence on the tapes, he'd change his mind and dump the woman. Pronto!

And maybe not.

Rico looked Dominique up and down and conceded that she was one hot-looking babe, despite her obviously trying to play her figure down somewhat this morning for whatever reason. But he'd seen her in clothes other than the conservative outfit she was wearing at this moment, and she had the sort of curves designed to make men's heads turn.

At her sharp reply, his own tongue was eager for a workout. "Charles usually does twenty laps of his pool every morning before breakfast," he countered. "I've never known him to be up later than seven. But, of course, that was before he got married. Before...you."

"Meaning what?" she snapped.

"Meaning things have changed and they'll never be the same again. Tell Charles I couldn't stay. The first race is at twelve-fifteen today. Here's the report I promised him." And he handed her the bulky envelope which contained more than enough evidence to have her out on her ear without a single cent.

But would Charles use it?

Rico certainly hoped so. If he didn't, he just might have to do something about this situation himself. He couldn't let this lady continue to con his best friend. Charles had his faults but he was a genuine gentleman, highly respected by everyone who knew him. Rico had known him for several years now, and would have trusted him with his life. He wasn't about to let Charles throw away any more of his life—and his pride—on some mercenary-minded vamp.

"Oh, yes," she said smugly. "The report. Charles told me all about it."

Rico was stunned. "He *told* you about it?"

She clasped the envelope to her chest, her eyes

flashing defiance at him. "Yes, of course. Why shouldn't he? I'm his wife."

Rico couldn't make held or tail of what was going on here.

"Why look so surprised?" she threw at him. "Have you forgotten I used to work for Charles myself? Don't you think I'd care if one of the people he'd employed and trusted turned out to be a con-artist and a liar?"

Aah…now Rico understood. Charles had invented a half-truth story to explain the report. How clever of him. How devious. How…devilish.

Maybe he was worrying about his friend for nothing. Maybe Charles was more than capable of handling his money-grabbing wife and having some rightful vengeance at the same time. Rico understood all about rightful vengeance. He was Italian, after all.

"You know, Rico," she said, those big blue eyes of hers glittering away frostily, "I'm fed up to the teeth with your looking down your supercilious Italian nose at me. What *is* your problem with me? Is it that you think I'm some sort of fortune hunter who's only with Charles for his money? Charles told me about your experience with your ex-wife, so I suppose that has to be it. But let me tell you this: I *love* my husband. No, that's understating things. I *adore* him. He's my life. What worries him worries me. What distresses him distresses me. So do me a favour in future and keep your cynical suspicions to yourself!"

Rico stared at her. What a tiger she was when crossed! And how convincing she sounded. If he didn't know better, he might have believed her.

He'd have to warn Charles never to let things go to court, because some damned fool male judge just *might* believe her. She could argue that she'd been a fortune hunter up till the moment she met Charles, then whammo, true love struck and she changed overnight into a loyal and ever-devoted wife.

Men could be suckers when it came to a beautiful woman. He knew that only too well.

"Don't forget to give Charles that report," Rico said with a rueful little smile. "Tell him I'll give him a call tonight and we'll discuss it. See you, Dominique."

Dominique pulled a face at his broad back as he walked away.

Wretched man. And a troublemaking one too. If he had his way, he'd break my marriage up. All he wants is his best mate back, so that he can go places with him. He doesn't give a damn about Charles's happiness, only his own.

"Was that Rico?"

Dominique spun to see Charles hurrying along the hallway towards her, pulling on a jumper as he did so. She quickly closed the door to prevent his running after the man. It would only take a few seconds and Rico would be on his way downstairs. Their private lift would be there, at the ready, for him.

"Yes, he had to dash," she replied. "He said he

was late for the races. Here's the report he left.'' And she handed the bulky envelope to her disgruntled-looking husband.

''No other messages?''

''He said he'd ring you tonight.''

Charles nodded, then stared down at the envelope which he was turning over and over in his hands.

''You're not going to read that right now, are you?'' she asked. ''You must be hungry. I know I am.''

He glanced up, and smiled at her. ''You know, you have an amazing appetite for a girl who worries about her figure like you do.''

Dominique shrugged. ''I work hard so that I can enjoy the good things in life.''

''Yes. Yes, I can see that. In that case, I'll just put this in my den and we can be on our way.''

''On our way where?'' she asked as she trailed after him down the other hallway which led to the room Charles liked to call his den. But it was more of a study-cum-office, fresh and modern with pale grey walls, carpet and furniture. The interior designer who'd done out this penthouse obviously had a thing for each room having the same colour throughout. Even the ceiling in here was painted the same pale grey. The vertical blinds too. Charles wasn't all that keen on the décor but Dominique liked clean, simple lines and pale colours. She rarely wore bright colours herself, preferring neutrals and pastels.

''I thought we might stroll down to the Rocks area

and have brunch there,'' Charles said, tossing the envelope onto the top of his grey desk before turning to draw her into his arms. ''Then I'll call up a real-estate agent I know and have him show us some houses. How's that?''

''Wonderful!'' She cupped his cheeks and kissed him.

Charles's heart lurched, reminding him of his ongoing vulnerability to this woman. He shouldn't have taken her in his arms. It had just seemed a natural thing to do. He almost kissed her back, wanting to feel the soft surrender of her mouth under his, wanting to forget everything but the pleasure to be found in her body.

But he didn't. Still, it was a close call, Charles having a struggle to resist temptation. Hopefully, after he read that report tonight his desire for revenge would be right back on track.

''Let's go,'' he said brusquely and, drawing back, he took her elbow and propelled her out of the room.

CHAPTER SIX

"SO WHAT do you think?" Charles asked, then waited for Dominique to gush.

It was four in the afternoon and this was the third harbourside property the agent had taken them to inspect, but the first to be empty of all furniture and inhabitants. It was brand-new, and had taken two years to build, the builder having bought an old dump on the site which he'd then torn down to build a home more in keeping with this exclusive area. The asking price reflected the bank balances of the neighbours. Fifteen million dollars.

"Well?" Charles prompted when Dominique remained silent.

They were standing in the huge living area at one of the bay windows which overlooked the terrace and the resort-size pool. Further on were the formal gardens and on one side the maintenance-free tennis court.

There was no yacht moored at the private jetty which jutted out into Sydney Harbour at the bottom of the gently sloping lawns, but Charles had no doubt Dominique would want one of those too, in due course.

Her lovely high forehead crinkled into a frown. "I

don't know, Charles. It's so big! I mean…I'm sorry, but I don't think I want a house as big as this.''

Charles couldn't believe it. The place was gold-digger paradise. It had everything. And all within a stone's throw of the city.

''I want a real family home,'' she went on, ''not a showplace.''

Charles stared at her. *This*, from a woman who'd only married him for his money? Something wasn't right here. What game was she playing now?

''But we could throw some wonderful parties here,'' he pointed out, waving his arm around the luxurious and spacious living area.

Dominique looked surprised. ''I didn't think parties would be such a big priority with you from now on. I thought you wanted a family life.''

''I did. I *do*,'' he insisted. ''But that doesn't mean I won't have to entertain sometimes. If you're worried about the price then don't be. I can easily afford it.''

''What? Oh, yes, yes, I'm sure you can, but that's not the point. Can I be blunt, Charles?''

''By all means.''

''I'm sorry, but I just don't like this place. It's over-the-top and not you at all.''

''Not me…''

''Yes, you're not a show-off. You're rich, yes, but you don't flaunt it. Your penthouse is fabulous but it's not decked out like some rich playboy's pad. I'll bet you bought it more for its convenient location than any other reason.''

Actually, she couldn't have been more right. Charles had always hated to waste time on travelling to and from the office. Before the penthouse he'd lived on the other side of the harbour on one of the far northern beaches, and had resented the time it took him every morning and evening, battling the traffic which flooded across the bridge.

"I can understand you want a quality home," Dominique continued. "But this isn't a home. It's just a setting for the kind of man who would want to live here. Maybe you should tell Rico it's on the market. He'd be the perfect owner."

"You really don't like Rico, do you?"

"What came first, the chicken or the egg?" she countered. "He disliked me at first sight. It's difficult to like someone who shows you nothing but disrespect."

Charles was alarmed. "Rico's been openly disrespectful to you?" He knew he should have been there when Rico arrived this morning. But he'd been in the darned shower.

"No, I guess not," she admitted, somewhat reluctantly. "He's clever enough not to be openly rude. But I can feel his disapproval just the same. He thinks I'm after your money."

Charles sighed his relief. Rico hadn't really said anything, then. "Rico is going through a very cynical phase where women are concerned."

"Don't make excuses for him," she snapped.

"I'm not making excuses. I'm just explaining

where he's coming from. He was very hurt by his ex. She spent his money like water whilst he was married to her, flatly refused to have children, then ripped him off for more money during the divorce.''

''Maybe she didn't want children. She does have that right, you know.''

''Yes, but she'd said she did want children *before* the wedding. Remember that Rico's Italian. He'd never knowingly marry a woman who didn't want children.''

''I see. Well, I guess he was hurt. But that's no reason to take it out on me. Besides, I *want* to have your children. Have you told him that?''

''Actually, I have.'' And she wouldn't be too thrilled with his reaction, Charles thought wryly. But he could see now that Rico had to be right in his assessment of the type of gold-digger Dominique was. Her game plan was nothing like Jasmine's. Her plan was to play the devoted wife and even have a baby, after which she would be in an invincible position when it came to demanding a huge divorce settlement. After all, she would be the mother of his child.

The thought popped into his head that she might be vetoing this property because she didn't want him tying up so much cash in a house which might prove difficult to sell. Buyers of fifteen-million-dollar harbourside mansions didn't come along every day of the week. This particular property had been on the market for a few months already.

Charles had difficulty hiding the bitterness his

thoughts evoked. It welled up inside him, like bile on the rise. How could someone so beautiful be so wicked?

And she looked extra-beautiful today, dressed as she was in that simple yet classy outfit. He found her no less sexy for her having hidden her voluptuous curves. Perversely, it made him want her all the more.

Whenever he looked at her, he kept thinking how much he would enjoy stripping her of that super-conservative suit later this evening; how he would insist she swim with him in the nude, under the moon-light. The nearby offices would be shut, so there were no worries about their being seen. He could do ex-actly as he liked.

His heart thudded at the thought, and the thought of all the other scenarios to come.

The time had arrived, he realised, to make sure that no baby would be conceived during his month of ven-geance. The real-estate agent was outside, taking a call on his cellphone. They had time to talk.

"Speaking of having children, darling, would you mind if we put off trying for a baby for a little while?"

His request clearly dismayed her.

"But why?" she protested. "I thought you were as anxious as me to get started on a family."

"I'm only talking about a month or two." He smiled and took her in his arms. A painful necessity if he was to act normally around her. "Call me selfish but I want you to myself for a little while longer. I don't want you feeling sick every morning and telling me to get lost. We've only been married a month, after all, and it's not as though we were sleeping together before the wedding. I can't get enough of you at the moment, my darling,'' he said truthfully. ''Why do you think I'm taking next week off work? It isn't only to look at houses. Be patient and try to understand. I'm a red-blooded man in love for the first time in his life. I'm sure my needs will lessen in time…''

Hell, he hoped so or he might go insane. Just taking her into his arms had made his desire move from his brain to his body. The ache was unbearable.

She slanted a coy look up at him. ''Do you want me to keep taking the Pill the way I have been?''

''Can you?'' During their honeymoon, she'd skipped the week of white pills which brought on a period, going straight on to the next month's red pills. Her doctor suggested the idea, knowing she was going away on her honeymoon.

''It shouldn't be any problem for another cycle. But after that, I'm stopping. You're not getting any younger, Charles, and neither am I. I *want* your baby. Fair enough?''

Something twisted inside Charles. Oh, if only she was speaking the truth. But Rico was probably right. What she wanted was an insurance policy.

''If you insist,'' he said.

''I insist. Now, let's go find the real-estate agent and see if he has something more cosy on his books.''

"Cosy," Charles repeated drily. "She wants cosy."

Dominique smiled. "Cosy compared to this, anyway. I won't object to water views, or a pool in the back yard. But I don't want it to be so large that we'd have to employ live-in staff to look after it. I would hate that. I wouldn't mind a cleaner coming in one day a week, like you have at the penthouse. But on the whole I want to look after my own home. And you, my love. I didn't get married to have someone else do all the cooking and cleaning. Which reminds me, I don't want to go out to dinner tonight. I want to cook us a meal at home. Your cupboards and freezer are full of ingredients and I'm a really good cook, even if I say so myself."

Charles didn't give a hoot about dinner at that moment. His hunger went in an entirely different direction.

Still, having her cook for him was far better than having to sit through a slow meal at a restaurant.

"I didn't get married just to be your legal mistress, you know," she tossed off airily.

Too bad, he thought. Because that was exactly what she was going to be for the next month. He'd paid for the privilege of unlimited access to her body and that was exactly what he was going to have! Still, if she wanted to throw in some home cooking then he wasn't about to object.

Charles glanced at his watch. "Time's getting on. It'll be dark soon. The days are so short at this time of year. How about we put off any more house-hunting till tomorrow and I take you home? We could relax and have a few drinks together whilst you wave your magic wand in the kitchen.''

She laughed. ''You don't fool me, Charles Brandon. It's not wine or food you want.''

He smiled. ''You've caught me out.''

''That's all right, darling,'' she whispered, then reached up on tiptoe to press a softly teasing kiss on his lips. ''I feel exactly the same way.''

His arms swept around her, pulling her hard against him, flattening her breasts against his chest and wrapping the soft swell of her stomach around his by now bursting erection. Their eyes locked and for the life of him, he could have sworn he was looking at real passion in hers. The way they dilated, then smouldered.

''Charles,'' she choked out, sounding almost desperate with desire.

It came to him then that maybe, just maybe, he'd touched something in her that no man had ever touched before. Maybe she wasn't faking. Maybe she'd become a victim of her own cold-blooded plan.

He didn't imagine for one second that she loved him. Women like her didn't love anything except money. But he supposed even the most mercenary creature was capable of enjoying sex. Rico had never said Jasmine faked it in bed. Rico had always believed his ex liked having sex with him.

Another thought followed, a much darker but more

logical thought. Maybe their passionate lovemaking last night had unexpectedly turned her on?

Charles decided to test his theory, right then and there.

''You do realise I can't wait till I get you home,'' he told her, and watched her lips fall apart. Shock, he wondered? Or instant arousal?

''I'll tell the agent we're going upstairs to look at the main bathroom once more,'' he went on, his own heart racing. ''You won't have to get fully undressed. He'll never know. And if he does, who cares?''

''But...''

''No buts,'' he said forcefully. ''Let's go.''

CHAPTER SEVEN

"YOU'RE angry with me," were her first words when they finally got home.

Charles closed the door behind them then looked deep into her agitated eyes. "No," he said quite truthfully. "I'm not angry with you." Bewildered was more the word.

She'd refused to let him make love to her when he'd taken her up to the *en suite* bathroom in that house. Quite adamantly. She'd stated she couldn't possibly with that man downstairs. When he'd pressed the issue, she'd seemed so genuinely distressed that he'd stopped. Maybe she'd been acting. Maybe not. He could no longer tell.

Whatever, so much for his theory. Or his expectation that she'd do anything he asked. Clearly, there was a limit to her co-operation.

"You had every right to refuse," he said, doing his best to sound calm rather than confused. "I would never force you to do anything you didn't like."

She shook her head. "You don't understand. It wasn't that I didn't want to. I did. Too much," she muttered under her breath as she turned away from him and began to walk disconsolately across the foyer.

He grabbed her by the shoulders and spun her back round to face him. "What? What did you say?"

Her eyes whipped up to his. "You heard me, Charles," she cried. "I wanted you to do it, *way* too much. I've been wanting you way too much ever since I met you. I...I've never felt anything like what I feel when I'm with you. It frightens me sometimes. I'm not used to not having control over my life, or my feelings. Do you understand what I'm saying, Charles?"

"Yes," he choked out as a wild elation rushed through his veins.

She *did* feel something for him. Maybe not love, but lust, yes. And right from the start. She hadn't lied about that. She'd wanted him as she'd never wanted any other man. He could feel her trembling even now, feel her fear of losing control.

She *was* putty in his hands, as he'd once imagined.

What a wildly corrupting thought! Much better than thinking he could make her do what he wanted through greed. Greed had obviously taken a backstep in her life whilst desire reigned supreme.

His hands tightened on her shoulders as he dragged her mouth up to his, his kiss savage and uncompromising. She stiffened but she didn't struggle and soon she was responding to the fierce probing of his tongue. Not till he was confident that her control was totally shattered did Charles lift his mouth from hers. His own control began to slip at the way she just stood there, eyes dazed, whilst he stripped her naked.

"Charles," she whimpered when he finally drew her quivering nudity against his still fully clothed body.

"Soon," he promised thickly. "Soon."

There was something incredibly erotic about just holding her like that. Even more so when he noticed their reflection in the wall mirrors which flanked the front door. Her buttocks were so pale against his dark grey trousers. He ran his large brown hands over the soft globes of flesh, lifting them, squeezing them. She buried her face into his neck and moaned. The ache in his own flesh was acute but he was determined not to rush things. He wanted to wallow in his new discovery that she wasn't pretending, at least where sex was concerned. Finally, he turned her round so that he could see himself caress her.

"Oh," she gasped once her glazed eyes connected to their mirrored images, groaning hard, then flinching slightly when he rubbed the centre of his palms over her already hard nipples.

"Oh, Dominique!" he cried, his hands dropping away. She was obviously still very sore after last night. He shuddered at the thought.

She blinked, then picked his hands up and put them right back on her breasts. "They're all right," she said thickly. "They don't hurt that much. Don't stop, Charles. Please don't stop."

Her blind excitement excited him unbearably, but he couldn't bring himself to touch her breasts again. Now he remembered how sore she'd said her nipples had been this morning. At the same time, he did what she wanted. He did not stop, his hands travelling down over her tensely held stomach, pressing her bottom back against his rigid sex, sliding his fingers down towards the V of blonde curls between her legs.

"Oh, God, yes," she begged, even before his fingertips slipped through her dampness in search of that spot which invariably sent her over the edge. He was perilously close to his own edge by then. If he moved his hips, he'd be a goner. He kept himself deathly still whilst his hand moved on.

Her whole body froze, her head falling back against his shoulder, her mouth gaping wide. She trembled violently, her cry the cry of a lost soul, her lower body jerking against him.

Charles couldn't help it. Hearing and feeling her was bad enough. Watching it in the mirror at the same time was too much. His release was involuntary, and for a few moments all thought ceased. But as soon as the wild heat of the moment subsided, his mind began to torture him.

What *was* he going to do with this woman, this woman he still craved? There was no point in kidding himself. His love for her hadn't turned to hate and his need for cold, hard vengeance was already beginning to wane. His initial desire to make her pay had just been a reaction to finding out she was a gold-digger. He'd wanted to strike back as any man would.

But everything had changed now, he realised as he swept her limp body up into his arms. She did have feelings for him. Maybe they were largely sexual but so what? A man could go a long way to find a wife who responded the way she did. So she wanted his money as well as his body. He could learn to live with that. And she was at least willing to give him a child.

Of course, Rico would say he was a fool to even consider not divorcing her. A desperate, Dominique-obsessed fool. And maybe Rico was right. But Rico *was* going through an extra-cynical phase. Dominique might not have any intention of asking for a divorce after she had his baby. She might be quite content to hitch a ride on his gravy train for life. If so, why would he want to get rid of her? Hell, he *loved* her.

Yes, but she doesn't love *you*, came back the argument for the defence. Her fancying you was just a twisted act of fate. She still lied to you, deceived you, played you for a fool. Can you really live with that forever without saying anything to her, without letting her know you know the truth?

Charles wasn't sure. His pride had always been both an asset and a weakness where he was concerned. He would hate to think she really thought him a fool.

Clearly, it was high time for him to read that report for himself, see in detail the evidence against her. Then he could make a more informed decision.

Meanwhile, he had to do something about the state of his underwear. ''I have to shower and change,'' he said as he carried her down the hallway which led to the master bedroom. "And you, madam, have to put some clothes on."

"Why?" she murmured dreamily, and he laughed.

"Because having you naked is an irresistible temptation. And I have to go read that report. Didn't you say Rico was going to ring me later this evening? He'll want to know what I think of it and I can hardly tell him I haven't had time."

"You pander to Rico too much," she said.

"He's my best friend. And a very astute business-man. I like to discuss things with him."

Her eyes suddenly cleared of their passionate haze to show the intelligence which lay behind her beauty. "I'm your wife and not exactly a dummy. Why not discuss that report with me? After all, I worked for Brandon Beer as well."

"Yes, but not any more," he said, and gave her a light peck on the forehead. "I don't want you wor-rying your pretty little head about business matters."

Her nose crinkled up. "Don't start treating me like some blonde bimbo, Charles. I wouldn't like that."

"What a shame. I always wanted a blonde bimbo for a wife." He smiled in an effort to make light of their discussion, and to deflect her away from talking about that report. He sincerely wished he'd never told her about the darned thing now.

"You don't mean that," she chided.

"Don't be too sure," came his laughing reply, and, dumping her in the middle of the bed, he whirled and strode straight for the bathroom.

"What would you like to have for dinner?" she called after him before he could escape.

You again, came the automatic thought.

"Anything," he called over his shoulder. "I'm easy."

Too easy where you're concerned, he realised bitterly. Any other man would have tossed her out on her ear by now. But what was he doing? Making excuses for her, clinging to any train of thought which would accommodate his desperate desire to keep her as his wife, and to keep having her body. It had to stop. He had to read that report, talk to Rico again for some balance of opinion, then hopefully make some tough decisions.

As soon as the bathroom door was safely shut, Dominique rolled over on the cream satin quilt and buried her face in her hands. She was perilously close to crying, yet she wasn't sure why. There was no real reason for her to be afraid like this again, no reason to worry that her marriage was heading for disaster.

Yet she *was* worried.

Was it because of the kind of sex Charles was suddenly wanting? Or was the fear still her own inner panic over loving anyone as much as she loved her husband?

She'd been cripplingly close to letting him have his way with her this afternoon in that ghastly mausoleum of a house. His forcefulness had excited her, there was no doubt about it. On top of that, they hadn't made love all day and she'd been wanting him badly. Clearly, she'd become addicted to his touch.

What had just happened out in the foyer was a perfect example of his power over her body, and her ever-escalating vulnerability to his. That was why she'd said no up front this afternoon. Because she'd been afraid that once Charles started, she would have been incapable of refusing him and she soon would not have cared if the real-estate agent *had* walked in on them.

That kind of loving was anathema to her. She wanted to flee from it, yet at the same time she was perversely drawn to it. She couldn't help being attracted to the woman she became in his arms, the uncontrollably passionate creature who was nothing like the cold-blooded mercenary-driven robot she'd become over the years. It was a relief to be driven by desire alone, and not the desire for money.

Money...

Dominique rolled over and stared up at the ceiling.

Did she even want money any more? Yes, yes, of course she must. Nothing would ever rid her of the fear of being poor. Her worrying that she would have married Charles, poor or not, was a really stupid train of thought. Charles was Charles because he *was* successful and smart. A man amongst men in every sense of the word, impressive and decisive, with a strong sense of self which she found overwhelmingly sexy.

Charles...

She needed him, needed his arms around her and

his mouth on hers. Only then would she feel safe again—and completely satisfied.

Tears flooded her eyes as the need to be with the man she loved struggled with her shame at appearing so needy in his eyes. It was no wonder he'd been surprised when she'd rejected him this afternoon. When had she ever said no to whatever he wanted? And he was wanting more and more from her lately. Last night seemed to have released a different Charles, a darker, more demanding man. What would she say when he made further demands?

Dominique was afraid her answer would always be yes.

With a raw cry of defeat she sprang off the bed and hurried to the bathroom door. Her grimace as the knob turned easily in her hand reflected her inner torment. Why hadn't he locked it? Why did he have to make it so easy for her to give in to this escalating weakness?

She opened the door and walked in, each step an exercise in humiliation. The tears spilled over and ran down her cheeks.

She found Charles standing under a stinging shower spray, his head bowed, his palms flat against the cream tiles. He didn't see her standing there, watching him through the steamed-up screen. Her sliding back the shower door sent his head jerking round.

"What the…?" He stared at her tear-stained face, his eyes flaring wide. "What is it? What's wrong?"

What's wrong? Dear God, if only he knew...

"I...I need you to make love to me, Charles," she choked out. "Now. Properly. Please..."

A tremor rippled down Dominique's spine when she saw his body respond to her plea, instinctively, automatically, as if he had no say in the matter. Her eyes widened at the realisation that he was as much in her power as she was in his.

"You want me too," she whispered, awed by his instant erection.

"Always," he said thickly, and held out his hand to her.

She placed her hand in his, then smiled shakily at him through her tears. "You do love me, don't you?"

"How can you doubt it?" he said, and pulled her into the heated enclosure.

I won't in future, she vowed as he kissed her, the hunger in his mouth as reassuring as the strong arms around her. I'm going to stop this negative nonsense once and for all. I'm going to be happy and secure in Charles's love from now on. No more fear. No more worrying.

"Dominique," he groaned when his mouth finally lifted from hers.

"Yes, yes, here," she concurred even as he was pushing her back against the tiles.

Oh, the glory of his flesh filling hers, lifting her up onto her toes, taking her mind and her soul with him.

"Charles," she choked out, her arms lifting to wind around his neck. "Kiss me some more."

He kissed her some more and made her whole, scattering her fears, taking her with him to that place where nothing existed but the two of them, together. Her heart sang with joy and her body thrummed with pleasure.

Charles loved her and she loved him. What more could she ever ask for?

CHAPTER EIGHT

HER real name was Jane Cooper, the report revealed, the only daughter of Scott and Tess Cooper, two seventeen-year-old teenagers who had run away from their small Tasmanian country town to live together in Hobart and who were never accepted back into either family fold. A magistrate had allowed them to marry when Tess became pregnant at eighteen.

Jane was born in Hobart but the young family of three soon moved to Keats Ridge on the west side of Tasmania, where her father worked for several years on the building of a nearby dam. Once the dam was built, however, employment opportunities dried up in the area and Keats Ridge was reduced to little more than a ghost town. The family lived on social security from the time Jane was eleven.

Charles frowned over this. Why didn't the man just move on to a place where there *was* work? What was wrong with him? Didn't he have any guts? Any goals? Any gumption?

Apparently not.

Charles's eyes dropped again to the report and he read on.

Jane's mother had never worked, except briefly as a waitress in a local tea shop. Although no photographs of her could be located by the investigator, locals said Tess Cooper was a very beautiful woman with lovely, long blonde hair and a great figure. They said the daughter, Jane, was the spitting image of her mother.

Jane attended the local primary school then the regional high school, where her attendance record was abysmal. She did pass her school certificate—just— but never completed her higher-school certificate. Her mother died when she was seventeen, the death certificate saying lung cancer. Locals remembered that Tess Cooper had been sick on and off for years. Rumour had it that her cancer had started elsewhere and finally spread to her lungs, which proved terminal. They said that towards the end Jane had left school permanently to nurse her mother, who died when she was just thirty-five and Jane seventeen. Scott Cooper, again according to the locals, had been a dead loss to his family, spending most days drinking at the one and only hotel still operating in town.

After her mother's death Jane moved to Launceston, where she worked in a fish and chip shop. At eighteen, she moved to the mainland, where she found work as a housemaid in a Melbourne hotel. Shortly thereafter, she changed her name to Dominique and started going to night school, doing secretarial and computer courses to begin with before later moving on to various sales and marketing diplomas.

Over the next six years she had worked her way

up in the hospitality industry, holding various clerical and guest-relations positions in Melbourne hotels before securing the job as PA to Jonathon Hall when she was twenty-six. That position had lasted two years.

Charles didn't need to read what had happened when she moved to Sydney. He knew that part.

The factual details of Dominique's childhood and working life were followed by edited transcripts of the taped interviews with various people of Dominique's past acquaintance, ten in all. Charles didn't have time to listen to the tapes just then—Dominique had said dinner would be ready in an hour—so he skimmed through the edited transcripts.

The first three interviews featured women who'd worked at the same hotels as Dominique during the years she was working on the reception desk in hotels. All described her as a clever but conniving creature with one aim in life. To become rich. They spoke of her flirting with the wealthier male guests, and probably sleeping with them—though when closely questioned they admitted this last was an assumption on their parts. They had no real evidence. Yes, Dominique had had boyfriends during the time they knew her, and they supplied a few names.

Four of these had been found and interviewed. All were working-class lads, all younger than Dominique. They all admitted to having been mad about her and all claimed they had slept with her.

One of them had said, ''It was love she didn't like.

The day after I told her I loved her, she broke up with me, said I was getting too serious. She said she was sorry, she liked me a lot but she didn't want to marry me.''

Charles shook his head in dismay at reading this. Dominique's unfortunate background had elicited some sympathy and understanding from him. But how could you forgive anyone who used young men with such callousness? It was obvious that they were just research material in her quest to find out how to be good in bed. It amazed him that each of her so-called boyfriends held no bitterness towards her. All four said that they wished her well.

Her female colleagues, however, had shown absolutely no sympathy for her. The three of them had thought her a mercenary piece of work who only wanted one thing in life and made no bones about it. They all hoped she would be miserable.

It wasn't till Charles moved on to reading the first of the interviews with the three girls Dominique had flatted with in Melbourne—the first flatmate's name was Sandie—that he suspected jealousy might be influencing some of the women's views on Dominique. As he read on, he found it impossible to separate the truth from sheer malice.

Charles stopped reading at this juncture, deciding that maybe listening to the tone of this Sandie's voice would uncover the truth of the matter. Once he found the tape marked ''Dominique's Melbourne flatmates'', he swung round on his office chair and slotted it into the portable player he kept in the book shelves behind his desk. Changing the mode from CD to tape, he pressed play then settled back to listen.

It didn't take Charles long to see he'd been right. Talk about catty! Sandie was clearly relishing putting the knife in. She especially loved telling the investigator what Dominique had supposedly said about her next marital target being older, less handsome and more grateful than Hall.

"So what's happened?" she herself wanted to know. "Has Dominique seduced some rich old sucker up in Sydney and his family is all up in arms?"

Charles was grateful that the investigator had declined to answer.

The second flatmate, named Tricia, was even worse. Her comments were vicious. "Of course, females like her have ice in their veins, not blood. I've never met anyone more fake than Dominique Cooper. You only have to look at her hair and her boobs to know that. She was just one big fake!"

Charles winced, though not because either of those last accusations was true. Aside from his own up-close and personal knowledge of the subject, it was obvious from this report that Dominique had inherited her blonde hair and lovely figure from her mother. Her beauty was a matter of genes, not surgery, or a dye job.

Still, he could not discount the fact that a lot of what the two flatmates said was probably true, and his dismay increased.

"She took endless courses, you know," Tricia went on, her tone scathing. "Anything which would make her into a better man-trap. Deportment and grooming. Art and wine appreciation. Even cookery. When I asked her why she was doing a cookery course, she laughed and said that if sex didn't work, she might have to resort to food as the way to a man's heart. Well, perhaps she should have tried the cooking angle with Jonathon because obviously her fake brand of sex didn't do the trick. He dumped her in the end, didn't he? I have to confess I was never happier about anything in my whole life!"

Only one of the three flatmates interviewed proved to have more balanced views. Less black and white. Less condemning and more sympathetic. It was Claudia, Rico's cousin.

"You have to understand," Claudia said at one stage, "that Dominique was a damaged person. She confided in me one night that no one who hadn't lived her life could understand her attitude to money. It wasn't just that she'd been poor as a child. There was something about her mother's death which affected her greatly and which she hinted at but never explained. I gather her mother had been ill for a long time before she died. I don't think Dominique ever got over it."

Charles had no doubt this was the case. His own mother's death had been just as tragic in its own way and had affected him greatly. He could well imagine that nursing a terminally ill mother all those years under financially deprived circumstances could have twisted a young girl's mind. Dominique might have believed money would have saved her mother. Which it might very well have.

"I think she was a very sad girl underneath," Claudia went on to say, with considerable insight in Charles's opinion. "I felt sorry for her. She's not a bad person. I actually liked her a lot, but the other girls in the house hated her. Of course, they were just plain jealous. I mean…Dominique is simply stunning, isn't she? All their boyfriends tried to come on to her. Not that Dominique did anything to encourage them. She actually wasn't the flirty type. But heck, let's face it, she only had to walk into the room and all the men's mouths would drop open. Her body, I guess. Not to mention her hair, eyes, lips, legs, skin. I could go on and on but I'm sure you get my drift. Actually, I don't have much pity for this man she married. From what I gather he's filthy rich and not exactly a spring chicken. He probably only wanted a trophy wife on his arm and that gorgeous body in his bed. Rico told me he married her in no time flat, so what did he expect? The man should have got to know her first. But he didn't really want to get to know her, did he? He just wanted to get into her pants."

Charles flinched at this brutal statement. Because it was partly true. He hadn't bothered to really get to know Dominique. He'd never probed into her past. Maybe, subconsciously, he hadn't wanted to know.

He'd chosen to keep things superficial. He'd deceived himself, more than she had.

"She got what she wanted and he got what he wanted," Claudia pronounced with brutal frankness. "Sounds like a fair exchange to me. Marrying for love isn't what it's cracked up to be, anyway. I know. I've tried it and it sucked. Hey, I hope Dominique isn't going to hear any of this. Rico said she wouldn't. I would hate her to think she thought I didn't like her because I did. I would have liked to be her real friend, but she never let anyone get that close. She was afraid of love, I think. Yes, definitely afraid of it."

That's it! Charles realised, jumping to his feet. That explains everything. She was afraid of love, afraid to love him.

But she *did* love him. Why else would she have been crying when she came to him in the bathroom earlier? Why else would she worry that she wanted him too much?

Had he soothed her fears with his more tender love-making, first in the shower then back in bed? He seemed to have. She'd been like liquid in his arms afterwards, her skin all soft and glowing.

"Tell me you love me," she'd murmured as she'd gazed up into his eyes.

He was glad now that he had said he did, even if his motivation hadn't been clear at the time. He'd still been hedging his bets, not sure if he'd been going to hang in there with this marriage, or not.

Now he knew what he was going to do.

Charles clicked off the tape and pressed rewind on the tape deck. He was slipping the page of the report back with the other two tapes into the envelope when he heard Dominique's footsteps coming down the tiled hallway towards the den. He just had enough time to drop the envelope into the top drawer of his desk before she popped her head in the door.

"Can I come in or is the cloak and dagger bit still on?"

He tried to act naturally and not as if he was really seeing her for the first time. "All finished," he said.

"And?" She pushed open the door and moved further into the room.

Charles tried not to stare. Her blonde hair was swept up into a pony-tail and she was wearing a pale blue polar fleece track suit. Her face was free of make-up, except for some pink lipstick. She looked fresh and young and heart-stoppingly beautiful. All her earlier tears had vanished and she was smiling a warm and very relaxed smile.

"I take that back," she hurried on. "I don't want to know anything about that infernal report until you're happy to tell me. Did Rico ring? I didn't hear the phone."

"No. Not yet."

"Then why don't you ring him and get it over with? The last thing I want is that man interrupting our evening together."

"How long till dinner?"

"Around ten minutes or so."

"And what gourmet delights am I to look forward to?" he asked.

"Chicken and mushroom risotto followed by some decadent passion-fruit-topped cheesecake I found in the freezer, all washed down with that lovely bottle of Margaret River Chardonnay you had hiding at the back of the fridge. I know you prefer red but you can't possibly have red with risotto, Charles. I forbid it."

Charles did his best not to think negative thoughts about her wine and cooking skills, but it was difficult in the light of what he'd just heard.

"Rico would agree with you," he tossed off.

"Rico, Rico," she said irritably. "I'll never know what you see in that show-pony."

"Rico has depths you would never imagine."

"Rico? Don't make me laugh. Now, you have depth, Charles. Rico is all shadow and no substance. I'll bet he can't even cook!"

"You're wrong but I'm not going to argue with you."

"No, please don't. I'm far too happy tonight to argue with anyone. Now, don't be too long. Time's getting on and my poor little tummy's rumbling. You have fifteen minutes at most."

"I'll be with you in ten."

"I'll hold you to that."

Suddenly, she was gone, but her perfume lingered, as well as the memory of her wonderful smile. He could not dispute her claim of happiness. She had looked happy.

Had she decided she wasn't afraid to love him any longer? She'd said she loved him during their love-making in the shower and afterwards, back in bed. She'd told him over and over.

And he'd done the same. How could he not when his love for her welled up inside him all the time he was with her? The truth was he'd never been happier than since he'd met Dominique. What did it matter what forces had brought them together? Who cared if she'd been just after his money to begin with? He felt confident that her agenda had changed, that *she* had changed.

Of course, Rico would not believe a word of that. He would call it sentimental crap. He'd say Charles had been well and truly conned.

Charles didn't want to listen to Rico's arguments. Rico would learn the truth about Dominique eventually. By their tenth wedding anniversary he might even come to believe it.

Meanwhile, he would avoid any further discussions over Dominique for a while. He would let Rico think he was keeping her as his wife just till he got her out of his system. It was better than having to listen to his friend go on and on about how he should get rid of her all the time.

Charles reached for his phone and punched in Rico's number. No answer. He tried Rico's mobile and was about to hang up when the man himself answered in slurred tones.

Oh, dear. Rico only drank occasionally when he was upset over something.

"Charles here," Charles said with a sigh. "I see you didn't win at the races."

Rico laughed. "Actually, I did. Money-wise."

"So in what way *didn't* you win?"

"Let's just say the merry widow spoiled my day."

"How?"

"The usual way. God, but she's sarcastic."

"Did you know she was going to be there?"

His reluctance to answer confirmed what Charles already suspected.

"You did know," Charles said emphatically. "That's why you went. You're hung up on her, aren't you?"

"Don't be ridiculous! I can't stand her. She's everything I despise in a woman."

"Yes, I know," Charles said drily.

"Have you read the report?" Rico asked abruptly.

"Yes."

"And?"

"It looks damning."

"Too right it does. So what are you going to do about her?"

"Nothing. For now."

"I just knew you were going to say that. Be it on your head, then, Charles. You've been warned. Just remember. Revenge is a tricky path to take. You could end up getting even more hurt.''

"I appreciate your concern. And I appreciate the report. Sorry about going off at you last night. You were right to tell me.'' This way, his marriage now had a real chance of surviving. Because he was going to make a point of getting to know Dominique, and he would start by telling her more about himself. He would take her fully into his confidence about things he'd never told anyone, not even Rico. Then one day, when she was secure in his love, she might tell him all about herself.

"I wish someone had told me about Jasmine,'' Rico muttered. ''*Before* the bloody wedding.''

"You wouldn't have taken any notice. You were besotted.''

"It's a failing I have, falling for the wrong type. No, forget I said that. I have not fallen for the merry widow. I'd just like to...''

"Get into her pants,'' Charles finished for him.

"Hell, no. I don't want her wearing pants. I don't want her wearing anything.'' He groaned. "Forget I said that, too. I've been drinking.''

"So I noticed. I hope you're not driving anywhere later.''

"Don't go big-brothering me, Charles. I can look after myself. For your information I'm in the foyer bar at the Regency, the one I took you to the other night. I came in a taxi and I won't be going home till tomorrow morning. Leanne will be here shortly.''

Charles's eyebrows shot up. "Who's Leanne?"

"A very nice blonde I met the other night. Not unlike your Dominique to look at, except Leanne is already filthy rich. All she wants is my body. Which is a very nice change."

Charles sighed. "Renée was wrong the other night. Money *is* the root of all evil. But sex runs a close second."

"True. Otherwise you wouldn't be hanging on to that gold-digging wife of yours, pretending it's revenge. Talk about pathetic. I hope she's worth it, mate, because every day you keep her from now on is going to cost you. Chicks like that don't go quietly and the family law court judge you eventually front will wonder why you didn't get rid of her once you had that report in your hot little hands. You'll lose your best weapon if you continue to cohabit with the enemy. You do know that, don't you?"

"It's my life, Rico. I don't tell you what to do. Don't tell me."

"Right. Fine. Be a fool, then. See if I care." And he hung up.

Charles winced. Was he being a fool? Was Dominique still conning him?

No. No, he refused to believe that. She loved him, and he loved her. They just didn't know each other very well. Yet.

But time would remedy that. Starting tonight.

CHAPTER NINE

DOMINIQUE was proud of the table she'd set and the meal she'd cooked. That cookery course she'd once taken had finally come in useful. Up till now, she hadn't had the opportunity to cook for Charles, except at breakfast. And she'd hardly have needed to take an advanced cookery course in international cuisine to manage such simple fare. After all, she'd been cooking since she was thirteen.

"This looks marvellous, Dominique," Charles said. "Somehow I feel underdressed for the occasion."

"I like you in what you're wearing," she complimented as they sat down opposite each other on the glass table which fitted beautifully into the penthouse's hexagonal-shaped dining alcove. Three of the five walls enclosing them were glass through which you could see the city below, with its bright lights and busy streets. Saturday night was *the* night in Sydney, the many theatres and restaurants drawing lots of people.

"You have the right body for jeans," she went on. "Tall and lean, with long legs and a nice tight bottom. Yummy."

"Dominique! Really!"

"You're blushing," she said with a teasing laugh.
"Are you deliberately trying to embarrass me?"

"Would I do that?" She laughed again. If Charles
had one flaw, it was a tendency to be a bit stuffy
occasionally. Though goodness knew he hadn't been
stuffy the last day or so. Not in the bedroom, or out
of it.

"I don't know," he replied.

She blinked, taken aback at the odd note in his
voice. "What do you mean?"

He picked up his wine glass, which she'd already
filled with the nicely chilled Margaret River
Chardonnay. "I've been thinking how little we actually know about each other."

Dominique's whole body sucked in sharply, panic
gripping her till she realised Charles hadn't meant
anything sinister by it. He was sipping his wine and
looking quite relaxed. Her automatic recoil at his remark, however, highlighted the fact that, no matter
how happy and secure she felt in Charles's love, underneath she would always be worried that he might
one day uncover the truth about her past. How could
she ever explain the person she'd been before meeting
him? Or the totally false family background she'd
given him?

She couldn't. That was the truth of it. And the in-
cessant worry.

Still, she at least had distance on her side. Charles
would never be able to talk her into going back to
Melbourne, or Tasmania. Never! And Charles himself

was not a gadabout, or much of a traveller, even with his business interests. Like the intelligent man he was, he hired top people, then delegated. Recently, he admitted he hadn't been interstate in ages, despite Brandon Beer having a branch office in Melbourne. Now that he was married and about to become a family man, he would stay put in Sydney even more. The chance of his meeting anyone from her past who could paint her in an unflattering light was unlikely.

No, she was being paranoid again. All she had to do was keep to her original stories about her past and everything would be fine. Nothing would ever be achieved by confessing everything to him. He would simply never understand.

Even if he did travel to Melbourne, who was there after all who knew anything concrete? A few old workmates and flatmates whom she might have opened her foolish mouth to on occasion. Jonathon certainly wasn't a danger. No way would he talk about her in a derogatory way. He'd been the guilty one at the end of that relationship, not her.

Besides, Charles already knew all about him. She'd pretty well told the truth about Jonathon, except for the inference that she'd been in love with the man. She'd had to do that or end up sounding like a tramp.

In fairness to herself, she'd been very seriously attracted to Jonathon. She'd admired his energy and ambition, and had even enjoyed sleeping with him. Up to a point. That had been somewhat of a shock, since he was a very experienced lover, much more so than the boys she'd known before him.

Dear God, it had been a long time since she'd thought about those early boyfriends. Had she hurt them? She hoped not. They'd all been very sweet, and very nice to her, unlike the people she'd been working with at the time. She hadn't been totally callous. Each one had been her friend as well. And everyone needed a friend sometimes. She couldn't seem to make close girlfriends the way other girls did. Other women always found her looks threatening.

"You're not eating your dinner," Charles said, breaking into her thoughts. "And it's delicious. I can see I'm going to enjoy coming home to this every night."

"What? Oh, yes, that's nice." Dominique had to force herself to blot out those infernal worries about her past and concentrate on the present. She'd wiped the slate clean when she'd met and fallen in love with Charles. Now her priority had to be her husband, and their future together. This constant worrying over things she could not change was a waste of time.

A warm smile crossed her mouth with this sensible resolve. "I'm glad you like it. And the wine?"

"Perfect. I will defer to your excellent judgement on such matters in future."

"Now, now, don't start patronising me again, Charles," she said, but with a smile on her lips. "I know you know heaps about wine and food and all things cultured. I'm just a philistine by comparison.

But that's all right. You can teach me all the things I don't know.''

''My pleasure,'' he murmured, and smiled over the table at her.

Dominique's stomach curled over. There it was again, that new and quite wicked gleam in his eyes. suddenly, she was fiercely aware of her braless breasts underneath her clothes, her naked nipples peaking hard against the fleecy-lined material.

This was another of her concerns, this…this change in Charles, plus her own avid willingness to accommodate whatever he had in mind. The memory of his tender and reassuring lovemaking in bed less than two hours ago receded in her mind, replaced by the stirring of an excitement over what he might want later this evening.

Sex with Charles had always been unlike any she'd ever experienced before. Everything was more intensified. As a lover, Charles was by far the best she'd ever had. He could make her melt with a single kiss.

But Charles in this new rakish mode seduced her mind as well as her body. Once he'd set his eyes on her the way he had at this very moment, she had difficulty thinking of anything else but what he was going to do to her after this meal was over.

If they lasted that long, that was…

Suddenly, she was sitting there like a cat on a hot tin roof, her appetite for food gone. She picked up her wine glass and took a deep swallow, then another, knowing that wine sometimes stimulated her appetite and relaxed her at the same time. She desperately needed both.

Fortunately, Charles dropped his eyes and resumed eating the risotto with irritating gusto. Wasn't it just like a man, she thought irritably, that nothing stopped him from eating? Dominique finally picked up her fork again, though not with much enthusiasm. Her mind was still on other things.

"Not hungry?" he asked on glancing up after clearing his plate and seeing that she was only toying with her food.

"I'm saving some room for dessert," she lied. "Cheesecakes are a weakness with me."

Abruptly, she stood up, and was about to whisk away both the plates from the table when he asked her to sit down again.

"What's wrong?" she asked, that now familiar panic churning away in her stomach.

"Just sit down again, please, Dominique," he repeated.

Charles watched her worried eyes as she sank back down into her chair. He'd originally been going to wait till after dessert before trying to get Dominique to exchange confidences about the past. Such a touchy project required a degree of subtlety and finesse, and he'd been hoping that by then the food and wine would have disarmed her.

But she'd hardly eaten any risotto or drunk more than two mouthfuls of the wine.

"I have a confession to make."

''Oh?'' Her lovely pink lips pulled back into a shaky smile. ''What have you done? Don't tell me you've been having an affair with the merry widow all along.''

Charles's head snapped back in surprise. ''Goodness, no. No, whatever would make you even think such a thing?''

''You've never slept with her, even before me?'' she persisted.

''No,'' he stated firmly, despite feeling pleased over her jealousy. Gold-digging wives wouldn't be jealous of their husbands. Why should they be when they didn't really love?

''Good,'' she said. ''I don't think I could have stood that, especially with you playing poker with her every Friday night. So what other dreadful thing have you done?''

''Nothing dreadful. But I didn't tell you the total truth about my mother's death.''

Her mouth dropped open. ''She…she didn't die from kidney failure?''

''She did, but only because of the cocktail of sleeping tablets and whisky which she'd swallowed the night before.''

''Charles! Oh, my God…oh, how awful for you!''

How perverse, Charles thought as his heart twisted. He'd honestly believed he was over his mother's suicide.

Apparently not.

But of course, now that he thought about it, why

would he keep her suicide a deep, dark secret if he was over it? He wasn't much different from Dominique, really, hugging the skeletons in his family's closet to himself. He'd told her the truth about his father's death—he'd fallen onto a crevasse whilst skiing on a New Zealand mountainside—but he'd never said a word about the man's profligate ways, or his mother's ongoing depression over the state of her marriage.

"Yes," he agreed, and picked up his glass of wine. "Yes, it was awful."

"Would you like to talk about it?" Dominique asked gently.

He looked deep into her sympathetic eyes as he sipped some more of the wine.

"You don't have to if you don't want to," she added, her eyes soft and kind. "I would understand if you don't."

He found it tellingly difficult but he told her. The whole, awful truth. His mother was an abused wife. Not physically, but emotionally. His father had only married her because she'd been pregnant with him and his own father had threatened to disinherit him if he didn't.

Jason Brandon had not been good husband and father material. He'd been a womaniser and a wastrel. He'd been left a healthy company when his own father passed away, but by the time Jason Brandon died in his late forties Brandon Beer had been close to bankruptcy.

At that time Charles had been at university, living on campus, happy to be anywhere but at home. It had been just twelve months since his mother's supposedly accidental death and Charles wanted nothing more to do with his father. It wasn't till he was going through his father's private desk the night after the man's own funeral that Charles had found his mother's last diary—she'd always kept one—detailing her escalating depression and despair, and the reasons behind her suicide. Apparently, his father had become addicted to call girls during his forties and would often have them visit the house to entertain him all night whilst his mother, poor, weak woman that she was, was banished to the guest room.

Discovering that his father was utterly amoral and cruel besides being lazy and incompetent had come as a great shock to Charles. Shocking too was the added revelation that the reason his mother had never had any more children after Charles was born was because his father refused to sleep with her after their wedding night. According to the poor woman's diary, he had denounced his bride the morning after their wedding night as disgustingly ugly and utterly boring in bed, crushing her self-esteem and shattering her illusion that he really loved her.

After that their marriage had been just a charade, with his mother putting on a brave face for the sake of her son, and his supposed inheritance.

Charles admitted to Dominique that he'd been kept in ignorance of his parents' marital problems all his life, being sent away from home a lot, first to boarding-school, then to summer camps during the school holidays, then finally to live on the university campus. He'd never got to know his father at all on a personal basis and he knew little more of his mother, although he knew she was unhappy.

"Why Dad kept that damning diary, I will never know," he ground out. "Maybe he liked looking at it. Maybe he liked reading about his exploits through my poor mother's tormented eyes."

"Oh, surely not, Charles. Surely no one could be that wicked."

"He *was* wicked. I hate to think I carry his genes. I sometimes take comfort from the fact I don't look like him."

"Maybe you take after your grandfather. He sounds as if he was a hard-working man."

"Yes, he was. A good man, too. Who knows why my father turned out the way he did? So which of your parents do you think you take after?" Charles asked, hoping that his confession and confidences might inspire Dominique to offer the same.

The kindness in her eyes clouded to a bleak unhappiness. "I...I don't like talking about my parents, Charles."

"Why's that? Because they were killed so tragically?"

"No. Because they're the past. I hate the past. At least, I hate the past before I married you. I like to think of our wedding day as the first day of my new life. All that went before wasn't worth remembering."

"Your mother wasn't worth remembering?" Charles probed gently. "That's an odd thing for a daughter to say."

Her eyes showed agitation. "Please, Charles, can we talk about something else?"

Charles sighed. So much for his idea of exchanging confidences. Clearly, it was too soon. Still...

"The last thing I want to do is upset you," he said. "It's just that I've been thinking how little we really know about each other. I mean...I know your taste in things like food and wine and books and movies. I know you're a hard worker and a perfectionist when it comes to your appearance. I know you like pale colours and you don't like men who swear. I know you're intelligent and good in bed. But I don't know what makes you tick, down deep."

Charles leant back in his chair, holding her eyes with his. "Who and what we are usually comes from our childhood. And from our parents. My mother was a sensitive but weak woman. I grew up thinking I was sensitive and weak too, mainly because my father kept telling me I was. It wasn't till my mother died that I stopped believing anything *he* said. He didn't even have the decency to grieve. After the liberation of *his* death, my real self started to come to the fore. To my surprise I had many hidden strengths, a tunnel-vision drive and limitless ambition. Sure, I was still sensitive in some areas. I hadn't inherited my father's looks or charm, you see, so my early encounters with the opposite sex were not a raging success.''

''I find that hard to believe!'' Dominique broke in, her expression genuinely startled. ''You're just being extra-modest for some reason.''

''See? You don't know me as well as you might think you do.''

''I know you're a marvellous lover. And you *are* good-looking. At least, you are in my eyes. Everyone has a different opinion over what good-looking is, Charles. You have the sexiest eyes, do you know that?''

He didn't. But he could almost believe it when she looked at him the way she was looking at him at this moment. As his flesh stirred Charles gave up the idea of coaxing the truth out of Dominique tonight. It probably *was* too soon, anyway. She needed more time to trust him with such sensitive information. It wasn't every day that a wife would readily confess to her husband that she'd been a gold-digger before she met him. She might *never* admit it.

Meanwhile, tonight's agenda had changed.

''Why don't we skip dessert for now, take this bottle of wine with us and go skinny dipping in the pool?'' he suggested.

Her eyes gleamed at the idea, then darkened momentarily. ''But do we have total privacy out there?'' she asked. ''Are you sure no one will see us? I mean…aren't some of the nearby buildings taller than this one?''

"Yes, but they're office blocks. No one will be working this hour on a Saturday night."

"How do you know?"

How odd, Charles thought, that her reluctance to go along with his idea was now annoying him. He should have been pleased. Instead, he felt nothing but frustration.

"Well, if there are some idiots working back, then they'd have to be serious workaholics and will hardly be peering out of windows. You can wear a costume if you want," he said. "But I'm not."

"You've become quite wicked just lately, do you know that?" she said, her voice a mixture of excitement and exasperation. "You know I won't be able to resist. You *know* it, you devil!"

Yes, he realised with a rush of dark triumph. He did. But he still wasn't absolutely sure of her; still couldn't quite dismiss all that he'd read in that rotten report.

He wouldn't be sure of her till everything was out in the open, something which might never happen. Meanwhile, he had to content himself with the satisfaction of seeing her as helplessly turned on as she was at this moment.

Oh, yes, she couldn't hide her aroused state. The evidence of her desire was there for him to see, in her glittering blue eyes and fiercely erect nipples. Her need for him would overwhelm any qualms over their being seen. His own need would do the same.

Just thinking about it sent hot blood charging

through his veins, swelling his pained flesh even further. He would not take no for an answer this time. She would do what he wanted, where he wanted. She would be his, tonight and forever. To hell with the past. To hell with everything but being with Dominique. His wife. His love. His torment!

CHAPTER TEN

"IF YOU like it so much, it's yours."

Dominique whirled from where she'd been practically drooling over the all-white kitchen, her eyes wide with surprise. As much as she liked everything about the house, not just the kitchen, Charles had seemed unimpressed.

"You mean it? Even though you'll have to cross the bridge to go to work?"

"I'll tolerate the inconvenience."

They'd looked at house after house in the eastern suburbs all morning and nothing had taken Dominique's eye. The homes had either been too large or too small. After lunch in a city café, Charles had suggested a change in real-estate agencies. This time, a lady had come to their aid.

Her name was Coral, she was in her forties and had the brains to be more interested in what the wife had in mind, rather than the husband. The first thing she did before launching them back on to the inspection road was ask Dominique to describe her perfect house.

Dominique rattled off her requirements from the list in her head. At least four bedrooms, with the master bedroom having walk-in wardrobes and a spacious *en suite*; a study for Charles and formal lounge and dining areas for entertaining. Critical was a large family room and an equally large kitchen which overlooked a garden with a safely enclosed solar-heated pool and some room left over for children to play in, plus at least a two-car garage with some off-street parking room for visitors. Dominique added that architecturally and décor-wise, she preferred clean, simple lines, tall ceilings, lots of windows, no stairs and no bright colours. Oh, and air-conditioning, if possible.

When asked if she wanted a harbour view, Dominique declined the idea. As much as it sounded very nice, she noticed from viewing various harbourside homes that their back gardens and water-facing balconies were invariably windswept and cold. Maybe they'd be fine to live in in the summer, but she was after a functional family home which would be comfortable all year round.

She'd thought it was a tall order but Coral brought her straight to this property at Clifton Gardens—a suburb not far north of the bridge—and *voilà*, it was as though a genie had conjured the place up from what Dominique had described. Everything was there. Absolutely everything, including air-conditioning. Even the outside of the single-storey residence found favour, being cement-rendered and painted cream with a black trim around the windows and guttering. Classy and elegant-looking.

Better still, it was empty with the owner keen to

settle as soon as possible. He was a television anchor man and had recently taken a job in Hong Kong. He and his family had only been gone a few days and the place still had a nice, clean, lived-in smell about it. A happy feel, too.

Dominique was surprised when this thought popped into her head. She did not believe in ghosts, or superstitions, or atmospheres. She'd always been a pragmatic and very practical person. Houses didn't have souls—or give off auras—in her opinion.

Yet this house felt just right.

And she said as much to Charles.

He smiled at her. "If you say so, Goldilocks."

"Goldilocks?"

"Yes. That house was too large," he mimicked in a little-girl voice. "And that other house was too small. But this house is *just* right."

Dominique laughed and so did Coral.

"Your husband has a sense of humour," she said.

"Her husband is sick of house-hunting already," Charles said drily. "Can we go home now, if I promise to put a deposit on this place first thing tomorrow morning?"

Dominique tried not to get too excited too soon. "But you haven't even asked how much it is."

"How much is it?" he asked Coral.

"Er—the owners are looking for two-point-five million."

Dominique was staggered whilst Charles remained cool. "Is it worth it?" he asked.

"Every cent," the real-estate agent replied confidently. "It's a very big block of land and a top position. But I'd still only offer them two mil to start with. They're very keen to sell quickly."

"No. No offers. No haggling. I'll pay the full sum. Here's my card."

Coral stared down at it, then up at him. "You're Charles Brandon, of Brandon Beer."

"That's right."

"I didn't recognise you. Silly me. Oh, wow!"

"Wow what?"

"Wow, I'm going to come first in commission this month because you're really going to buy this place, aren't you?"

"Sure am, Coral. My solicitor will be in touch first thing in the morning. Now, if you'll excuse me, it's been a long day so far and I'd like to go home."

"I know what you'd like," Dominique whispered as he shepherded her towards the still open front door.

"I have no idea what you mean," he returned smoothly, but the corner of his mouth lifted in a devilish smirk.

Dominique broke out into goose-pimples. For this man, no time was the wrong time, no place sacrosanct against his escalating desires. He wanted her in all sorts of places and all sorts of ways. Out in the pool last night for instance. Now, *that* had been one wild experience.

Dominique shivered at the memory. As exciting as

it had been, she'd felt embarrassed afterwards. Never again, she vowed.

She was about to tell Charles that making love in the pool was not on when a sound distracted her, a piteous meow, coming from somewhere above their heads. They'd come through the front door and had just stepped down onto the curving front path which wound its stylish way through the almost mainte-nance-free Japanese-style garden.

Dominique spun round and looked up. There, on the roof, was a slender, reddish-brown cat with slightly oversized ears and the sweetest little face.

"Oh, look, Charles, it's a cat!"

Charles rolled his eyes at her. "Yes," he said in droll tones. "I do believe it is. Come on. Let's go."

She pulled away from his urging grip and stood her ground. "But it looks hungry and lost."

"Dominique, I doubt that very much. It has a collar and tag around its neck."

The cat meowed piteously again and Dominique decided to go with her gut instinct and ignore Charles's quite logical observation. "No, she's in some kind of trouble and I'm going to help her. She probably can't get down from the roof and has been up there for days. She's very thin."

"What makes you think it's a she? It could be a he."

"With that face? No, it's a girl cat. I'm sure of it."

"Come to think of it, so am I. A boy cat would have more sense."

"Did I hear you say there was a cat on the roof?" Coral said as she joined them outside.

"Yes. Up there. Look." Dominique pointed to where the cat was peering plaintively down at them over the black guttering. Clearly, she wanted to get down but was wary of doing so.

"Goodness, that's the owners' old cat. We've met several times before. Her name's Rusty. She's part-Abyssinian."

"In that case, what's she doing still here, all alone?" Dominique said, distressed. "Oh, no, they just left her behind, didn't they?"

"I don't think they would do anything like that. The Jenkinses are very nice people. The day before they left, they gave Rusty to some friends of theirs in Newport because they couldn't take pets with them to Hong Kong. The apartment block they'll be living in doesn't allow it. I'll bet the poor old thing's run away and come home. She's not young—I think she's eight or nine—and this is the only home she's ever known." Coral sighed. "I'll have to ring the Jenkinses in Hong Kong and find out the name and number of their friends and organise for them to come and get her."

"But that won't work," Dominique said agitatedly. "She'll just run away again. Next time, she might not make it back here in one piece. Newport is miles away! She might get run over or attacked by a stray dog!" Dominique saw in a flash what she had to do. "We'll take her home with us," she announced. "I'll keep her inside till we move in here. Then she can live out the rest of her years in the home she knows and obviously loves.''

''Hey, hold it there!'' Charles protested. ''You can't do that. We're not supposed to have pets in our building, either.''

''Oh, phooey. We can smuggle her in. And it's not for very long. Only a few weeks at most. Didn't you say the owners wanted to settle this sale quickly, Coral?''

''Yes, indeed. That's a wonderful idea, Dominique. And so very good of you. I know Mrs Jenkins will be relieved. She was very upset at having to leave Rusty behind. I don't think *Mr* Jenkins understood her feelings at all.''

''Some men can be very insensitive,'' Dominique agreed. ''Not many of them are like my darling husband,'' she added, batting coy eyelashes up at Charles as she linked arms with him and drew him close to her side. ''Agree with everything I say, Charlie-boy,'' she whispered under her breath, ''or there'll be no hanky-panky for you when we get home.''

Charles smiled, but whether from amusement or necessity he wasn't sure. The boot was definitely on the other foot for the moment. She had him jumping through her hoops, not the other way around as it had been last night. Hell, he shouldn't have thought about that. Talk about wicked.

''Now, up you go, darling,'' she was saying. ''And get Rusty down for us.''

He turned disbelieving eyes her way. "You want me to climb up on that roof?"

She batted those baby blues up at him. "Uh-huh."

"How?" he demanded to know. "The place is empty. No ladders in the garage, or anything else, if I recall. I'm not a superhero, you know. I can't fly."

"You'll find a way," she said. "You're a very inventive man." And her eyes sparkled mischievously at him.

It was at that point Charles gave up and surrendered himself totally to this woman he'd married. Strangely, it was an extremely liberating experience, accepting the fact that he would always love her, no matter what. But it was the choosing to believe that she really loved him back which brought the most surprising peace of mind.

Suddenly, all those lingering doubts and fears which had been niggling away at him were gone, as well as the need to keep testing her in various ways.

"Right," he said, and went in search of whatever he could find to help his rescue mission. The wheely bin around the side of the house was just the thing. Once manoeuvred into position over the garages—that was where the guttering was at its lowest—he hauled himself up onto the roof quite easily. Just as well he was wearing jeans, however, and fairly fit. It took an extra minute or two to gain the cat's confidence, but eventually, with a few soft words and the odd stroke or two, Rusty eventually let him lift her

up and lower her gently into Dominique's waiting arms.

The way his wife looked up at him at that moment
moved Charles more than the way she looked at him
when they were making love.

"Thank you," was all she said, but those two simple words said *I love you* better than any impassioned
declaration of love ever could.

By the time he'd made it safely down again, the
cat had snuggled into Dominique's arms as if it had
been there all its life.

"Oh, isn't she a darling, Charles?" Dominique said
when Rusty started to purr.

"Yes," he said, but he was looking at her, not the
cat.

"We'll have to go shopping for some house-cat
things," she said happily. "She'll need a couple of
kitty litter trays. We wouldn't want her not to be able
to find one when she needed it. And a bed. One of
those raised trampoline styles are best, I'm told. And
some bowls for food and water. And some food, of
course. Oh, and we'll have to find a vet tomorrow,
Charles. Have her checked over. Coral, could you
ring me later tonight with Mrs Jenkins's phone number in Hong Kong? I'll give her a ring and find out
what Rusty likes."

Charles shook his head whilst Coral nodded. "I'll
do that. You have a good woman there, Mr Brandon.
Very kind. Not many people would bother."

No, he realised. Not many would.

"I'm not being kind," Dominique denied. "I'm being totally selfish. I've always wanted a cat but I've never had one.

"You don't mind, do you, Charles?" she asked him once they were back in his car, and alone. By then the obviously very tired cat was almost asleep in her lap.

He smiled over at her. "No. Of course not. You have whatever you want."

She gazed at the house again through the passenger window. "I can't tell you how much it means to me, Charles, to have a house like that to raise my children in. If you saw the shack I lived in as a child... No, no, I don't want to think about that. That's dead and gone."

She reached over to touch him on his arm, her eyes lifting to lock with his. "I am *so* lucky to have found a man like you."

He leant over and kissed her softly on the lips. "I think I'm the lucky one in this car."

Charles was alarmed to find tears in her eyes when his head lifted.

"I...I do love you, Charles," she said in a tone which betrayed doubt in his belief of that fact.

"I know," he returned warmly. "And I love you. Now let's go home."

He was glad to turn his attention to driving the car. Tears always made him feel uncomfortable. His mother had cried a lot.

''We're going to be very happy in that house, you know. It's a happy house.''

''A *happy* house? That's an odd thing to say. What makes it a happy house?''

''It's just a feeling I got when I walked in. Maybe that's why Rusty came back. Because she felt it too.''

Charles smiled. ''I didn't realise you were such a sentimentalist.''

''I'm not. Not usually. But I think I'm in danger of becoming one since marrying you.''

''That's sweet. There again, you are sweet.''

''No one has ever thought so before,'' she said with a sigh as she continued to stroke the cat in her lap.

''Not true. Coral thought so.''

''That's a first, believe me. Women usually can't stand me.''

''I would imagine a less mature woman might be jealous of your looks. But I can assure you that Renée likes you. She called you a lovely girl the other night at poker.''

Charles was touched by the look of surprise on his wife's face.

''Did she *really*?''

''Absolutely.'' It wasn't really a lie, although Charles was pretty sure Renée had been talking about Dominique's beauty.

''I...I'd like to become better friends with her,'' Dominique said. ''But she's a bit...formidable, isn't she?''

Charles laughed. ''I know what you mean. The

merry widow doesn't suffer fools gladly. She gives poor Rico a hard time.''

"Pardon me if I don't feel sorry for *poor* Rico.''

Charles knew where Dominique was coming from. He really had to straighten Rico out where his wife was concerned; had to make him see that she hadn't married him just for his money.

He wasn't stupid enough not to think his money added to his attractions, or that Dominique would ever have married a poor man. But that was a far cry from believing her a cold-blooded gold-digger. She obviously had complex issues where money was concerned, and a deep-rooted sense of insecurity.

"Charles...''

"What now?''

"You're going the wrong way. I doubt there are any pet shops open in the city on a Sunday. We'll have to find a shopping mall in the suburbs.''

Charles swore, at which Dominique placed her hands over Rusty's ears. "Not in front of the cat, dear.''

He groaned. "I think I'm going to regret letting you have that damned cat.''

"No, you won't. Because it's made me love you all the more.''

"Just because I let you have a cat?''

"Yes." She sighed an almost weary sigh. "When I was about fourteen, this bedraggled kitten wandered into our back yard and cried and cried at our back door. When I went to give it some milk my father

yelled at me not to, then shooed the cat away. He said
we couldn't afford to feed it. But we could afford his
going down to the pub every day, couldn't we?'' she
added bitingly.

Charles didn't know what to say. Best perhaps not
to say a thing, he decided. Best to just let her talk.

"He was a drunk. A pathetic drunk. And I really
don't want to talk about him any more. Even thinking
about my father is enough to put me in a bad mood.
And I don't want to be in a bad mood today. Today,
I'm happy and I'm going to go on being happy.
Please don't ask me any more about him, Charles.''

"All right," he said gently. He wished she'd told
him more but even the little she had said was important. Bit by bit the pieces of the puzzle which was his
wife were coming together.

What hell she must have gone through as a child,
with her mother dying a slow, painful death and her
father obviously being a hopeless alcoholic.

Dominique would no doubt be shocked to learn
how her father had turned his life around during the
past decade. Though shocked might not be the word.
Charles suspected she'd be furious. She would not
understand why he couldn't have done that when she
and her mother had needed him.

No, she would not be pleased at that little piece of
news. Still, she was unlikely to ever find out. Charles
couldn't see her ever going in search of her father
again, and *he* had no intention of telling her. How
could he ever explain how he knew?

No, he could never reveal anything he'd found out from that report. And he'd have to make sure Rico never did, either.

Rico…

Now, Rico could present a bit of a problem. He really had it in for Dominique. Fortunately, their paths wouldn't cross this week, but come next Friday night he would tell Rico straight that his marriage was a goer, he'd advise him that he'd bought a house and was going ahead with the baby idea, and he was to change his attitude towards Dominique, or else!

Or else what? Charles pondered.

Was he prepared to give up his friendship with Rico for Dominique? Maybe even his Friday-night poker game altogether? His partnerships in the race-horses he shared with the man?

Yes, he realised. Such was the measure of his love for his wife, and his faith in her. She had to come first with him. Today, tomorrow and forever!

CHAPTER ELEVEN

"I CAN'T believe it's only a week since you last went to play poker," Dominique said as she watched Charles get dressed. "It seems so much longer."

Charles smiled a wry smile. "I can see it's time for me to go back to work. Time always goes slowly when you're in boring company."

Charles rather liked seeing the shock his self-deprecating remark brought to her beautiful face.

"Don't be ridiculous, Charles. You know that's not what I meant. It's just that it's been such a full week, what with deciding on the house and looking at furniture and..."

"And playing mother to that infernal cat I was weak enough to let you keep," he finished for her, his eyes flicking ruefully at the bundle of contented fur curled up next to her on the bed.

So much for his edict the first night that the cat was banned from their bedroom. One little meow at the door and Dominique had been up like a flash. Of course, once Rusty's newly purchased trampoline bed—the deluxe model complete with built-in heat pad—had been brought into their room, all the meowing had miraculously ceased.

Within twenty-four hours of the cat's arrival, Rusty

had the run of the whole penthouse, with Dominique her devoted slave. Nothing was too much trouble for her darling puss.

Not that Charles really minded. He rather liked seeing Dominique's maternal side. She was going to make a marvellous mother. And, to be truthful, Rusty was actually an independent old dear and not much trouble after that first night. By Tuesday, the cat didn't care where she slept, as long as it was warm and comfortable. During the day, she would find herself a sunny spot on the carpet, curl up and go to sleep. The lounge chair closest to the TV was her favourite spot at night. She seemed to genuinely enjoy watching the television.

Charles happily left the television on all night for her so that he didn't have those curious cat's eyes on him whilst he was making love to Dominique. Bad enough that their bedrooom activities had been curtailed somewhat during the day, not so much because of the cat's presence but because Dominique had become obsessed with her plans for the house. She spent hours on the internet, looking at furniture and furnishings and other home-wares. Charles had perhaps foolishly given her a blank cheque over the decorating, which she wanted to do herself, and she was taking the job very seriously.

By mid-week, he'd begun to feel more jealous of that darned house than the cat. By today, he'd been so frustrated he'd pounced on Dominique mid-afternoon and thrown her across his desk for some very hot lovemaking. She'd been a bit stunned by the speed of things but no less enthusiastic than usual.

"So what are you going to do whilst I'm gone?" he asked as he slipped his wallet and keys into his trouser pocket.

"Oh, just woman things. My hair could do with a moisture treatment and my nails badly need redoing. But first, I'm going to run myself a big bubble bath and just relax for an hour or two. Pamper myself. By the time you get home, I'm going to be all gorgeous and glowing."

"You're always gorgeous and glowing in my eyes," he said, bending to kiss the top her head.

"You're just saying that so that I'll forgive you for attacking me in your study this afternoon."

He laughed. "I didn't hear you saying no."

"You were too fast for me to say anything!"

"Not too fast for you not to enjoy it, I noticed."

Her blush was endearing.

"I still don't know how you do that."

"How I do what?"

"Charles Brandon, stop being such an egotist! You know exactly what I mean."

"Why worry about it? Just lie back and have a good time."

"Huh. Hard to lie back and seriously have a good time when you've got Biros and things sticking into your backside. Next time, clear the top of your desk first."

"With pleasure. And the first thing to go will be that infernal computer."

"Don't you dare. I *love* that computer."

"What you love is the online shopping! You're never off the darned thing."

"I know. I have been rather obsessive about it this week, haven't I? How about I promise not to go on the internet even once over the weekend? I'll leave all that till you go back to work on Monday."

"Cross your heart and hope to die?"

"Absolutely." And she made the gesture.

"Great. I'll look forward to it."

"But you have to promise to take me out as well."

"As well as what?" he asked, feigning an innocent look.

She pulled a face at him. "I hope you bluff better than that tonight at poker."

"I happen to be a superb bluffer."

She chortled. "You lost last week, if I recall."

"Tonight is another night entirely. I'm going to be right on my game tonight."

"That's what you said last Friday night when you knocked me back in this very room. If you lose again tonight, try not to go too primitive on me when you get home."

"What? Oh, yes," he said, guilt rushing in as he recalled what had happened the previous Friday night. Thank heavens she'd never find out what had been going through his mind at the time. "Right. I promise. Better go. Don't want to be late."

"Heaven forbid."

Dominique watched him hurry off. What was the attraction with that game? she wondered. She'd never liked cards herself, let alone playing them for money. There again, gambling in any form was not something she'd ever do. She'd always hated the idea of risking her hard-earned money. Still, Charles obviously enjoyed it.

There again, he probably considered playing poker more entertainment than gambling. She doubted he was seriously trying to win money when he played cards, or placed a bet on one of his racehorses. He was already fabulously wealthy. Winning and losing would be more a question of ego with him, rather than money. Charles was very competitive, as all successful businessmen were.

Dominique rose from the bed, leaving Rusty to sleep. She made her way into the bathroom, humming happily as she went about turning on the taps and pouring in the scented bubble bath. She was really looking forward to lying back in the water and listening to some of her favourite music.

What a change from her mood the previous Friday night, when she'd been worried sick about Charles playing poker with the merry widow. Amazing, really, what a difference this past week had made. She'd never felt happier, or more confident in the future. Charles really loved her and Renée was no longer a threat in her mind.

Then there was that wonderful house Charles had

bought, and her lovely cat. All she needed now to make her life perfect was a baby.

This last thought brought a frown. She really didn't want to keep taking that Pill for another cycle. For who knew how long it might take her to get pregnant? Just wanting a baby did not always produce one.

She'd read it was more a matter of timing and abstaining till the time was right. Too much sex and the male sperm count went down, according to the article she'd read at a hairdressing salon the week before her wedding. By then, she'd been drawn to articles like that.

With a sigh, Dominique realised Charles would not be happy about abstaining just yet. Hopefully, he'd get over it once he went back to work next week. Maybe she could help by giving him more lovemaking than he could handle this weekend, starting with when he arrived home tonight.

Dominique smiled at the deviousness of her plan. By Monday Charles would be running to the office for a rest and more than willing to go along with her going off the Pill and trying for a baby next month!

Just the thought of having their baby put her on a high. And to think that seven days ago she'd been worried that something might go wrong; that her loving Charles as much as she did was a sure recipe for disaster.

Falling in love with Charles, she realised, was the best thing that had ever happened to her. Even though she hadn't appreciated it at the time. The

Dominique she'd been back then could not handle love. She'd reacted with panic and fear. Even as recently as last week, she'd still been afraid. Now she had finally accepted that love did not necessarily equate with weakness and foolishness. Love—and being loved back—could be wonderful and warm and the most secure feeling in the world.

Rico was the only potential fly left in the ointment, and he too didn't seem to be such a problem any more. Charles hadn't even rung the man all week. Maybe he'd decided to cool their friendship somewhat, now that he was a married man, and soon to become a family man. Maybe he was as sick of the Italian playboy's cynicism as she was.

Whatever, Dominique wasn't going to think about Rico tonight. Nothing was going to spoil her good mood, or the prospect of a lovely, quiet evening pampering herself to the greatest degree before she launched into Project Love Overload!

Once the bubble bath was ready, Dominique collected a couple of her favourite CDs from Charles's huge collection in the living room. Then she went along to his study to get the portable CD player she'd noticed he kept in his bookcase behind the desk. With that in hand, Dominique returned to the bathroom, where she positioned the player on the shelf above the corner of the spa bath and plugged it into a nearby power point. Slotting the first CD into the player, Dominique stripped off and slowly climbed into the steamingly fragrant water. It wasn't till she'd lowered herself beneath the frothy bubbles that she realised she hadn't pressed play.

With a groan, she peered up over her head and decided she could just reach the play button on the side without fully getting out again. It was a stretch but she made it, unaware that the button she pressed was not the CD-play button but the cassette-play button. Not many people used tapes any more and it hadn't occurred to Dominique that the player even had a tape section or that it would be set on to tape. When a male voice echoed through the bathroom, her first reaction was surprise. But surprise quickly gave way to shock when her name was mentioned, and a woman started talking.

"Sandie?" Dominique gasped, and sat bolt upright in the bath, her head spinning as she tried to work out why Charles would have a tape with her Melbourne flatmate talking on it.

There was no doubt in Dominique's mind that it was Sandie. Her voice was quite distinctive with its abrasive delivery and nasal whine. But the things she was saying, and all about her!

Dominique had always known Sandie didn't like her, especially after Sandie's boyfriend had made a rude suggestion to her and Dominique had complained about it. But this wasn't dislike she was hearing. This was hatred, and condemnation, and contempt.

Tricia followed, with more damning opinions, all branding her a heartless fortune hunter.

The trouble was Dominique could not deny the basic truths of what they were saying. Behind the hostility and viciousness lay fact, not fiction. She had been everything they accused her of being. Heartless. Mercenary. Ruthless.

Dominique sat there, frozen, in the bath, yet her heart was going like a jack-hammer inside her chest.

"Oh, God," she kept saying over and over.

The realisation that Charles must have had her investigated at some stage both appalled and bewildered Dominique. The blood began pounding in her temples and she could hardly think. Shock was scrambling her normally sharp brains and she struggled to make sense of it all.

If he'd known all this, then why had he still married her?

It wasn't till the tape rolled on to the interview with Claudia—the third of Dominique's Melbourne flatmates—and the girl mentioned Rico, that the penny finally dropped.

Rico! It was *Rico* who'd had her investigated, not Charles. That was what that report was all about last weekend. It had nothing to do with some crooked executive at Brandon Beer. Rico had been delivering the evidence against *her*.

Yet that didn't make total sense, either. If that report had been about her, why would Charles have waited till Saturday night to read it? Surely curiosity would have overtaken him to find out what was in it, post-haste.

And then the second penny dropped. He didn't have to rush to read it because he already knew what was in it. Rico had told him everything the previous night. That was why he'd come home in such a black mood, not because he'd lost at poker but because he'd found out that his wife was a cold-blooded gold-digger.

All the not-so-cold blood drained from Dominique's face as she looked back on that night from this new perspective. The things Charles had done. The things he'd made *her* do. She'd found them exciting at the time. Now she was consumed by disgust. And dismay.

A shudder ran through her as she buried her face in her hands in horror. She didn't want to think about those things. She'd thought he loved her, that his powerful needs and desires came from that love. Now she saw his actions as nothing of the kind. He'd been driven by hate, not love. And revenge. The most terrible revenge.

More things fell into place. His putting off their having a child. His probing into her past.

He must truly hate her!

Yet if that was the case, then why had he bought her that house? And let her have Rusty?

Not everything made sense. A man intent on just revenge wouldn't have done some of the really nice things he'd done this past week.

Hope filtered in beside the horror in her heart. Maybe, just maybe, his love *hadn't* turned to hate.

Maybe he'd listened to some of the surprisingly in-tuitive things Claudia had said about her. Maybe he'd decided in the end to give their marriage—and her—a second chance.

Hope did spring eternal, Dominique realised as she scrambled out of the bath and reached for a bath-sheet. But she had to find the rest of that report and see what else it said about her. Only then would she know what to do, and how to act when Charles got home.

CHAPTER TWELVE

RICO scowled at his cards. Truly, he'd had dreadful cards all night. Impossible to bluff successfully when you never got a good hand. Even so, Renée inevitably knew when he was bluffing, regardless of his cards. He wasn't sure how.

"I'm out," he said and tossed his hand down onto the table in disgust.

The sound of a tinkling "Happy Birthday" tune coming from somewhere on his person had three pairs of irritated eyes snapping towards him.

"Sorry," he said sheepishly. "That's the new ring my nephew chose for me to programme into my cell-phone. He's only seven."

"We're supposed to have all phones turned off whilst we're playing," Renée reminded him tartly as Rico dived into his pocket.

"I was expecting an important call." A total lie. He'd just forgotten to turn the darned thing off. He was beginning to forget lots of things whenever he was around his nemesis these days.

"I'm out of this hand, anyway," he said as he rose, scraping back his chair. "I'll just go take this in the powder room."

No way did he want the merry widow to hear him

154

begging off from meeting Leanne again. She was sure to make some caustic remark about his lack of commitment with women.

Most men would think he was foolish not to take full advantage of the uncomplicated relationship which Leanne wanted with him. But Rico had found that on his second night with the blonde he'd started thinking of Renée all the more. By the time he'd said goodnight to her, he'd realised he'd much rather spend one minute in Renée's abrasive company than all the nights in the world with the likes of Leanne. He'd told her last Saturday night it was over between them but she was just the type to make a pest of herself. Spoiled, she was, and used to getting her own way with men.

"Rico," he said curtly into the phone in anticipation of the caller's identity.

"Don't let Charles know it's me on the phone," a woman's voice said abruptly. "Don't say my name."

Dominique? What in God's name was she doing ringing *him*?

"Don't worry," he ground out. "I won't."

"Can you talk freely?"

"Pretty well. I'm sitting out this hand. I came into another room to take this call so I wouldn't annoy the others. I naturally didn't think it would be you."

"Naturally. Don't worry. This conversation is going to be brief. I have just one question, Rico. Why? Why did you have me investigated?"

Rico sucked in sharply at the realisation that the

revenge Charles had been enjoying with his wife was
about to come to an end. Which was all for the better
in Rico's opinion. When you played with fire, you
often got burnt. And Dominique was the worst kind
of fire. It was way past the time that Charles got that
witch out of his life, once and for all.

"I gather you found the report," he said drily. Typical, though, that she'd go snooping around as soon
as Charles was out of the house. She'd probably been
looking for his bank statements.

"Yes. I've read it. And listened to the tapes. *All* of
them."

She sounded upset and outraged, which was no surprise. It hadn't been pleasant reading, and even less
pleasant listening.

"Good," he said. "I'm glad. I never agreed with
Charles not telling you up front. But trust me, he was
going to. Eventually. Don't go thinking he was planning on letting bygones be bygones, because he
wasn't. And don't go thinking you'll get a cent of his
money because you won't succeed there, either. The
game's up, Dominique. I suggest you cut your losses,
take whatever expensive gifts and clothes Charles has
no doubt lavished on you and run, unless you like
your husband making an even bigger fool of you than
you made of him for a while. Because that's what
he's been doing since he found out, you know, getting
his money's worth of the only wares you have worth
peddling before he dumps you cold."

Her shocked gasp echoed down the line.

"That hurt, did it?" Rico snarled. "Good. Because you should have been there when I told Charles the truth about you last Friday night. I'd never seen such hurt before in my life. The man was shattered."

"Oh, God. Oh, poor Charles. But you...you're wrong about me, Rico. And I think you're wrong about Charles. I have no doubt he *was* hurt by this report and I could never explain how much I regret that. He might even have wanted revenge to begin with, but I think he changed his mind about me this past week. He saw that I really did love him. He understood where I was coming from when I was the person in that report. He bought us a house, did you know that? A house to raise a family in. Does a man planning on dumping his wife do that?"

Rico was momentarily taken aback by this news. Charles hadn't said a word to him about a house. There again, they hadn't had an opportunity to talk this past week. He'd been flat out filming the next few episodes of *A Passion for Pasta*. Then tonight, he'd deliberately cut the timing fine so that he arrived at the presidential suite right on the dot of eight and didn't have time to engage in any idle chit-chat before the game started. Repartee with Renée pre-cards was always a hazardous activity.

Still, if Charles had changed his mind about Dominique's character, surely he would have rung him and told him so. No, she was just grasping at straws.

"Are you quite sure of that?" he threw back at

her. "It's very easy to put a deposit on a home, you know. Quite another thing to go through with the sale and exchange contracts. He's just stringing you along, honey, keeping you sweet for a while longer. Trust me when I tell you there will be no house and no family for you. Not with Charles."

"I...I don't believe you," she said, though she sounded shaken. "Charles would never do something as vile as that."

"Really? Why don't you ask him when he gets home tonight?"

"I...I won't be here."

"Excellent idea."

"No doubt you think so. Charles might not. But everything's ruined now. I can see that. Our marriage might have worked if you hadn't been around."

"You mean if my cousin, Claudia, hadn't been your flatmate."

"Your *cousin*! Oh, oh, I see. Yes, I see."

"I doubt it. Women like you see nothing but your own selfish agendas. You don't see the human wreckage you leave behind. All men are just suckers in your eyes."

"Charles said you were going through a cynical phase, but he was wrong," she said. "You're warped. Totally warped. I love Charles and I'm never going to say differently. It's you who's hurt him, Rico. You're the one who's shattered his life. He could have been happy with me. We could have been happy. And now it's all been ruined."

''You don't honestly expect me to believe that crap, do you? You *never* loved him.''

''You're wrong. I did. I do. I always will. Falling for him came as a surprise, that's true. I *had* targeted him as a candidate to marry for money but all that changed the moment I met the man.''

''Bullshit. You and I both know that if Charles had been some ordinary guy working for a wage, you'd never have married him.''

''If Charles had been some ordinary guy I wouldn't have fallen in love with him in the first place.''

''Oh, right. That's convenient logic for you. And one I've heard before, how it's easier to love a rich man than a poor man,'' he sneered.

Her sigh sounded weary. ''I know I'll never convince you. I'm not really trying to. You've won, anyway. My marriage is over. I can't stay with Charles now because he'll never really believe in my love. There will always be that part of him which doubts. I couldn't bear that. I'll leave Charles a note saying why I've gone. And I'll tell him to go ahead with a divorce. You don't have to mention this call or the rotten things you said about him. I won't. But he'll need a good friend after I'm gone. Maybe you could be that for once instead of such a narrow-minded, cynical, self-centred bastard. Goodbye, Rico. Good luck. You're going to need it.''

She slammed her phone down, leaving Rico without the opportunity of a final word. Frustrating, that.

Angrily, he switched the cellphone right off then

headed back to the card table, telling himself that it was good riddance to bad rubbish. The wormy feelings wriggling around in his stomach had nothing to do with guilt. He was hungry, that was all.

"Time for supper, isn't it?" he said to the others on his return. They'd obviously finished the hand with Charles gathering the pot over to his side and flashing him a happy smile.

Rico's stomach churned some more.

"Who was it on the phone?" Charles asked.

Rico opened his mouth, then closed it again.

"A female, no doubt," Renée said drily.

"Leanne, was it?" Charles tried.

"No."

"And who's Leanne?" Renée asked.

"Some blonde Rico's been seeing," Charles supplied, which raised Renée's finely plucked brows.

"Really? That's surprising. I thought only gentlemen preferred blondes."

"I'm stopping this before it starts," Ali said firmly. "Back to cards. Supper will be at ten-thirty as it always is, Rico. Now *deal*."

He dealt, but the call from Dominique remained at the forefront of his mind, and his revolving stomach did not settle. He kept wondering if he could possibly have been wrong where Charles's wife was concerned. What if she *had* loved him? What if Charles had discovered that for himself this past week and decided against a divorce? This would better explain his buying her a house rather than the cruel and callous motive *he'd* attributed to that move.

Charles would never be that cruel or callous. It wasn't in his nature...

Rico looked across the table and hoped like hell he hadn't just done his friend the most appalling disservice.

CHAPTER THIRTEEN

CHARLES had never seen Rico play worse. Something was on his mind. That phone call. Had he been lying when he'd said it wasn't from Leanne?

Possibly.

When supper came, he pulled Rico slightly to one side. "All right, I want the truth now. That call was from Leanne, wasn't it? You just didn't want Renée to know."

"No. It wasn't from Leanne," Rico repeated, his body language betraying agitation.

"Then who? Come on. Out with it!"

"Did you or did you not buy a house this week?" came his surprising words.

Charles blinked. Good lord! Who *was* that on the phone? The real-estate agent?

"Have you decided *not* to divorce Dominique?" Rico swept on. "*You* give it to *me* straight."

Charles was glad to. He'd only been waiting for the right opportunity. "No. I'm not going to divorce Dominique, and yes, I have bought us a house."

Rico's uncensored expletives had Renée's head snapping round from where she was still sitting at the card table, sipping her coffee.

"What is it?" she asked, sounding concerned. "What's happened?"

"Nothing," Charles returned brusquely. "Just a personal matter between us boys."

"You mean it's about women and sex," she muttered in a caustic tone.

"No, it bloody well isn't!" Charles countered. He too was growing tired of Renée's sarcasm. "It's about women and love. We men do know the difference, you know. And we occasionally embrace the latter."

She flushed whilst Rico groaned. Charles didn't like the sound of that groan. It carried far too much guilt.

"I'm beginning to get worried, Rico," he growled in low tones. "I think you should tell me what this is all about and stop playing word games. Who was that on the phone and what did they want?"

Rico looked stricken and Charles began to panic.

"It was Dominique," Rico blurted out. "She…she found the report."

Charles's expletives surpassed Rico's. He grabbed Rico's arm and shook him. "Tell me what she said!"

"She said she won't be there when you get home. She said she wants a divorce."

Charles imagined there'd been a lot more said than that. Rico's obvious remorse spelled out a far more lengthy and volatile exchange than that. But he didn't have time to find out the details right now.

Charles whirled to face his host, who was staring at him from across the room. Charles appreciated that his uncharacteristic swearing just now would have shocked Ali, who was such a gentleman. "I have to go, Ali. And I have to go *now*."

He was already off and sprinting for the door before he'd uttered that last shouted word. The ride down in the lift was sheer torment but he ran again once the lift doors whooshed open on the ground floor. He didn't stop for the parking valet to collect his car. That would take too much time. He bolted down the ramp and out onto the city street, racing for home.

He made the apartment block in three minutes flat, the security guard in the foyer looking startled as he charged in.

"Have you seen my wife tonight, Jim?" he demanded to know as his chest heaved.

The man frowned. "No, Mr Brandon. I haven't. But my shift only started at ten. Is there something wrong? Anything I can do?"

"No. No, nothing you can do," Charles muttered and hurried over to the lift well.

One minute later he was letting himself into the penthouse and feeling as if he was going to be sick. The place had some lights on but it sounded quiet. *Too* quiet.

Charles was almost afraid to go further in. He didn't want to find out what he already suspected. He was too late. She was gone.

The sudden appearance of Rusty curling around his

feet brought a surge of desperate hope. Surely she wouldn't have left her beloved cat behind?

"Dominique?" he called out, appalled at how frightened he sounded. But that was the truth of it. He was terrified that he'd lost her. No, *more* than terrified. His soul was screaming inside.

Bending to pick up the cat, he held her tight as he made his way reluctantly down to the bedroom. That would be the first sign. If her clothes were still there, then so would she be.

They were there.

Charles almost cried with relief. Now he hurried back to the living area, calling her name as he went.

But the living room was empty, as was the kitchen, the terrace. Everywhere. Maybe she'd just gone out for a walk, or possibly to a hotel for the night as a kind of protest. She'd be back soon, or in the morning. No way would she leave Rusty behind permanently.

For the first time since he'd entered the penthouse, his heartbeat slowed a little from its frantic pace and he began to have some real hope. Lowering the cat gently onto her favourite chair, Charles turned on the television then hurried to check his study and the guest suite to make sure Dominique wasn't in any of those rooms.

The letter was in the study, on his desk, weighed down by the black jewelry box he'd bought for her the previous Friday night. Charles approached both objects with the dread of certainty in his heart. He *was* too late. She *was* gone.

He lowered himself onto his chair in something of a daze, shock now taking over. His hands shook as he slid the two handwritten pages from under the box and began to read.

My darling Charles.

I do hope you don't mind my calling you that because that is what you will always be to me. My darling Charles. First, let me explain how I came to find that report. I didn't pry into your desk, if that's what you're thinking. I wanted some music to listen to whilst I was having my bubble bath and borrowed your portable player from your study. I pressed the wrong play button without even realising that there was a tape already in it or that it even played tapes...

Charles groaned. The tape! He'd left the damned thing in there. God, what a stupid thing to do!

...Naturally, once I heard what was on that tape I put two and two together and realised the report Rico had given you last Saturday had been about me, although when I thought about it some more, I guessed he'd already told you what was in it the night before.

Charles, first let me say how sorry I am that my past behaviour hurt you as much as it obviously did. I can only imagine how upset you must have been at the time. So I don't condemn you for what you thought of me and what you did that night, or during this past week. I understand how pain makes people do things they wouldn't normally do. I wasn't going to mention this but I rang Rico to-night when you were playing cards because I wanted to find out why he had me investigated. I was a tad upset myself at the time. Anyway, when Rico suggested that your buying the house might have been a part of some kind of revenge and that you probably never meant to go through with the sale, I have to confess I felt sick for a moment...

"Oh, no," Charles groaned, hating for her to think that.

But in the end, I chose not to believe Rico's idea. I chose to believe you'd already discovered you still loved me as I loved you. Of course, that doesn't mean that your love for me can possibly survive. It can't. Of course it can't. And I am en-tirely to blame. I took a path in life which was as warped and twisted as the path Rico is currently taking. People who act like he does—and how I did for years—have their own private hells. You brought me out of my hell, my darling. You re-stored my faith in the human race. You even made me see that money—or the lack of it—is not what brings happiness or unhappiness.

It is so easy to condemn others for what they do, especially when there is no sympathy or understanding. Rico has lost the capacity for sympathy and understanding. I actually feel sorry for him and hope that one day he meets a woman who will truly love him for himself. I just hope he believes her when she comes along.

But time is hurrying by and I really want to get going. I don't want to still be here when you get home. I don't want you persuading me to stay when I know I should go.

I am leaving you Rusty for two reasons. To show you that I believe you don't hate me. Not down deep, in your heart. And secondly because I don't think it's fair on Rusty to give her another change of home. She likes it there. Keep her, Charles, as a memento of me, and when you look at her, think only of how much I truly loved you. It was never a question of money. Even I can see that now. It was always a question of love.

I've left behind all the clothes and things you bought me because to take them would be to prove Rico right. Thankfully, I still have my own car and some savings. I will be in touch after a period of time so that you will know where to send the divorce papers. Needless to say I also don't want anything in the way of alimony, so please don't go making any generous gestures. I'll just give it all away. See? I've grown up at long last.

I must go. I've already stayed too long.

Don't be too hard on Rico. He probably thought he had your best interests at heart. All my love,

Dominique.

Charles slumped back in his chair, the pages resting limply in his lap. What was he going to do? What *could* he do?

He leant forward and opened the black box and there lay the necklace in all its corrupting glory. But it wasn't the necklace which moved him to tears. It was the sight of his wife's wedding and engagement rings resting with the circle of gold and opals.

There was something awfully final—and heart-wrenching—about a woman leaving her rings behind.

The doorbell ringing jolted him out of any self-pity and sent him racing to answer. She'd come back. She'd changed her mind and come back!

"Dominique!" he cried out as he wrenched open the door.

It wasn't Dominique. It was Rico, standing there looking as bleak as Charles was suddenly feeling again.

"Oh," Charles said flatly. "It's only you."

Rico visibly winced. "I remembered Dominique said you'd need a friend. So I came straight away."

Charles laughed, its hollow, brittle sound echoing in the marble-tiled foyer. "I think you've been a friend too much already, don't you?"

"I'm sorry, Charles. I really thought she was bad

for you. You have to agree the evidence looked damning.''

Charles sighed. Rico was right. That report had been damning. ''She left me a letter,'' he said wearily. ''Maybe you should read it.''

Rico glanced up after he'd finished, his eyes sad. ''She sounds so different from what I always imagined.''

''She was.''

''I think she really loved you.''

''I *know* she really loved me.''

Saying it out loud gave Charles a spurt of much needed energy, and resolve. ''I'm going to go after her and get her back.''

''Good idea,'' Rico agreed. ''But where do you think she's gone?''

''Probably to some city hotel for the night to begin with. We'll start ringing around.''

They rang every hotel but no one by the name of Dominique Brandon had booked in.

''Maybe she's using a different name,'' Rico suggested.

''And maybe she's not in Sydney at all,'' Charles returned thoughtfully. ''Maybe she's driven well away from here.''

''To where?''

''I don't know. I'll have to think. She would have a plan. Dominique would always have a plan.''

''I think her first priority was to just get well away

from here, Charles. And you. Given the size of Australia, she could be anywhere.''

''I might have to hire that detective again to find her. The one you hired for that report.''

''Do you honestly think that's a good idea?''

''Yes. I have to find her, Rico.''

Rico sighed. ''I don't think she's going to be happy with your hiring some PI to track her down. I think you should wait till she gets in touch. She said she would. She needs time, Charles.''

Charles groaned. Maybe Rico was right. But maybe he was wrong.

''I'm so sorry, Charles,'' Rico apologised again. ''I didn't mean to hurt you like this.''

Charles patted Rico's arm. ''It's all right. You meant well, but perhaps you shouldn't be so hasty to judge people in future. Look, I'll do what you suggest and wait a little while. But no more than a month. If I haven't heard from her by then, I'm going to go and find her myself!''

CHAPTER FOURTEEN

THE day was bitter, the watery sun providing no warmth at all. But the west side of Tasmania was like that in the winter. Dominique buttoned up her overcoat, then opened the back door of her car and lifted out the flowers she'd brought with her. Yellow roses, they were. Her mother's favourite flower.

She trudged over the spongy earth, trying not to look at the tumbled-down headstones. But it was hard not to notice the general state of neglect in Keats Ridge cemetery. Still, it was no different from the town itself, which was even more run-down than she remembered.

She headed straight for the spot where she knew the grave was located, fearful now that her mother's resting place might not even *have* a headstone. She hadn't been back here in ten years and had no idea what her father had done after she'd left.

No idea what he'd done where her mother's grave was concerned that was, she thought bitterly. She knew what else he'd done. He'd gone and got himself a decent job, then a new wife who'd given him two new sons whom he obviously supported very well. That was what he'd done.

Dominique was still struggling to understand that

part of the report. Why hadn't her father been able to do that for her mother, and for her? Why had he left them both to cope alone whilst he'd drunk what little money there was?

Whatever the reason, it would have to remain a mystery. Because no way was she going to look him up and ask what miracle had caused this massive turn-around, despite the mining town he now lived in being less than an hour's drive away. She just wouldn't know what to say to him. She'd hated him too long to trust herself to even be polite. No, there was no point in fronting up there, just out of curiosity. She was going to go straight back to the mainland today, where she might have the courage to ring Charles and find out how *he* was coping.

Just on a month it had been since she'd left him. It felt like an eternity. She'd spent most of the time in a guest house in a small seaside village to the west of Melbourne, a place she'd visited once and found peaceful.

But there was no peace for the wicked and Dominique had found her days and nights plagued with never-ending feelings of remorse and regret. Reading that report and hearing Rico say how much it had hurt Charles had really brought home to her how unconscionably she'd acted in the decade since her mother's death. She'd used people, perhaps not callously, but selfishly and insensitively. And she'd had only one goal. Money.

As much as she would have liked to wallow in self-pity that her marriage to Charles had failed, she could find none. She'd been as guilty as hell of the gold-digger tag Rico had given her. There were no excuses, really, only reasons. And the main reason lay here, in this cemetery, in...

Surprise ground Dominique to a halt. Because before her lay not what she'd feared. Not a ramshackle mound with grass and weeds growing over it and a cheap cross marking the site, but a beautifully kept grave covered by a full marble slab in a lovely grey colour with a large matching headstone.

The simple words carved into it touched Dominique deeply.

Tess Cooper, beloved wife of Scott Cooper, beloved mother of Jane Cooper. A beautiful woman. May she truly rest in peace.

She sank down onto her knees beside the grave, her hand reaching out to touch her mother's name. Guilt flooded in over the reality that this was the first time she'd visited here since the funeral. Ten years ago today her mother had been buried. Ten *years*, and she hadn't been back. Not once.

"Oh, Mum," she cried softly. "Forgive me..."

Yet someone had visited not that long back. There were some dried-up flowers in the built-in vase, which indicated someone had come here not all that long ago.

"Forgive me," she choked out again, tears flooding her eyes as she took the dead flowers out and replaced them with her own.

"I hoped and prayed I'd find you here today."

Dominique gasped and jumped to her feet, spinning round at the same time.

"Charles!" she exclaimed, lifting her hands to dash away her tears and focus on the man she loved. Dear God, he looked thin. And tired. And every one of his forty years. "But how—?"

"Don't ask," he interrupted, his voice thick with emotion. "And don't argue. Just come home."

"Come home," he repeated when she just stood there, stunned. He'd come all this way after her. He must really love her if he still wanted her back, even now.

"But..."

"There are no buts," he ground out. "When I married you I married you for better or worse, for richer or poorer, in sickness and in health till death us do part. That report was the worse but I am not going to divorce you, Dominique. I love you. I will always love you, no matter what. If you truly love me then you will come home with me. Today. Because I cannot bear another day without you. And neither can Rusty. We're both pining for you, my darling. We need you. Come home with me. But first...just come here." And he reached out to her.

She burst into tears then fell into his arms.

He gathered her in close and hugged her till she didn't have enough breath to keep crying.

"No more tears now," he ordered. "We're going to go home together and be happy in our happy house. Yes, I really did buy the place. I always meant to. Rico has been mortified over what he implied about that. There was no revenge in my heart after that first night, Dominique. That's the honest to God truth. The contracts were exchanged on the house last week and I've already moved the furniture in from the penthouse, which actually looks quite good. Rusty was ecstatic to be back in her own home, till she discovered you weren't there. Then she went off her food again."

Dominique pulled back to gaze up into her husband's drawn face. "You look like you've been off your food too, Charles."

He smiled. "I need you to cook for me."

"Who's looking after Rusty whilst you're down here?"

"Rico volunteered for the job. Poor man. Renée's not speaking to him at all now. She blames him for breaking up our marriage. Friday nights at poker have been very quiet, I can tell you. And a tad boring. I didn't realise how entertaining Rico and Renée's spats were till they stopped. But then..."

"Jane? *Jane?* Is that you?"

Dominique whirled in Charles's arms, sinking back against him once her eyes confirmed what her ears had already told her.

"It *is* you?" her father said. "Good God, I'd forgotten just how much like Tess you were."

Dominique stood there, staring at the man before her. He looked good. No, be honest, damn you. He looked great, despite his greying hair and a few added pounds. There again, he wasn't all that old. He'd only been eighteen when she was born. Which made him...what? Forty-six. Not much older than Charles.

She stared first at his face, then at the bouquet of yellow roses he was holding.

"It was you, then, who's been visiting here?" she asked, disbelief in her voice.

He nodded and came forward to put his roses in with hers. They made quite a show.

"I come every couple of months or so," he said. "Make sure everything's kept nice for her. You know how she liked everything to be nice."

Dominique remembered. So particular her mother was, with her person, and her home. Too bad that home had only been a shack.

"How can you bear to come here?" Dominique blurted out. "Today of all days! How can you face her after what you did?"

She felt Charles's hands tighten on her upper arms. "Remember what you said in your letter," her husband told her gently, "about there always being reasons for people doing the things they do. Give the man a hearing, darling. He deserves that, at least."

"Thank you," her father said. "I appreciate that. And you are?"

"The name is Charles Brandon. I'm Dominique's husband."

"Dominique? But…"

"I changed my name after I left here," Dominique said sharply, and her father nodded. Slowly. Sadly.

"I understand. You wanted to forget. I don't blame you. I wanted to forget, too."

"You seemed to have managed that quite well," she threw at him. "A new wife. Two new sons."

"You know about them?" He was very taken aback.

"I know everything. I know all about your wonderful new job as well. So tell me, Dad, how did you manage all that, given that when I left here the day of Mum's funeral you were nothing but a pathetic drunk with no pride and no guts?"

"For pity's sake, Dominique," Charles said with a groan.

"No," her father said. "She has every right to feel the way she does. I had become exactly what she said. A pathetic drunk. I couldn't cope with her mother's illness, or her fears. I should never have promised her what I promised her in the first place. It was weak of me, but then I was always weak where Tess was concerned. I loved her too much to go against her wishes, especially after I'd lost my job. I felt…powerless. Useless. Drinking was the easy way out and I took it. I took it and I left it to my teenage daughter to carry the load which should have been mine."

"You're not making any sense," Dominique snapped, having no patience with him at all. "What wishes are you talking about? What fears? Mum was very brave when she was dying. Much braver than I could ever be. And much, much braver than you!''

''Yes, she was brave. But it was a bravery that was so unnecessary.''

''You can say that again. If only you'd taken her to some decent doctors, she might not have died at all.''

''You think I didn't want that? I begged her and begged her to get medical help but she refused. She wouldn't go to doctors. Not after her experience when she was having you.''

''What kind of experience?''

''She said the doctor who looked after her during her pregnancy touched her in not a nice way whenever he was examining her. She didn't tell me about it till after you were born. When she did she cried and cried for days. After that, she began to be afraid of lots of things. The city. Crowds. Most men. We went to live in Keats Ridge because it was so remote. Unfortunately, some of her fears came with her. Her fear of men, and doctors. Yet the doctor there was a very good man. You knew him, Jane. Dr Wilson. Tess would take you to him but she never went to him herself. Not once. When she kept miscarrying I begged her to go and see him and have one of those pap smear tests but she refused. She said she'd get better all by herself and she did for a while, although she never did fall pregnant again. Around the time I lost my job she got a lump in her breast. She said it couldn't be cancer because it didn't hurt. But she wasn't well. Then eventually, the pain started. I think the cancer had gotten into her bones by then. Finally, it went to her lungs and that was the beginning of the end.''

Dominique could hardly believe what she was hearing. ''But Mum told me she *had* gone to the doctor. She told me he said there was nothing they could do, it was too late to operate. When I asked her why you didn't take her down to the hospital in Hobart and see a cancer specialist for a second opinion, she said you said we couldn't afford it.''

Her father's face reflected true horror. ''But that's not true! I would have taken her in a flash. And it wouldn't have cost a thing, since I was unemployed. She just wouldn't go. She wouldn't even leave the town so that I could find work. Her fear of the outside world and doctors was greater than her fear of death, I tell you.''

''But that's crazy!''

''Yes, I know. It was. And it almost drove *me* crazy, watching her die like that. But you don't know what she was like when you weren't around, the way she would beg me to stay here and not do anything. In the end, I was beyond doing much, anyway, as you well know. I did get some morphine tablets for her, which gave her some relief from the pain. After she died and you left, I took all the rest of the tablets and almost died myself. But I didn't. Doc Wilson saved me then brought in a social worker for some counselling, as they do in all attempted suicides. She was very kind. Very…understanding. Her name was Karen and she helped me get my life back on track. I moved over to Holt Mountain, went to AA, got myself a job and two years after Tess died Karen and I were married.''

Dominique didn't know what to say. As much as her father's story had answered a lot of questions, she still could not put aside the hatred she'd lived on for most of her life. ''How nice for you,'' she bit out.

His eyes looked terribly sad and she began to hate herself.

''I'm sorry, Jane. Sorry I let your mother down. But especially sorry I let *you* down. It's troubled me a lot these past ten years, thinking of how angry and bitter you were at your mother's funeral and knowing how much you despised me. I see now you must have thought I was entirely to blame; that I could have saved Tess if only I'd been stronger and taken her down to Hobart and made her see a doctor. And you're right. That's exactly what I should have done. But I didn't and I can't go back. What's done is done. All I can do for Tess now is come here and make sure her grave is as she would have liked it to be.''

When he took a step towards her, she shrank back into Charles, her face warning him to keep his distance.

He shook his head slowly in an attitude of defeat. ''I can't tell you how many times I've hoped to find you here. Just seeing you here today, seeing that you're alive and well…'' His throat convulsed. His hands balled into fists at his sides. "It…it means a lot to me, Jane. I have worried about you so much, although I dare say you don't believe me. I wasn't much of a father. But if you could find it in your heart to forgive me, I…I…"

He broke off, his shoulders shaking as his eyes dropped to the ground. "Oh, God," he sobbed.

How she found herself in his arms was a mystery and a miracle. Had Charles propelled her there or had she gone herself, driven by the need to forgive her father so that she could forgive herself for all the things *she'd* done during her life, and deeply regretted?

"It's all right, Daddy," she cried, hugging him close and sharing his very true pain. For both of them had a lot to feel remorseful over. "I do forgive you. I *do*. It's all right. It's all right."

Charles watched them with tears in his own eyes. But his tears were tears of relief, not distress. Because Dominique's emotional refrain carried the ring of truth. It *was* going to be all right. For her father. For her. And for him.

Wonderfully, incredibly all right.

CHAPTER FIFTEEN

"I...I FEEL nervous," Dominique said as Charles angled her silver car into their new driveway at Clifton Gardens.

It had taken them three days to make it home from Tasmania. One getting back to the mainland by boat from Devonport, then two days driving from Melbourne to Sydney with a stop over in a motel outside of Goulburn.

"Nervous about what?" Charles asked after parking next to Rico's fiery red Ferrari.

"About facing Rico."

"There's nothing for you to be nervous about. He was thrilled about our being back together again when I rang him the other night."

They both climbed out of the car and walked together up the front path.

Dominique sighed as she mounted the front porch. "Somehow I find that hard to believe."

The man himself wrenched open the front door before Charles could produce a key.

"And about time too," he grumped. "I could have driven to Timbuktu and back in the time it's taken you two to get home."

183

"Dominique doesn't like me driving her car too fast," Charles explained.

"What? Oh, yes, you flew down there, didn't you? And rented a car. Hi there, Dominique. You're looking extra well. Am I glad you've patched things up with Hubbie here. You've no idea how impossible he's been without you. Your cat's been just as bad. At least she *was* till this morning, when she suddenly decided to stop whining and eat. Must have known you were coming home. Anyway, she's asleep in front of the television after devouring two tins of that super-duper spoiled-kitty-cat food Charles bought for her. Look, sorry to cut and run but I'm way behind in my filming schedule for this week, as you can imagine. See you tomorrow night at poker, Charles. And don't forget, I will expect a dinner invite soon to make up for all I have endured this past month or so. But don't serve pasta, Dominique. I'm sick to death of the stuff. *Ciao!*"

Sweeping up an overnight bag he had at the ready, Rico was gone before Dominique could say boo, the tyres on his Ferrari screeching a little as he backed out, then zoomed up the street.

"Goodness!" she exclaimed. "Is he often like that?"

"Only when *he* feels nervous," Charles said with a wry smile. "But don't worry. He'll be back to being his normal obnoxious self in no time."

"I dare say. But I'll still invite him to dinner. Maybe he can bring Renée with him."

Charles laughed. "Over Renée's dead body."

"She *really* doesn't like Rico?"

Charles pondered that question, trying to see if there might be some unwanted attraction behind Renée's hostility. "I'm not sure," he said in the end. "Look, I'll extend an invite to them both tomorrow night and see what happens, shall I?"

"Yes. Yes, do that, Charles."

"I'd better go and bring in our cases."

"No, don't do that yet. Take me for a tour first and let me see what you've been doing with my house."

"Not much, I can assure you. I just filled up the cupboards in the kitchen and had the penthouse furniture brought over."

Dominique walked down the central hallway into the kitchen and then the family room, letting the atmosphere she'd first felt in the place wash through her. Rusty woke as she passed and jumped down from the lounge chair to follow her, curling around Dominique's legs when she finally stopped in the master bedroom.

Smiling, she bent down to pick her up. "I was right, Rusty, wasn't I?" she murmured as she placed the cat on the bed and stroked her ears. "It *is* a happy house."

"It will be now that you're in it," Charles said, and Dominique turned to him, her eyes glistening.

"What a lovely thing to say. But then...you're a lovely man. How can I ever begin to thank you for coming after me? And for loving me, despite everything? I...I don't deserve it."

"Yes, you do. You deserve the very best and I aim to make sure you always have it. You had a rotten time of it as a kid, Dominique. I do understand what made your father act the way he did, but I can't condone it. He can't, either. It was generous of you to forgive him. *Very* generous."

"How could I not when you forgave me?" she choked out. "Besides, he wasn't always a bad father. I'd forgotten how good he was in my younger years, when he had a job, and before Mum got sick. People have a tendency to forget the good bits and only remember the bad."

"That's true."

"I wish I'd understood my mother more. I wish she'd confided in me instead of letting me think the things I thought."

"She couldn't, Dominique. She would have been too afraid to tell you the truth. She would have been worried about losing your love, and your respect."

"Yes, yes, I can see that now. I just wish that... Oh, I don't know what I wish."

"Your father said it all, Dominique. You can't go back. He can't go back. What's done is done. All we can do is learn from our mistakes and forge a better future than our pasts."

"Promise me you'll always tell me the truth," she said, her voice catching. "Promise me."

"I promise."

"Me too." Dominique swallowed. "What…what did you do with my rings?"

"They're here, waiting for you." Drawing them out of his jacket pocket, he came forward and slipped them back onto her left hand.

"For better or worse, Dominique," he said, lifting her hand to his lips. "For richer or poorer. In sickness and in health… Forever and ever."

MISTRESS FOR A MONTH

MIRANDA
LEE

CHAPTER ONE

RICO MANDRETTI jumped into his shiny red Ferrari and headed, not towards Randwick Racecourse, but straight for his parents' place on the rural outskirts of Sydney. His plans had changed. Last night had changed them.

'Not today,' Rico muttered to himself as he sped out through Sydney's sprawling western suburbs, oblivious of the second glances he received from most of the women in the cars he passed, and *all* of the women in the cars he was forced to idle next to when the lights turned red.

Only one woman occupied Rico's mind these days. Only one woman did he crave to look at him as if he was a man worth looking at and not some prima-donna playboy with no substance at all.

For over five years he'd endured Renée Selinsky's barbs over the card table every Friday night, as well as at the races on a Saturday afternoon.

Five years was a long time to tolerate such treatment. *Too* long.

Yet he had to confess that till last night he'd enjoyed their verbal sparring in a perverse fashion, despite the fact Renée usually got the better of him. When she'd temporarily subjected him to the cold-shoulder treatment a few months back, he'd hated it. Rico discovered during that difficult time that he'd rather have his buttons pressed than be ignored.

Still, Renée had pressed his buttons one too many times last night.

Be damned if he was going to be on the end of that woman's caustic tongue again today at the races. Enough was enough!

The lights turned green and he floored the accelerator. The Ferrari leapt forward, tyres screeching slightly as he scorched up the road. But, given the speed limit on that section of highway, and the regular traffic lights, there was no solace for Rico's frustration in speeding, and no escape for his thoughts.

Soon he was idling at the next set of red lights, practically grinding his teeth when his mind returned once more to his nemesis.

She'd be at the races by now, probably sitting at the bar in the members' stand, sipping a glass of champagne and looking her usual cool and classy self, not caring a whit that he hadn't turned up, whilst he was sitting here in his car, stewing away, already regretting his decision not to go. He *loved* the races. They were one of his passions in life. And one of hers, unfortunately.

That was how he'd met Renée in the first place, through their mutual love of horse racing. Just over five years ago she'd become the third partner in the syndicate he and his best friend, Charles, had formed with the help of Ward Jackman, one of Sydney's up-and-coming young horse trainers.

Rico could still remember the first day he met the up-till-then mysterious Mrs Selinsky. The three co-owners had gathered at Randwick races to see their first horse race, a lovely chestnut filly named Flame of Gold.

Before that day, Rico had only known of his lady

co-owner's existence on paper. He'd no idea that she was also Renée, the owner of *Renée's* modeling agency and the widow of Joseph Selinsky, a very wealthy banker who'd been almost forty years his second wife's senior, and who'd passed away the previous year. He *did* know she was a rich widow, but he'd pictured an overweight, over-groomed madam in her sixties or seventies with more money than she could spend in the beauty salon, and a penchant for gambling.

Nothing had prepared Rico for the sleekly sophisticated, super-stylish and super-intelligent thirty-year-old which Mrs Selinsky had proved to be. And certainly nothing had prepared Rico for her instantly negative reaction to him. He was used to being fawned over by the opposite sex, not the exact opposite.

Looking back, he'd been attracted to her right from first sight, despite his having another woman on his arm that day. His fiancée, in fact. Jasmine. The bright, bubbly, beautifully blonde Jasmine. He'd thought himself in love with Jasmine, and he'd married her a month later.

It was a marriage which had been doomed from the start. God, if he'd only known then what he knew now.

But would that have changed anything? he pondered as he revved up the Ferrari's engine in anticipation of these lights turning green. What if he'd realised Jasmine was an unfeeling fortune-hunter before their wedding? Or that his so-called love for her was the result of his being cleverly conned and constantly flattered? What if he'd broken up with his faking fiancée and pursued the enigmatic and striking Renée instead?

Renée's reaction to him might have been very different if he'd been single and available five years ago, instead of engaged and supposedly besotted with his fiancée.

After all, he was Rico Mandretti, the producer and star of *A Passion for Pasta*, the most successful cooking show on television. The merry widow—as he'd soon nicknamed Renée—obviously knew the value of a dollar, given she'd already married once for money. Rico could not imagine a woman of her youth and beauty marrying a man in his sixties for *love*.

Whilst Rico hadn't had as many dollars in the bank as Renée's late husband at that stage, he'd still been well-heeled, with the potential for earning more in the years to come, which had since proven correct. His little cooking show—as Renée mockingly liked to call it—was now syndicated to over twenty countries and the money was rolling in, with more business ventures popping up each year, from cookbooks to product endorsements to his more recent idea of franchising *A Passion for Pasta* restaurants in every major city in Australia.

Aside from his earning potential, he'd also only been twenty-nine back then, brimming with macho confidence and testosterone. In his sexual prime, so to speak.

Rico liked to think Renée would have fallen into his arms, but he knew he was just kidding himself. He'd been split up from Jasmine for two years now, his divorce signed and sealed over a year ago, and Renée's negative attitude to him hadn't changed one bit, If anything, she'd grown more hostile to him whilst his desire for her had become unbearably acute.

It pained Rico to think that she found nothing attractive in him whatsoever. In fact, she obviously despised him. Why? What had he ever done to her to cause such antagonism? Was it his Italian background? She sometimes sounded off about his being a Latin-lover type, all hormones and no brains.

Rico knew there was more to himself than that. But not when he was around her these days, he accepted ruefully. Lately, whenever she turned those slanting green eyes on him and made one of her biting comments, *he* turned into the kind of mindless macho animal she obviously thought him. His ability to play poker suffered. Hell, his ability to do anything well suffered! The charm he was famous for disappeared, along with his capacity to think.

Aah, but he could still *feel*. Even as his blood boiled with the blackest of resentments, his body would burn with a white-hot need. That was why he was avoiding his nemesis this weekend. Because Rico suspected he was nearing spontaneous combustion where she was concerned. Who knew what he would do or say the next time she goaded him the way she had last night?

'Now, if you'd married someone like Dominique, Rico,' Renée had remarked after Charles announced his wife was expecting, 'you'd have a baby or two of your own by now. If you're really as keen on the idea of a traditional marriage and family as you claim, then for pity's sake stop dilly-dallying with the Leannes of this world and find yourself a nice girl who'll give you what you supposedly want.'

Rico had literally had to bite his tongue to stop

himself from retorting that he took women like Leanne to bed in a vain attempt to burn out the frustration he experienced from not being able to have *her*.

Somehow, he'd managed an enigmatic little smile, and experienced some satisfaction in seeing her green eyes darken with a frustration of her own.

Mark one up for Rico for a change!

But for how long could he manage such iron self-control? Not too much longer, he suspected.

Charles and Ali wouldn't know what hit them if and when he exploded. Rico might have been born and brought up here in Sydney, but he was Italian through and through, with an Italian's volatile temperament.

A peasant, Renée had once labelled him. Which was quite true. He did come from peasant stock. And was proud of it!

Rico's other two Friday-night poker-playing partners were blue-blood gentlemen by comparison. His best friend, Charles, was Charles Brandon, a few years older than Rico and the owner of Brandon Beer, Australia's premier boutique brewery. Ali was Prince Ali of Dubar, the youngest son of an oil-rich sheikh, dispatched to Australia a decade before to run the royal Arab family's thoroughbred interests down under.

Both men had been born into money, but neither was anything like the lazy, spoilt, silver-spoon variety of human being whom Rico despised.

Charles had spent years dragging his family firm back from the brink of bankruptcy after his profligate father died, leaving Brandon Beer in a right old mess.

That achievement had taken grit, determination and vision, all qualities Rico admired.

Ali didn't act like some pampered prince, either. He worked very hard, running the thoroughbred stud which occupied over a thousand acres of prime horse land in the Hunter Valley. Rico had seen with his own eyes how hands-on Ali was with running and managing that complex and extremely large establishment.

It had been Ali, actually, who'd brought the four poker-players together. He was the breeder of Flame of Gold. After she'd won the Silver Slipper Stakes, the three ecstatic owners and one highly elated breeder had had a celebratory dinner together. Over a seafood banquet down at the quay, they'd discovered a mutual love, not just of racehorses but also of playing cards. Gambling of various kinds, it seemed, was in all their blood. They'd played their first game of poker together later that night and made a pact to play together every Friday night after that.

Being ill or overseas were the only excuses not to show up at the presidential suite at Sydney's five-star Regency Hotel every Friday night at eight. That was where Ali stayed each weekend, flying in from his country property by helicopter late on a Friday and returning on the Sunday.

Rico smiled wryly when he thought of how, when he'd been hospitalised with an injured knee after a skiing mishap last year, he'd insisted that the others come to his hospital room for their Friday-night poker session. The evening had not been a great success, however, with Ali having a couple of security guards trailing along.

Looking back, he could see that his own insistence

on playing that night, despite his handicapped condition, highlighted his rapidly growing obsession with the merry widow. He hadn't been able to stand the thought of not seeing her that week. Now he wasn't sure if he could stand seeing her again at all! He was fast reaching breaking point. Something was going to give. And soon.

Rico's stress level lessened slightly once the more densely populated suburbs were behind him and his eyes could feast on more grass and trees. He breathed in deeply through his nostrils, smelling the cleaner air and smiling with fond memories as the city was finally left behind and he drove past familiar places. The small bush primary school he'd attended as a child. The creek where he'd gone swimming in the summer. The old community hall where he'd taken dancing lessons, much to his father's disgust.

As far back as he could remember, Rico had been determined to one day be a star. By the time he turned twelve, he'd envisaged a career on the stage in the sort of singing, dancing, foot-stomping show he adored. But whilst his dancing technique was excellent, he'd grown too tall and too big to look as elegant and graceful as shorter, leaner dancers. On top of that, his singing left a lot to be desired. Once that career path was dashed, he'd focused his ambition on straight acting, seeing himself as an Australian John Travolta. People often said he looked like him.

His early acting career had been a hit-and-miss affair, especially after he'd failed to get into any of the élite and very restricted Australian acting academies. He did succeed in landing a few bit parts in soaps, plus a couple of television advertisements and one minor role in a TV movie, but at a lot of auditions he was told he was too big, and too Italian-looking.

Although not entirely convinced, Rico finally began looking more at a career behind the camera rather than in front of it. Producing and directing became his revised ambition, both on television and in the booming Australian film industry. He learned the ropes as a camera and sound man, working for Fortune productions, who were responsible for the most popular shows on TV back then. He watched and observed and learned till he decided he was ready to make his own show.

With backing from his large family—Rico had three indulgent older brothers and five doting older sisters—he started production on *A Passion for Pasta*, having noted that cooking and lifestyle programmes were really taking off. But the Australian-Italian chef he hired for the pilot episode turned out to be a bundle of nerves in front of the camera, with Rico constantly having to jump in and show him what to do, and how to do it.

Despite his not having any formal training as a chef, it soon became obvious that he was a natural in the part as the show's host. Rico had finally found his niche. Suddenly, his size didn't matter, his Italian looks were an asset and the Italian accent he could bung on without any trouble at all gave a touch of authenticity. It also helped that he really was a very good amateur cook, his mother having taught him. It was Signora Mandretti's very real passion for pasta, and her creativeness with the product—feeding her large family on a tight budget required more than a little inventiveness—which had inspired the show's title and content.

A Passion for Pasta was an instant success once Rico had found a buyer, and he hadn't looked back.

Not that any of his successes ever impressed Renée. They had certainly impressed Jasmine, however. She'd known a good thing when she saw it.

Rico pulled a face at the memory of the gold-digger he'd married. He was still flabbergasted over how much the family law court judge had awarded her for the privilege of being a pampered princess for three years.

Still, it had been worth any price in the end to get Jasmine out of his life, although he'd deeply resented her demanding—and *getting*, mind you—both their Bondi Beach apartment *and* his favourite car, a one-off black Porsche which he'd had especially fitted out with black leather seats and thick black carpet on the floors.

Black had always been Rico's favourite colour, both in clothes and cars. He'd bought the red Ferrari he was now driving on a mad impulse, telling himself that a change was as good as a holiday, an act which had rebounded on him when Renée had recently seen him getting into it in the car park at the races.

'I should have known that the red Ferrari was your car,' she'd said with a sniff of her delicately flaring nostrils. 'What else would an Italian playboy drive?'

On that occasion—as was depressingly often the case these days—he hadn't been able to think of a snappy comeback quick enough, and she'd driven off in her sedate and stylish BMW with a superior smirk on her face.

His mind returning to Renée once more brought a scowl to his. He'd promised himself earlier he wasn't going to think about that witch today. He'd already given her enough thought to last a lifetime!

The sight of a very familiar roadside postbox coming up on his right soon wiped the scowl from his face.

His parents' property wasn't anything fancy. Just a few acres of market garden with a large but plain two-storeyed cream brick house perched on the small rise in the middle of the land. But Rico's heart seemed to expand at the sight of it and he found himself smiling as he turned into the driveway.

There was nothing like coming home. Home to your roots, and to people who really knew you, and loved you all the same.

CHAPTER TWO

Teresa Mandretti was picking some herbs from her private vegetable and herb garden—the one *she* planted and personally tended—when a figure moved into the corner of her eye.

'Enrico!' she exclaimed on lifting her head and seeing her youngest child walking towards her. 'You startled me. I wasn't expecting you till tomorrow.'

The first Sunday of the month was traditionally family day at the Mandretti household, with her youngest son always coming home to share lunch with his parents, plus as many of his siblings and their families that could make it.

'Mum.' He opened his arms and drew her into a wrap-around hug, his six-foot-two, broad-shouldered frame totally enveloping her own short, plump one.

How he had come to be so big and tall, Teresa could only guess. His father, Frederico, was not a big man. When the family back in Italy had seen photos of Enrico at his twenty-first birthday, they said he had to be a throwback to Frederico's father, who'd reputedly been a giant of a man. Teresa had never actually met her father-in-law. Frederico Senior had been killed in a fight with another man when he was only thirty-five, having flown into a jealous rage when this other fellow had paid what he called ''improper'' attention to his wife.

Teresa could well imagine that this was where

Enrico got quite a few of his genes. Her youngest son had a temper on him, too.

'Have you had lunch?' she asked when her son finally let her come up for air. He was a hugger, was Enrico, like all the Mandrettis. Teresa was from more reserved stock. Which was why she'd found Frederico Mandretti so attractive. He'd taken no notice of her shyness and swept her off to his bed before she could say no. They'd been married a few weeks later with her first son already in her belly. They'd migrated to Australia a few months after that, just in time for Frederico the Third to be born in their new country.

'No, but I'm not hungry,' came her son's surprising reply.

Teresa's eyes narrowed. Not *hungry*? Her *Enrico*, who could eat a horse even if he was dying! Something was not right here.

'What's wrong, Enrico?' she asked with a mother's worried eyes and voice.

'Nothing's wrong, Mum. Truly. I had a very large, very late breakfast, that's all. Where's Dad?'

'He's gone to the races. Not the horse races. The dog races. Down at Appin. Uncle Guiseppe has a couple of runners today.'

'Dad should buy himself a greyhound or two. The walking would do him good. Get rid of that spare tyre he's carrying around his middle. I think he's been eating too much of your pasta.'

Teresa bridled. 'Are you saying your *papa* is fat?'

'Not fat, exactly. Just well fed.'

Teresa suspected Enrico was deliberately diverting the subject away from himself. She knew all her children well, but she knew Enrico even better than the others. He'd come along when she'd thought there would be no more *bambinos*. She'd already had eight children, one each year or so, three boys followed by five girls. After giving birth to Katrina, the doctor had told her she should not have any more babies. Her body was exhausted. So she'd gone on the Pill with her sensible priest's permission, and for the next nine years, had not had the worry of being pregnant.

But the Pill was not perfect, it seemed, and another child had eventually been conceived. Although she was worried, a termination had not even been considered, and fortunately Teresa had been blessed with a trouble-free pregnancy that time and an amazingly easy birth. Enrico being a boy was an added bonus after having had five girls in a row.

Of course, he'd been very spoiled, by *all* of them, but especially his sisters. Still, despite the temper tantrums he threw when he didn't get what he wanted, Enrico had been a loving child who had grown into a loving man. Everyone in the family adored him, not the least being herself. Teresa would never have admitted it openly, but Enrico held a special place in her heart, possibly because he was her youngest. With the ten-year age gap between Enrico and his closest sister, Teresa had been able to devote a lot of time to raising her last baby. Enrico had followed her around like a little puppy, and mother and son were very close.

Enrico could *never* fool her. Aside from his suspicious lack of hunger today, she knew something had to be up to take him away from the races on a Saturday afternoon. With a mother's intuition, she sensed it had something to do with a woman. Possibly with that Renée lady he often spoke about but whom she'd never met, the one he played poker with every

Friday night and who was part of his racing syndicate. Teresa had sensed an odd note in his voice whenever he mentioned her.

And he mentioned her quite a bit.

Teresa would have liked to ask him about her but suspected that the direct approach would be a waste of time. At thirty-four, her youngest son was long past the age that he confided matters concerning his personal and private life to his mother. Which was a pity. If he'd consulted her before he'd become tangled up with that Jasmine creature, she could have saved her son a lot of heartache.

Now, *there* was a nasty piece of work if ever there was one. Clever, though. Butter wouldn't have melted in her mouth around the Mandrettis till the wedding, after which she'd gradually stopped coming to family functions, making poorer and poorer excuses till there weren't any left to be made.

Fortunately, she was now past history. Though not generally believing in divorce, Teresa was a realist. Some divorces were like taking the Pill. A necessity. Still, Teresa didn't want Enrico repeating his mistake by getting tangled up with another unsuitable woman.

'Did you play cards last night?' she asked as she bent to pull a few sprigs of mint.

'Of course,' came her son's less than enlightening reply.

'Charles well, is he?' Charles was the only one of Enrico's three poker-playing friends whom Teresa had actually met, despite her having invited the trio to several parties over the years. That Renée woman was a bit like Jasmine, always having some excuse not to come. The other man, the Arab sheikh, had also always declined, though his refusals Teresa understood.

Enrico had explained that Prince Ali kept very much to himself, because of his huge wealth and family connections. Apparently, the poor man could never go anywhere in public without having a bodyguard accompany him. Sometimes *two*.

What a terrible way to live!

Enrico had to cope with a degree of harassment from the Press and photographers himself, but he could still come and go as he pleased without feeling he was in any physical danger.

'Charles is very well,' her son answered. 'He and his wife are going to have a baby. In about six months time, I gather.'

'How lovely for them,' Teresa enthused as she straightened, all the while wondering if that was what had upset Enrico. He'd always wanted children of his own. Most Italian men did. It was part of their culture, to father sons to proudly carry on their name, and daughters to dote upon.

Teresa had no doubt Enrico would make a wonderful father. He was marvellous with all his nephews and nieces. It pained Teresa sometimes to see how they always gravitated towards their uncle Rico, who was never too busy to play with them. He should be playing with children of his own.

If only she could *say* so.

Teresa suddenly decided that she was too old and too Italian for the tactful, indirect approach.

'When are you going to stop being silly and get married again, Enrico?'

He laughed. 'Please don't hold back, Mum. Say it like you see it.'

'I do not mean any disrespect, Enrico, but someone has to say something. You're thirty-four years old and not getting any younger. You need a wife, one who will be more than happy to stay home and have your children. A man of your looks and success should have no trouble finding a suitable young lady. If you like, we could ask the family at home to look around for a nice Italian girl.'

That should spur him on to do the looking around for himself! Enrico might have Italian blood flowing in his veins but he was very Australian in many ways. Look at the way he always called her *Mum* and his father Dad, whereas his older brothers and sisters always called them Mama and Papa.

Naturally, arranged marriages were anathema to her youngest son. He believed in marrying for love, and, up to a point, so did Teresa.

But best not to tell him that.

Her son's look of horror was very satisfying.

'Don't start that old-fashioned nonsense, Mum. When and if I marry again, it will be to a lady of my choosing. And it will be for love.'

'That's what you said the first time, and look where it got you!'

'Hopefully, not every woman is like Jasmine.'

'I still can't understand what you saw in that girl.'

He laughed. 'That's because you're not a man.'

Teresa shook her head at her son. Did he think she was so old that she had no memory of sex? She was only seventy-three, not a hundred and three.

'She might have had a pretty face and a good body but she was vain and selfish,' Teresa pronounced firmly. 'You'd have to be a fool not to see that.'

'Men in love *are* fools, Mum,' he retorted with a

self-mocking edge which Teresa immediately picked up on.

She stared up at Enrico but he wasn't looking at her. He was off in another world. It came to her that he wasn't thinking of Jasmine, but some other woman. Teresa's heart lurched at the realisation that her youngest son, the apple of her eye, was in love with a *new* woman.

Dear God, she hoped and prayed that it *wasn't* his card-playing friend. Despite never having met the lady, Teresa had gleaned quite a few facts about her from Enrico's various comments. She was a widow for starters, a wealthy widow, whose late husband had been a much older man. An ex-model, she was also a highly astute businesswoman who ran a modelling agency in the city. To cap it all off, she was in her mid-thirties and had never had any children. Probably hadn't wanted any. A lot of career women didn't.

In other words, she was not good daughter-in-law material for Teresa Mandretti.

'I won't be coming home for lunch tomorrow, Mum,' Enrico said abruptly. 'I have somewhere else I have to go.'

'Where?'

'The man who trains our horses is having a special open day at his place for all his owners to celebrate the arrival of spring, and presumably get everyone in the right mood for the imminent spring racing carnivals.'

'Like a party,' his mother said.

'Yes. I suppose you could call it that,' Rico agreed.

Earlier this year, Ward's very savvy personal assistant, a smart little piece called Lisa, had instigated the increasingly popular tradition amongst horse trainers of having an open day for the owners every Sunday where they could visit their horses, discuss their valuable charges' prospects with the trainer or his stable foreman, then enjoy each other's company afterwards over a buffet lunch. But tomorrow was going to be extra-special, with the best of champagne and food.

Rico hadn't been going to attend, the same way he never attended any open day which fell on the first Sunday of the month, because it clashed with his monthly family get-together, an occasion which was far more important to him than socialising with the rich and famous, or having another clash with Renée.

But tomorrow was different. Tomorrow was D day. Desperation day.

'I see,' his mother said thoughtfully. 'Will Charles be there?'

'Probably not. He's not as interested in the horses as he once was.'

'That is understandable, Enrico. He has more to think about now that he has a wife and a little *bambino* on the way. What about your sheikh friend? *He's* not married. Will he be there?'

'No. You know Ali rarely goes to functions like that.'

Which left...the widow, Teresa deduced. Unless this horse trainer had a blonde girl jockey in his employ.

Enrico was partial to blondes. But tall, curvy ones, come to think of it, not teenie-weenie skinny ones. Which begged the question of what this Renée looked like.

She had to be tall, since she was an ex-model. And probably blonde, since her son was attracted. Maybe even busty, as Jasmine had been. Gone were the days when models had to be flat-chested.

'What about your other card-playing friend?' Teresa couldn't resist asking. 'The lady. Renée, isn't it? Will she be there?'

He smiled. He actually smiled. But it wasn't a happy smile. More a wryly resigned one.

'Oh, yes. Sure to be.'

Which gave Teresa the answer she was looking for. Enrico *was* in love with this Renée, but the lady didn't return his feelings.

Now Teresa didn't know what to think, or to feel. That any woman could resist her Enrico annoyed her considerably. Her youngest son was irresistible, in her opinion. At the same time, the last woman she would want him getting tangled up with was another creature like that gold-digging Jasmine.

So perhaps it was just as well this Renée didn't fancy him. But truly, she had to be some kind of blind fool. Enrico was a magnificent man. A man amongst men. What kind of stupid woman would not want him in her bed, and in her heart?

Teresa dropped the sprigs of mint she'd picked into the front pocket of her apron and linked arms with her handsome son. 'Come, Enrico. I have another pasta recipe to show you. A brand-new one.' And she drew him towards the back door, chattering away all the while, showering him with her love and approval.

Rico allowed himself to be cosseted and comforted, because he knew that, come tomorrow, he would be going into battle again with his nemesis. His decision just now to attend the open day showed how addicted he was to that witch's company. He simply could not go a single weekend without seeing her. Avoiding her at the races this afternoon hadn't worked at all.

It was a deplorable state of affairs. But what could he do about it? How could he change it? How could he change *her*?

He couldn't. All he could do was change himself. But how, was the problem. How did you stop yourself craving what you'd become addicted to?

He'd tried the out-of-sight, out-of-mind method, and that hadn't worked. Going cold turkey didn't apply, as he hadn't yet had the pleasure of having what he craved. There was counselling, he supposed, but he just couldn't picture that working, either.

So tell me, Mr Mandretti, what is it about this lady that you like so much?

Let's see, now, Doc, he could hear himself replying. *First there are her eyes. The slanting green ones which gleam with contempt every time they look at me. And then there's her gorgeous mouth, which cuts me to ribbons every time she opens it. But mostly there's her long, tall, far-too-slender body, which I shouldn't find incredibly sexy but I do!*

He'd be diagnosed a masochist with obsessional compulsive disorder and sent home with a swag of antidepressants, an appointment for a therapy session every week into eternity and a bill you couldn't climb over.

No, he wasn't going to try counselling.

Which left what?

The answer really was quite simple…if you were prepared to embrace the joys of rejection. He could ask the merry widow out. On a date.

He had asked her out before, of course. Many

times. But under the guise of a general invitation to one of his mother's parties.

Renée had always refused. Oh, she'd been polite enough on those occasions, but the bottom line was always the same. Clearly, she didn't want to spend any more time in his company than that which she presently endured.

To ask her out on a one-on-one basis was true masochism. But damn it all, what did he have to lose?

Tomorrow, he would jump right into the lion pit and put his head in the lioness's mouth. What happened after that was anybody's guess.

CHAPTER THREE

AROUND twelve-thirty the following day, a gut-tightened Rico left his new penthouse apartment—the one he'd snapped up from Charles when he relocated to the North Shore—and rode his private elevator down to the basement car park. There he strode quickly over to his Ferrari, jumped in behind the wheel, shoved in the key and started the engine.

He was running a bit late, considering the invitation stated from eleven onwards, but it wouldn't take him long to get there. Fifteen minutes at most. That was one of the great things about Charles' old place, aside from the views. Its location down near Circular Quay was so darned convenient.

Rico hadn't exited the underground car park and driven more than a block before realising that having the top down on his car was downright uncomfortable. The day was not a picture-perfect spring day, unlike yesterday, which had been lovely and warm.

As he grudgingly zapped the top up on his car, Rico told himself that the grey skies were not an omen of the day ahead, just typical of Sydney in early September. He still marvelled how the Sydney Olympics—which had been held in that same month—had been blessed with such consistently magnificent weather. Most of the time you never knew what you were going to get in spring in Sydney till you stuck your head out of the window in the morning. Relying on the weather forecast the night before was as silly as thinking Renée was actually going to say yes to his asking her out today.

Rico still could not believe he was actually doing this. Talk about masochistic!

But all the self-lectures in the world were not going to change his mind. Rico had always believed in going after what he wanted, at least till it was irrevocably certain that he could not have what he wanted, such as a career on the stage. Then and only then did he move on from such a goal, putting his energies into something more attainable.

So till Renée looked him straight in the face and said *no way, José* to going out with him, Rico harboured some small hope that he might succeed in his mission improbable. He even managed to convince himself during the brief drive over to Randwick that he had a reasonable chance of success.

After all, the merry widow had no permanent partner. If she had, such a partner would surely have accompanied her to the races sometimes. Yet she always came alone. Added to that was the interesting fact that, except on the rare occasion she'd gone overseas on a business trip, she *always* showed up to play poker on a Friday night. What woman involved with, or living with, some man would be so consistent?

Not that Rico imagined for one moment Renée was leading a nun-like lifestyle. She had to have had men friends since becoming a widow. Lovers, in other words. It had been over five years after all, far too long a time for a woman like her to have spent every night alone.

For some reason—possibly self-protection—Rico hadn't given much thought in the past to whom Renée actually slept with. Suddenly, this subject was the sole focus of his brain. After discarding all sorts of scenarios from secret affairs with married men to one-night stands with commitment-phobic divorcees, he decided she probably enjoyed strictly sexual flings with the toy-boy variety, selected from the huge stable of young male models who were contracted to her modelling agency.

Rico could easily see Renée in that kind of relationship. She would always want to be the boss, to always be on top.

The thought of her being on top of *him* did things to his body which hadn't been done so swiftly or so savagely since he was a teenager. He winced then tried to rearrange the bulge in his trousers to ease his discomfort, but it was a lost cause. Nothing was going to solve his problem, nothing except full body contact with Renée.

As Rico turned into the Randwick street where Ward's home and stables were located, he vowed to succeed in making Renée go out with him—*and* go to bed with him—even if he had to sell his soul to the devil to do so!

The sight of her blue BMW parked at the kerb right outside Ward's front gate gave Rico's black resolve a momentary jolt. She was there, waiting for him to make a fool of himself. No escape now, not unless he wimped out. And Rico was no wimp.

For a split-second the car-lined street almost gave him an excuse to drive on, to forget this insane mission. But then a gap presented itself in between a silver Jag and a dark blue Merc. Ward's owners were not short of a dollar. With a resigned sigh, Rico expertly angled his Ferrari into the rather tight spot and cut off the engine.

After a glance at his watch—it was getting on for one—he dragged himself out from behind the wheel, slammed the door and zapped the immobiliser. Almost as an afterthought, he checked his appearance in the side-mirror, finger-combing his messy hair back from his face before frowning at the dark stubble on his cheeks and chin. He never shaved on the weekend—something Renée had no doubt noticed in the past—so he hadn't wanted it to seem as if he'd been sprucing himself up specially for her.

Still, given he was planning to ask her out—view full sex at the end of the night—this now seemed a stupid train of thought. Totally…utterly…stupid! Which meant he was running true to form. Once Renée came into the equation in anything he did, off went his head and on went a pumpkin.

But faint heart never won fat turkey, Rico reminded himself doggedly. Or the hand of the fair lady. Not that he wanted to marry the merry widow. He wasn't *that* crazy! All he wanted was a few nights in her bed, after which he was sure that this perverse sexual obsession he'd been suffering from these past five years would burn itself out.

He didn't love her. Lord, no. No way! What was there to love? She was no better than Jasmine, really. Just another hard-nosed, hard-hearted, mercenary madam who specialised in making fools of men, namely him.

With that charming thought in mind, Rico slid his hands into the pockets of his black trousers and walked somewhat reluctantly back up the street to Ward's establishment, throwing Renée's BMW a testy look as he passed by. She must have been the first guest to arrive to get such a prize spot.

Rico stood for a moment at Ward's front gate, staring blankly up at the trainer's very stylish two-storey home and trying to get his brain into gear. All the owners would have finished visiting their horses by now. They'd all be inside, tucking into the champers and caviare. All except...Renée.

More than likely she'd still be at the stables, fussing over their syndicate's most expensive purchase to date, a three-year-old black colt which they'd bought from Ali as a yearling but which had gone seriously shin-sore during his first preparation and been turned out to mature. He'd been back in training for a few weeks, and Ward's PA had told Rico on the phone the other night—the notoriously taciturn trainer rarely spoke to owners in person over the phone—that Ebony Fire had come back a treat and was working the place down. No doubt Lisa had relayed the same news to Renée.

Although Rico knew surprisingly little about Renée on a personal basis, he knew how she felt about the horses she owned and part-owned. She loved them. Loved being around them. Loved touching them and talking to them. On the couple of occasions that he *had* come to an open Sunday prior to today, Renée had been difficult to pry away from the stables.

'I don't come here to eat,' she'd snapped at him once when he'd suggested going inside for lunch. 'I come here to visit with my horses.'

Rico smiled wryly at the memory. Oh, yes. She would not have gone inside yet. He was sure of it.

Which was a comfort. The prospect of propositioning the object of his desire in privacy was infinitely preferable to doing so in a roomful of people where others might hear her hysterical laughter. This way, he could keep his humiliation to himself.

Scooping in a deep and hopefully calming breath, he spun on his heels and headed for the side-path, which bypassed Ward's house and led round to where the stables were located at the rear of the property. At the end of this path was a gate which was always manned by a security guard. Today's man was called Jed, a big, beefy fellow who knew all of Ward's owners by sight.

'Afternoon, Mr Mandretti,' Jed said as he opened the gate to let Rico in. 'You're running a bit late. All the others have gone in to lunch.'

Rico's heart sank, till he realised Jed couldn't possibly know that for a fact from where he was stationed. Ward's stable complex was shaped in a square with an internal courtyard. Each side of the square housed six stalls along with feed and tack rooms at the ends of the rows, with staff quarters on the floor above.

Whilst Jed could peer through the gap at the nearest corner into the courtyard beyond, he couldn't possibly see inside the stalls, which was where Renée always ventured. It was never enough for her to stroke her horses' heads over the stall doors. If the horse was docile enough, she would be right in there, up close and personal.

'No worries, Jed,' Rico replied as he walked on in. 'I haven't come to eat today. See you.'

The courtyard was deserted except for one stable-hand, who was hosing away the last of the horsy deposits from the pavings, legacies of their having been walked around on show for their owners.

'Working hard there, Neil, I see,' Rico said as he approached.

The young lad glanced up with surprise and pleasure on his face.

'Why, hello there, Mr Mandretti,' Neil replied, swiftly turning off the hose so that their esteemed visitor could pass by without getting anything splattered on his very smart and expensive-looking black clothes. If there was one owner Neil liked almost as much as he liked Mrs Selinsky, it was Mr Mandretti. For one thing, he always remembered his name, not like a lot of the *hoi polloi*. You'd never know he was a famous TV star by the way he acted. He was so nice and friendly. Of course, no one was as nice as Mrs Selinsky. Now there was one genuine lady. Generous, too. Every time one of her horses won any prize money, she gave all the grooms a bonus.

But it wasn't just her handing out cash which made everyone here warm to her. It was the way she was with the horses. She really cared about them. Even the boss liked Mrs Selinsky. You could tell because he actually talked to her. And the boss was not one for idle chit-chat.

'You'll be here to see your colt, I suppose,' Neil said. 'Mrs Selinsky's still in there with him. I think she'd sleep in that stall if the boss'd let her.'

Rico decided then and there that if there was such a thing as reincarnation he wanted to come back as one of Renée's racehorses.

'What stall is Blackie in?' Rico asked. Blackie was Ebony Fire's stable name.

'Number eighteen. The last on that row over there. I know it's not for me to say, but if he runs as good as he looks this time in, you'll have a class-one winner there for sure.'

'Let's hope so, Neil. But there's many a slip twixt the training track and the winner's circle.'

'Aye. That there is. But then that's the way of the racin' game, isn't it? It's all a gamble. A bit like life.'

Rico nodded. Neil was right. Life *was* a gamble. Sometimes you won and sometimes you lost. Knowledge, however, increased your odds of winning. Suddenly, he wished he knew a lot more about Mrs Renée Selinsky. But it was too late to worry about that now. The time had come to take his chances. To gamble on winning the Maiden Stakes. Trouble was, he was a long shot and long shots didn't win too often.

Despite his growing inner tension, he waved a jaunty goodbye to Neil before making his way straight for stall number eighteen.

Several of the horses whose heads were hanging over the doors whinnied to him as he strode past. Ebony Fire, however, was not one of them. At first glance, stall number eighteen seemed empty. But, once Rico's eyes adjusted to the dimmer light inside, he saw that the black colt was standing on a thick bed of straw in the far corner, having his flank stroked and being talked as if he were a much loved child.

'You are such a beautiful boy,' Renée crooned as her right hand continued its rhythmic petting. Her left arm was curled round the horse's neck, with the side of her head resting against his glossy black mane. 'Ward says there's no sign of that shin soreness coming back and you'll be ready for your first race soon. *And* he says you'll win. I did tell him that you might be a little nervous to begin with and we shouldn't expect too much too soon, but he said you didn't have a nervous bone in your body. He said you were a born racehorse. A potential champion. Oh, I do so wish you were all mine, my darling. But I suppose one third of you is better than nothing.'

Rico didn't know whether he felt jealous of the horse on the receiving end of Renée's caresses. Or of Ward Jackman. It sounded as if the man said one hell of a lot more to Renée than he did to him, or anyone else for that matter. Could it be that Renée's relationship with Jackman extended beyond trainer and owner?

Suddenly, Renée's BMW being parked right outside Ward's front gate took on a different and more ominous meaning. Maybe she hadn't arrived first today. Maybe her car had been there all night...

Rico swallowed the bile which leap into his throat and tried to look at this appalling idea more rationally and without panic. There'd never been a hint of intimacy shown between them that he'd noticed. No telling glances, or untoward touching.

But their being lovers would certainly explain the uncharacteristic amount of chit-chat which obviously had been going on between them about Ebony Fire. Even the most taciturn men were prone to pillow talk.

The thought of Renée sleeping with the ruggedly handsome horse trainer stabbed deep into Rico's heart. His fists curled over by his side, his nails digging into his palms. Theoretical lovers were a whole different ball game to an in-your-face, flesh-and-blood one. If what Rico suspected was true, then it was no wonder she never brought a boyfriend to the races. He was already there!

He stared at the way she was cuddling and petting

the horse, but his brain didn't see Ebony Fire as the recipient of her caresses any longer. His mind's eye was picturing Ward Jackman, naked and aroused, beneath her hands.

A violent shudder ran down Rico's spine.

The colt suddenly swung his head Rico's way as he spotted him standing there at the stable door and neighed a welcome to his new visitor. Renée whirled, her eyes widening when she saw who that new visitor was.

For a few moments her usual composure seemed to desert her, her body language showing agitation as she hurried over to the stable door, the horse hot on her heels.

'What on earth are *you* doing here?' she snapped as she wrenched open the bottom half of the stable door and slipped out of the stall, quickly closing the door behind her before the colt could follow. 'Don't you usually go home to the family on the first Sunday of the month?'

The way she said the word, *'family'*, suggested he was a member of the Mafia, rather than the son of an honest, hard-working market gardener.

'And hello to you too,' Rico returned, impressed at how cool he sounded in the face of the jealousy and fury raging inside him. 'The thing is, my dear Renée, I just couldn't go another day without a dose of your charming company,' he added in a mocking tone which masked the truth behind his words.

She totally ignored him as she concentrated on shoving the bolt home on the door before finally raising cool green eyes to his. 'In that case, why weren't you at the races yesterday?'

Rico smiled. 'Aah, so you noticed I wasn't there. I'm flattered.'

'Don't be. I had a very pleasant afternoon. I picked several winners as well.'

'In that case, why are you so sour today? Or is that always your disposition around me?'

Rico could feel his tongue running away with him, along with any hope he had of Renée ever accepting an invitation to go out on a date.

Not that he was going to ask her now. Not until he discovered what was going on between her and Jackman. No man liked to make a total fool of himself, not even when that man was as desperate as he was.

His gaze swept over the object of that desperation, trying not to ogle the way the tight camel-coloured trousers she was wearing hugged every inch of her long, slender legs. Her neat white T-shirt was equally snug-fitting and showed more bust than he realised she had. Either that, or she was wearing a padded bra.

No, no padding, he realised on a second glance. Damn, no bra at all! Her nipples were starkly outlined against the thin white cotton, as long and hard as bullets.

Maybe their erect state was due to her being cold—the day still hadn't warmed up much. Or maybe their condition was the result of her having spent all night in Jackman's bed.

His stomach crunched down hard at the image of the other man sucking on Renée's nipples. He could not bear it. He should leave. Right now, before he did or said something he would really regret.

But he couldn't.

'Would you mind if I asked you a personal question?' he grated out, struggling not to sound the way he was feeling.

'Would it stop you if I did?' she flung back at him.

'No.'

'I didn't think so.'

'Are you and Ward lovers?' he demanded to know, his eyes glued to hers.

There was no doubt her face registered shock, her finely arched brows arching even further over rapidly blinking eyes, her red-glossed mouth dropping slightly open.

Her recovery was swift, however, with her face resuming its characteristically self-contained, slightly superior expression. Ignoring him again for a few moments, she bent to pick up the black leather jacket and matching bag which he hadn't noticed sitting on the ground next to the stable wall. The movement swung her smooth curtain of thick, shoulder-length brown hair across her high cheekbones, momentarily hiding her face from him. When she straightened it fell back into perfect place, a testament to the expertise of her hairdresser. Tilting up her chin slightly, she fixed her slanting green eyes on his own eyes, her gaze cool and steady.

'Why do you ask? Has someone said something about us?'

'No. But I heard you talking to Blackie here just now and it sounded like you were pretty chummy with Ward. Let's face it, it's hard to get two words out of that man at the best of times, but he seems to have told you plenty about the horse's progress.'

'So you jumped to the conclusion that he told me in bed.'

'Well, did he?'

'I don't think that's any of your business,' she said quite coldly, and turned back to start stroking Blackie's head once more.

'I'm making it my business,' he bit out.

'Why?' she said indifferently, not even bothering to glance his way. 'What's it to you who I sleep with?'

'I don't like you sleeping with Jackman,' he ground out.

Now she did stop stroking the horse to look at him, her expression curious. 'But why?'

What could he say? I don't like you sleeping with *any* man. I want you in my bed and my bed only.

She would laugh in his face.

His pride simply could not stand that degree of humiliation.

'He's the syndicate's trainer,' he snapped instead. 'I don't like the idea of you getting inside information which should be shared with all the partners.'

She gave a small, dry laugh. 'Typical. I should have known the reason would be something like that. For your information, I'm *not* sleeping with Ward. If you had any brains at all, or any powers of observation, you'd know that he and Lisa are madly in love. She's even moved in with him. The only reason Ward talks to me more than you is because he knows I genuinely love my horses. I'm not just in racing for the status, or the socialising. Satisfied now?'

When she went to move away, he grabbed her arm. She stiffened and shot him a look which would have shriveled a lesser man. Rico's fingers tightened.

'Why do you dislike me so much?' he demanded to know. 'What have I ever done to you?'

She stared down at the hand circled on her arm till he let her go, at which point she actually shuddered.

Rico knew then that she would never go out with him, let alone go to bed with him. Not willingly. He repelled her for some reason.

It was the most appalling realisation of his life, worse than discovering Jasmine was a gold-digger. Much worse than anything he could imagine.

Now *he* was the one who shuddered. But not visibly. Inside. Deep, deep inside.

'You don't want me to answer those questions,' she replied tartly. 'Trust me on that.'

'But I do,' he ground out. 'Trust me on *that*.'

Her green eyes frosted over further, if that was possible. 'Very well. I'll tell you. The reason I dislike you so much is because you represent everything I despise in the male sex. You're selfish and self-centred and appallingly shallow. You say you want substance in your life but you continually choose shadows. You also make snap judgements about people without ever looking beneath the surface. When I think of how you nearly ruined Charles's marriage…'

Her top lip curled up in contempt and Rico cringed. OK, so he'd made a terrible mistake in accusing Dominique of being the same kind of heartless gold-digger Jasmine had been. But the evidence *had* seemed damning at the time.

'All because you couldn't see past your own pathetic marital experience,' Renée continued caustically. 'Like I said, selfish and shallow. Of course, most really good-looking men are tarred with the same brush. You imagine that you're so irresistible, just because you were born with a great body and loads of sex appeal. You think I don't know that your arrogant Italian nose is put out of joint because I don't swoon every time you come into the room? Or that you're seriously irritated by the fact I can play poker better than you can? I might have more respect for you, Rico Mandretti, if just *once* you behaved with some depth and sensitivity. But no, you just keep on keeping on in your usual superficial playboy fashion, acting like a spoiled brat when you don't get your way!'

By now her voice had risen slightly and Rico cast a desperate glance around, relieved to see that Neil had finished his hosing down and was nowhere in sight.

'But most pathetic of all,' Renée swept on, regardless, 'is the way you go from one blonde bimbo to the next, then bemoan the fact you haven't got what Charles has got. Grow up, Rico. Get a life, and a nice girl for a wife. *Have* that family you claim you want. Then maybe I might grow to like you. No, maybe not,' she added scornfully. 'Liking you is something I'll never do. But at least I'd have some respect for you.'

At last, her tirade was finished. And so was Rico.

He had never been on the end of such a brutal character assassination in all his life. Not even Jasmine at her most venomous had managed to make him feel so utterly worthless.

He could have lashed back, he supposed. Could have torn strips off Renée's own less than perfect past. But somehow, he had a feeling that might backfire on him as well. Though goodness knew how. No one would ever convince him she'd married that old geezer for love. Still, possibly money hadn't been her motive. Maybe his believing her a gold-digger was one of those snap judgements she'd referred to.

'I did warn you,' she stated brusquely when he just stood there, silent and shattered. 'Don't make me feel guilty for speaking the truth. Don't you dare! It's not as though you give a damn what I think, anyway. Men like you don't give a damn about anyone but themselves.'

And with an angry toss of her hair she pushed past him and stalked off.

Well at least she thinks I'm good-looking, Rico thought bitterly as he watched her go. Clearly, she's repelled more by my characterless character than my great body or my arrogant Italian nose. That was something, wasn't it?

'Yeah, right, Rico,' he muttered bleakly and, sliding his hands deeply back into his trouser pockets, he trudged back across the still blessedly deserted courtyard, murmured a desolate goodbye to Jed at the gate then headed wearily for his car, and home.

CHAPTER FOUR

CHARLES glanced across the card table at an unusually quiet Renée, then sidewards at a very grim-faced Rico, and wondered what on earth had happened between those two during the past week. They'd been in good form last Friday night, hitting off each other with their usual savage but highly entertaining wit.

But tonight was a different story entirely. Tonight they were both tight-lipped and tight-fisted. The pots so far had been small, the betting abysmal. Neither Rico nor Renée seemed interested in trying to out-bluff each other the way they usually did. Rico was particularly dull. Even when he had a fairly good hand, he didn't raise the stakes to his usual daring degree.

All in all, it was turning out to be one of the most boring poker nights Charles had ever sat through. He would much rather have stayed home with Dominique. Frankly, he couldn't wait for the evening to end. Yet it was only ten-twenty. At least they'd be stopping soon for supper.

'It's your turn to deal, Charles,' Ali reminded him. 'We'll make this the last hand before supper.'

'Good,' Charles said.

Rico agreed. All he wanted to do was finish this torture and get out of here. With a weary-sounding sigh, he started picking up the five cards Charles had dealt to him. The first was the queen of hearts. The second, the jack of hearts. When the third turned out

43

to be the king of hearts, his own heart gave a little flutter. When the fourth proved to be the ace of hearts, his heart ceased to beat altogether.

Holy hell!

At that point, mathematical probability told Rico all he could seriously hope his last card to be was one more heart of any kind, giving him a flush. Or possibly a ten—again of any suit—completing a straight. To think that it could possibly be the ten of hearts, completing a royal flush, was a million-to-one chance. He'd heard of it happening but never seen it, let alone experienced it personally.

His fingertips clipped the edge of the table as he went to pick up his last card. Renée's eyes immediately flicked his way. Before Rico could think better of it, his head turned and their gazes connected.

It was the first time he'd looked straight at her all night, other than when she'd first walked into the presidential suite right on eight o'clock, looking elegantly sexy in cream woollen trousers and a pale green twin set.

He *had* been thinking about her constantly since last Sunday's fiasco, wondering what to do about his escalating frustration. And he'd come here tonight, still not sure what action to take. His body's immediate and involuntary response to just the sight of her had swiftly made up his mind.

This was going to be his last night playing poker with the merry widow. Charles and Ali would have to find someone else. He would opt out of the racing syndicate as well. On top of that, he aimed to leave Sydney and go overseas for a while. He'd been offered the opportunity to take his show on the road to

Italy. He intended to do just that. He had to get right away from this scene before he self-destructed.

His decisions, though sensible, had depressed him, and the evening's card-playing so far had passed in a fog. But the four cards he now held in his hand could not help but set the adrenaline flowing in any poker player.

This time, when he looked at Renée, his excitement was not of the sexual kind.

Her smile, when it came, startled him. Was it an apology? A peace offering?

No, he swiftly realised. It was far too wry, and knowing. Clearly, she had sensed his sudden tension, and was waiting to see his reaction to his last card. Rico noted that she was already holding all five of her cards, so she knew the state of her own hand.

How cold-blooded, and clever she was!

His eyes dropped away from hers, but he felt her watch him closely as he picked up his fifth and last card.

Did he manage to hide his reaction? He believed so, but every internal muscle he owned stiffened with the effort of keeping his hands still and his expression poker-faced. After all, how often did you pick up the one card which gave you not just a great hand, but also an unbeatable one?

Unbeatable!

His heart thudded heavily in his chest as he battled to remain outwardly composed. Blood pounded through his temples. His mouth went dry.

'How many cards do you want, Rico?' Charles asked him somewhat impatiently.

Quite deliberately, he hesitated, before relaxing back into his chair and adopting an attitude of over-confidence. This was not how he usually acted when he had a really good hand. His aim in adopting such a manner was to confuse his opposition, to convince the others he was bluffing, otherwise they would all fold and he wouldn't win a single cent.

And what a criminal waste that would be!

'I think I'll sit on what I've got,' he said, tone smug, mouth twitching at the corner.

Ali frowned over at him, dark eyes puzzled. Rico smiled back at him, thinking that he would enjoy taking a few thousand of Ali's oil-rich millions off him. The trouble was Ali was no fool. He rarely lost much at the card table. Would he smell a rat and fold, regardless?

'So Enrico is alive tonight after all,' Ali murmured, and discarded three cards. Charles dealt him three more. Unfortunately, Ali didn't look thrilled with what he picked up, which meant he probably wasn't going to take part in the betting, no matter what he thought Rico was up to. Ali wouldn't have shown his disgust if he'd been planning on bluffing.

Now it was Renée's turn. 'I'll sit too,' she said in that soft, silky voice which Rico found impossible to read. Sometimes she was bluffing. At other times, she held a full house, or at least three of a kind.

No matter this time. Whatever she had, she could not possibly win. Rico's body fizzed with elation as he looked over at her.

I'm going to go out a winner here tonight, madam, Rico thought with a savagery born of a severely bruised male pride. I hope you've got a full house. Or even four of a kind. Either that, or I hope you think I'm bluffing and you bet every cent you've got.

'I'm taking two,' Charles said, which suggested he

could be holding three of a kind. But possibly not. Charles often sat on a pair and a high card. He seemed pleased with what he drew. But that could mean anything. Charles was a very sneaky poker player when he was on his game.

Rico was right about Ali. He dropped out of the hand straight away. Renée stayed in, continually raising the stakes. Rico did the same. Charles folded when the pot reached the six-figure mark.

'This is too hot for me,' he said as he closed his hand and placed it face down on the table. 'You two can fight it out.'

'I think Rico should save his money and fold now too,' Renée advised coolly. 'Unless, of course, he enjoys losing. I suspect he must, the way he's been playing tonight.'

It was the wrong thing to say, especially with Rico holding the cards he was holding, and feeling the feelings he'd been feeling all week.

Suddenly, his winning Renée's money wasn't enough. He wanted to strike at her pride, as she had shattered his last Sunday.

The sheer wickedness of the wager which sprang into his mind sent his heartbeat into overdrive. If Renée wasn't bluffing—and he suspected she wasn't—she would not be able to resist his proposal.

And then she was would be his. *His*, where he'd always wanted her. In his bed.

Just the thought of it gave him an instant erection.

'If you're so confident,' he said smoothly despite the dark excitement racing through his veins, 'how about we raise the stakes?'

'You mean increase the maximum bet?' she returned, her finely plucked brows drawing together in a frown.

'No. I was thinking we could wager for something other than money.'

Her head jerked back, long eyelashes blinking rapidly. 'Like what?'

'Yes, like what?' Charles piped up.

'Whatever we fancy. Renée can choose something she wants which I can give or buy her. And vice versa. Anything at all.'

Her eyes flashed scornfully. 'I can't think of *anything* you could give me that I couldn't buy for myself.'

'*Can't* you? I got the impression at the open day last Sunday that that wasn't the case...'

He locked eyes with hers and saw the penny drop. His share of Ebony Fire. She wanted that all right. He could guess what was going on in her devious mind. If she won his third, it would be relatively easy to buy out Charles' share. He was already losing interest in the syndicate. Then she would have her dearest wish. To own *all* of her precious colt.

Rico knew Renée would not be able to resist the temptation. She would agree to the bet and fall right into his trap.

'I'm not so sure about this,' Charles said, ever the gentleman. 'It doesn't sound right.'

'Mind your own business, Charles,' Renée snapped, showing Rico that she was already on the slippery slide to hell. 'This is between Rico and myself. So how do you suggest we go about this?'

'We write our heart's desire down on separate pieces of paper,' Rico suggested. 'Then we put each in its own envelope and place them both next to the pot. We then show our cards at the same time and the winner takes the pot. The loser is then handed the winner's envelope and has to deliver whatever the winner wants.'

'So we don't have to say up front what we're actually betting for,' Renée said, her expression thoughtful. 'It's a secret.'

'Yes. It's more exciting that way, don't you think?'

'What happens to the loser's envelope?' she asked him, green eyes narrowed.

'She—or he—can take it back, if they like, sight unseen by the other.'

Her frown deepened. 'I just can't imagine what you could possibly want from me.'

'Maybe it's the same thing you want from me.'

She stared hard at him. 'Maybe,' she said at last. 'But somehow, I doubt it. Still, it might be…interesting…to find out.'

'Provided I win, of course,' Rico added, pretending that the result wasn't a foregone conclusion. 'If I don't, I'll certainly be taking *my* envelope back.'

Her eyes shot him a look which he would have given anything to read. But that had always been her skill, hiding the truth from him when she wanted to. That was why he never knew when she was bluffing or not.

'Let's get the paper and envelopes, then,' she said crisply.

'I'm still not sure I like this idea at all,' Charles grumbled.

'Why not?' Rico returned with a shrug of his broad shoulders. 'What's the harm? It's just a bit of fun.'

'I suppose so,' Charles said grudgingly. 'By the

look of you tonight, you certainly could do with some lightening up.'

'But we won't make a habit of this kind of wager,' Ali inserted with his usual authority, never liking things to become personal at his card table. 'This is a one-off. *James*,' he called to the butler who was at that moment preparing supper over in the adjoining sitting room. 'Bring Mr Mandretti a notepad, two pens and two envelopes.'

'Yes, Your Highness,' the butler replied and walked over to the writing desk in the corner of the sitting room, where he gathered the required objects and delivered them with his usual aplomb.

Rico ripped off the top page of the hotel notepad and handed the rest of the pad to Renée, along with a Biro and an envelope. She wrote quickly, clearly knowing exactly what she wanted to ask for. Rico, however, found himself suddenly in a quandary. How much to ask for? One night with her? Two? Or every night for a week?

Not enough, he decided darkly as his flesh grew even harder. Not nearly enough. So he put his pen to paper and wrote.

'You are now my mistress for a month, starting tonight.'

His hands trembled slightly as he folded the sheet of paper and shoved it into the remaining envelope. On the outside he scrawled his name, then tossed it on top of Renée's envelope.

Yes, on top, he thought with another overwhelming rush of desire. That was where he was going to be every night for the next month. On top of Renée. Except when he ordered her to take that position herself. Mistresses could be ordered into whatever position or activity which took their lover's fancy. That was their role in life, wasn't it, to keep the men who kept them sexually satisfied, to accede to their every demand?

Of course, Rico understood he would have to pay for the privilege. Mistresses did not come much cheaper than gold-digging wives. But it would give him great pleasure to spend money on Renée. To shower her with jewels and dress her in designer clothes. She wore trousers far too often for his liking, despite the fact they suited her tall, willowy figure, and made her lovely long legs look even longer.

Still, he wanted to see what she looked like in soft, floaty dresses and low-cut evening gowns and black satin nighties with tiny straps which yielded to a mere flick of a finger. He also wanted to see what she looked like wearing nothing at all except that subtly musky perfume which sometimes drove him mad. But most of all he wanted to see what she looked like when she came.

That would be the ultimate triumph, and the best salve for his male pride, to make her lose control, to watch her mouth fall open as he listened to her moans of unexpected ecstasy.

Rico knew that if there was one talent he had, and which had not been God-given, it was his skill in the bedroom. Admittedly, those naturally born good looks which Renée had scorned last Sunday *had* made it easy for him to get women into his bed. Frankly, the opposite sex had been coming on to him in droves since he was fourteen.

But, as was his nature, he hadn't been content to just ''Do it.'' Rico never saw the point of doing anything unless he did it to the best of his ability. So he'd made a point of learning everything which could be learned about giving and receiving sexual pleasure. He'd set out to discover what women really wanted in the lovemaking department. Gradually, he'd uncovered their secret desires and acted upon them, with great success. Jasmine might have married him mainly for his money, but she had certainly enjoyed herself in their marital bed.

Rico was confident Renée would enjoy herself with him just as much, once he got past her defences.

Because, of course, she wasn't going to be pleased when she read his demand. She was, in fact, sure to be downright furious.

Too bad. A bet was a bet. You had to pay up. In full. Renée knew that.

Rico didn't doubt the merry widow would deliver. But not happily, or willingly. At least, not to begin with…

His challenge was to bring her round, to make her see that being his mistress was a very pleasurable way to spend the next month. The thought of seducing her totally to his sexual will was almost as exciting as looking at the unbelievable hand he was holding.

'Come on, then,' Charles said impatiently. 'Let's see your hands.'

Charles' speaking at this juncture jolted Rico. He'd forgotten what his best friend's reaction would be once his less than gentlemanly demand was made public. Charles would be shocked, and disapproving. Ali, not so much, Rico imagined. His ideas on women and sex were along more primitive lines. Whenever Ali met a young lady he fancied at the races here in Sydney, he often invited her to accompany him home here to the presidential suite for the night, then on to his property for the following week. But she was always returned the following Friday. And was never invited again.

Despite his one-week affairs being common knowledge around Sydney's racing set, he still had no trouble finding willing companions. Frankly, Ali had even less trouble getting women to share his bed—even on this temporary basis—than Rico. Jasmine had once described the Arab prince as sex on legs.

Of course, his billions added considerable impetus to his sex appeal, as it did with all seriously wealthy men. But if the women who went with Ali thought they would ever catch him for a husband, then they were sorely mistaken. Ali had once confided in Rico he had no interest in marriage. Or having children. His horses were his children and women were just a pleasant diversion.

No. Ali would not be shocked by Rico's demand. Not one iota.

Charles, however, was another matter.

Too late to worry about that, however. It was time to put his cards on the table. Time to claim his prize.

CHAPTER FIVE

'TOGETHER, then?' Rico suggested, too excited now to care what anybody thought.

Renée's shoulders lifted in a seemingly nonchalant shrug but he detected a flash of something in her eyes. Surely not panic. Was she afraid, suddenly, that she might lose?

Her hand trembled slightly as she placed her cards down just before his. So she *was* worried.

She had every right to be, came the devilish thought when he saw her cards. Four nines was a good hand. But not nearly good enough.

'Hope you're not bluffing, pal,' Charles said as Rico exposed his own incredible hand.

Renée sucked in sharply whilst Charles openly gaped.

'My God!' he exclaimed. 'A royal routine. You know, I've never seen one of those before.'

'I have,' Ali said drily. 'How wicked of you, Enrico, to trick Renée into such a wager with such a hand.'

'Renée didn't have to agree,' Rico retorted, his elation refusing to give way to guilt. 'It was up to her to gauge what kind of hand I was holding. She should have known I wasn't bluffing.'

'I did,' Renée said, composed once more. 'I just didn't realise your hand was unbeatable. I did have pretty good cards myself, you know.'

Rico frowned over at her. She should have been more disappointed. More angry with him.

Still, she hadn't read his demand yet. What would happen when she did? If Rico was any judge of character at all—something Renée insisted he wasn't—he would bet that she wouldn't make a scene. She would be cool and controlled, till she got him in private. *Then*, she'd let him have it.

In a perverse kind of way, he was looking forward to that moment. The only thing about last Sunday that he'd enjoyed was seeing her in a temper over him.

Heated dislike was much preferable to cold uninterest. Her admission that she thought him physically attractive had not been forgotten, either. Hell, he was depending on it!

When she reached for the two envelopes, his stomach suddenly twisted into the most awful knot. But she bypassed the one which had his name on it and picked up the other one.

'I can have this back now, can't I?' she said with a saucy tilt of her chin. 'That was the deal. The loser gets to keep his—or her—heart's desire secret.'

'It's no secret from me,' Rico snapped, irritated by the delay in her opening *his* envelope. 'I know exactly what you asked for.'

'You only think you do,' came her cryptic comment.

Rico could not believe it. Even in his moment of triumph, she had to make some smart remark which would distract him and make him wonder. He wished now that he hadn't made that particular condition of the bet. He would have preferred to see for himself exactly what she'd written. As much as he was pretty sure that she would have asked for his share of Ebony Fire, now he'd never know for certain.

And she'd never tell him. He knew Renée well enough to know that!

'This is all getting too much for me,' Charles grumbled. 'Just open Rico's envelope, for pity's sake, and let's see what he wants. But I hope you've got plenty of money, Renée, because with that hand Rico could have asked for the world!'

'I doubt our Italian friend would have asked for anything which could be bought,' Ali said quietly and with his usual insight. 'I suspect it will be something only Renée could give him.'

'My thoughts, exactly,' Renée remarked, coolly taking her time putting her envelope away in the handbag she always kept at her feet before finally picking up the envelope with Rico's name on it. 'Are we right, Rico?' she asked, a small, knowing smile playing around her mouth as she turned her gaze on to him.

Rico battled to stop his face from burning, a mammoth effort considering his body was on fire and his brain besieged by the most humiliating of realisations. She knew. *Knew* what he'd asked for. In essence, anyway. Ali suspected as well.

Had he been so obvious these last couple of years? Had they all known how much he'd wanted her, how he'd sat there every Friday night in a torment of desire and need?

Charles had guessed Rico's supposedly secret feelings for the merry widow some time back, but Charles was his best friend and privy to Rico's confidences. Rico hadn't realised the other two had known what he was enduring as well. It was mortifying in the extreme.

Once again, she'd struck at his pride. He tried not to glower at her, tried to keep his face from betraying the resentment raging within him. But he could never hide his feelings the way she could. He could feel his eyes blazing and his heart pounding with fury. He vowed to make her pay, in the only way he could.

Some time during the next month he'd reduce her to begging for him. He'd make her whimper with need, and moan with desire. He might even make her fall in love with him!

What a delicious revenge that would be for the way she'd constantly belittled him over the years; to have the merry widow surrender her soul to him, as well as her body.

Even as she opened his envelope, he already knew what to expect. No visible reaction whatsoever. No shock. No anger. Not on the outside, anyway. She would protect *her* pride at all costs. To hell with his, though.

'Well, well, well,' was all she said, with just the slightest raising of her right eyebrow, the one she always cocked when she was being her usual sarcastic self. 'I'm surprised, Rico. If that was all you wanted, you only had to ask. You didn't have to wait for a million-to-one chance to have your heart's desire.'

Rico gritted his teeth and willed the angry flush away. 'You mean you would have said yes if I'd just asked?'

'Asked what?' Charles demanded to know. 'What has he asked for, damn it? Or aren't we allowed to know that either?'

'Don't get your dander up, Charles,' Renée said

soothingly. 'Of course you can know. It's nothing worth hiding. Rico just wants me to go out with him.'

Rico could not deny her answer stunned him. He'd been sure she'd drop him right in it. But then the truth surfaced. Of course! She was protecting *her* pride again. She didn't want the others to know what she'd be doing for the next month.

'But that doesn't make any sense,' Charles said with more than a touch of bewilderment in his voice. 'If you wanted to ask Renée out, then why didn't you just ask, like she said?'

'Because he didn't want to risk her saying no,' Ali explained. 'No man likes to be rejected.'

'Renée wouldn't have said no,' Charles said firmly. 'Would you, Renée?'

'Absolutely not, Charles,' Renée returned in that seemingly polite but cleverly mocking tone Rico knew only too well. 'How could I possibly have resisted Rico's charm?'

'I *have* asked her out before,' Rico pointed out through gritted teeth, his temper only just under control.

'Only to family affairs,' she countered. 'Not on an intimate, one-on-one basis.'

When she said one-on-one, her eyes met his and Rico could have sworn that he glimpsed a glitter of excitement, not mockery, in their depths.

No, no, he had to be mistaken. She couldn't possibly *want* to sleep with him. OK, so he *was* bargaining on her not finding him physically repulsive, but she'd made it quite clear last Sunday she didn't like him one little bit. He'd be the last man on earth she'd choose for her lover.

'Dominique is going to be tickled pink,' Charles

said with a delighted smile. 'You two won't be able to refuse her dinner invitations in future.'

'We're just going out a few times, Charles,' Rico pointed out. 'See if we can get along. Don't make plans for our future just yet.'

'Surely we could manage one little dinner party, Rico,' Renée shocked him by saying. 'I still feel guilty over refusing Dominique's last invitation for us to go to dinner. Tell her to give me a call, Charles, and we'll set a date soon.'

Rico sat there, smiling his agreement on the outside but fuming on the inside. He didn't want to have to pretend to be a real partner to Renée in front of his friends. That was not his plan. She was to be kept for the darkness of the night, to be used strictly for his private pleasure. When he took her out, it would be for drinks and dirty dancing in dimly lit clubs, dressed as only a mistress would be dressed. He didn't want to have to play the gentleman. Not for a single moment.

Somehow, he would wangle his way out of that dinner invitation.

'James has supper ready,' Ali announced, and began to rise from his chair.

Supper on poker nights was nothing heavy, just a tasty selection of sandwiches and pastries and coffee, all set up on the large coffee-table where the four of them could sit on the surrounding seating and serve themselves. Except for the coffee part. James did the honours there, then hovered to one side with the coffee-pot, ready for top-ups.

Rarely did supper last longer than half an hour, the drinking and eating usually interspersed by trips to the powder room. Renée always used the last ten

minutes or so to have a couple of cigarettes on the
balcony that came off the dining area, a hangover
from her modelling days, when she'd used smoking
to keep her weight down, one of her few revelations
about her past.

That night, she bolted her first cup of coffee down,
Rico noticed. Didn't touch any food then carried a
second cup of coffee out onto the balcony. He would
have followed her out there if Charles hadn't kept
blathering on about how he still couldn't believe that
hand and that bet.

'Hell, Rico, you could have asked for anything.
Anything at all. But all you wanted was a date. I
didn't realise you were such a romantic.'

'All men are romantics,' Ali said. 'If they meet the
right woman. Unfortunately, that's where the problem
often lies. Meeting the right woman.' He placed his
empty coffee-cup down, then waved the butler back
when he stepped forward to refill. Ali could drink
coffee with the same gusto Rico downed his Chianti.
'No more tonight, James. I'll be back shortly, my
friends, then we can get back to the card table.'

When Ali left the room and Charles pulled out his
cellphone to ring Dominique, claiming he couldn't
wait to get home to tell her about Rico's hand and
his amazing wager, Rico used the opportunity to join
Renée out onto the balcony.

As he passed the outdoor table on which she'd put
her bag and her coffee-cup, Rico noticed that the ashtray sitting in the middle was filled with recently burnt
paper. The realisation that she'd hurried out here to
physically destroy her own heart's desire piqued
Rico's curiosity further, but he determined not to
mention it. He also determined not to weaken and let

her off the hook, no matter how much guilt was currently swirling in his stomach.

The sight of her leaning against the railing in an attitude close to defeat sparked even more guilt within him. How can you possibly go through with this, Rico Mandretti? he asked himself.

The answer was a very complex one. But, in a nutshell, he didn't have a choice. Having her at least once was a compulsion, a necessity. Expecting her to accommodate him for a month, however, was definitely beyond the pale.

'What are you thinking?' he asked as he leant against the railing next to her.

She didn't look his way, or answer him, just kept on dragging on her cigarette.

'One night,' he grated out at last, regretting the words even as he spoke them. 'I'll reduce the bet to one night.'

Slowly she exhaled, then turned to face him, her expression haughty and scornful. '*Pity*, Rico? From *you*? I'm surprised. But sorry, darling, I must refuse your gallant gesture. A bet is a bet. You demanded I be your mistress for a month, so your mistress for a month I will be. Not a day less. Not a day more.'

Her contrariness jolted him. Was this her pride still talking, or did she have some other secret agenda? Whatever the case, experience had taught Rico never to try to second-guess Renée, so he just shrugged.

'Fine by me.' Far be it from him to lessen her sentence. She'd made her bed now. Let her lie in it.

'You might think that tonight,' she replied. 'You might think differently in a month's time.'

'Is that a threat, Renée? Or a challenge?'

'It's a promise. I don't just dislike you now, Rico. I despise you.'

'If you despise me so much, then why didn't you tell Charles what I really asked of you? Why save me with a lie?'

'Oh, good God!' she exclaimed impatiently. 'I didn't lie for *you*. I just didn't want Charles to find out what an out-and-out bastard his best friend is.'

'Why would you bother?'

'Because the foolish man likes you, that's why. And I like him. Why should he be upset by any of this? You've caused him enough hurt this year, don't you think? This battle is strictly between us, and that's how it's going to stay.'

'Battle? That's an odd word to use.'

'I think it's very appropriate. We are at war, you and I. We have been for a long time.'

'Maybe it's time we stopped, then. Maybe it's time we made love, not war.'

'Make *love*?' she scoffed. 'You must be insane. You don't want to make love to me any more than I want to make love with you. You want revenge, that's all, for what I said to you last Sunday.'

Rico saw with a sudden and quite blinding insight that revenge *wasn't* his first and deepest wish where she was concerned. He would have much preferred her to like him, and respect him, and, yes, desire him for the man he was.

But he knew that wasn't about to happen.

So he wasn't going to belittle himself further by putting his stupid heart on his sleeve.

'Believe what you will, Renée. I will be booking us a room here in the hotel as soon as the evening's poker is over. I will expect you to accompany me.

And to stay the whole night. Given you don't want dear Charles to know what an out-and-out bastard I am, then I suggest you meet me in the lobby, *after* he's left the hotel.'

She didn't even turn a hair. Not visibly, anyway. Rico began to wonder if she was a living, breathing woman, or some evil robot designed by the devil and sent to earth to torment and torture fools like him.

'Fine by me,' she said, echoing his dismissive words earlier. 'Just one question before we go back inside. There are mistresses, and mistresses, Rico. What, exactly, will you be requiring? The I'll-do-anything-you-want-when-you-want-it sex-kitten type of mistress, or the seriously kinky, black-leather-wearing, whip-wielding variety?'

Rico was truly taken aback. Then slightly intrigued. 'What if I chose the latter?'

Her smile was pure ice. 'I'd be most gratified. I've always thought a good beating or two was what you needed most in the world.'

Rico couldn't help it. He laughed. This was the Renée who aroused him most. The sarcastic spitting cat. 'Then perhaps it's just as well that that scenario doesn't appeal to me,' he replied, still smiling. 'I would like to survive this month with my skin intact.'

'Ah, yes, but what about your soul?' she countered snakily. 'Do you really believe you can go through with this and live with yourself afterwards?'

For a moment, his conscience *was* pricked. Rico understood full well that what he was doing was wrong. But he was way beyond right and wrong where this woman was concerned.

'You're quite right,' he said, feigning a contrite face and enjoying her momentary look of surprise. 'I have no doubt I will feel very badly afterwards. But I can always run along to Confession if needs be. Come along, my dear Mrs Selinsky,' he went on, abruptly whipping the cigarette out of her hand. 'It's time to return to the card table.' He stalked over and stabbed the cigarette to death in the still smouldering ashtray before lifting glittering eyes to hers once more.

'Not that I'll be able to put my mind back on poker. I'll be too busy picturing as a—how did you describe your role for the next month?—a you'll-do-anything-I-want-when-I-want-it sex-kitten type of mistress. The mind boggles how you're going to manage it, given you despise me so much. But I recall reading once that models have to be marvelous actresses as well as clothes-horses. So just do what I'm sure you did very well when you were strutting your stuff on the cat-walk, *and* when you were married to Mr Selinsky. *Act.*'

CHAPTER SIX

'WHATEVER possessed you to book one of the honeymoon suites?' she said quite angrily as he unlocked the door.

Rico gave her a satisfied look. She was nervous, he realised. Good. Because he was nervous, too. All that bravado he'd displayed on the balcony earlier had dissipated during the remaining hour's poker, leaving him in a right royal mess.

'Don't complain,' he advised brusquely. Or explain, he told himself. She doesn't need to know that you didn't want to take her to one of the standard rooms where you'd taken Leanne; that you'd wanted something special for their first night together, romantic fool that he was.

The lights came on the second he slotted his keycard into the gizmo next to the door. Not bright, overhead lights. Subtle wall-lights and lamps.

Renée's sharply sucked-in breath was an echo of what Rico thought as he glanced around. Wow. It was romantic all right.

'I don't believe this,' Renée said as she strode across the black marble foyer and through an ornate archway into a sitting room which looked like something out of *The Arabian Nights*. Rico followed, equally startled by the decor.

Crimson carpet underfoot. Walls papered in the deepest blue. Ceiling covered with draped swathes of black silk shot with gold. Incredible all right.

The furniture and furnishings were equally exotic. Aquamarine silk curtains adorned the large picture window, each fall tied back with matching sashes, decorated with huge gold tassels which hung to the floor. The low curved sofas were just as colourful, arranged around a black lacquered circular coffee-table on which sat a gold-plated ice-bucket filled with the obligatory bottle of chilled champagne. Next to it were two gilt-edged crystal glasses and a platter of cheeses and fresh fruits which must have been dispatched and delivered whilst they were riding up in the lift. The Regency was renowned for its swift room service.

'This is like something out of fantasy-land,' Renée said drily as she put her handbag down on a black lacquered side table and walked over to another wider archway on the right.

'My God,' she gasped as she entered the bedroom, Rico still trailing in her wake.

If the sitting room was out of fantasy-land then the bedroom surpassed it. The carpet in there was emerald, and thick as lush grass. Rico could only imagine how it would feel in bare feet. The walls were papered in what looked like silver foil. The four-poster black lacquered bed was raised on a platform in the centre of the room and totally surrounded by gauzy white curtains, the kind that dressed the bedroom settings in the desert film epics of the fifties. The quilt was white satin shot with silver, with a countless number of matching pillows and scatter cushions leaning against the curved headboard. The ceiling, Rico noted with raised eyebrows, was totally mirrored.

The desk clerk had said something about all the

honeymoon suites being themed but Rico had been too agitated at the time to listen properly.

Both their gazes finally left the bed to scan the rest of the room, simultaneously landing on the two naked statues that flanked the archway through which they'd just walked. Lifelike in size, both were made in pale grey marble and both were blatantly erotic.

It was impossible to look at them without thinking of sex. An already painfully erect Rico didn't need any further stimulation. Or any further delay.

Renée kept staring at the impassioned carvings and didn't hear Rico come up behind her. She jumped when he curled his hands over her shoulders. But she didn't say a word in protest. His hands tightened as he pulled her back against him, bringing just the whisper of a moan from her lips.

'Sexy, aren't they?' he murmured into her hair, his own lips making contact with her right ear.

Her shudder told him what he needed to know. Not revulsion this time. Or even nerves. Excitement, pure and simple. Or not so pure, perhaps.

He purred seductively, 'I'm big and hard, Renée, and I'm hot. Very hot. Can't you feel me?' He pressed himself against the softness of her buttocks. 'See how much I want you? Don't you want me back, just a little?'

A cry escaped her lips as she spun round in his arms then glared up at him with the most telling colour in her cheeks. 'I *hate* you, Rico Mandretti,' she declared, even as her arms wound up around his neck and she lifted her parted lips towards his.

Rico heard her declaration, but actions spoke louder than words. And her actions told him she did want him. Maybe more than a little.

'I like your brand of hate,' he returned, and, sweeping his arms tightly around her, he crushed her body against his just as his mouth crashed down on hers.

His kiss was savage, but she didn't shrink from it. If anything, she met him more than halfway, taking his tongue avidly into her mouth, sucking on it, displaying a hunger every bit as wild and uncontrollable as his. He kissed her and kissed her, then kissed her some more till she was like dough in his arms and he himself was incoherent with desire and need. Finally, he dragged her down into the plush green pile and began pulling at her clothes.

Did she help him? Or was it all his doing? Whatever, they were both soon naked from the waist down and he was pushing her legs wide apart and touching her there, there where she was wet, oh, so wet. He groaned, then touched her some more, thrilling to the evidence of her arousal. She surely wouldn't be able to say afterwards that she hadn't wanted him. His fingers slipped easily inside her and she moaned, her head threshing from side to side on the carpet.

'No, no,' she began whimpering, but he knew she didn't mean for him to stop. She wanted him inside her, not his hands. And that was where he wanted to be too, despite knowing he was going way too fast. Where were all his supposed skills in the bedroom now? He wasn't going to be able to control himself much longer here. He had to have her. *Now!*

Within a heartbeat, he was pushing into her, filling her to the hilt. He gasped at the rush of wild elation which ricocheted through him. What delicious heat, what sweet surrender.

But the surrender was going to be all his. And soon.

Perhaps if her long, lovely legs weren't already wrapped tightly around him and she wasn't urging him on, her nails digging into his already tensed buttocks, he might have stood a chance of lasting. As it was...

'Oh, hell,' he muttered when his thighs and belly tightened and he knew from experience that he was about to come. Years of practising safe sex finally sent warning bells clanging through his bedazzled brain but it was already far too late.

They groaned together, then came together, fierce violent spasms worthy of five years of foreplay. His back arched, as did hers, and then he was clasping her to him, holding her tight as his seed pumped away inside her, recklessly refusing now to care about the consequences.

So what if he made a baby with her? It wouldn't be the end of the world. It might, in fact, Rico started thinking as his orgasm gradually began to fade away, be the beginning of a brave new world. For him. For her.

He'd always wanted children. And he'd always wanted Renée, from the first moment he'd set eyes on her.

She slipped her legs away from his waist with an exhausted sigh, her arms also abandoning his body to flop out by her sides. He levered his body weight up onto his elbows and stared down at her flushed face, which was tipped sideways, her eyes shut but her lips still apart. Her breathing was shallow, but slowing.

'Are you all right?' he asked softly.

Her head turned to face him and her eyes opened, as cool and calm as ever. 'You mean, am I lying here worrying myself sick because I've just had unsafe sex with a notorious playboy?'

Rico gritted his teeth. Nothing had changed. Once sarcastic, always sarcastic.

'I am not,' he ground out, 'and never have been a notorious playboy. But, that aside, let me assure you this is the first time I've had unsafe sex since leaving Jasmine. And before you ask, yes, I had myself cleared with blood tests once I realised what kind of creature *she* was. What about you?'

'You needn't worry, Rico,' she said with a weary sigh. 'About anything.'

'You mean you're protected against pregnancy?'

'Trust me when I say there will be no baby. What do you take me for?' she snapped. 'A complete fool?'

Rico gnashed his teeth. What kind of fool was *he* for even considering a future with this woman? What kind of wife would she make? Or mother, for that matter?

'What about everything else?' he persisted. After all, just because she hadn't been sleeping with Wade Jackman didn't mean she hadn't had other lovers. Obviously, she had a pretty high sex drive, the way she'd just carried on. She scorned him for being a playboy but that modelling world she moved in wasn't exactly renowned for being conservative in the sexual department. They were an incestuous lot from what he could see, a bit like the acting world.

'If you must know, this is the first time I've had unprotected sex in so long it doesn't matter. Given I'm a regular blood donor, I can guarantee I'm safe.'

'Well, aren't you a goody two-shoes?' he mocked.

'And aren't you glad that I am? Just think. A whole

month of condomless sex if you like. Now, that's a male fantasy these days, if ever there was one.'

Rico had to confess that the idea did appeal to him. A lot. He stirred at the thought of being able to have sex with her at any time without the worry or awkwardness of using protection, his response reminding him he was still inside her, his flesh encased snugly in hers. *More* snugly by the moment.

Her eyes flared wide. 'You can't be,' she said disbelievingly. 'Not this soon.'

'We playboys can just go and go,' he said with a superb poker-face. 'Or should that be come and come? Whatever, the result is the same. Very happy partners. But let's try it with the rest of your clothes off this time. I've always wanted to see you naked.'

Colour zoomed back into her cheeks, pleasing Rico no end. He liked seeing her rattled. He should have known, however, that she'd soon recover.

'You too, then,' she countermanded. 'I'm not going to be the only one in my birthday suit.'

'My pleasure,' he said, and whipped his top off in a flash.

There was no doubt she liked what she saw.

'I knew you'd have a lovely hairy chest,' she murmured as she slid her fingers slowly and sensuously through the centre of his hair-matted chest. Her eyes, which had been sharp and clear a moment before, clouded over and she appeared quickly lost in another world. Her focus was all on the dark curls which covered his chest then formed an arrow that ran downwards. When her fingers started following that arrow, his stomach sucked in sharply. But she only went as far as his navel before retracing her steps upwards. Any relief was short-lived, however, when she discovered his already hardened nipples and started playing with them. Rico gasped, then grabbed her wrists.

'No more of that,' he growled, 'or this will be over before it begins.' Hell, she turned him on quicker than any woman he'd ever been with. He was already fully erect again. Maybe hate was an aphrodisiac.

'Like the first time, you mean?' she scoffed.

'You were just as quick,' he reminded her. 'Now take off the rest of your clothes. But do it slowly. I want to watch.'

Her eyes flashed. 'You're a wicked devil, do you know that?'

'Just stop talking and get your gear off, mistress mine.'

She glared at him as she struggled out of the pale green cardigan, not an easy process when you were pinned to the floor. She had even more difficulty pulling the short-sleeved jumper up over her head and he had to help.

'I'm going to buy you some far more accessible clothes,' he muttered darkly. 'Either that, or I'll just keep you naked all the time you're with me.'

She stared up at him whilst he stared down at her bra.

It was made of pale pink satin, a nothing-thing not designed to enhance or exaggerate. He'd been right about her not being flat-chested. She wasn't nearly as busty as Jasmine, or Leanne, or a lot of the women he'd dated over the years, but what he was seeing through that pink satin looked nicely round and soft, with hard centres, the way he liked his chocolates.

Her hands went to the front-opening clasp before hesitating.

'Don't be shy,' he said thickly. 'You must know you're beautiful.'

'I...I always thought you preferred voluptuous women,' she said a bit shakily.

Her sudden lack of confidence touched him.

'And blondes!' she added more stroppily.

He smiled. 'I do. You're the exception. Here. Let me do it.' He brushed aside her reluctant hands and undid her bra, slowly peeling the cups back to reveal exquisitely shaped breasts with deliciously dark aureoles and large, fiercely erect nipples. Once he'd wriggled her right out of the garment and tossed it aside, he couldn't resist bending to suck them. She didn't stop him, arching her back at first contact, then cradling his head at each breast as if he were a much loved infant.

Rico found the experience incredibly sexy, yet at the same time amazingly comforting, like being wrapped in a big, warm towel after a long, hot bath. He could have stayed suckling on her breasts forever.

His hair suddenly being tugged upward brought a cry of shock from his lips. He lifted his head and frowned questioningly down at her flushed face.

'No more,' she said huskily. 'Or I'll come.'

He blinked. No kidding? From just doing that?

And then he felt it, her insides squeezing then releasing him, over and over. Her need for another orgasm, he realised, was acute.

'Just how long has it been since you've been with a man?' he asked her.

Her face twisted into a grimace almost like pain. 'Please don't start asking me stupid questions,' she choked out. 'At least a week, OK? Now, just do it, will you? Do it hard and fast.'

Once Rico had decided that her crack about a week had to be sarcasm, he fell to the task with gusto. Hard and fast she wanted it. Hard and fast was what she was going to get.

'Oh, God,' she groaned after several thrusts, which spurred him on to more vigorous efforts.

'God help me,' she cried and clasped him to her, inside and out.

God help me too, Rico thought. For how was this going to cure him of his sexual obsession for Renée Selinsky? He'd never been with a woman like her. So contradictory. So intriguing. So…exciting. All this would do, he feared, was make him want more. And more. And more.

But then he remembered he could have all he wanted of her for the next month. A month was quite a long time.

He just hoped it would be long enough…

CHAPTER SEVEN

RICO woke to silence, and no one in the bed with him. The empty champagne bottle was propped up on what had been her main pillow, a rolled-up sheet of notepaper funnelled into its neck.

Snatching it out, he unrolled the paper onto the crumpled sheets and read what she'd written.

Dear Don Juan,

it began.

Sorry I can't stay for breakfast, or afters. I have an appointment at André's in town at eight. If you know anything about the popularity of André's beauty salon, you'll understand why I refuse to cancel. Then I have some shopping to do afterwards before heading off to the races, as usual. I'm sure you'll find me there. You know my regular haunts. I presume you have something in mind for this evening, so, being a good little mistress, I'll arrange to be free.
    Ciao,
    Renée
    P.S. Don't shave!

Rico frowned down at the postscript. Don't shave. What did she mean by that? Was she being sarcastic again?

Hell, was she ever anything else?

Rico crushed the note in his hand, his mood instantly black. If ever a woman had the knack of spoiling things, it was her. They'd had a fabulous night together. More than fabulous, damn it! And what had she done? Run out on him the first chance she got!

Any other female would have still been here, in this bed, cuddled up to him and wanting more of what he had finally expertly delivered. He'd had her purring with pleasure for hours, and sighing with satisfaction over and over. The least she could have done was stay.

'But no!' Rico snarled as he brushed aside the curtains around the bed and climbed out, forgetting in his temper that the bed was on a stupid platform. His foot suddenly found air instead of carpet, his language extremely colourful as he slipped down the steps and crashed to the floor, not far from where he and Renée had first had sex.

Winded but not hurt, he lay there for a moment before glaring balefully up at the nearby statues.

As much as Renée had seemed startled by his ability to bounce back, she'd been very happy to take full advantage of his unabating desire for her. Very, very happy! No wonder she hadn't wanted him to reduce their bet to one night. She probably got off on the idea of having a lover like him on tap for a month, one who would bust his britches to satisfy her, and be prepared to pay for the privilege as well. The woman was wicked, he decided. Wicked and perverse and more lusty than any woman had a right to be!

Scrabbling up from the floor, he staggered into the black marble bathroom, only to be confronted with more evidence of their decadent evening together. Two empty champagne glasses sat beside the huge spa bath, which was still full of water, though the bubbles were long gone. The almost empty food platter was on the floor, alongside a pile of crumpled towels. Rico pulled the plug on the bath and picked up the platter before leaning on the vanity and peering into the mirror at his bleary, bloodshot eyes.

The memory of other eyes in that mirror immediately jumped into his mind. Green eyes, dilated with desire as their owner clung to the vanity-unit edge, staring wildly at him behind her whilst he did what she liked most, being taken that way.

The memory disturbed him. Because it wasn't what he *really* wanted, just being her stud. Yet that was what he'd reduced himself to last night, he realised. Him, just servicing her every which way. Him, trying to outdo himself each time.

No wonder she'd mockingly called him Don Juan. Clearly, that was all she thought he was good for. There'd been no meaningful conversation between them, nothing but provocative banter designed to keep their minds focused on sex and their bodies ready to accommodate their thoughts. In the end, he'd proved himself to be exactly what she'd always accused him of being. Shallow!

But not selfish, he conceded ruefully. She had to give him that. Her pleasure had been his first concern.

Or had it?

Had he pulled out all the stops *just* to satisfy her, or to *show* her how darned good he was in bed? What part had his male ego had to play in last night's many and varied performances?

A lot, he finally accepted and winced at the realisation.

'Oh, Rico, Rico, Rico,' he said, shaking his head

at the man in the mirror. 'What kind of man are you really? The essentially decent guy your mother thinks you are? Or the superficial, self-centred rake that Renée sees when she looks at you?'

Serious soul-searching was something Rico hadn't attempted in a good while. He'd been forced to have a partial look at himself a few months back when he'd jumped to hasty conclusions about Charles' wife and caused the poor devil no end of trouble. But all he'd discovered about himself at that time was that he'd become a cynic about beautiful women. With good cause, too.

There were a lot of mercenary females out there with their eye on the main chance, namely a rich husband.

Renée had once been one of them.

Not any more, apparently. She didn't seem even slightly interested in catching herself another Joseph Selinsky. Or a Rico Mandretti. Yet she must know she could if she wanted to.

It wouldn't take much to tip his lust for her into full-blown love. Hell, he only had to remember that moment when he'd thought she might have conceived to know his feelings for the woman ran deeper than desire.

Who knew why? It was truly perverse. And he was truly sick to death of thinking about her.

Clearly, she wanted to remain footloose and fancy-free. She wasn't remotely interested in remarrying or ever having a family. All she wanted from the men in her life was what he'd given her last night.

The *men* in her life?

Rico scowled, then spun on his heel and hurried out into the bedroom to where he'd thrown the crumpled note. Scooping it up from the carpet, he smoothed it out again and reread the part where she said she'd arrange to be free.

His whole insides contracted. Did that mean she would have to cancel a date tonight?

'At least a week,' she'd said to him when he'd asked her how long it had been since she'd had sex. He'd thought she was joking. With hindsight, he conceded that she might not have been. A woman with her obviously high sex drive probably had a hot date every Saturday night.

A black jealousy ripped through Rico at the thought of her doing the things she'd done with him last night with any other man. He couldn't change the past and obliterate her previous lovers, but he aimed to make sure she understood there would be *no* other men during the next month. Mistresses gave their lovers *exclusive* rights to their bodies.

At least, they were *supposed* to.

But mistresses didn't always do what they were supposed to do, Rico accepted. And neither would Renée. She would run her own race, make her own rules. He hadn't stipulated exclusiveness on that piece of paper. A bad mistake on his part.

He wouldn't mind betting she hadn't made any mistakes with her *written* demand.

It really annoyed him that she'd destroyed her darned wager. He'd like to have seen exactly how she'd worded her demand for his share of Ebony Fire. As he recalled, she hadn't taken long to write it down. He'd had more difficulty, both over the wording and the fact the Biro hadn't worked well because he had nothing underneath his sheet of paper except the felt-topped card table, whereas she had had the rest of the notepad for support.

A light suddenly went on in Rico's brain. The notepad! What Renée had written might still be visible on the notepad. He'd seen how detectives handled such things on television and in the movies. They rubbed a pencil softly over the next page sideways, making sure the carbon didn't sink into the indentations of the writing and, pronto, the words that had been written on the missing page were magically revealed!

Rico raced over and snatched up the phone and dialed Reception, where he gave his name then asked to be put through to the presidential suite. James answered, making Rico wonder if the man ever slept. Still, it was after nine. Not all that early.

'It's Mr Mandretti here, James,' he announced, trying not to sound as excited as he was feeling. 'I need to speak to Ali, if he's up.'

'His Highness is having his morning coffee out on the balcony. I will take the phone out to him.'

Ali eventually came on the line.

'Good morning, Enrico. To what do I owe the honour of your call?'

'I need to ask a favour.'

'Of course. If it is within my power to grant it.'

Rico rolled his eyes. Ali's formal way of speaking sometimes irritated him. But he was such a great guy otherwise that Rico tolerated his being slightly pompous.

'I need to come up and have a look at that notepad which we used to write our bets on last night,' he confessed. No point in trying to pull the wool over Ali's eyes. No need to, either. Ali would understand perfectly why he wanted to know what Renée had written.

'Come up from where? Oh. Oh, I see. You spent the night here in the hotel. I presume, then, that the lovely Mrs Selinsky did not stay the whole night with you?'

Rico shook his head from side to side. As he'd just been thinking. No point in trying to fool Ali.

'She had an early hairdressing appointment,' Rico replied. 'We're meeting up again at the races this afternoon.'

'Now, what is that saying? You don't let grass grow under your shoes?'

'Under my feet,' Rico corrected. 'And you're right. I don't. I've always lived by the motto of not putting off till tomorrow what you can do today.'

'Or last night,' Ali said, his tone drily amused.

'Exactly.'

'I won't be uncouth and ask you how things went. I will be able to judge for myself shortly. So yes, do come on up, my friend, and have coffee with me. I'll get James to locate the notepad and have it waiting. I presume you also want a pencil. Soft-leaded?'

'Yes, that'd be great. I knew I could count on your co-operation. And your understanding.'

The laughter down the line was deep and rich, a bit like Ali's bank accounts. 'We men have to stick together. Especially when the lady concerned is both beautiful *and* complicated.'

'You can say that again,' Rico muttered. 'I won't be a tick. I just need to put some clothes on.'

He could hear Ali chuckling as he hung up.

CHAPTER EIGHT

RICO rarely admired other men's looks. But as he walked out onto the balcony of the presidential suite, it was difficult not to notice that Ali lounging back in the morning sunshine in cream silk pyjama bottoms and nothing else was a sight to behold. If his Arab friend ever decided to become a movie star, then a remake of *The Sheikh* would be the perfect vehicle for him. Not totally surprising, since that was what he was. But not all real sheikhs looked like the Hollywood version.

Ali did. He had it all. The rich olive skin. Jet-black hair and eyes. High cheekbones and hawkish nose. A lean, well-honed body and a predator's mouth. Plus sufficient hair on his chest to be primitively sexy without being beast-like.

Rico could well understand why the ladies threw themselves at him. They were the same reasons women had thrown themselves at *him* over the years.

But looks were not the be-all and end-all, Rico had come to realise, more so lately than ever before. A man had to be more than the sum total of his inherited genes.

He wondered if Ali's good looks had been more hindrance than help to him in *his* life. One day, Rico would ask him. But not this morning. This morning, Rico had other things on his mind.

'Good morning, Enrico,' Ali said with a flashing smile which would not have gone astray on a Barbary

Coast pirate. Yet if you closed your eyes he sounded like an English aristocrat. A most unusual mix. 'You do look well, if a little frazzled. Sit down. Some coffee? Or do you want to uncover your lady's secret straight away?'

Rico sat down at the table and picked up the notepad that was lying there, waiting for him, along with a pencil.

'She's not my lady. Not really.'

Ali frowned. 'I'm not sure I understand. If she spent the night with you, then surely she—'

'That was part of my prize for winning the hand,' Rico broke in. He had decided to confess everything on the way up in the lift. He needed another man's opinion, and he couldn't talk to Charles about his situation with Renée. Charles would not have been sympathetic at all. Ali, on the other hand, lived his own life by less conventional rules than those society dictated, especially when it came to his relationships with the opposite sex, so surely he would not be quite so judgemental.

'I didn't ask for Renée to go out with me,' Rico went on. 'She lied about that. She was protecting Charles' sensitivities. I demanded she be my mistress. For a month. Starting last night.'

Ali's eyes showed more shock than Rico had anticipated.

'My friend,' Ali said carefully, 'I admire your boldness, but that is a dangerous game you're playing, especially with a woman like Renée.'

'I realise that now. That's why I have to see what she wrote; what *she* wanted from *me*.'

'What do you think she wanted from you?'

'My share of Ebony Fire. She loves that horse more than anything. She covets *all* of him.'

'As you coveted all of her.'

No point in denying it. 'Yes.'

'So you dangled your share of the horse as a carrot to tempt her to make that wager, knowing full well she would lose and have to become your whore.'

'My *mistress*,' Rico protested. 'Not my *whore*.'

'In my culture, it is the same thing. A mistress is a kept woman. She accepts money and gifts to make her body available for sex. That makes her a whore.'

Rico was beginning to think he'd made a mistake in confiding in Ali. It seemed he was more like Charles than he'd realised. 'We don't look at mistresses like that in the west,' he pointed out a tad irritably.

'I can't see how you can look at them any other way,' Ali countered. 'But, that aside, why are you so anxious to see what Renée asked for, when you already know?'

'I now think she might have asked for something else.'

'Why? Because she melted in your arms?'

Rico laughed. 'I wouldn't say melted, exactly. But she didn't object.'

'Such modesty, my friend. I'm quite sure she melted. You have a reputation for being…shall we say…more than adequate in the bedroom?'

Rico stiffened in his chair. 'Where in God's name would you hear something like that?'

'Without being indiscreet, I have to inform you that we shared a certain lady during the past year.'

'My God, who? Oh, of course. Silly of me not to guess. Leanne.'

'There is no need for us to exchange names, or notes. We are gentlemen, are we not? Let me just say that this certain lady raved about your—er—technique. But being a man as well as a gentleman, I was forced to demonstrate at length that Arab men of good breeding and culture are *never* surpassed in the bedroom.'

Rico could not help but be amused. So he'd been right in the first place. Ali was more pirate than gentleman. And a competitive, arrogant pirate at that. 'Just as long as we haven't shared Renée,' he said warningly.

'Only an Italian would be fool enough to take on a woman such as your merry widow,' Ali said quite seriously. 'Now, pick up the pencil and satisfy your curiosity. *And* mine.'

Rico wished his hand had been steadier. He didn't want to look more of a fool in Ali's eyes than he already did.

'Well?' Ali prompted when Rico finished and just stared down at the piece of paper. 'What does it say?'

Rico remained speechless. With a bewildered shake of his head, he handed the revealed note over to Ali. 'It doesn't make sense. It's crazy.'

'"*Marry me,*"' Ali read aloud, then glanced up, his own face puzzled. 'If you had asked her to marry you, then I would not have been surprised. But this…this is indeed a strange request from a woman who has done nothing but argue with you for the past five years.'

'You can say that again.'

'Could she possibly be secretly in love with you?' Ali asked.

'You *have* to be joking! She can't stand a bar of me. You know that.'

'No. I do not know that. What women say and what they *feel* are two entirely different things.'

'Renée does not love me,' Rico stated quite firmly. 'Trust me on that.'

'She *is* attracted to you, though, isn't she?'

Was she? Or was she attracted to and turned on by any good-looking guy who knew what he was doing in bed? 'She likes my looks and, yes, my technique, to coin your phrase. That's all. She told me last Sunday how much she dislikes me. And last night, she added that she now hates me.'

'Whereas you are madly in love with her.'

'What? No, no, I'm not. Definitely not. Why on earth do you say that? Or think it?'

'I've seen the way you look at her when she doesn't know you're looking at her. I know that look. It's the way I looked at a woman once. I recognise the symptoms of the disease. And it is a disease, being in love like that. It possesses and obsesses you. You can think of nothing else but being with her. You will do anything, risk anything, even your honour, to lie with her, even if it's just the once.'

Rico was taken aback by this unexpected confession. At the same time he was totally in tune with the emotions expressed. Ali understood. He'd been there, done that. But Rico still did not agree with him that he was truly in love with Renée. He wasn't madly in love at all. Just madly in lust.

'Who *was* she?' Rico asked.

Ali smiled the saddest smile. 'The one woman I could never have. My eldest brother's wife-to-be. The crown prince's betrothed.'

'Hell, Ali, that was rotten luck. So what happened?'

'What happened? Nothing happened,' he bit out. 'I was exiled here to Australia, my brother married my beloved, and their marriage remains a brilliant success to this day. They even have a handsome son and heir to prove it.'

The bitterness in his words and the abject bleakness in his eyes filled Rico's heart with pity for this man whom the world would perceive as having everything. Everything but the woman he loved. No wonder he never wanted to marry or have children. No wonder he had never fallen in love with any of myriad women he'd bedded since coming to Australia. His heart remained in Dubar, that was why. Either that, or it had been irretrievably broken.

'So why do you think Renée asked you to marry her?' Ali resumed, his eyes and his attention returning to the piece of paper he was holding. 'If not love, then what? Money?'

'That doesn't make sense, either. She's a very wealthy woman already. If she wanted to marry me for my money, she hasn't gone about achieving that end with any intelligence. You know how she acts around me. No, now that I've had time to think about, it's more likely to be spite.'

'Spite!' Ali repeated with surprise in his voice. 'I can't imagine many women marrying for spite. Still, Renée is not your usual woman. She runs very deep, that one.'

'Tell me about it. I can't work her out at all.'

Rico could work out the spite part, however. He remembered how she knew last night that he would demand sex as his prize. Had she decided to go one better, ask him for the one thing which she thought he would never want to give her? A wedding ring? Had it been a spur-of-the-moment burst of vengeance, something she had instantly regretted?

That certainly fitted the facts. And the woman. Rico recalled how he thought he'd detected relief in her when she hadn't won. She might have become afraid that he would relish marrying her, just to spite *her*.

'Going back to the motive of money,' Ali said, interrupting Rico's train of thought, 'I wouldn't dismiss that motivation out of hand. Renée might not be as wealthy as we presume. She might have had some bad luck on the stock market. There have been some mammoth losses recently, both locally and overseas. Also, her own business might not be going well. Remember, she lives high and likes to gamble. Maybe she's frittered a lot of her dead husband's money away. It might be worthwhile for you to find out the exact state of her finances.'

Whilst Rico believed he'd already worked out the reasons behind Renée's surprising demand, he conceded that Ali did have a point. It was worth checking out. No way would he want to risk ever falling into the hands of another devious fortune-hunter.

'I agree with you wholeheartedly. But how am I going to do that? I can hardly ask to look at her bank statements.'

'Use that detective agency you hired to check up on Charles' wife,' Ali suggested, leaning forward to refill his coffee-cup from the pot. 'They'll be able to do it quite easily. They have the right contacts and the right computer equipment. They can find out things which ordinary people can't.'

Rico's first reaction to this suggestion was negative in the extreme. Renée had gone right off her brain when she found out he'd had Dominique investigated. If she ever discovered he'd done the same to her, she would...

What? Rico asked himself irritably. What would she do? Hate him some more? She already hated him.

Besides, there were things other than her financial status which he would like to know. Like how many other men she had slept with since her husband died? And who?

'There is another reason which brings women to the altar,' Ali said. 'Could she possibly want a baby?'

Rico stopped breathing. A baby...

'The woman is thirty-five years old,' Ali went on. 'She doesn't have too many more child-bearing years ahead of her. You are always saying you want a family. And, despite what Renée has said to you in the past, we all know you would make a good father and possibly even a good husband. You're Italian, after all,' he said with an engagingly warm smile. 'Maybe that's her secret heart's desire. To have a child.'

Rico swallowed. Could Ali be right? And if he was, could Renée still be intent on securing her heart's desire, *without* the wedding ring?

A month of condomless sex, she'd promised him. But what if her reassurances over her being safe had all been lies? What if a baby *was* her secret heart's desire?

If so, what else had she lied about last night? Or faked?

No, no, he couldn't accept that reasoning. Renée's responses to him had not been pretence. She'd enjoyed the sex. *All* of it. No woman who was faking orgasms went that far.

No, a baby was not what she wanted from him,

Rico decided, despite not *wanting* to come to that conclusion. The idea had excited him momentarily, as it had last night. But it was a false and futile excitement, born of a desperate desire to believe his relationship with Renée could become more than a one-month forced affair. Renée would never choose him as the father of her baby, if a baby was what she wanted. Frankly, he'd be the last man on this planet she would choose.

No, *spite* was the odds-on favourite reason for her asking him to marry her. Money was the second favourite, although still a rank outsider. But worth looking into. Leopards didn't change their spots. She'd married once for money. If her chips were down, she'd do it again. She might not be broke as such, but women like Renée had one credo in life. You could never be too rich, or too thin. Just as Ali said, she was a high-maintenance gal.

'You're right,' Rico said. 'I'll have her finances investigated.' Amongst other things. He was curious to see just who she *had* been sleeping with since her husband died. And how many.

Meanwhile…

He ripped off the top sheet of the notepad and stood up. 'You won't mind if I keep this, will you?' he said as he slipped it into his trouser pocket.

'What are you going to do with it?'

'Nothing. Yet. But it seems silly to destroy evidence.'

'Why don't you just tell her you love her and ask her to marry you?'

Rico stared down at Ali then burst out laughing. 'Would you, if you were in my shoes?'

'If I were in your shoes, I would have made marriage my prize in the first place, not just sex. Then I would have had both.'

Rico laughed again. 'I see you've not become fully acquainted yet with the ways of the western world. Marriage in this country does not give a man automatic rights to his wife's body.'

Ali looked truly taken aback. 'Then why marry?'

'Exactly. You might have noticed that more and more Australian men are not exactly rushing off to the altar.'

Ali shook his head. 'A sad state of affairs if a man can't make love to his wife when he wants to. I would not enter into that kind of marriage. Was that a problem with your first wife?'

'No.'

'No, I didn't think so. A piece of advice, then, my friend. If you find money is not the issue here and you still want Renée as your wife and not just your mistress, why don't *you* try to get her pregnant? Women can change their attitude to a man once a baby comes into the picture,' he added with a touch of irony, Rico imagined.

'That's a thought, but I don't have control of the contraception part. She's on the Pill. And yes, I know if you were in my shoes you'd probably kidnap the object of your desire and whisk her off to some remote hideaway where there was no Pill and nothing to do but make your beautiful captive pregnant.'

God, but that *was* a good idea. He'd be tempted if Renée wouldn't eventually have him arrested for kidnapping and rape and goodness knew what else.

Ali smiled. 'I might have done something like that once. But not now. Now I content myself with passing pleasures when it comes to the ladies. I suggest you do the same with the merry widow. Enjoy her for the next month, then be done with her.'

'This could mean the end of our Friday-night poker games,' Rico pointed out.

Ali shrugged his broad brown shoulders. 'All good things come to an end, my friend. But let's cross that bridge when we come to it. A good philosophy for life, don't you think?'

CHAPTER NINE

ACTUALLY, Rico did not agree. He liked to anticipate any upcoming bridges. He was a planner as well as a doer. He could never just sit back and not worry about future difficulties, if he thought he could change or solve them in advance in some way.

Which was why his first job after checking out of the hotel and walking back to his new city address was to contact IAS and give them the job of finding out Renée's present financial status, along with a full report on her private life over the past five years. He needed to know what he was dealing with here. And asking Renée for the information herself was not an option. She would not tell him the truth. On the contrary, he could guarantee that she would lie her spiteful little tongue out.

The boss of the investigation agency—his name was Keith—told Rico over the phone that he could expect to know the lady's financial status within the week, but it would take another couple of weeks before they could fully report on the other matter.

'Such enquiries take time, Mr Mandretti,' the man informed Rico. 'Especially since you said it was vital Mrs Selinsky not find out people were asking personal questions about her.'

Rico finally hung up, satisfied that he was at last using his brains where Renée was concerned. Amazing what a little distance could achieve. Ali was wrong about his being madly in love with the woman.

The disease he was suffering from was strictly sexual in nature. So far. Hopefully, he would be cured before it changed into anything else.

Meanwhile, he had to protect himself from any weird and wonderful agenda Renée might still have where he was concerned. Her demanding marriage on that piece of paper had really thrown him for a loop there for a while. She must have been momentarily out of her mind. He hoped so, anyway.

With a dry laugh he padded across his main living room and clicked open the sliding glass door which led out onto the wide, sun-bathed terrace which ran around three sides of the penthouse. Stepping out onto the terracotta-tiled floor, he walked over to lean against the tubular steel railing which framed the shatter-proof glass panels beneath.

Rico had always liked this place, inside and out. Its central location, along with its heated lap-pool and the spectacular views, put this particular penthouse in a class of its own. There weren't many apartments, even right on the harbour, where you could see so many Sydney icons from so many vantage points. The opera house. The bridge. Circular Quay. The Rocks. And, of course, the city itself.

Rico was admiring it all when the sun suddenly went behind a heavy bank of cloud, casting an instant gloom over the buildings and water below. When a cool breeze started ruffling his hair he turned and went back inside.

Shaking his head once more at the fickleness of Sydney's spring weather, he made his way over to the kitchen and set about cooking himself a belated breakfast. Food had been the last thing on his mind lately, his body and his brain having other priorities.

But, now that he thought about it, he was damned hungry. Clearly, his energy stores had been severely depleted by last night's activities. He would need to refuel if he was going to keep up with Renée tonight. He had to give the witch credit for one thing: when she honoured a bet, she sure as hell honoured it!

In no time, Rico had a king's breakfast in front of him and fresh coffee perking away, filling the air with its mouth-watering aroma. He settled himself at the breakfast bar and tucked in to a calorie-laden plateful of bacon and eggs, mushrooms, grilled tomato and French toast.

'Great kitchen, this,' he muttered to himself between mouthfuls.

With the preparation of food having become so much of his life, Rico was very appreciative of a good kitchen. This one was state-of-the art, with sleek white cupboards, black granite benchtops and the latest in stainless-steel appliances. It was also a pleasure to cook in. Very well designed in a U-shape, with an internal island and this very handy breakfast bar along one side, complete with comfy stools.

Actually, no, it hadn't come complete with these stools. Charles had taken all his furniture with him to his new home in Clifton Gardens. *He'd* been responsible for the purchase of these stools, which were very modern, in keeping with the kitchen. Steel-framed, with red leather seats.

They also matched the new dining and lounge suites he'd bought, along with the rest of the furniture, although he hadn't personally chosen a single thing. He'd commissioned a small but well-recommended interior-design company to do the job for him, telling the lady boss the style of furniture he liked—clean lines and modern Italian. Plus the colours he liked—primary. And presto, three weeks later he'd walked right in to a totally user-friendly home.

The designer had taken care of everything. Linen, crockery, cutlery, glassware as well. All stylish and classy. She'd even had the kitchen cupboard stocked with food. Rico had been impressed, and very pleased.

He'd been renting a furnished apartment since his divorce and hadn't owned a single household item. Jasmine had been awarded everything of that nature, claiming those things had meant more to her—the little housewife at home—than him.

What a laugh. Jasmine hadn't even been able to cook. He'd done all the cooking—when they'd stayed home for meals, that was—and the cleaning service that came in every morning had done everything else.

Looking back, Rico had to agree that he'd been a short-sighted fool to marry Jasmine. He'd been seduced by his ego—and other parts of him—into thinking she loved him, and vice versa. He should have known that if he'd truly loved her, he would never have been so attracted to Renée.

Renée…

Back to her again. He had that woman on his brain. Well, at least he *had* done something about the situation with her. Not that his mistress-for-a-month solution would necessarily solve anything. He had an awful suspicion that come the end of the month, his sexual obsession with Renée would have grown, not dissipated.

Don't shave.

The provocative P.S. on her note this morning

jumped into his mind, and he reached up to rub the stubble on his chin.

Impossible to put anything but a sexual connotation on that request. Impossible not to start wondering what erotic fantasy had inspired it. Over which erogenous zone did she want him to rub his hair-roughened skin? The same places he'd poured champagne over last night, then licked it off?

His stomach crunched down hard at the images that sprang into his mind. Last night had turned out very differently from what he'd anticipated. There'd been no need to seduce her—not after those initial few moments. She'd been with him all the way. And then some.

There'd been times when she'd astounded him with her passion, and her need. She simply couldn't get enough of him.

That was why he'd been so put-out when he woke this morning to find she was gone. Because he'd begun to believe—or hope—that it was him personally that she wanted and needed. Clearly, that wasn't the case. Clearly, she was simply a highly sexed creature who'd possibly gone too long without a man. He would be very interested to find out exactly how long it had been since her last lover.

Rico suddenly realised he'd been sitting there for ages without eating. When he tried another mouthful, he grimaced before reluctantly swallowing. Everything was stone-cold. Oh, well, at least he'd finished most of it. And there was still the coffee.

Getting up, he walked round to the sink and scraped the rest of the food down the disposal unit, then put all the utensils tidily into the dishwasher before pouring himself a corpse-reviving mug of very strong coffee. After he added a hefty slurp of milk and three teaspoonfuls of sugar he set off for the master bedroom, sipping as he went.

Time was slipping away and he didn't want to be late for the races. He didn't want to miss a second of being in Renée's stimulating company.

As it turned out, however, Rico *was* late for the races. He'd forgotten that they were not on at Randwick that Saturday afternoon, but at Rosehill Gardens, which was on the opposite side of the city. He'd almost reached Randwick and had just turned on the car radio to the racing channel when an announcement made him realise his mistake. Cursing, he swung the Ferrari into a U-turn and headed west. But by the time he arrived and parked his car, the first race was already under way. He could hear the cheering as he hurried across the car park.

'Damn and blast,' he muttered frustratedly to himself.

Once inside the members' enclosure he headed straight for the members' stand and the bar where Renée was most likely to appear between races. A drink was called for by then, something long and cold. A beer. Not that the weather was hot, or even warm. That cloud earlier had thickened and the day was overcast and cool.

Not so Rico. He felt as if he had a furnace stoking up inside him.

By the time he'd finished his beer there was still no sign of Renée, so he wandered out onto the veranda, which overlooked the grounds below, his gaze scanning the groups of people still standing around on the expanses of lawn or leaning against the saddling-enclosure fence. The horses had by then returned from the track, with the jockeys dismounting to go inside to be weighed. The four place-getters were standing in their parallel-placed stalls, steam rising from their flanks. The winner's trainer was beaming and the happy owners—a large group of middle-aged suits—were chatting and laughing together.

Rico envied them for a moment. There was nothing like leading in a winner. But then his eye was caught by a sight that drove all thought of winning races from his mind.

Renée was standing on the lawn, chatting away with some strange man. But not the Renée Rico was used to seeing at the races. Not the one who always wore a tailored trouser suit in some bland colour, along with sensible pumps, little make-up and a simple, smooth hairstyle. This Renée was totally different.

She was wearing a dress for starters, a smart black wrap-around coat-style dress with padded shoulders, deeply cut lapels and a black leather cummerbund belt that pulled her already tiny waist into a double handspan size. The end result was an hourglass shape that drew the eye, first to the amazing amount of cleavage she had on display, and second to her legs, those gorgeous long legs that had been wrapped so deliciously tightly around him last night.

Usually, she kept them hidden under trousers. Today they were encased in shimmering black pantihose and easily admired, courtesy of the shortness of her hem and the height of the killer shoes she was wearing. Black too, of course, with tall heels, pointy toes, cut-out sides and ankle straps. Quite wide, they were, as was the black satin ribbon she wore around her throat.

Rico could hardly believe his eyes. And the changes did not stop there. Her hair was different as well, both in colour and style. Jet-black now instead of walnut-brown. Still shoulder-length but layered and feathered around her face, as was the current fashion.

Rico couldn't say that it didn't suit her, because it did, as did her more extravagant eye-make-up and the scarlet gloss that shone brightly on her mouth, that mouth which had kissed him all over last night and which was at this very moment talking and laughing with another man, a rich-looking grey-haired gentleman, whose eyes were glued to her cleavage. Rico was less than fifty feet away so he knew damned well where that dirty old man was looking, and what he was thinking.

Had she sensed him standing up there at the railing, glowering down at her? Must have, for she lifted her face and their eyes connected, his instantly dark and dangerously jealous, hers sassy and sparkling.

She waved up at him before saying goodbye to her companion and heading towards the flight of steps that led up to where Rico was still standing, fists curled tightly over the railing. He remained right where he was, struggling to regain his composure, knowing full well that her appearance today was designed to torment him, not please him. She'd lost the bet last night but was still trying to win the war between them. How better to beat him than to turn him into a jealous, gibbering idiot as well as a bewitched, besotted fool.

She was the one intent on doing the seducing and the corrupting, he realised with sudden insight. That was what last night was all about, and what today was all about.

Rico's breathing quickened at the boldness of her counter-attack. He had to admire her. She had guts all right. And spirit. But it was a dampening thought that she *might* have faked a few things last night. Maybe she wasn't as enamoured of his technique as he'd imagined.

Whatever, he simply *had* to take her vamp-like appearance in his stride this afternoon or fall right into her trap. He thought he had himself under control again, but, as he turned to watch her join him on the veranda, her right knee lifted to take the final step and that action, combined with a puff of wind, flapped back the wrap-around slit in her skirt, giving him a gut-churning glimpse, not of pantihose but of lace-topped stockings and black suspenders, sensuously stretched against her soft, pale thighs.

The effect was instantaneous, and mortifying, Rico's only consolation being the fact he was wearing one of his more casual and loosely fitted black suits. Still, he moved swiftly to button up the jacket and hide his humiliation. To have Renée see the state she'd reduced him to so easily would have been the last straw. But it underlined to Rico that his imagining that a mere month would cure him of his desire for the merry widow was laughable.

Be damned, however, if he would ever give her an inkling of how he really felt. She wanted to tease and torment him? Play erotic games with him? Fine. He would wallow in every perversely pleasurable moment in private, then leave for Italy the moment the month was up, before she could deliver her *coup de grâce*, which of course would be to cut him dead.

One moment she'd be taking him to hedonistic heaven. And the next? Nothing. Zilch. Zero.

He wasn't sticking around for another five years of hell. No way. He would be out of her reach like a shot.

Not today, however. Today, she was all his. And he meant to take full advantage of the fact. He would play the game her way. But at the same time, *his* way. She wasn't going to get the better of him yet.

'My goodness, Renée,' he said silkily as she sashayed towards him with that lethal weapon of a skirt still flapping slightly open. 'When you take on a role you really like to get into the part, don't you? That outfit has sex-kitten mistress written over it, with just enough dominatrix built in to be tantalising. But don't you think you might have gone a little too far? Surely you don't want *every* old geezer you meet here today thinking you could be his, at a price. Or do you?' he went on before she could draw breath and reply. 'Maybe you've always been a little whore at heart.'

It was a low blow, inspired perhaps by some spite of his own. But she didn't seem to mind. She just laughed.

'I think you could be right, lover. How else do you explain my enjoying being with *you* last night?'

Aah. So she *did* mind. Her sarcasm gave her away. Yet for some reason he wasn't offended this time. Perhaps he'd moved beyond that, now that he'd held her in his arms and made love to her, and, yes, watched her come. Thinking back, he was pretty sure her many orgasms couldn't have all been faked. Perhaps her sarcasm was now a mocking not so much of him but of herself.

'Once I accepted I had this undeniable penchant

for bad boys,' she continued blithely, 'I decided to go with the flow, so to speak. Have some fun instead of resenting the situation. So when I left you this morning I thought, what the heck, Renée? Go for broke. I'd seen this little number last week in a boutique window and you said you wanted me to wear accessible clothes. Well, you don't get much more accessible than this, I can assure you.'

She leant close enough for him to get a more direct eyeful of cleavage and a noseful of her musky perfume.

And then she leant even closer.

'Are you game to see just how accessible, darling?' she murmured as her lips pressed against his cheek. 'We could find a relatively private corner somewhere here, I suppose. Or do you want to wait till tonight, when we're both climbing the walls?' Her lips moved over to brush his earlobe before she stepped back and eyed his quickened breathing with satisfaction. 'Or maybe you're climbing them already,' she added, and ever so gently pressed her hand between them, right over his straining erection.

He smiled. He had to, or scream. 'Now, now, Renée...' He took her hand equally gently and dropped it back by her side. 'Have some decorum. And please...don't forget who's the master here, and who's the mistress. I make the rules, not you. Which reminds me, how much do I owe you for this quite astonishing make-over?'

She shrugged, the movement momentarily lifting her already pushed-up breasts to more provocative heights. 'Not a cent,' she said. 'I'm a very cheap mistress.'

'*You* said that. *I* didn't. By the way, who was that gentleman you were just talking to?'

'An old friend of my husband's. Why?'

'He couldn't take his eyes off you.'

'I know.'

'You *like* old men ogling you?' he asked, his tone far too sharp.

'I like *you* ogling me,' she returned huskily.

His breath caught before he could stop it. Their eyes met, and this time, neither of them said a word. But it shimmered between them. The heat. The need.

A male hand clamping over his shoulder interrupted the sexually charged moment. 'Rico! Well, fancy running into you! Long time, no see. But aren't *you* doing well these days?'

Rice had turned to find that it was a man he'd worked with years ago in television. For a second he couldn't even remember his name. And then it came to him. Davidson. Ian Davidson.

'Not too bad, Ian,' he replied. 'And you?'

'Can't complain. I'm into wildlife documentaries now. They're always popular. A bit like cooking shows.'

'True.' Rico knew he should introduce Renée but he just didn't want to. He was already tired of the way men were looking at her today. Ian was no exception. He wasn't some old codger, either. He was relatively young, reasonably attractive, and his eyes were all over her.

'I heard you'd got divorced,' Ian said with another glance Renée's way.

'Yep,' was his abrupt reply.

'Aren't you going to introduce me to your lovely lady-friend?'

'No,' he replied curtly. 'I don't think I am.'

Renée rolled her eyes at him, hoisted the long strap of her black bag over her left shoulder and extended her right hand towards the still admiring Ian.

'I'm Renée,' she said.

Rico clenched his teeth when Ian eagerly shook the outstretched hand, then held it far too long.

'Renée,' Ian repeated, a smirk on his mouth. 'So, Renée, are you and Rico an item? Or just good friends?'

'Actually, I'm Mr Mandretti's mistress,' she said, perfectly poker-faced.

Rico couldn't help it. He laughed. Both at her gall and at Ian's sharply indrawn breath.

'Renée, darling,' Rico said, 'how naughty of you. She's not really my mistress, Ian. I just won her in a bet.' Two could play at being outrageous, his eyes told her. And Ian meant nothing to him. He could think what he liked.

Ian looked both perplexed and intrigued. 'Er—am I in the middle of some kind of game here?'

'I'm afraid you are,' Rico said. 'Renée is partial to games. And to gambling.'

'Now, that's the pot calling the kettle black,' Renée countered, green eyes glittering. 'Rico's the compulsive gambler here, Ian. But he's grown bored with betting for money. So he's upped the stakes to sex and sin. Next thing you know, he'll be wanting to play strip-Jack-naked with me right here in the stand.'

'Er—sounds fascinating, folks, but you'll have to excuse me for a moment. I happen to still like betting for money and there's a horse I want to bet on in the next race.'

'Good luck!' Renée trilled after him as he hurried off.

'You too, honey,' he called back over his shoulder with one last leer at her chest. 'Don't go away, now. I'll be back!'

Rico decided then and there that he could not tolerate any more of this type of banter—or encounter—this afternoon. Not in public, anyway. None of their horses were running today. There was no compelling reason for them to stay. But there were compelling reasons to go. Aside from his almost crippling need to make love to Renée again—and very, very soon—the thought of running into Ali with Renée dressed up like some expensive tart did not sit well on Rico. He really didn't want to have to smack his Arab friend right in his royal mouth, but he might if Ali started talking about whores again. *He* was the only one who could call Renée a whore, because he didn't really mean it.

'I don't want to play strip-Jack-naked,' he growled after Ian's departure. 'I want to play strip *Renée* naked. But not here in the stand. We're off to my place. Now.' When he took her arm in a firm grip, her eyes flashed green fire at him.

'And if I said no?' she snapped, the old Renée surfacing once more.

His fingers tightened as his eyes gleamed with dark resolve. 'I'd kiss you right here and now till you said yes.'

Was that a flicker of alarm that skittered through her eyes? If it was, it was gone in a flash.

'You would too, wouldn't you, you wicked devil?'

she said, but she was smiling. The new, go-with-the-flow, determined-to-have-fun Renée was back.

'You can count on it.'

She laughed. 'OK, so you've won this little skirmish. But the war is not over yet. Not by a long shot!'

CHAPTER TEN

'SO WHERE have you parked *your* car?' Rico asked as he guided Renée swiftly through the open-air car park towards his Ferrari. Rico having been late for the races, his car was not exactly close.

'I didn't bring my car,' she confessed breathlessly. She was having some difficulty in keeping up in those ridiculous shoes. 'I came in a taxi.'

'Why's that?'

'It seemed silly to bring my car when I knew you would be taking me home after the races.'

'Aah. A girl who plans ahead. I like that.'

'Oh, I always plan ahead.'

I don't doubt it, Rico thought cynically, but didn't say so. They'd reached his car and he didn't want to start an argument.

'I expect you to stay with me for the rest of the weekend,' he told her as he helped her into the passenger seat.

She jerked her head up to stare at him, and again that odd moment of panic flashed into her eyes. But it was gone as quickly as it had come. 'In that case, I'll need you to take me home first.'

'Why's that?'

'I'll want a change of clothes. And some night-wear.'

He closed the passenger door and walked round to climb in behind the wheel before he looked at her again.

'You won't be needing any nightwear,' he said firmly, his eyes brooking no opposition.

Her blush astounded him.

He wanted to kiss her at that moment, but he knew if he did he would not be able to stop. And the front of a Ferrari was no place for lovemaking at all, let alone the kind he had in mind.

'Unless, of course,' he added, hoping to break the tension of the moment with some humour, 'you own a clinging black satin nightie with no back, even less front, and straps that refuse to stay on your shoulders.'

His goal was achieved because she laughed, her eyes sparkling with return mischief. 'No, but I do own a black satin corset, which has a built-in half-cup push-up bra and is so high-cut I had to have a full wax this morning before I could wear it today.'

Rico groaned and tried not to picture how she would look when he peeled that dress off her.

'I also have some red chiffon baby-doll pyjamas which you can see right through and which I've lost the panties to.'

'Stop!' he protested, then grinned and shook his head. 'And you called *me* a wicked devil.'

'I'm just being a good little mistress.'

'I think you're trying to make me fall in love with you,' he jested, then worried she might be doing just that.

Her startled expression showed he was way off-base.

'Then you'd be dead wrong, lover,' she confirmed.

'What about my money?' he asked, using the opportunity to pry a little. 'You interested in that?'

'Even less than I am in your falling in love with me. Look, we could go tit-for-tat here for ages, like

we usually do. But, quite frankly, I'm sick and tired
of all that. We've been acting like children around
each other for far too long. If it makes you feel any
better, I don't dislike and despise you as much as I
thought I did. I'm sure you'll also be flattered to know
that I've always found you disturbingly sexy. That's
one of the reasons I used to have a go at you all the
time. Because it bothered me how much I wanted you
to f...'

She broke off and smiled a rueful little smile. 'Tch-
tch. Have some decorum, Renée,' she lectured herself.
'Four-letter words are not really your style. I should
have said it bothered me how much I wanted to sleep
with you,' she amended sweetly.

Rico was more than flattered with this news. He
was elated. But he did his best to remain cool and
suave on the surface. 'I wish I'd known that. I thought
I was the only one sitting there every Friday night in
an agony of frustration.'

'Oh, no. I think I can safely say there were moments when I wanted to taking a running jump off
that very high balcony.'

He grinned. 'I'm rather glad to hear that.'

'I don't doubt it. You're as egotistical as you are
wicked. Oh, dear. I'm doing it again. Sparring with
you.'

'Old habits do die hard.'

'Indeed. But honestly, Rico, let's not spoil the next
month with silly spats and trying to get one over each
other. Let's just enjoy each other for a change.'

'Sounds good to me. Like I told you once before,
I'd rather make love than war.'

'Heavens, let's not go *that* far. What we're doing
here is playing a game. And a pretty erotic game at

that. But no more talk of love, please,' she swept on with a shudder. 'Or falling in love. I can't think of anything worse.'

Rico was taken aback, and tellingly hurt. But be damned if he was going to show it. 'That's an unusual thing for a woman to say,' he commented as he set about starting up the engine. Best to keep his expressive eyes away from her right at this moment. 'Love is usually the first thing a woman thinks of. And wants.'

'I'm an unusual woman,' she said offhandedly.

And a secretive one, Rico realised. Like Ali, she rarely revealed any details of a personal nature. This morning was the very first time his Arab friend had told him anything about his past, or his personal feelings. Renée was just as reticent.

'You know, Renée, I've known you for five years and I still have no idea what makes you tick.'

She presented him with one of those beautifully bland faces that she did so well. 'But you don't have to, Rico. Just concentrate on what you're going to do to me when you get me home. Mistresses aren't meant to be understood, just…used. Now there's an acceptable four-letter word. Used. You…*used*…me with incredible skill last night, Rico. Quite frankly, I've never had better.'

She possibly meant it as a compliment. But all Rico heard was his being compared with innumerable other lovers. On top of that, her mocking tone sounded both insulting and patronising. She was relegating him to the role of mindless stud again. A role he was beginning to have mixed feelings over. Because it wasn't enough.

Damn it! Had Ali and Charles both been right after

all? *Did* he love this woman? It didn't *feel* like love when he looked at her. There were no warm, fuzzy feelings in his stomach. Neither did he want to be sweet or gentle with her. He wanted to ravish her. And often. If that was love, then it was a darned peculiar kind. Powerful, though. Darned powerful.

'Sounds like you've had a lot of experience,' he couldn't resist commenting as he reversed out of the car park.

She slanted him a dry look. 'I'm thirty-five years old, Rico. I was a model for ten years, during which time I had several boyfriends. I even lived with one for a while. Added to that, I married an older man-of-the-world type when I was in my late twenties, and I've been a widow since I was thirty. So what do *you* think?'

'I think I don't want to know,' he snapped. 'Just tell me where you live. I *have* to know that if you want me to take you there.'

She sighed, the sound echoing his own frustration with the way they always ended up snapping and snarling at each other, no matter what promises they made.

'I have a town-house in Balmain.'

'Balmain,' he repeated, surprised. He thought a woman with her money would have lived somewhere more ritzy, like Double Bay, or on one of the northern beaches.

Admittedly, Balmain had become a much more up-market address than it had once been. All inner-Sydney suburbs, even the ones in the west, now commanded top prices for their homes. Balmain had long made the leap from working class to yuppie heaven, with its elegant rows of trendily renovated terraces and the opening of cafés and restaurants on every other corner.

'Don't you know where Balmain is?' she said, misinterpreting the surprise in his voice. 'I would have thought the *Passion for Pasta* king would be well acquainted with the place, since Balmain sports more Italian restaurants than Leichardt.'

'I know Balmain,' he said. 'I have friends there.'

'In that case, I won't need to give you directions till you get closer.'

'Fine,' he said, then fell broodingly silent. She did likewise, which was a relief to begin with, but then a torment. Their lack of conversation and his familiarity with the roads through western Sydney meant that his mind was left idle. The devil, it seemed, found just as much work for idle minds as idle hands. Rico soon started thinking about what he *was* going to do to her when he got her home, not the best train of thought when driving, as evidenced when he almost ran up the back of a truck.

'Keep your eyes on the road, will you?' Renée chided.

'My eyes *are* on the road,' he retorted. 'It's my mind that's gone AWOL. Look, Balmain's not far away. Start giving me directions.' Anything so that he stopped picturing her in that black satin corset and nothing else. Except the stockings and shoes, of course. He'd want her to keep those on as well for a while.

Geez, even getting road directions didn't do the trick!

Fifteen minutes later he sat outside her town-house in the car, tapping the steering wheel impatiently whilst she went in to collect what things she thought she needed.

'Don't be long,' had been his parting advice.

'I'll have to feed my goldfish,' she'd curtly informed him through the passenger-side window before whirling and wiggling her way across the pavement and up some steps onto a covered walkway that led into a small but exclusive-looking town-house complex.

He watched her disappear into the one furthest from the road. It was just like all the others. Cream brick, two-storeyed and quite stylish. But again, a lot less than a woman of her wealth could afford.

He'd be very interested in seeing that report on her financial status at the end of the week. But not so interested any more in seeing how many men she'd slept with during the past five years. She'd already admitted she'd been very sexually active. All that was left for Rico to find out, really, was with whom. Although he already had ideas on that. He'd bet London to a brick that they'd all be younger than her. Younger and easily dispensed with. Men she met through her work. Possibly male models or advertising executives or aspiring fashion photographers. The toy-boy type, as he'd thought before. It was clear Renée liked sex, but she liked it unencumbered with emotional involvement.

The thought riled him, as did the time she was taking in getting her damned things. If she was in there changing out of that black dress and black satin corset, he was going to strangle her.

Rico was just about to leap out and pummel on her front door when the lady herself made a reappearance, thankfully still in the same sexy gear, and carrying a reasonably large navy gym bag. Now he did leap out, meeting her before she reached the steps and sweeping the gym bag out of her hand.

'You're only staying for the weekend, Renée,' he said drily on feeling the weight of the bag. 'Not the whole month.' Though, having said it, Rico thought that wasn't a bad idea. But he knew she wouldn't go for that. He'd already pushed things, demanding she stay the weekend. Frankly, he'd been surprised when she'd agreed. Although of course her motivation was strictly selfish. She wanted more of what she'd waited so long for. More sex. More fun and games.

Come Monday morning, however, she'd be back to work. And so would he. He had a heavy schedule next week. Several episodes to shoot. Meetings with his accountant and solicitor about the restaurant franchises. And discussions with his television crew about the road-tour of Italy he was going to propose.

Oh, yes, that was definitely still on. Rico could already see the writing on the wall where Renée was concerned. He'd be out on his ear at the end of the month, no matter how well he performed in the bedroom. Except on the million chance she was after him for his money. If that was the case, then he certainly wouldn't be waiting around to become her next victim.

No. This month was all they were going to have together. Given that, he aimed to enjoy himself to the full. And to hell with silly worries about falling in love with her, or whatever other weird and wonderful agenda she had in mind.

Sex was the name of the main game. And it was a game he was eminently qualified to participate in. Same as the woman walking beside him.

Rico's gaze raked over that incredible black outfit again, putting his body right back on red alert for action.

'What in hell were you doing that took you so long in there?' he asked as he slung the bag into the boot. 'Besides packing the kitchen sink, that is.'

'I told you. I had to feed the goldfish.'

'How many have you got? Two thousand?'

She sighed. 'I went through the message bank on my phone as well. Made a few return calls.'

'Who to?'

'I don't think that's any of your business.'

'Fine,' he said through gritted teeth. 'Let's get going, then,' he added, resolving to shelve every thought about Renée for the next thirty-six hours except sexual ones. She wanted him in no other role except Don Juan? Fine by him. He could do that.

He started playing his part the second his front door was shut behind them and he'd disposed of her gym bag on the foyer floor, leaving his hands free to pounce. Her cry of protest when he pushed her up against the nearest wall failed to impress, as did her feeble attempt to shove her shoulder bag between them. That bag quickly joined the gym bag, leaving her with no weapons against him but her tongue. And *that*, he swiftly found after some serious French kissing, soon totally lost its usual caustic edge.

'You kiss very well,' she purred when he finally lifted his head.

'I do most things well,' he growled and stepped back just far enough to do what he'd been wanting to do since he first clapped eyes on her that day.

It was a struggle to keep his fingers from fumbling as he undid the leather tie that secured the cummerbund. But he managed, although his already pounding heart became even more erratic as he slowly unwound the darned thing. Her chest was rising and falling rapidly too, he noticed. Yet her face had grown quite pale, as if all the blood had run from her head.

'Don't you dare go fainting on me,' he warned just as the leather wrap ran out and slipped from her body, leaving the dress to hang more loosely around her but still secured in some way.

Press-studs, he soon found out.

He could have simply ripped the two sides of the dress apart, but he didn't want that. He wanted to torture her as much as himself. Her eyes had already grown wider and he could feel her tension, as well as her excitement. He knew how she was feeling, because he was feeling the same way, torn between the desire to draw out these exquisite moments of anticipation, and the urgent need to see everything at once, *do* everything with delay.

The knowledge that she wouldn't stop him doing anything he wanted at this stage gave him patience, and a wicked resolve to have her lose control first. Yes, to make her beg as he'd once vowed to make her beg. So he undid each press-stud slowly, taking his time, making sure his hands didn't brush against a single thing other than the soft black lightweight wool the dress was made out of. There was no accidental touching of exposed flesh, although he went darned close at times. She stood there silently and very stiffly, every muscle held exquisitely tight, both inside and out, he imagined.

At last every press-stud had yielded and he was peeling the dress back, back off her slender shoulders, giving up the secrets of what lay beneath.

His eyes didn't know where to wallow first, but inevitably they raked downwards.

Dear God. She hadn't lied about that corset being high-cut. There was nothing but the narrowest strip of black satin between her legs.

He wrenched his gaze upwards as he felt his own control beginning to slip. But the sight of her breasts pushed up and together in that decadently designed built-in bra did little to help. Every time she breathed in—which was often—her nipples tried to escape their confinement. He could already see a good proportion of each aureole.

There was no doubt the whole corset was a mastery of erotic engineering, boned to pull her waist right in, automatically making her hips flare out and her breasts look larger than they were. The choice of black satin was spot-on as well, the colour a perfect foil against her pale skin, the slick, shiny satin more feminine than leather but just as arousing. To him, at least. She could not have chosen better if she wanted to reduce him to mush.

A strictly emotional term, of course. His body was far from mush. It was like granite and screaming for release.

His eyes dropped downwards again, taking in her long, long legs and those devastatingly sexy suspenders. The screws on his own sexual tension tightened a notch. Truly, there was no safe place to look. Even if he closed his eyes, the memory of her in that outfit would stay with him.

'Wicked,' he murmured, then laughed. 'I don't even know where to start. Or what to do next. How many times have you done this to a man with this amazing outfit?'

'Never.'

'Huh?'

'I only bought it this morning. Like the dress. And the shoes. Everything…just for you, Rico,' she said thickly, her green eyes glazing over.

He couldn't decide if she was for real, or just playing with him. Maybe even lying to him.

If she was, he didn't want to know. Not right now. He reached out to smooth his hands down the sides of the corset, tracing the shape of her very feminine figure. When his hands spanned her tiny waist and squeezed, she gasped, quivering when he let her go. His hands continued their journey down the outside of her bare upper thighs then across the lace-topped stockings before starting up the inside towards the ultimate goal.

'Move your legs apart a little more,' he commanded, his voice sounding as if he were talking underwater.

'You…you can undo it,' she said shakily as she did what he wanted.

'Undo what?'

'Between my legs. There are snaps at the front and back. You can remove that part altogether.'

His eyes flicked up to hers then back to the task at hand. If his hands had fumbled before, they were all fingers and thumbs now. But it wasn't rocket science and the strip of satin which had so tantalisingly but inadequately covered her private parts was finally dispatched to the floor of the foyer.

He stepped back to view his handiwork, and to try to keep his brain working, even whilst his body was fast racing towards overload. She looked incredible. Stunningly sexy and beautifully bad. But not bad enough, he decided darkly, and reached out to tuck the bra-cups down against the undersides of her breasts, exposing all of her nipples. Already rock-hard, they were. And so eagerly awaiting his attention.

She gasped when he gave each a tweak before stepping back once more to see how she looked now.

'That's better,' he said, and took no notice whatsoever of the look in her eyes, or the way she was pressing her palms against the wall beside her as if she was some kind of virgin sacrifice, pinned to the wall against her will. What an actress!

This was *exactly* what she wanted, what she'd planned to happen all day, to torment and arouse him unbearably with her choice of clothes and underwear, firing an insatiable appetite in him so that he would, yes, use her as she wanted to be used.

'Like I said,' he muttered, 'wicked.'

'Rico, I—'

'Hush up,' he snapped. 'I like my mistresses silent. Except when they're begging, of course. Is that what you were going to do, Renée? Beg?'

Their eyes clashed. Slowly the panic left hers, replaced by a dark and bitter resolve which almost eclipsed his. But not quite. Rico in full-on fury mode was an unstoppable and unsurpassable force.

'I'd die before I'd beg anything from you,' she threw at him.

He smiled. 'We'll see, sweetheart. We'll see. Don't go away, now.'

He delighted in the anguish that immediately filled her face. 'Where…where are you going?' she choked out, levering herself away from the wall. Clearly her leaning position had been supporting her because, once away from the wall, she swayed dangerously on her heels.

'To my bedroom,' he informed her. 'To slip into something more...comfortable. Don't worry. I'll be back. But before I go...' he strode over and pressed her back hard against the wall, palms splayed wide as before '...perhaps a little taster of what's to come...'

He clasped her face with one hand and held it captive, watching her eyes whilst he touched her with his other hand, touched her there between her legs, where she was silky smooth but shockingly wet. Touched her inside and out. Touched her everywhere but right on that spot he knew would send her screaming into a climax. Touched her till her iron will broke and he saw an anguished pleading enter her eyes. It wasn't verbal begging but it was almost as good.

When a moan broke from her lips he let her go.

'I won't be long,' he said with a final patronising peck on her panting mouth.

'You bastard,' she spat. 'If you think I'm going to stay here and wait for you to come back like a good little girl, then you can think again.'

'You *will* stay. Or I won't *be* back. I'll walk out of here right now. There are plenty of women who can give me what you're giving me here, sweetheart. You choose. Either you do exactly as I say, when I say it, sexually speaking, or this is over.'

He was bluffing, but for the first time since he'd met her he was doing it superbly. His face wasn't totally unreadable, but it remained convincingly hard and cruelly cold.

'Well? What's it to be?' he snapped.

She didn't say a word. She just glared at him, then turned her face away and stayed put.

Rico's moment of triumph felt somewhat shallow. Perhaps because underneath he knew only her pride was hurting. Underneath her outburst, she *wanted* to stay, not like a good little girl but like a bad little girl. A very bad little girl. This was the kind of fun and games she obviously liked. She just wasn't used to the man running the show. As he'd once thought, Renée liked being on top, not under a man's orders, or pushed up against a wall.

Rico determined not to hurry back despite it not taking more than thirty seconds to strip himself naked. He took his time going to the toilet, washing his hands, cleaning his teeth, applying some expensive cologne. He even contemplated having a shower but decided that might be going too far. After a good ten minutes his own frustration won the day so he slipped on his black silk bathrobe, sashed it then strode casually back down the carpeted hallway to the foyer.

She wasn't there. She'd gone. Fled. Escaped. Run out on him.

He swore, and was about to wrench open the front door and follow her—a rather stupid plan of action in his present attire—when he noticed that her things were still there. Her bags and her clothes. No way would she have taken the lift down to the lobby in the get-up he'd left her in. She'd be arrested for indecent exposure.

So where was she?

A door suddenly opened down the other hallway, the door to the guest bathroom, just this side of the study. Renée emerged then sashayed slowly back towards him, her eyes calm and composed.

He gulped at the sight of her in slow motion, his eyes riveted first at her still boldly bared breasts, then to the smooth naked mound between her thighs. All his controlling anger shattered, replaced by a desire so hot and so fierce that it frightened him.

'You were gone so long,' she explained coolly on reaching him. 'I simply had to go to the loo. I was desperate. Don't worry. I'll go right back to where I was, as ordered.'

When she went to brush past him his hand shot out to grab her nearest wrist, spinning her back then yanking her hard against him.

'Put your arms up around my neck,' he told her, which she did, eyes flaring wide, lips gasping apart.

With her wearing such high heels, there wasn't much between their height—Renée was a tall woman—so the juncture of her thighs was in just the right place for him. No time to waste now, he realised, the brakes he'd been exerting on his body up till now no longer working. He was beginning to lose control. His hands ripped open his robe, then moved down to push her legs apart, just wide enough for him to angle his erection away from his stomach and into the liquid heat between her legs. Dared he rub himself against her before slipping inside? He did, and the effect was well worth it. She stiffened against him, then cried out.

But not in pleasure. More in pain, the pain of knowing you were cripplingly close to coming. Did she feel like him? he wondered. Desperate to come but already resenting the moment of release.

'Look at me,' he whispered, and she did, just as he surged up into her.

'Oh,' she cried again, this time in stunned surprise.

He was big. Never bigger in fact. She'd done her job well, if this was what she wanted.

'Rico,' she sobbed.

'What?'

'Nothing. Just…just do it.'

Just do it. God, but he hated it when she said that. That was what she'd said last night. Didn't she know that this was special, him being inside her? That *she* was special, to *him*?

No, he thought savagely as he clamped his hands over her bare buttocks and began to pump up into her. She didn't know that. Any man would do, as long as he had the right equipment and knew how to use it. Use it and use *her*.

Her orgasmic cries were like daggers in his heart, as was the way her flesh convulsed violently around his. His immediate counter-climax was inevitable. How could he hold out against such stimulus?

But his own cries and shudders of physical ecstasy somehow shamed him. This was not how it should be between them. This was not what he wanted. He wanted to make love to her, not use her. Couldn't she understand that?

Obviously not. Her aim in all this—today at least— was sexual gratification. Which she was getting, if the length and intensity of her climax was anything to go by. Eventually, her body calmed and her arms sagged around his neck, her head drooping into the crook of his neck.

He reacted poorly when her mouth brushed his throat in a seemingly tender gesture. Hypocrite, he thought. She didn't want tenderness. She just wanted to be well and truly screwed.

When her knees started going out from under her,

he scooped her up and carried her down the hallway on the left, which led to the master bedroom. She wanted sex? She would get sex. She wanted to be in control for a change? He could do that, too. And he'd enjoy every single moment.

CHAPTER ELEVEN

RICO woke to the sound of the shower running, his head shooting up from the sheets to glance at the clock radio on the bedside table. Six fifty-three. He hadn't been asleep long. Only twenty minutes or so.

Relieved, he rolled over from where he'd been lying face-down on the bed, heaved himself up onto the pillows by the headboard, pulled a sheet up over his lower half, then hooked his arms behind his head.

Well, at least she hadn't run out on him this time. And why would she? He'd even surpassed his top-class performance of last night.

It had been five hours, give or take a few minutes, since they'd got here. Five hours and a lot of sex, and a lot of foreplay and afterplay in between. He'd used everything he'd ever learnt about women to keep her in a state of abandoned surrender.

Renée, he'd discovered to his surprise, *did* like to relinquish control. At least, with him she did. He'd been the one firmly in charge of the action, doing the seducing and the demanding and the taking. Yes, she'd been on top, but only at his command, and not for too long. He didn't want her getting ideas that she could be the boss in *his* bedroom. But she'd been a glorious sight, riding him, her head tipped back, her eyes shut, her mouth wide open as she gasped in much needed air. For a few moments he'd just lain back and watched her and wondered who she really

126

was, this woman who captivated him so. Captivated and corrupted him.

Because this wasn't him, this dark and domineering master who was already planning more things to do to her, with only one ultimate aim in view: to coerce her into agreeing to be his permanent mistress, not just a passing one. If she wouldn't let him love her, then by God he was going to own her. He'd become a predator, a primitive, primal animal who'd found his mate and wasn't about to let her go. He had a month to stake his claim, to brand her, so to speak, to show her that he and only he could totally satisfy her. He would appeal to her dark side, and her intelligent side, but especially her female side, which seemed extra-vulnerable to his being a forceful lover. He must have tapped into some secret fantasy of hers, because a woman like Renée would not normally be so submissive, or co-operative. Yet not once had she said no to him this afternoon.

Oh, yes, soon he would have her exactly where he wanted her. Maybe not in love with him, but seriously in lust. Lust was almost as powerful as love, Rico believed. Sometimes even more powerful.

The water stopped running in the bathroom and his insides immediately tightened. Rico snorted in disgust at himself. So much for all his dark vows. He was the one who was afraid. Afraid of losing her.

What to do for the best? he worried. More sex at this juncture seemed like overkill. Better she be made to wait a while. Restoke her fires. And his fuel. He was just a man after all, not a machine.

He would take her out to dinner somewhere. That would kill two birds with one stone. Give them both a rest and force her to make small talk with him.

Talking could be just as effectively seductive—and as intimate—as lovemaking. Talking broke down defences, created bonds, dispensed with misconceptions and brought about understanding. Rico was dying to find out more about her. Maybe this was his chance, whilst she was all soft putty in his hands. Or she *had* been before he'd foolishly fallen asleep.

Yes, a good strategy that, taking her out to dinner.

He reached for the bedside phone and made a booking for seven-thirty at a nearby seafood restaurant where he was well known and wouldn't be turned down, regardless of his call coming so late on a Saturday afternoon. It was just a short walk away, down on the waterfront. He wouldn't have to drive, or worry over having a couple of glasses of wine.

By the time the bathroom doorknob turned ten minutes later, Rico was feeling reasonably confident about his plan of action for this evening. No sex for a while, just dinner and chit-chat. A good plan, till she actually walked back into the room, wrapped in one of his thick, thirsty navy bathsheets and looking like a bride the morning after her wedding night. Glowing was the word that sprang to mind. Glowing and gorgeous and, oh, goodness, there he went again.

She spotted the movement under the sheet straight away and shot him a shocked look. 'You can't be serious,' she said as she stared at the phenomenon. 'That's impossible!'

'Apparently not,' he said drily, hauling himself up into a sitting position against the headboard then lifting his knees to hide his erection. 'Just ignore it for now. I've booked us a table for dinner at seven-thirty. That gives you over an hour to be ready.'

'Ignore it,' she repeated, clearly agitated. She gave

a little shudder and lifted her eyes back to his face. 'What was that? Oh…oh, yes, dinner. I…I don't have to get dressed up, do I? I've only brought casual clothes with me and I don't want to wear that black dress again. Or these,' she added, bending to scoop up the corset, stockings and killer shoes from the floor.

'Why not?' he asked.

'You know why not,' she snapped. 'Wearing them did things to me. Bad things.'

'Wasn't that the idea when you bought them?' he commented, thinking ruefully that she was back. The old Renée.

'No.' She dumped everything on the chair next to the bedside table, the one he sat on to put on his shoes every morning. 'They were supposed to only do bad things to *you!*'

He laughed.

'You can laugh. All that sexy stuff cost me a bomb.'

'I did offer to recompense you but you refused. Now, do stop complaining. You've been enjoying the after-effects of your purchases all afternoon. So I'd say they were a good investment, wouldn't you?'

Oddly enough, she aroused him more in what she was wearing at this moment. Just one snatch of an outstretched hand and she'd be standing there stark naked. Rico had found earlier in the afternoon that he preferred her that way. That corset had been a real turn-on, no doubt about that. But nothing beat having access to all of her body, every dip and curve, every erogenous zone, every intimate, deliciously responsive part. He loved stroking her smooth, soft stomach and kissing it and, yes, rubbing his stubbly chin over it. And elsewhere. She liked that, too. It had driven her wild.

Hell, stop thinking about sex, you fool, he ordered himself, painfully aware of the worsening situation in his nether region.

'You never did answer my question,' she said impatiently as she stood beside the bed and shook out her damp hair with her fingers, making it more tousled and incredibly sexy-looking.

'What question was that?' Rico replied coolly whilst his lower body raged white-hot. That short nap had certainly revived him.

'Can I wear trousers and a jumper to this place you've booked?'

'Sure. It's only casual. And it's only a five-minute walk from here. We won't have to leave till nearly half past seven.'

'Good. In that case, I'm going to go make some coffee before I get dressed. Would you like some?'

'Not right now. I'm heading for the shower myself.' A long cold one.

'Fair enough.' She turned and padded from the room in her bare feet, shaking her hair some more with her fingers as she went.

Rico bounced out of bed as soon as she was out of sight and headed, post-haste, for that hopefully life-saving shower. Five minutes later a teeth-chattering Rico switched off the icy water and grabbed the one remaining bathsheet, aware that the cold shower had worked all right. He'd not only lost his erection but everything else down there as well.

It seemed, however, that his neutering was only temporary, everything gradually dropping back to normal by the time he'd dried himself, sprayed on deodorant, combed his hair and cleaned his teeth.

'Now, I want you to behave yourself for a while,' he lectured his still twitchy penis as he slipped on the navy towelling robe he kept hanging on the back of the door. 'I'm trying to get to know the woman for the next few hours. And I'm not talking biblically here. So just cool it, will you?'

Rico was surprised when he re-entered the bedroom to encounter Renée there, standing over at the French doors, her hands clasped around a steaming mug of coffee, staring out at the view. An innocent enough sight. The trouble was that darned towel had slipped. Any more and her breasts would pop right out over the top, nipples and all.

'Down, boy,' he muttered under his breath.

'I'd go outside on the terrace,' she said on seeing him, 'and enjoy more of the views. But it's too cold. Nicely warm in here, though.'

And getting warmer by the minute, Rico thought irritably.

'I took myself on a brief tour around the other rooms after I made my coffee,' she went on. 'I hope you don't mind.'

'Not at all,' he said.

'I really like what you've done with the place. Your choice of furniture, I mean. I can see you haven't changed the wall colours or the carpet. But creams and greys go with just about anything, anyway, don't they? That red leather in the living areas looks fantastic, but I really love the rich, warm-coloured wood you've used in here,' she raved on, walking back to the bed, where she held her mug in one hand whilst she ran the other over the curved headboard. 'So much nicer than the bland cream-painted stuff Charles had.'

Rico blinked, then stared at her. It had never occurred to him till that second that Charles might have been one of Renée's past lovers. Yet, once it had, he could see that it was a distinct possibility. Till Charles had met and fallen in love with Dominique late last year, he'd been somewhat of a man about town. Frankly, he'd had more women than Rico, who was not the playboy Renée had always believed.

'Was Charles one of your lovers?' he asked, a huge lump forming in his throat at the thought of it. Please, anyone but Charles.

'What?' She glanced up from where she was caressing that stupid bloody headboard, her eyes momentarily off in some other world. Probably thinking about the last bed that had stood on this very spot, and the last man she'd screwed in it. His best friend!

Her dreamy expression cleared to one of exasperation. 'Oh, don't be silly. Of course not.'

'Then how come you know what this bedroom looked like when he lived here?'

'For pity's sake, Rico, I've been here several times over the past few years. To parties and to Charles' wedding more recently. I'm a woman, which means I'm a snoop. I peeked in here, all right?'

Sounded reasonable. Brother, was he relieved! 'I guess so. So why did you say of course he wasn't your lover. Is Charles too old for you, is that it? You like your lovers young, I suppose. Young and randy. They'd have to be to keep up with you.' As the jealous and insecure words tripped out of his mouth, Rico would have given anything to take them back. But too late. The damage had been done.

She took another sip of coffee, then sighed. 'Look, could we possibly not get into this kind of conversation? It's such a waste of time. I'm here with you now, and I'll be here whenever you want me to be here for the next month. I'm your mistress for that span of time. But that doesn't give you the right to give me the third degree about what lovers I've had in the past, or anything else. I'm happy to chat with you on a wide range of topics. Work. The weather. Religion. Politics. Your decor. And, of course, sex. But I will not discuss my personal life. Which includes my past.'

'I see,' he bit out, frustrated on all levels. Taking her to dinner clearly wasn't going to achieve what he'd hoped. Not if she stubbornly refused to open up to him on a personal level. They still had to eat, but no way was he going out with a hard-on like the one he was trying to hide. His masochism where Renée was concerned was now over. For the next month at least.

'OK,' he said, adopting a cavalier attitude. 'If that's the way you want it. In that case, put down that coffee, take off that towel and get your sweet fanny around here to me. Pronto!'

He enjoyed her shock, then took advantage of her hesitation, disposing of his own towel and showing her what was waiting for her. She stared. No doubt about it. Then swallowed convulsively. He could see the movements in her throat. When she licked her lips, he knew he had her.

'Do you do this to all your women?' she threw at him angrily.

'Do what?'

'Corrupt them.'

He had to laugh. 'No. Only green-eyed witches who've given me curry for bloody years. Now, put down that mug and do as you're told, mistress mine!'

She didn't move a muscle for a long moment. Then slowly, haughtily, she put down the mug and removed the towel, tossing it well away from her. It was the first time he'd seen her standing up in the nude. Heavens, but she was lovely. Tall and sleek, with long, elegant curves. A thoroughbred through and through. If she'd been a horse paraded around a sale-yard, she would have commanded top dollar.

What a pity he couldn't actually buy her.

Suddenly, he hoped that report would show she was in some financial difficulty. Then he might have some bargaining power to keep her in his bed. But somehow he doubted it. All he could count on with Renée was the next month, and this moment.

'Now come round here,' he commanded, his voice as thick as treacle.

She obeyed, walking as he imagined she'd once done on the catwalk, with long, slow strides and that snooty look on her strikingly sculptured face. She came right up to him, her lovely green eyes locked to his, flashing fire and defiance and, yes, hatred still.

'So what do you want me to do, lord and master? Should I just lie back, or do you want me on my knees, perhaps? I'm sure you'd like that. But lo and behold, he's suddenly not saying anything. Can't make up your mind, lover? Let me make it up for you.' And she dropped to her knees before him.

He watched, fascinated and appalled, as she stroked him with one hand whilst she cupped and squeezed him with the other. The pleasure was electric. Blinding. *Compelling!* When her head bent and her lips made intimate contact, he gasped, then groaned. How easy it would be to let her do this, take him all the way. He almost let her. He *did* let her for a while. Too long, almost. But at the last second, he grabbed her by the arms and hauled her to her feet. Was it decency? Or despair which stopped him? He wasn't sure. He just knew that he could not let her do that to him in anger. He only wanted that from her in the heat of her passion.

'No,' he growled when her stunned eyes questioned him. 'Not that. And certainly not like that. I...I want to make love to you, don't you understand?' he said, shaking her. 'I want to take you in my arms and kiss your breasts and whisper sweet nothings in your ear. I want...I want...'

He broke off his impassioned speech and just kissed her, kissed till, yes, she moaned and melted in his arms. They fell back onto the bed together, mouths still fused, limbs tangling, hands frantically seeking intimate places. There was no skilled foreplay on his part this time, just wild, urgent action. His mouth abandoned hers, only because he needed air. She seemed just as desperate, her legs lifting to wrap high around him, opening her body wide to his. He slipped inside her like a knife through hot butter, her muscles grabbing at him and pulling him in deep.

'Oh, God,' she groaned. 'Why am I letting you do this to me?'

'Do what?' he ground out through gritted teeth. 'What am I doing to you?'

'You're driving me insane,' she panted. 'This is crazy. I can't. Not again,' she moaned, but she grabbed at his buttocks, digging her nails in hard as she pulled him in even deeper, her rocking hips driving him on and on. 'Yes, yes,' she urged. 'Like that. I...Oh...' And she came with a rush.

He gasped, then tore her hands away and lifted them high, high above her head, stretching her upper body tight, then tighter. With a raw moan, he lowered his full weight onto her, his chest crushing her breasts flat between them, their straining stomachs glued to each other. Inside her, he forced himself to be still, wanting to wallow in her abandoned surrender. Why, he wasn't sure. Perhaps because this was the only moment when he felt superior to her.

But all the while she kept spasming fiercely around him, taking him inexorably closer to his own climax. It was a fight to the end, but she won, her name bursting from his lips as his body exploded, his heart bursting with emotion at the same time whilst his head whirled with dismay.

Driving *her* insane, was he? How ironic. Didn't she know that she'd driven him insane eons ago? Why else did making love to her never satisfy him? Why did he start thinking about the next time almost before this time was over? What name did you give such a self-destructive desire? Addiction? Obsession? *Love?*

He didn't know what to call it any more. All he knew was that Renée was going to be his woman. Not just for this weekend. Or this month. For a long, long time. He wanted her here, under his roof, in his bed, every night, and he would do everything in his power, use every trick in the book, by fair means or foul, to achieve that end.

CHAPTER TWELVE

'I'M NOT going to let you go, you know,' he told her as they sipped the very nice Chablis he'd ordered, and waited for their barramundi in lemon butter to arrive. They'd skipped the entrée and gone straight to the main course. Renée had claimed she never ate entrées. Rico just wanted to get her straight back home to bed, where at least he always felt on top of things. Once she'd put her clothes on—the classy but conservative ones she normally wore this time—she'd immediately changed back into the Renée he had difficulty handling.

'You're mine now, Renée,' he added with considerable bravado. 'All mine.'

Her wine glass had stilled, mid-air, for a moment, but then she laughed and took another sip. 'Watch it, Rico. Your Italian blood is showing.'

'Meaning what?' he snapped.

'Meaning Italian guys, I've noticed, have this tendency to be excessively jealous and possessive over the women they've—er—been with.'

He glowered over the table at her, feeling exactly what she accused him of feeling. Yes, he was jealous, *and* possessive. She'd given him her body so completely and with such intense passion that surely he could be excused for thinking she could never have been quite like that with any other man before.

Soon, she'd realise that he was as special to her as she was to him. Meanwhile, he simply *had* to find out more about her. He couldn't wait for that stupid report. Despite her proclaiming she would not talk about her personal life, she'd just given him an opening.

'You've had an Italian boyfriend before, have you?' he asked.

She sighed an exasperated-sounding sigh. 'Might I remind you, Rico, that you are *not* my boyfriend? See what I mean? Spend one night or two with an Italian and they think they own you. Now, could we change the subject, please?'

'*You* brought it up. Look, we have to talk about *something*. So you had an Italian boyfriend once. Big deal. Tell me about him.'

She sighed again, and started twisting her wine glass round and round in her hands. 'His name was Roberto,' she said at last. 'He was a model, like myself at the time. He was very handsome. Like you,' she added with a rueful flick of her eyes at him. 'And good in bed. Like you.' Another dry glance. 'And a total, *total* bastard.'

Rico waited for her to add, like you. But she didn't. Instead, her eyes shimmered momentarily before she lifted the wine glass to her lips and drained it dry.

'I think I need another drink,' she said, her voice cold and hard, her eyes alone betraying her distress.

Rico reached for the bottle, which was resting in a portable wine cooler by his elbow, all the while struggling not to show *his* emotions. But he wanted to kill this Roberto for being the one responsible for making his Renée like this, for making her hostile to him from the start, just because he was Italian.

'What did he do that was so bad?' he queried casually as he refilled her glass.

'It doesn't bear repeating in detail. Let's just say he was totally and utterly selfish.'

'I'm not *totally* and utterly selfish,' he pointed out with a covering smile. Instinct warned him to keep things very light or she'd clam right up.

'That's a matter of opinion.'

'I never leave you unsatisfied.'

'True. I'll give you that. But I'm not talking about sexual selfishness. I'm talking about the capacity not to know, or care, how other people feel.' She fixed him with an uncompromising gaze. 'One month, Rico. That's the deal. Don't, for a moment, think this is going to go on any longer than that.'

'What if you find *you* don't want it to end in a month's time?'

Her eyes glittered with dry amusement but its meaning eluded him. What did she find so funny? 'I don't have long relationships with *any* man any more, Rico. I certainly won't be having one with you.'

'Why? Because I'm Italian?'

'Because it's not what I want.'

Rico decided to play the only trump card he held in his hand at the moment. 'Then why did you ask me to marry you for your prize last night?'

She almost spilled her wine.

After her initial knee-jerk reaction she just sat there, frozen with shock, whilst he fished the sheet of notepaper out of his trouser pocket and handed it over to her. She put down her glass, a bit clumsily, then stared down at the clearly outlined words that she'd written with her own hand.

'Very clever,' she muttered, then crumpled the piece of paper into a small ball.

'Well?' he prompted impatiently when she declined to say any more. 'Care to explain that to me?'

'No,' she bit out. 'We had a deal, Rico, and you haven't honoured your part of it. You weren't supposed to know what I asked for.'

'Why not? What's the big secret? It's not as though you're madly in love with me. Which leaves what, Renée? Spite? Money? *Sex?* What motivated that request, I'd like to know?'

'It was just one-upmanship,' she snapped. 'I knew that you were going to ask me for sex, so I went one better. I regretted writing it the moment I had. It was a stupid thing to do. I was relieved when you won.'

Rico recalled that this was true. She *had* been relieved when he'd won, for whatever reason.

'So it wasn't my money you were after?'

Again, she looked taken aback. 'You know, Rico, that's the second time you've mentioned money. Look, I know you think I married Jo for his money and that you believe most good-looking women who marry rich men are gold-digging tramps, but trust me, I am not interested in your money. Aah, here comes our food...'

She was relieved again, Rico thought, this time by the arrival of their meals. She also hadn't denied that she'd married dear old Jo for *his* money.

Yet, strangely enough, Rico was beginning to believe that she hadn't. There was something innately honest about Renée. She was secretive, yes. But not devious. And there was a difference.

Rico fell to eating his meal whilst he decided on his next brilliant topic of conversation and had only taken a few mouthfuls of the mouth-watering barramundi when his cellphone rang.

'Should have turned the darned thing off,' he muttered as he fished the phone out of his pocket and answered.

'Rico,' was all his mother said, but it was enough for every nerve-ending in Rico's body to go on emergency alert.

'Yes, Mum, what is it?' he asked, trying not to sound sick with instant worry. But his voice must have betrayed a considerable amount because he'd never seen Renée look at him with such concern before.

'It's your *papa*,' his mother went on. 'He was having bad chest pains after dinner, but he didn't want me to do anything. He said it was just indigestion from my cooking. But he looked so bad, Rico. Bad colour. Bad breathing. I took no notice of Frederico for once and called the ambulance. I am at Liverpool Hospital now and the doctors, they…they are doing tests. They won't say much but they look worried, Rico. I think you should come. They will talk to you.'

'I'm on my way.'

He was already on his feet, his heart racing, panic a heartbeat away. Not his dad. Not yet. Not before he got there, at least.

'I have to go, Renée. My dad's in hospital with a suspected heart attack. I'm sorry. I just have to go.'

'I'm coming with you,' she said, and jumped up too.

'No. You won't be able to keep up. I have to run home and get my car first and I'm not going to slow down for anything.' He was already on his way, throwing a hurried explanation at the *maître d'* as he bolted past, breaking into a run as soon as he was outside.

You could have knocked him over with a feather when she not only caught up with him but also kept up with him, all the way to his apartment building. He didn't waste any energy asking her how till they were in the Ferrari and on their way. Even then, he didn't speak till they were forced to stop at a set of lights. He was too out of breath.

'Care to tell me how you managed that?' he asked her at this point. Hell, she wasn't even puffing!

'Running is my exercise of choice,' she replied. 'I go in the City-to-Surf fun run each year. And other fun runs. I'm one very fit gal.'

He nodded in wry agreement, not really wanting to talk. He'd just been curious.

'Just drive, Rico,' she said, surprising him with her insight. 'And don't speed. You don't want to have an accident, or get pulled over. That won't get you to your father's bedside any quicker, will it?'

His glance carried gratitude for her sense, and sensitivity. Then he just drove in concentrated silence, not speeding, but taking every short cut he knew, all the while trying to keep the panic at bay, reassuring himself with the thought that lots of heart-attack victims survived these days, if they got to the hospital in time. He just hoped his dad would be one of them. He prayed he would be.

The drive took forty minutes, with Rico not sure where to go when he got there. His stress level by this time was extreme, his decision-making powers not what they usually were.

'In there,' Renée advised, pointing to the casualty sign. 'That's where your father will be. You get out and I'll park the car for you. Then I'll come to Casualty and find you. OK?'

He did exactly that, stopping briefly to give her a peck through the window before he rushed off. 'Thanks,' he said.

'Good luck,' she called after him. 'I'll start praying for your dad.'

'You do that,' he called over his shoulder, then forged on into the casualty section. He'd already been praying all the way there.

It was bedlam inside, the waiting room chock-full of patients. Saturday night, of course, was the busiest night for any casualty section in a large hospital. It took some time for Rico to be seen to, then shown to where his father lay, eyes closed, ashen-faced, in a narrow hospital bed, his mother sitting by his side.

She looked very relieved to see Rico.

'How is he?' Rico asked straight away as he hugged her.

'I am fine,' his father answered grumpily, his eyes opening. 'I told your *mama* it was nothing. But she is a stubborn woman, and here I am, having lots of silly tests when I could be home, sitting in my favourite chair and watching my favourite television show.'

'What tests have they done?' he asked, directing the question at his mother. 'You be quiet and rest,' he ordered his father when he opened his mouth to answer. 'I'm talking to Mum here.'

'You are getting too big for your boots, Enrico,' his father muttered, but closed his eyes and fell silent.

'I don't know,' Teresa told her son worriedly. 'Lots of machines and wires and things. And they gave him some medicine. I don't know what.'

Rico swept up the chart from the bottom of the bed and did his best to decipher what was on it. Not easy.

Such a scrawl! 'Mmm. Looks like they did an ECG and an ultrasound. Blood pressure very high. I doubt it's just indigestion, Dad. But you don't seem to be dying just yet.'

'Mandretti men do not die before ninety,' his father retorted. 'Only if they are murdered.'

Teresa was startled by a soft laugh coming from a woman who had suddenly appeared beside her son at the foot of the bed. A tall, strikingly beautiful woman with jet-black hair and lovely green eyes and the nicest smile. Teresa was one of those people who either liked or disliked people on the spot. This woman, she liked.

But who *was* she?

'Aah, you found us,' Enrico said, turning to smile at the woman.

'I had to tell them I was your fiancée before they would let me in,' the woman returned, her pretty green eyes sparkling. 'I see your dad's not doing too badly. That's good. My prayers must have worked.'

Now Teresa liked her even more. A woman who prayed was not only nice, but also good.

'Mum, Dad, this is Renée. My horse-racing and poker-playing friend. We were having dinner together when you called, Mum. Renée was nice enough to come with me and stop me from getting a speeding ticket.'

Teresa could not have been more taken aback. *This* was Renée? Why, she didn't look a day over twenty-five! And she was nothing like her son's usual woman. Not blonde. Or bosomy. Or showy. And she'd been having dinner with her son. Must have come to her senses after all!

'It is lovely to meet you at last, Renée,' Teresa

replied, coming forward to give her a hug and a kiss on the cheek. 'I have heard so much about you from Enrico, but you look so much younger than I pictured. You must come and visit us at home soon. Isn't that right, Papa?'

'*Sì*. If I ever get out of here.'

'Well, that won't be tonight, Mr Mandretti,' the doctor said as he bustled in. 'We will be wanting to keep a close eye on you for a couple of days yet. Now...'

Whatever he was going to say was interrupted by the noisy arrival of Katrina, Teresa's youngest daughter and the apple of her father's eye. Katrina was the only other one of her offspring whom Teresa had rung, not wanting Frederico to be overwhelmed by visitors and noise. But Teresa knew that Katrina would never have forgiven her if she hadn't been notified at once that her beloved *papa* was ill. Unfortunately, Katrina had brought her youngest child with her, Gina, who was four and given to crying at the drop of a hat.

Gina took one look at her grandpapa in bed and started howling.

'Hush, darling. Hush,' Katrina said, looking very harassed. 'Sorry, Mama, but Paulo had to work tonight and I couldn't leave Gina with the other kids. They don't know how to handle her.'

Rico was of the opinion that no one could handle Gina. Katrina certainly couldn't. Spoilt through and through, that child was.

'Here. Let me take her,' Renée offered, and scooped the wailing child out of his sister's highly ineffectual hands. 'I'm Renée,' she told an open-mouthed Katrina.

'My fiancée,' Rico added drily, then laughed when Katrina's mouth fell even more open. 'I'll explain later.'

'And I'll be out in the waiting room,' Renée said.

Katrina's head swivelled from one to the other. 'But…but…'

'Don't worry,' Renée reassured her. 'I'm very good with children.'

Rico could see it was a statement of some truth, since the little devil had immediately stopped crying. Renée was constantly amazing him tonight.

'Thanks again,' he said.

She smiled, then walked off, chatting away to the child in her arms as she went. Rico stared after her for a second before dragging his mind back to his father's health. That had to be his first priority at this moment, even though it did look as if his dad wasn't in any immediate danger.

The doctor told the family that Rico's father had had *not* a heart attack but a serious angina attack, the forerunner of a coronary. The plan was to move him shortly to a cardiac ward, where he would be kept for observation and treatment for a couple of days, during which time he would be seen by a specialist as well as a cardiac-care consultant. A change in lifestyle and diet would undoubtedly be prescribed, which brought a scowl from Rico's father and a quick rebuke from his mother.

'You will do what the doctors say,' she said firmly. 'You are the one who is stubborn. Not me.'

'And I'm going to buy you a couple of grey-hounds,' Rico butted in. 'Then you can walk them. Get your heart as fit as a fiddle and have some fun at the same time.'

'Walking and fun is excellent therapy for the heart,' the doctor concurred. 'You should listen to your wife and son, Mr Mandretti. They know what's best for you.'

Rico's father pulled a face. '*Sì, sì.* Enrico always thinks he knows best. If he is so clever then why didn't he marry that lovely lady who was just here, instead of that other one with the bleached hair and that silly laugh?'

Rico winced at this reminder that Jasmine had had a silly laugh. A high-pitched giggle that had been as false as the rest of her.

'I'll be back,' the doctor said, then scuttled off. No rest for the wicked, Rico thought, or Casualty doctors.

'But he *is* going to marry her, isn't he, Papa?' Katrina piped up, sounding puzzled. 'He said she was his fiancée.'

'Was just a silly joke,' the old man said scornfully. 'She does not want to marry this clever boy. Your *mama* told me so.'

Rico glowered at his mother, then scowled at himself. Because she was right. Renée didn't want to marry him.

Or *did* she?

She had asked him to marry her in that bet, hadn't she? OK, so she claimed it was one-upmanship, and that did ring true, given their history. But what if something else had been at play there? What if…?

For the first time, Rico began to consider the possibility that something was going on with Renée that he'd been blind to. Ali might have touched upon it when he said that what some women say and what they *feel* were two different things.

Rico had hard evidence of what Renée *felt* for him

when she was with him in bed, when her defences were down. Not just desire and need, but also passion. A deep and powerful passion, which drove her body to feel things that her mind resisted.

'I shouldn't be letting you do this to me…'

That was what she'd said shortly after she'd acted as if she didn't want to make love with him; that she was only obeying because she'd lost the bet.

But her body had been on fire for him. Her body had been on fire for him all along. Why? What would make a woman like Renée want a man so much if she supposedly hated him?

And then the solution came to him. The other side of hate. Love.

She's in love with me!

The thought blew his mind.

Could it possibly be true?

She would deny it, of course, even if it *was* true. Maybe she didn't even recognise what she really felt, as he hadn't recognised the truth of his feelings for her up till tonight. Maybe her silly pride was getting in the way, or those old tapes she had in her head about Italian men.

Rico frowned and fretted over this last very real problem. He had to make her see that not all Italian men were like Roberto. He had to make her see that it wasn't just sex he wanted from her, but a future as well. A future and a family. She wasn't too old to have children. Not at all. She…

'Enrico,' his mother said, laying a gentle hand on his arm, 'The people are here to wheel your father's bed away.'

'Oh. Oh, sorry, Mum. I was off in another world.'

'I know…' She smiled one of her soft, understanding smiles. 'Perhaps you should go check how your Renée is doing with Gina.'

Their eyes met, mother and son.

She knows, Rico realised. Knows how I feel about Renée.

She patted his arm and smiled. 'Go to her and wait with her till your *papa* is settled in his room. And then the three of you can come, visit with him for a while. *Sì?*'

'*Sì,*' Rico agreed, and bent to kiss her cheek. 'Love you. Be with you soon, Dad,' he added more loudly. 'Don't worry about, Gina,' he told his sister. 'She'll be fine.'

Teresa watched her son hurry off, and for a moment her heart was full of sorrow. I've really lost him this time, she was thinking. He belongs to her now.

'Teresa,' came the oddly fragile plea from the bed, and she turned to see her husband of almost fifty years looking at her as he had never looked at her before. With fear in his eyes.

She hurried over and took his hand in hers. It felt cold, and old. 'It's all right, Frederico. I'm here. And you are going to get well. I will see to it myself.'

His face registered surprise, then pleasure. '*Sì,* Teresa. I know you will. A good woman, your *mama,*' he said to his daughter. 'A very good woman...'

Not so good, Teresa was thinking. A silly, selfish old *mama* who has finally grown up.

CHAPTER THIRTEEN

RICO found Renée in a far corner of the waiting room, talking to a thankfully quiet Gina, who was sitting on the plastic chair next to her and staring with rapt attention up into Renée's face. As Rico drew closer he could hear she was telling the child a story.

'And the big bad wolf put on one of Grandma's nighties and jumped into Grandma's bed just as Little Red Riding Hood…'

Renée broke off once she saw Rico, with the child immediately protesting. Rico swept a wailing Gina up from her chair and sat down with the child placed firmly in his lap.

'If you don't shut up, Gina,' he warned with deep authority in his voice, 'you won't hear the rest of the story.'

It was the right thing to say. Gina shut up immediately.

'Do go on,' he encouraged Renée. 'This is one of my favourites.'

'I imagine you like all stories that star big bad wolves,' she quipped drily before continuing.

Rico laughed, then listened. What a natural storyteller she was! He was impressed.

Unfortunately so was Gina, who wanted another one as soon as *Little Red Riding Hood* was finished. Renée launched into *The Three Little Pigs* without batting an eyelid, clearly knowing that story equally well. Fortunately, this time, Gina began to droop during the telling, and was sound asleep shortly after the last *I'll huff and I'll puff and I'll blow your house down*.

Renée immediately stopped and *Rico* protested. 'I've come this far. I want to hear the end.'

She gave him a droll look. 'You mean the bit where the big bad wolf gets his comeuppance?'

'Absolutely.'

'Mmm. What a pity real life doesn't echo fairy stories. I know a big bad wolf who could do with falling into a pot of boiling water. Scald his ego a bit.'

'Ouch. But seriously, though, Renée, how come you know these stories so well? You didn't miss a beat.'

'That's because I spent a good chunk of my teenage years reading those stories to my much younger cousins every single night.'

'How come?'

'How come? I was brought up by my aunt and uncle from the age of twelve.'

'How come?'

She sighed. 'You ask a lot of questions.'

'I'm interested.'

'I know *exactly* what you're interested in where I'm concerned, Rico Mandretti. But I suppose you can't indulge that appetite here so you want to feed your curiosity instead. Very well, if you must know. When I was twelve, I became an orphan. My parents were killed in a head-on collision, along with my younger sister. I was luckily—or unluckily, depending on your point of view—staying with my aunt and uncle that day. They took me in afterwards and I lived with them till I left school and came to Sydney to find work.'

'You weren't happy with them, though, were you?' Rico said, reading between the lines.

Renée shrugged. 'They did their best for me, I suppose. I mean…I wasn't their daughter, just a niece. But my aunt was not a motherly woman. Lord knows why she had baby after baby. I do know she liked having a ready-made baby-sitter in me. I looked after those babies from sun-up to sun-down some days. Not that I minded all that much. Her kids loved me, even if she didn't. And I needed someone to love me back then.'

Rico was shocked, both by her tragic story and the fact that till that moment he hadn't given a serious thought to Renée's family or her upbringing. Yet he claimed he loved her. Maybe he *was* as selfish as her other Italian lover. Or maybe *all* men were selfish. Whatever, it was high time he started thinking about her, instead of himself.

'You haven't mentioned your uncle. You didn't have any trouble with him, I hope.'

She looked startled. 'What do you mean? Oh…oh, no, not at all. Why do people always think awful things like that?'

Rico shrugged. 'It's just that you must have been a very good-looking girl, even at twelve.'

'Actually no, I wasn't. I never was the cute and pretty type, with baby-blue eyes and curls et cetera. I was always very thin and bony, with straight, mousy-brown hair, skin that didn't tan and these big pale green eyes. My nickname at school was Froggie. Then, around fourteen, I shot up far too quickly and became terribly awkward and gangly. All legs and no bust to speak of. I wasn't the kind of young girl that men look at and lust over. By the time I was eighteen

I'd improved somewhat, but I still had no style or poise. I used to go round with my shoulders hunched and looking down at the ground all the time.'

'I find that hard to believe. You walk so beautifully now. So proudly.'

'Thanks to a deportment and grooming course I was lucky enough to win after I came to Sydney. It was a prize in a raffle the women were running at work for charity. I was the mail girl at a plastics factory at the time. Anyway, the people running the course said I had the right look for a model and recommended me to an agency. I never expected to be taken on but I was, and in no time I was on the catwalk and doing fashion layouts. I never reached supermodel status—I'm not quite tall enough for that—but I did very well for myself.'

'I have to confess I only vaguely recall your name. But then, I wasn't into dating models.'

'Not enough boob for your taste?'

'Very funny. No. I think my ego was too large to compete with successful women. I was content with girls who said I was wonderful all the time, not the other way around. Hopefully, I've grown up a bit since then. I know you think I go from one blonde bimbo to another but that's not true. Not any more, anyway.'

She threw him a thoughtful look. 'You surprise me, Rico. It's a sign of real maturity to be able to look back at things you've done and understand why you've done them. I'm really glad you're not going to go back to dating girls like Jasmine. You deserve better.' Is this *me* saying *that*? Well, I did say you were driving me insane.'

Their eyes met and he wanted to kiss her again.

Very badly. But, of course, he didn't. Instead, he decided to press on with finding out more about her.

'So how did your parents' accident happen?' he asked gently. 'Under what circumstances?'

Her eyes saddened with the memory. 'Mum and Dad had to take my little sister, her name was Fay, to Sydney to see a specialist. She had scoliosis of the spine. We lived out in the country, on a farm, not far from Mudgee. Not many specialists out there. They'd driven down to Sydney early that morning, and been at the hospital all day. They stayed for a meal and didn't start the drive back till it was quite late. They weren't all that far from home when their car veered onto the wrong side of the road straight in front of a truck. They think Dad fell asleep at the wheel.'

Rico's heart went out to her. 'That's tough, Renée. Really tough. I'm so sorry.'

Their eyes connected and he hoped she would see genuine sympathy in his.

'You're not really a big bad wolf, are you?' she said with a frown.

He smiled, happy that she could see beyond the playboy tag at last. 'No. But I haven't been at my best the last couple of days. I have to admit that.'

'Wow, if that's not your best then I'm in for a few treats during the next month.'

Rico had to laugh. She had a wicked sense of humour. He was almost tempted to tell her right then and there that she didn't fool him. He *knew* she wanted more from him than sex. She wanted him to love her. *And* to marry her.

But it was neither the right time nor the right place for such a confrontation. He didn't want to risk losing her altogether by being impatient. He would wait till the time *was* right, till she was ready to accept his love. Meanwhile, he would keep on carefully asking her about herself. She'd started to tell him things now. There was no reason for her to stop.

'So what are they doing with your dad?' she asked first. 'He didn't look too bad from what I saw. A bit pasty-faced but well able to live till that ninety he said you Mandretti men live to. Unless they're murdered, of course. By jealous exes and vengeful mistresses, no doubt.'

He grinned, and was proceeding to update her on what the doctor had said when Katrina made an appearance, looking both surprised and pleased when she saw her little girl was asleep.

'I was getting worried,' she said. 'I see I didn't have to be. Thank you so much, but I'd better take Gina home now,' she went on, easing the child out of Rico's arms into her own. 'Papa's resting comfortably. I'll come and see him tomorrow. Nice to meet you, Renée. And thanks for minding Gina. I'm sorry you're not Rico's real fiancée. He could do with marrying someone nice for a change. Bye, Rico.' She bent to kiss him, whispering, 'You silly fool,' as she did so.

He grinned up at her as she straightened. Katrina had been like a second mother to him as he grew up and had spoiled and indulged him almost as much as she had Gina. For her to call him a silly fool was a very serious rebuke indeed. But it meant she approved of Renée as a potential sister-in-law.

He liked that idea. A lot.

'See you tomorrow, sis.'

She rolled her eyes at him and left.

'Are all your brothers and sisters as good-looking as you are?' Renée asked as Katrina walked off.

Rico thought about that for a second. 'Almost,' he said, and Renée punched him playfully on the upper arm. 'You're an arrogant sod.'

'Yeah. It's a problem we big bad wolves have in common. We're arrogant. So, shall we go see what the old man is up to?' He stood up and took her hand, pulling her to her feet.

'Would you prefer for me to wait for you in the car?'

'Absolutely not. Dad's always had an eye for a pretty woman. Seeing you again will keep his ticker going.'

'Flatterer.'

'That's another quality you can rely upon in a big bad wolf. We're all flatterers.'

'I already said you *weren't* a big bad wolf.'

'So you did. In that case, I'm not a flatterer. You must be really pretty, then.'

She gave him one of her droll looks. 'Lead on, Mr Mandretti.'

'I'll have to ask the nurse at the desk for directions first.'

He asked the nurse, got directions, then set off for the ward they'd moved his father to. The directions were rather complicated, and they got lost a couple of times, wandering down empty and echoing corridors before finally reaching the wing, and the right room. Rico was pleased to see it was a private room with only one bed in it. His father looked very settled, and much better, with some colour in his face. He was also sound asleep, courtesy of an injection he'd been given, his mother told them.

'There's no need for you to stay,' she told Rico. 'Come and visit tomorrow.'

'But what about you, Mum? You should get some sleep. I'll drive you home.'

'Thank you, Enrico, but no. They say I can stay. A nice nurse is going to bring in a stretcher bed. I sleep in here by your *papa*.'

Rico frowned. He didn't like the sound of that. It worried him. Why would the hospital let his mother do that? Unless it meant...

'It's fairly standard procedure these days in hospitals,' Renée broke in softly. 'Don't worry.'

He looked at her. 'How did...?' He shook his head. 'Never mind.' He liked to think she was sensitive to his needs, that they were already becoming attuned to each other, not just physically but emotionally. He gave his mother a goodbye hug and his father a kiss goodbye, just in case.

'Don't die on me, Dad,' he whispered. 'I love you.'

'He'll be all right,' Renée said as they walked together back to his car, Renée leading the way. 'He's in good hands.'

'I guess so.'

'But you'll worry all the same,' she said as they reached the Ferrari, which was standing alone in the main car park under a lit telegraph pole. 'You love your family a lot, don't you?'

'But of course. Family is everything, Renée.'

Her eyes turned instantly bleak and he could have kicked himself. 'Oh, God, I *am* a fool,' he muttered, and pulled her into his arms.

She went willingly, but with a sob. When she buried her face against his chest and wept, he just held her and stroked her hair. 'I shouldn't have said that,' he said regretfully. 'It was stupid of me.'

'No,' she choked out, shaking her head. 'No, it was beautiful.' And then she wept some more. Deeply. Despairingly.

He let her cry herself out, knowing that there was nothing he could say to make her feel better. Before tonight, he would have had no concept of what it felt like to lose both your parents so tragically. Going through this scare with his father had given him some idea. But not entirely, he conceded. How could he possibly know how she'd felt as a twelve-year-old, being told that her whole family had been snuffed out? And then having to live with people who didn't really want or love you?

'I don't know about you,' he said when she finally stopped crying. 'But I could do with something to eat. Do you think they might have kept our barramundi warm?'

'Why don't we go to my place instead?' she offered, her eyes still looking lovely despite their red rims. 'I have a whole heap of ready-made meals in my freezer that wouldn't take long to heat up in the microwave. Not supermarket muck, either. Good food that I've cooked myself.'

'Sounds great to me,' he said, hiding his surprise that she bothered to cook at all.

Her town-house was even more of a surprise. Country-style furniture and very comfy, where he'd envisaged either ultra-expensive antiques or that cold, minimalist stuff you saw in style magazines. In no time he was sitting on floral-cushioned wooden chairs and forking spicy Thai chicken and noodles into his eager mouth, washed down with some refreshing Chinese tea.

'You've no idea how much I enjoy eating food other people have cooked,' he said between mouthfuls.

'You've no idea how much I enjoy seeing someone else *eat* my cooking,' she countered. 'It's always just me.'

He let that information sink in whilst he downed some more of the simply delicious food. There was so much he didn't know about her.

'Why did you marry a man so much older than yourself, Renée?' he asked when both their plates were empty. 'And please...don't give me some bull-dust answer. I want the truth.'

'The truth,' she repeated slowly, then leant back in her chair, her face taking on a resigned expression. 'You really are extra-curious tonight, aren't you? All right. Perhaps it's time you heard the truth, anyway. I married Jo because he loved me. And because he didn't want children.'

Rico could not have been more startled. Or more worried.

'It had absolutely nothing to do with his money,' she added wryly.

'Fine.' Rico nodded slowly. 'OK. I believe you. But why didn't *you* want children?'

'I didn't say that, Rico. I said *Jo* didn't.'

'I'm sorry. I'm confused.' Utterly.

'I am only telling you this because I have an awful feeling where all this is heading. The total truth is, Rico, I *can't* have children.'

Her baldly delivered statement struck him like a physical blow, obliterating in one fell swoop everything he had been planning. How could he marry her and make her the mother of his children if she couldn't have any?

Rico sat there with his mouth hanging open and his hope for their future together disintegrating on the spot.

'How…how long have you known?' he asked at last, when he could think again.

'Since I was twenty-six. I had an ectopic pregnancy. Twins. One in each tube. There were complications, along with a severe bacterial infection. After the operation necessary to save my life, I was told the good news.'

Rico didn't know what to say. He knew her sarcasm hid a lot of pain. He could see it in her eyes. The surgeon must have had to give her a hysterectomy. Dear God, what devastating news for a woman in her twenties!

But it explained so much. Her marriage to Joseph Selinsky. Her decision to never have a real relationship since becoming a widow. Her reluctance to talk, or even *think* of love.

'Roberto was the father, wasn't he?' he said with further insight.

'How did you guess?'

'So what happened? He just dumped you after he found out you couldn't have any more children, was that it?'

'Heavens, no, Roberto was much more selfish than that. He pretended to be sympathetic. Told me it didn't matter, that he still loved me madly and we would still get married. He continued to sleep with me. Naturally. But he began going overseas a lot. Modelling assignments, he told me. Around that time,

I started up the modelling agency and soon found out through contacts that Roberto hadn't been working in the business for ages. He was away when I discovered this piece of puzzling news. I rang him immediately and tackled him over what was going on. He confessed over the phone that he'd been spending all his time in Italy with his new wife, his new *pregnant* wife.'

Rico sucked in sharply. The bastard went and got himself married!

'She was from a very wealthy family,' Renée continued, then smiled a travesty of a smile. 'The funny thing is he could not understand why I was so upset. He said I couldn't possibly expect him to really marry me. He said he still loved me and wanted me to continue being his lover. He said his father-in-law was in the shoe business and had given him a job in the export-sales division and that he would be coming to Australia regularly on business. He said it was a perfect arrangement and I was perfect mistress material, since I could not conceive and he wouldn't even have to bother with condoms. He promised me he would only sleep with me and his wife so everything would be perfectly safe.'

Rico could hardly believe what he was hearing. What kind of man did something like that? Or said such amazingly arrogant and incredibly insensitive things?

'So...what did you do?'

'What do you mean, what did I do?' she flung back at him. 'I told him to go screw himself and that if he ever came near me again I'd cut his balls off with a carving knife! What do you think I did?' she said, jumping up, her voice having risen hysterically. 'Do you think I just lay back and let him do what he liked when he liked? Give me credit for more pride than that. The only reason I'm telling you this is so that you won't go getting any silly ideas about my marrying you. Which you have been thinking of tonight, haven't you? You think you love me. You probably think I love you. And maybe I do. But whether I do or not is totally irrelevant, under the circumstances. You want children. I can't give them to you. End of story. End of affair.'

He stood up, walked round and took her trembling body into his arms. 'I don't just *think* I love you, Renée. I *know* I love you. I've always loved you. I love you and I want you to be my wife. To hell with your not being able to have children. They're secondary to what I feel for you.' And he meant it. How could he possibly do what Roberto had done? Marry some other woman, just to have children, when all the while his heart belonged to *this* woman, this incredibly brave, beautiful, proud, stubborn woman?

'No, they're not,' she wept. 'They're not secondary. They're one of the most important things to you. And you *don't* love me. Not really. It's just sex. Give you a solid month of sleeping with me, night after night, and this so-called love you feel will burn a little less brightly and you'll be grateful that I didn't say I'd marry you tonight. Even if you did really love me, any marriage between us is still doomed. You'd end up hating me.'

'I doubt that. I've already tried hating you and it didn't work. It didn't work for you, either. We love each other, Renée, and nothing is ever going to change that. We love each other and we should be together as man and wife. As for children…we can adopt them. I know there aren't many children up for adoption in Australia but there are other parts of the world where poor, neglected orphan kids are crying out for a good mum and dad. And we'll make very good parents.'

She stared up into his face, her green eyes luminescent with tears, and something else. It was wonder. Wonder and awe.

'You really mean that, don't you?'

'I do.'

'Oh, God, how...how can I say no? Yet I should say no. I know I should. This is all too quick. Too soon. You...you aren't thinking quite straight at the moment. Look, I'll make you a new deal. I'll be your mistress for the next month, as agreed. A month of wild, uncontained and constant sex, Rico. And then, after that month is up, if you still want me to marry you, I will.'

'No kidding?' Rico had difficulty containing his elation over her agreement, not about her promise of all that wild, uncontained and constant sex. Although, damn it all, that sounded pretty good too.

'No kidding.'

'You won't go back on that?' he growled, sweeping her up off the floor into his arms.

'Not unless you do something really terrible in the meantime.'

'Like what?'

'I don't know. Turn into a serial killer or start shaving on the weekends, perhaps,' she murmured, reaching to run her hand over his very stubbly cheek and chin. 'I think my nipples have become addicted to this...'

'Only your nipples?' he said wryly.

'Perhaps some other sensitive little bits as well.'

'You know nothing about addiction, lady,' Rico growled and started to carry her towards her bedroom. 'Let me show you what serious addiction is, and the only way to deal with it.'

Rico was making love to her for a second time when he suddenly remembered those reports he had commissioned.

'Rico,' she moaned softly when he stopped moving.

He kissed her shoulder. 'Just taking a breather, darling.'

God help him, he thought, if she ever found out. Should he ring Keith up tomorrow and cancel them? Not much point, really. What difference would that make now? Besides, he still wanted to know who she'd been sleeping with. And no way would Renée tell him that. As far as her finances were concerned…maybe he should put his mind totally at rest there as well.

'Rico…please…' Her hips wriggled against his, her breasts jiggling under his hands.

He groaned. Impossible to think of other things right at this moment.

His right hand slid down to splay over her stomach, his left staying clamped to her left breast. He pressed her back against him till they were two perfect spoons, curved around each other, their flesh as one. When she wriggled again, sharp flashes of electric pleasure shot through him. He was close to coming again. He rolled over onto his back and took her with him, his penetration not as deep now. When her legs moved restlessly apart and she continued her wriggling, he stayed very still inside her. Only his hands moved, his left playing with her fiercely erect nipples, his right moving down to where he knew she would be equally swollen.

Just the slightest touch there, and she gasped. A firmer stroke and she froze. A squeeze, and she cried out, then splintered apart.

'Mine,' he muttered, then came just as violently.

Mine...till death us do part.

Or until...

No, no, Rico vowed despairingly. That could not happen. He would not *let* that happen. Not now. Not ever! It would be his secret, carried with him to the grave.

CHAPTER FOURTEEN

RICO left the two reports on his glass-topped coffee-table and walked over to the corner bar to pour himself a drink. Selecting a heavy-based glass from the built-in shelves under the black granite bar-top, he half filled it with Glenfiddich, then added a few cubes of ice from the tray in the bar bridge. His hands shook as he did so.

Nerves.

Glass in hand, he made his way out onto the terrace, where he leant on the railing, sipped the whisky and tried to pull himself together. Dusk was falling and the city lights were rapidly blinking on. The evening promised to be coolish, with the night sky clear and dark and star-filled.

The quay below was still very busy with ferries leaving at regular intervals, carrying city workers home across the harbour. It was Friday, so lots more people had probably stayed on in town for end-of-week drinks and general carousing.

Renée was due home soon from a business trip to Melbourne. Unavoidable, she'd told him late last Monday as she'd headed for the airport. A staff emergency in the Victorian branch. He'd wanted to go with her but she'd said no, definitely not. Business and pleasure did not mix. Besides, she'd be back in a day or two. Each morning this week she'd promised to return that night, and each time something else had delayed her. But there would be no delay tonight, she'd assured him from Tullamarine Airport. She was on the six-o'clock flight and would catch a taxi straight from Mascot.

He'd missed her terribly these last four days. Renée had been virtually living with him since the beginning of their month's agreement three weeks back, only returning to her place to feed her goldfish and replenish her wardrobe. Her absence this week had highlighted to him how much he'd already come to depend on her company every night. And he didn't mean just the sex, although that continued to be incredible.

Rico understood, however, that their mutual urges to make love several times a night—or at regular intervals during the day at weekends—would eventually fade. They would not spend the rest of their lives unable to keep their hands off each other. Their love life would settle down to a more normal routine. Eventually.

That was why he was thrilled with how well they got along during their other times together. Charles and Dominique were astounded when they went to dinner at their place recently and didn't throw a single verbal dagger at each other, although Renée still liked to stir him a bit during their poker-playing evenings. They even behaved themselves at the races, not a difficult task so far, considering Ebony Fire had won brilliantly the last two Saturdays. Renée's pride and pleasure in her beloved Blackie had been touching to see. She'd cried with happiness. Rico understood that her horses were like the children she would never have, a situation he aimed to remedy. He'd already instructed his solicitor to investigate countries where legal adoptions could be fast-tracked.

Yes, all Rico's plans were falling into place. He had no doubt that Renée loved him, although she never said she did. And he had no doubt she would say yes to his proposal at the end of the month.

That was why, Rico realised as he downed his whisky in agitated gulps, he was so nervous at this moment. The woman he loved more than life itself would walk in the front door shortly. And what was he going to do? Risk his future with her by showing her those two reports, by confessing what he'd done.

He'd tossed and turned over this decision for the last few nights and found he could no longer live with the secret. Or his own curiosity. Frankly, the reports from the detective agency had created as many questions as they had solved. Not that they revealed anything bad. Just the opposite. The woman had to be a damned saint.

Yet Renée wasn't a saint. Who was?

The sound of the glass door sliding back behind him had Rico whirling round, the ice clinking in his glass.

'I didn't hear you come in,' he said, aware that he sounded strained.

Renée stayed standing in the doorway. 'I can see that. What's that you're drinking. Bourbon?'

'No, whisky. Would you like one?'

'Mmm. That would be nice. Flying always makes me strung-up.'

He felt her puzzled eyes on him as he brushed past and hurried over to the bar, where he mixed her a drink the way she liked it before dinner in the evenings. Whisky and ice, with a little soda.

'So what's made *you* so strung up?' she asked

when he handed her the drink. 'Something go wrong with your shooting schedule this week?'

'No. It went off like clockwork. Come and sit down, Renée. I have something I want to tell you and I don't think it can wait.' He knew if he procrastinated at all, he might wimp out. And that just would not do.

'Mmm. Sounds serious. Let me just get out of this jacket first,' she said, putting her drink down on the coffee-table right next to the reports and taking off the very tailored navy pinstriped jacket that went with the equally tailored trousers she had on. Underneath was a three-quarter-sleeve white shirt, which still looked crisp and smart, despite her travelling. Her hair was pulled back into a tight roll, and she was wearing a single string of pearls around her throat, along with simple matching earrings.

She looked chic and sexy, and Rico wanted desperately to change his mind and not do this and make love to her instead. But that would be the coward's way out.

'What's all this?' she asked, nodding towards the two reports as she picked up her drink again.

'It's what I wanted to tell you about,' he said.

'Oh?' Before he could stop her she'd put down her drink again, picked up the top report and started reading.

'Renée, please don't be angry,' he jumped in just as her head whipped up and around, her eyes blinking wide.

'You had me investigated,' she said disbelievingly. 'Like you had poor Dominique investigated.'

'Not quite.' With Dominique he'd asked them to

go right back, to the day the woman was born. 'There were just a few things I needed to know.'

'I can't believe this,' she raged, shaking the report at him. 'Why, you…you…'

'*Listen* to me before you go off at half-cock,' he ground out, hoping to sound firm and not panic-stricken. 'This was something I put into motion the morning after our first night together, immediately after I found out you'd asked me to marry you. That threw me, Renée. I couldn't work out why you'd ask for marriage. I was worried that your motive might have been money. I didn't know the real you then. Hell, I knew next to *nothing* about you. I still believed you'd married your last husband for money.'

'So what do you believe now?' she asked him with cold fury in her eyes. 'Are you satisfied after seeing this that I have enough money of my own? Or do you think I'm still looking for another gravy train to jump onto?'

'I'm satisfied you are a very wealthy but wonderful woman who gives heaps of money to charities and chooses to live reasonably simply. Other than the racehorses, of course. They cost a pretty penny. Try to understand, Renée, this was more about my emotional baggage than you. After Jasmine, I'd lost faith in beautiful women. When I met Charles' wife-to-be, *and* you, all I saw were two more mercenary gold-diggers willing to trade their bodies for financial security. You have to be honest, Renée. Both you *and* Dominique had bad track records. You can't blame me entirely for thinking what I did in the first place.'

She grimaced, then sighed, most of the anger leaving her face, replaced by reluctant agreement. 'No, I guess not. But you could have *asked* me, Rico, not set some professional to snoop into my finances and…and…' She broke off suddenly, then spun round to snatch up the next report, starting to read it before Rico had a hope of stopping her. He waited with trepidation for the next explosion.

It wasn't long in coming. Her head shot up, her face flushed. 'My God, you even had my personal life investigated! My…my *sex* life!'

'Only for the last five years,' he said apologetically.

'There is no *only* about this, Rico. This is unforgivable!' she said, throwing both reports onto the coffee-table and sweeping her drink back up with shaking hands. 'You must know that. Quite unforgivable. And downright typical.' She took a swift swallow of the whisky and soda. 'Bloody Italian men. You just can't trust them. Not a one. They don't love or trust you. They just want to own you and know all your sexual secrets and…and…'

'But you don't *have* any sexual secrets, Renée,' he pointed out, trying to stay calm in the face of her fury. 'You haven't *had* a sex life. Not since your husband died. There have been no men in your life during that time. Why, Renée? I want to know.'

'Oh, do you, now? Well, bully for you! I would have thought, being typically Italian, that you'd be pleased as punch that I'd been celibate all this time. I could almost qualify as a born-again virgin. You Italians like virgins, so I've gathered. Roberto wasn't at all pleased when I wasn't a virgin, though God knows how he expected me to be. Once the poor darling realised, he wanted to know the ins and outs of every boyfriend before him. And do you know what was even more pathetic? I thought his insane jealousy was evidence of the extent of his love for me. I thought he was crazy about me, and that he'd never look at another woman. I was so stupid. So abysmally, stupidly stupid!'

She began to pace the living room, taking swigs of the whisky as she did so. 'But I didn't stay stupid,' she threw over at Rico, who decided he'd best stay where he was. 'Post-Roberto, I knew *exactly* what men wanted from me and what they felt when they looked at me. Not love, Rico. *Never* love,' she sneered. 'Till Jo came along. I knew *he* really loved me. I knew it wasn't a question of lust with him.'

Rico snorted, his pretend calm finally giving way to his own emotional mayhem. If he was going to lose everything, then he would not go quietly. He'd go down fighting. 'Oh, really?' he scoffed. 'What makes you think that a man of sixty is any different from one of thirty? He *wanted* you all right. And he bought you, lock, stock and barrel. Don't start kidding yourself that all he was interested in was your mind, Renée. That's bull and you know it.'

'For your information, Jo was dying of prostate cancer when I met him,' she countered, stopping Rico in his tracks. 'His treatment had already left him impotent. Sex was *never* a part of our lives together. All he wanted from me was affection and caring and companionship. After Roberto and all the other sleazebags I'd been involved with, that seemed like heaven. OK, so I wasn't madly in love with the man,' she confessed. 'But I liked and respected him. He gave me a lot of happy moments. And he taught me how to give again. He was a nice guy and I won't have you saying he was some kind of dirty old man because he wasn't!'

Rico scooped in then let out a ragged sigh. 'All

right,' he said. 'But it might have been nice if you'd trusted me with that information, Renée. Then I wouldn't have just put my big foot in my mouth again, or had you investigated in the first place. You can't blame me for trying to find out some facts about you. If I waited for you to volunteer things about yourself, I'd wait a bloody eternity!'

At least his forcefully pointing out this truth stopped *her* in her tracks as well. Now her expression was a mixture of confusion and guilt. 'I...I'm not used to confiding in people,' she said defensively.

'Then it's time you learned. And I'm not *people*. I'm Rico, the man who loves you, damn it! The man who's going to marry you.'

Her chin whipped up, her eyes glittering once more. 'You think I could marry a man who had me checked out by a private detective?'

'Yes!' he roared back at her. 'You can and you damned well *will*!'

Her mouth dropped open and she stared, wide-eyed, at him. He glowered back, his knuckles white as they lifted his glass and downed the watery remains of his whisky and melted ice. 'I'm taking no more nonsense from you, Renée Selinsky,' he grated out as he slammed the glass down on a side-table. 'I'm not waiting till the end of the month, either. Tomorrow I'm going out and buying you an engagement ring, and we're going to go over to your place and move those rotten goldfish in here. Then, as soon as we can make the proper arrangements, we will be getting married. That's the new deal and I'm not asking you, I'm telling you!'

Her mouth finally snapped shut and a slow, almost

shy smile tugged at her lovely mouth. 'My, but when you're forceful, Rico, I...I just go to water.'

Rico almost went to water himself at that moment. His bluff had worked. Holy hell!

'Time you saw some sense,' he grumped. 'Now, get yourself over here, woman, and give your fiancé a proper hello kiss.'

She obeyed him, and kissed him, and he wanted to weep. His hands tightened around her and the kiss deepened, his hunger not sexual so much as emotional. He needed to hold on to her and never let her go.

'Rico,' she murmured against his mouth when he lifted his lips briefly for some air.

'Mmm?'

'There's something I have to tell you, too...'

His stomach instantly reverted to panic mode. His head lifted further, his eyes searching hers. 'What now?' he asked tautly.

She looked worried. No doubt about that. She pulled back to arm's length.

'Now, I don't want *you* to be angry with *me*,' she said somewhat hesitantly.

'About what?'

'When I told you about my not being able to have a baby, you—er—seemed to jump to the conclusion that I'd had a hysterectomy.'

'And?'

'My...um...womb is still intact. It's my fallopian tubes that had to be removed. It *is* theoretically possible for me to have a child through IVF, although of course there are no guarantees.'

Rico didn't know whether to kiss her again, or kill

her. Why couldn't she have trusted him with the truth? Why let him think she was totally barren?

But way down deep, he already knew the answers to those questions.

Roberto, again. Rico hoped he'd never meet up with that bastard, or he *would* be guilty of murder.

Still, Renée revealing there was some hope of their having a child together confirmed what he already knew. Renée having his natural baby *wasn't* his first priority in life any more. It would be wonderful. Yes. But it wasn't the only thing. First and foremost was spending his life with this deeply wounded, annoyingly complex but still wonderful woman standing before him.

'Please don't be angry with me,' she whispered, her eyes desperate. 'I…I had to be sure that you really loved me for myself; like you had to be sure that I wasn't a gold-digger. I thought that if after a month of no-strings sex you *still* wanted to marry me then you must truly love me, especially if you thought there was absolutely no chance of a baby. But there was one small hiccup I didn't think of and which cropped up last Monday.'

The penny dropped. 'Your period,' Rico said. 'You got your period.'

'Uh-huh. I didn't want you asking me awkward questions so I did a flit. I can't tell you how awful I've felt, lying to you all week. But I didn't know what else to do. I…I had to be sure of your love. I'm sorry, Rico. Perhaps you shouldn't marry me after all. Perhaps I'm far too screwed up to even think of being any man's wife. Look how terribly I've treated you all these years. Yet all the while I was madly in love with you. I must be some kind of sick sadist. Or masochist. I'm not sure which!'

Rico could not have been more stunned. Or flattered. 'You've loved me all along? You never said so. In fact, I don't think you've said you love me yet even once.'

'See what I mean? I still have difficulty admitting it. Yet I fell in love with you that first day at the races. I thought you were the most handsome, most charming, most exciting man I'd ever met.'

'So why were you so prickly to me? I thought you *hated* me on sight.'

'You had two fateful marks against you. You were Italian, and you were engaged to the type of woman who always brings out the worst in me. I thought...how could he possibly be in love with *her*? And then you looked at me and I knew you weren't. Because I knew that look. I thought...he doesn't love her. He's just marrying her to have babies. He'll be unfaithful. In fact, he'll be unfaithful with me if I let him.'

Rico didn't deny it, because maybe he would have been, if she'd given him an ounce of encouragement. He'd certainly have broken his engagement.

'It was always a battle in my mind,' she went on, 'every time I saw you. God, but I wanted you so much. It was easier to hate you rather than love you. To mock and stir you, *especially* after you got divorced. Your being suddenly available was the most dreadful torment, Rico. I knew I could have you then, but I'd vowed never to get mixed up with another Roberto-type and you seemed awfully similar.'

'I don't see how,' he refuted.

'Think! In my eyes, you were an Italian who married a woman just to have a family, then divorced her once she refused. I couldn't risk giving my heart to another Roberto. I asked you to marry me in that bet because I already knew you had the better hand—you never could bluff me at cards, darling—and I just wanted to see the words. It gave me a secret thrill. I almost wrote ''I love you'' on it as well, just to see *those* words. I never imagined you'd find out. Yet you did! That was awfully clever and very devious of you, Rico. But then, I can see you're a devious man.'

'No, I'm not,' he denied. 'I'm a very straightforward man. I love you and I want to marry you. And I don't want there to be any secrets between us. You're absolutely right, I didn't love Jasmine, but I didn't realise I didn't love her at the time. When you're young, and male, it's difficult to know the difference between lust and love. She also did a damned good job of convincing me that she loved me. We're all susceptible to being loved, Renée. You were with Jo Selinsky. It's a seductive thing, being loved. It was easier to believe that I felt love for Jasmine and only lust for you, rather than the other way around, especially when you were so hostile.'

'I was awful. I admit it.'

He grinned. 'No, you were great. I loved every awful, frustrating moment.'

She looked appalled. 'How could you?'

'I guess I've always liked a challenge. And you were the ultimate challenge. Man, when I got that unbeatable poker hand and you agreed to that bet, I was on cloud nine.'

'I was pretty excited myself. Because I knew what you were going to ask for. By the time we reached that honeymoon suite, I was in such a state. I knew you only had to touch me and I'd come. When I saw that statue, I kept thinking of how you would look without clothes on, and how you'd feel, deep inside me.'

Rico sucked in sharply as his body reacted to her evocative words.

'I couldn't wait to see how you'd look without clothes on myself,' he said, and reached out to start flicking open the buttons on her shirt. 'It's been four days since I've had the privilege and I think I need reminding.'

She didn't say a word till his fingers stopped on the last button. 'What's wrong?' she asked somewhat breathlessly. 'Why are you stopping?'

'Tell me you love me. I want to hear you say the words.'

'That's blackmail!'

'Yep. So speak up, honey, or I'm going to leave any lovemaking till after tonight's poker game. And trust me, I'll do it. Making you suffer comes high on my list of pleasures.'

She pulled a face at him. 'I always knew you were a sick sadist as well. That's why we clicked. OK…here goes. I…love…you.'

'Again, please. And put a bit more feeling into it.'

'I…*love*…you,' she said, and fluttered her eye-lashes up at him. 'Good enough?'

He smiled. 'Better.'

'Fine. Now get on with it, will you? We have to be at Ali's suite by eight and it's already after seven.'

'Tch, tch, such impatience.'

'Rico…'

He laughed, and got on with it.

CHAPTER FIFTEEN

SPRING had finally arrived, with Teresa's gardens never looking better. The wisteria was in full bloom over the back pergola and her prized azaleas were having a wonderful season with masses of pink, red and white blooms.

Australian friends had told Teresa not to plant azaleas in Sydney's west. Too hot and dry. But she knew exactly where to plant them—underneath the native trees on the gentle slope which surrounded the large back terrace. She always kept them well fed and watered, and everyone who visited the Mandrettis in spring admired them profusely.

'I've never seen azaleas like those, Teresa,' Renée had said on seeing them. 'I've never had any luck with azaleas myself. Even in pots.'

It was the first Sunday in October, with the traditional family get-together having been swiftly converted into an engagement party. Teresa had only had a week to prepare since Rico had informed her of his news, and she'd worked her fingers to the bone to make sure that everything was perfect for him. The food. The wine. The setting. Nothing was too good for her Rico, and his lovely bride-to-be.

The rest of the family had helped, of course, with the women promising to bring plates of freshly made salads and desserts today, and the men coming the day before to do the lawns and set up some trestles under the terrace. Frederico was still not allowed to do heavy work.

Over sixty guests were expected, most of them direct family. The happy couple had arrived first, as requested, with Enrico immediately taking his father off to discuss where he wanted the kennels and runs built for the greyhounds Enrico was determined to buy his father for Christmas. Frederico pretended to still be reluctant in this venture but Teresa knew he was secretly happy with the idea.

Once the men were out of the way, Teresa had poured herself and Renée a glass of *vino* and they were sitting on the outdoor seating under the pergola, relaxing together.

'People say I have the green fingers,' Teresa remarked.

'And they'd be right,' Renée agreed warmly.

Teresa smiled. 'Speaking of fingers, let me see your ring again.'

When Renée lifted her left hand and wiggled her fingers, the sunlight hit the central diamond, sending out starbursts of colour.

'*Magnifico!*' Teresa exclaimed.

Renée laughed. 'I know. It *is magnifico*, isn't it? Just like my Rico,' she added in a voice that betrayed more to his mother than she ever had to the man himself.

Teresa finally understood why her son had chosen to marry a woman who might never give him a child of his own. She'd been very shocked when he'd first told her about Renée's fertility problem. Shocked and worried. But also proud that her son could love so selflessly. Still, she'd always known that her *bambino* had more love in his little finger than most men did in their whole bodies. She'd been reassured when Enrico told her that they aimed to adopt a couple of children as well as try to have their own. Also, that they weren't going to wait with bated breath for that to happen. Plans were already underway for them to fly to the Philippines and visit several orphanages. Teresa thought that was an excellent idea. Parents who adopted often then had *bambinos* of their own.

'I...I hope you're not too disappointed, Teresa,' Renée added, sensing something in the other woman's silence. 'I know you would have liked a younger wife for your son. One who would pop out babies like clockwork.'

Teresa reached over the narrow trestle table and patted Renée's arm. 'All I want is for my son to be happy. And you make him happy, Renée. No mother could ask for more.'

Renée's eyes flooded. 'Thank you, Teresa. That makes me feel better. Oh, dear, I can hear a car coming up your driveway and I've just made my mascara run.'

'Come...It won't take you long and you will be looking your beautiful self again.'

Which was true. By the time their first guests rang the front doorbell, Renée's make-up was repaired and she was smiling again.

Teresa thought her future daughter-in-law looked even more beautiful than ever, dressed in a feminine and flowing green dress that matched her eyes and showed off her dramatically pale skin and jet-black hair, worn up that day with soft, feathery bits around her face.

But it wasn't Renée's outer beauty that quickly captivated the Mandretti family during the next few hours. It was her genuine warmth, her ease of conversation, plus her obvious love for their favourite son. They'd all lived through Enrico's relationship with that awful Jasmine, and were so happy to see him with a woman of substance and style.

Of course, Rico's own beaming happiness was very catchy. Now that he'd found true love, his natural exuberance for life was overflowing, sweeping everyone along in its rush of sheer joy. Even his best friend, Charles, who could be a serious type of man, could be heard laughing and joking a lot.

The lunch had been devoured and all the adults were sitting around, sipping some of Frederico's excellent homemade wine and feeling very mellow indeed, when a group of the older children came running round from where they'd been playing soccer in the huge front yard. The older girls were inside, talking boys and make-up, and all the younger children had been put to bed for a nap.

'There's this huge truck coming up the driveway, Poppa!' they told Frederico in chorus. Frederico gave his wife a questioning look but she just shrugged.

'Everyone who was coming has arrived,' Teresa told him.

'Let's go see,' Frederico replied and they all traipsed around the side of the house to see whose truck it was.

Rico suspected what was behind the mysterious arrival the moment he saw Ali's royal insignia on the side of what was a large livestock-transporter. He gave Renée a squeeze and said, 'I might be mistaken but I think you're just about to get a new heart's desire.'

She glanced up at him. 'A horse? From Ali?'

'I presume so.' Ali had declined to come to the party, as he declined all such invitations. He said the security measures he had to employ spoilt things for the other guests.

The truck came to a halt not far from the expectant crowd and the fellow driving it jumped out, along with his sidekick in the passenger seat. Both men wore big hats and big smiles.

'Got a horse here for a newly engaged couple named Enrico and Renée!' the driver said, grinning from ear to ear.

'That's us,' Renée said excitedly.

'Nice to meet you, ma'am, sir,' he said, tipping his hat at them. 'Congratulations on your engagement. His Highness, Prince Ali of Dubar, has sent you both a little present, namely one not so little horse. Here's his pedigree and papers.'

Renée gasped when she saw the horse's breeding. 'Rico, look, he's a two-year-old half-brother to Ebony Fire. The same dam but a different sire.'

'That's right, ma'am,' the sidekick informed her. 'And he's a flyer. The boss was gonna keep him himself, he was so fast in the paddock. You are one lucky couple, I can tell you. He's all broken in and been goin' through his paces a treat up home. Just needs some racin' polish. His stable name is Bobbie but his racin' name is Streak of Lightning.'

'Oh, I love that!' Renée exclaimed. 'Oh, I can't wait to see him. Can I see him right now?'

Rico loved seeing her so excited, and so happy.

'No trouble, ma'am. We've been told to get him out and parade him for you for as long as you like, then take him on to Ward Jackman's stables at Randwick.'

The colt was dark grey with a black mane and tail, and highly spirited. Either that, or he was grateful to get out of prison for a while. He reared up on his hind legs a couple of times and danced around, showing off shamelessly for his crowd of admirers. Clearly, the sidekick was an experienced groom because he handled the horse expertly.

'He will get a lighter grey as he gets older,' the groom informed them.

'I have to give Ali credit for his skill as a breeder,' Rico said after the horse had finally been reloaded and was on the way to its new home. 'That is one fabulous horse. And one fabulous gift. I must give him a call and tell him how thrilled we both are.'

He did, straight away, just catching Ali before he left the hotel to fly home. Renée spoke to him as well, thanking him and promising not to beat him at poker for at least a month.

Ali laughed. 'I am too smart a man to fall for that little bluff, Renée. I will now approach next Friday night with even more caution than usual.'

'I had no idea Ali could be so thoughtful, or generous,' Renée remarked on their drive home later that evening. 'He always comes over as rather cold.'

'Ali's not at all cold,' Rico replied. 'He's just another one of the once-bitten, twice-shy brigade.'

Renée shot him a sceptical look. 'I can't imagine the Ali I've seen eyeing up the ladies at the races ever being described as shy.'

'Perhaps shy is not the right word. Wary would fit the scenario better. Wary of opening up his heart, and his emotions. Ali was badly hurt once.'

'By a woman?'

'By a woman, and a man, and his whole family, I would guess.'

'You know a lot about him that I don't know, don't you?'

'Not a lot. Only a little. And only recently.'

'Are you going to tell me the full story?'

'Only if you promise never to tell another soul. Ali would not be happy for this to get around.'

'I promise.'

'I'll tell you after we get home. After we get into bed.'

Renée laughed. 'You have a one-track mind, Rico Mandretti. And that track always leads to the one place. Bed.'

'Actually, I have three tracks. Food, poker and sex. It's just that lately sex has taken precedence over the other two, for which you only have yourself to blame, madam. If you weren't so desirable, I wouldn't spend so much time quenching that desire.'

'I'm not really complaining,' she said, smiling.

'Mmm. Yes, I noticed that.'

'I love you, Rico Mandretti.'

He looked over at her and grinned. 'Well said, my darling. But that was only number seven. Remember, your quota for each day is ten.'

Renée laughed. 'When am I going to be let off that ridiculous quota?'

'When you get the hang of expressing your feelings for me properly.'

'I thought I did that every night.'

'Not in words. I like to hear the words.'

She laughed. 'OK. I love you. I love you. I love you. How's that?'

'Mmm. Not bad. But I think perhaps actions speak louder than words, after all.' And he put his foot down on the accelerator.

SOLD TO
THE SHEIKH

MIRANDA
LEE

PROLOGUE

HIS eyes had been on her all afternoon. Dark, beautiful eyes. Arrogant eyes. Presumptuous eyes.

Charmaine knew, soon after their introduction, that His Royal Highness, Prince Ali of Dubar, was going to make some kind of pass before the day's races were over.

From the moment she became aware of the sheikh's interest in her, Charmaine regretted accepting this particular job. The pleasure of being one of the judges for the 'Fashion-in-the-Field' competition during Flemington's spring racing carnival did not override the displeasure of being pursued by yet another international playboy.

But by the time she'd completed the job she'd been hired for—the final judging on Ladies' Day had been over by four—Charmaine had a firm handle on her irritation and began looking forward to that moment when her admirer put his mouth where his eyes had been, so to speak. Not literally, of course. The thought of such a man actually kissing her made her shudder. Nothing repelled Charmaine more than overly good-looking, overly wealthy men who thought any female they fancied could be had for the price of a dinner. Or even less.

And this one was more than overly good-looking and overly wealthy. The Arab prince and horse breeder was one of the most handsome men—and undoubtedly one of the richest—Charmaine had ever met. Taller and leaner in her opinion than most Arab princes, he was also clean-shaven and dressed that day not in traditional Arab dress, but a pale grey suit and brilliant white shirt which highlighted his richly olive skin and thick, jet-black hair. His face was as hard and lean as his body, his dark, deeply set eyes bisected by a strong nose that was underlined by a cruelly carved but not unattractive mouth.

He looked unlike any sheikh Charmaine had ever met. And she'd met a few. Supermodels met many of the world's wealthiest men, both in the course of their careers and their social lives. The rich and famous liked having the bold and the beautiful at their dos.

Being invited to be a special guest of Prince Ali in his private box at the races had not surprised Charmaine. Having the sheikh think what he had obviously been thinking about her all afternoon didn't surprise her, either. In her experience, billionaire Arab playboys had a tendency to overestimate their own irresistibility, as well as underestimate the morals of some western women. No doubt, in this sheikh's mind, supermodel equated with superslut.

Charmaine would take great delight in cutting Prince Ali down to size a little. His inflated male ego, she decided as she sensed him watching her again, needed pruning.

She was right. He *was* watching her, his eyes never leaving her as she made her way back up into the stand, burning their way through her figure-hugging silk dress, stripping her of every stitch and leaving her feeling stark naked and almost bitter over her undeniable physical assets. Not for the first time, Charmaine had a moment of burning resentment over the genes which had combined her father's height and

Nordic fairness with her mother's large blue eyes and womanly curves to produce a tall, head-turning blonde who'd first rocketed to modelling fame at the tender age of sixteen.

Nine years later, Charmaine's precocious beauty had blossomed into a more mature but still widely recognisable look with her striking figure and extra-long but perfectly straight fair hair. Hourglass shapes were supposedly out of fashion, but Charmaine's elegantly elongated version was eagerly sought after by designers, primarily because she could showcase their wares more effectively than her thinner colleagues. She was especially popular with swimwear and lingerie fashion houses and had made a small fortune being photographed in a state of dishabille.

Unfortunately, a side-effect of being seen on billboards and magazine covers in skimpy underwear and hardly there bikinis was that some men presumed her whole body was for sale, not just the image she projected. It was amazing how many wealthy men had thought they could buy her as their trophy girlfriend, or mistress, or even wife. Charmaine found this perversely amusing. Little did they know but she was the last woman on earth they would want in their beds.

The man staring at her at this moment would be severely disappointed if she agreed to whatever of those three intimate alternatives he had in mind. She was actually doing him a favour in rejecting his overtures.

With a small smile hovering on her lips, she lowered herself with an almost perverse pleasure into the seat he'd obviously kept clear for her, right next to his own and close enough for her to smell his expensive cologne and see that his black eyes were framed with the longest lashes she had ever seen on a man.

The rest of the box was empty, not even graced by the granite-faced bodyguard who'd either stood at the back or shadowed the prince everywhere he'd gone so far that afternoon. Clearly the bodyguard had encountered this particular scenario before, and knew to make himself scarce whilst his boss chatted up whatever lady his royal eye had fallen upon.

'I have been eagerly awaiting your return,' the prince said in that overly formal manner which only a British private-school education could have instilled in him. 'You have finished your judging for today?'

'Yes, thank goodness. I didn't realise how difficult a task it would be, picking the winner from so many beautifully dressed ladies.'

'If I had been the judge, there would have been only the one winner. And that is your lovely self.'

Oh, *please*, she thought wearily. Save it for a more impressed model.

Charmaine didn't give voice to her irritation. Not yet. Instead, she waited patiently for him to put his foot further into his mouth.

'I was wondering if you might be free this evening,' he went on predictably. 'I would very much like to have your company at dinner.'

What you'd like, my pompous prince, is to have *me* for dinner. Or afters.

Her eyes turned cold as his continued to smoulder.

'I'm sorry,' she returned with an upward tilt of her chin that lifted the brim of her picture hat and gave him a clearer view of her icy blue eyes, 'but I'm not free tonight.'

Her first refusal did not deter him, as she knew it wouldn't.

'Perhaps another night, then. I hear you live in Sydney. You may not be aware of the fact, but I am in Sydney every weekend.'

Actually, she hadn't been aware of much about the prince at all till today. Like a lot of sheikhs, he did not seek publicity. But a Melbourne racehorse-owning couple who were also guests of the prince today had been more than happy to fill her in when he was off presenting a trophy for one of the early races which his family had sponsored. Charmaine now knew he was in his mid-thirties and managed a huge thoroughbred stud in the upper Hunter Valley north-west of Sydney, a job he'd been doing very successfully for the last decade. Apparently, his royal family's interests in horse-racing spread far and wide and they had similar breeding establishments in Britain and America. Prince Ali, however, was solely in charge of the Australian branch.

She'd also been discreetly informed of his reputation as a ladies' man and a lover, although she wasn't sure if that had been a warning or an advertisement for her host's boudoir skills, a teaser meant to whet her appetite to experience the reality rather than the rumour. If so, his minions had been wasting their time. They'd definitely picked the wrong target today. And so had he.

She couldn't wait to enlighten him of his mistake.

'I will be back in Sydney by tomorrow afternoon,' he went on suavely, his eyes never leaving hers. 'I play cards with friends in my hotel suite every Friday night and attend the Sydney races every Saturday. To be truthful I rarely travel interstate. I only came to

Melbourne this week because I had a horse running in the Cup last Tuesday and another in the Oaks today. Unfortunately, neither of them won.'

'How sad for you,' she said without a trace of true sympathy in her voice.

He didn't seem to notice, however. Perhaps he could not conceive of the possibility that a woman would not hang on his every word, or feel anything but flattery over his obvious interest.

Charmaine almost smiled over the thought that Prince Ali of Dubar was about to have a new experience with the opposite sex. It was called...rejection.

'Would you be free to go to dinner with me this Saturday night?' he persisted, as she had known he would. 'Or do you have further commitments which will keep you down here in Melbourne?'

'No. I fly back to Sydney tomorrow morning. But I won't be free to have dinner with you that night, either. Sorry,' she added blithely.

His frown carried some confusion. 'You have another engagement?'

'No,' came her succinct reply.

His frown deepened. 'There is a lover who would object to your going out to dinner with me?' he ventured in his bewilderment. 'Or a secret patron perhaps?'

Charmaine's irritation reached new heights, prompted by both his stuffy manner of speech and his presumption that there had to be some man stopping her from going out with him. It could not possibly be that she *didn't* find him irresistible and didn't *want* to go out with him. What annoyed her most, however, was his last inference that she might already be some wealthy man's secret mistress.

'I have no lover, or *patron*, as you put it,' she replied curtly. 'The fact is, your royal highness, I will *never* be free to go out with a man like you, so please save yourself the trouble and don't ask again.'

His eyes flared momentarily with shock before going as hard as ebony, his dark brows gathering like clouds before the storm.

'A man like me,' he reiterated in clipped tones. 'Might I ask exactly what you mean by that?'

'You may ask,' she answered coolly, 'but you will not get an answer.'

'Surely I have a right to know why you have turned me down so rudely.'

Some of the fury that Charmaine had kept bottled up for years bubbled up in her throat and found voice.

'*Right?*' she snapped, and was on her feet in a flash. 'You have no *rights* where I am concerned. You asked me out. I declined. You asked me again, so I made it quite clear that any further attentions of yours are unwanted. I don't think that is rude. That is *my* right, to not be pestered by spoiled and arrogant men who have not had no said to them nearly often enough. My answer is and always will be no, Prince Ali. Hear it and take heed of it, because if you ever make contact with me again, I will have you arrested for stalking!'

She whirled and swept out of the box, swishing her way down the steps and out of the stand. She half expected him to charge after her but he didn't, for which she was grateful, because she knew if he dared lay a hand on her, she would strike him across his arrogant face. Her hands were gripping her handbag with white-knuckled intensity, but they would have loved any excuse to lash out physically at him. A verbal assault was not nearly enough to soothe her temper.

Charmaine didn't stop her angry retreat till she had reached the car park, and her car. But even as she climbed in behind the wheel of her rented blue car and started up the engine, she was still shaking inside.

The sight of the sheikh's stunned face suddenly filled her mind and she groaned. She had gone too far this time. Way too far.

Normally, she said her nos to such men much more politely and tactfully. Something about Prince Ali, however, had brought out the worst in her. She wasn't sure what. Possibly because he was armed with far too many attractions for most females to resist. Goodness, those *eyes*!

Charmaine imagined he'd been very successful in seducing then carelessly discarding many silly Australian girls in the past. Such thoughts had her blood heating in her veins again. When she went to reverse out of her spot, she did so recklessly and almost backed into another car. She must have missed it by an inch.

Giving herself a rigorous mental shake, Charmaine forcibly calmed herself before resuming her exit from the car park. The last thing she wanted was to have an accident. She had to be in Fiji on Monday, on a photo shoot for the cover of a sporting magazine.

Stop thinking about the man, she lectured herself as she drove off at a relatively sedate speed. And stop feeling guilty. Men like him don't have feelings like ordinary people. They have egos, and desires, both of which are well catered for. So he wanted you for a moment today. And he didn't get what he wanted for once. Big deal! He won't go to dinner—or to bed—

alone tonight. There will be some other foolish female to soothe his ego and satisfy his desires. You don't have to worry about him. Or even *think* about him.

But she *did* think about him, on and off for the next week. Guilt, she supposed. Being so openly rude was not part of her usual public persona. When out and about, she kept her feelings well hidden, covering the darkness within under a cloak of sweetness and light. The way she'd treated the sheikh had been quite uncharacteristic and strangely troubling.

Finally, however, all thought of him was gone, banished from her mind as she got on with her life and her life's work. Charmaine was on a mission these days, and that mission had no time for men. Certainly not men like Prince Ali of Dubar. She'd finished with that type many years before. More recently, she'd finished with the nicer types as well.

The media would be surprised to know that Charmaine, the Aussie model who'd been voted by more than one glossy rag as one of the sexiest women in the world, now lived a celibate lifestyle. There were no boyfriends or lovers any more. And definitely no secret *patrons*, she thought sneeringly. The very idea!

Of course, Charmaine had enough business nous to realise that news of her nun-like life would not do her career any good. Being seen as sexy and sexually active was part of her image. So she continued to be snapped by the media at premières and parties on the arms of handsome young men, usually hunky male models who had a sexual secret of their own, namely that they were gay. And she continued to model the most daring of clothes, often without any visible underwear.

Charmaine kept her public profile high, and her image extremely sexy. She earned more money that way. And money was the name of the game these days. It took millions, she'd found out since she started up the Friends of Kids with Cancer foundation, to fund cancer research, as well as make the lives of children already suffering from cancer more bearable, not to mention their poor families' lives. Millions and millions!

Sometimes, Charmaine surrendered to depression over the enormity of the mission she'd set herself. Could she really make a difference? But most of the time she was filled with the most dogged determination. She would do anything she could to raise money for her own very personal cause and crusade.

Anything at all!

CHAPTER ONE

OCTOBER, the second month of spring in Sydney, eleven months later…

'I have to admire your courage, Charmaine,' Renée said as she glanced up from where she'd been studying the lunch menu. 'Have you thought about what kind of man the highest bidder for your dinner-date-with-Charmaine prize next Saturday night could be?'

'A very rich man, hopefully,' Charmaine replied with a flash of pearly white teeth. 'My total target for the banquet and auction is ten million dollars.'

'He could be a right sleazebag, you know,' Renée warned. 'Or an obsessed fan.'

Charmaine smiled again over at Renée, who was not only the owner of the modelling agency she was currently contracted to, but a nice person, too. Even nicer now that she was happily married and expecting.

As much as Charmaine was cynical when it came to rich and handsome men, she had to concede that it looked as if Renée had found a one-off in Rico Mandretti. Who would have thought that the playboy king of cable-TV cooking shows would turn out to be good husband and father material?

But he had. When Charmaine met the *A Passion for Pasta* star in person for the first time the other night, he hadn't flirted with her one bit. A good sign. Not that she could be absolutely sure of Mr

Mandretti's loyalty and sincerity, she supposed. She and Renée did not mix socially so she didn't know Renée and Rico as a couple at all. Her own relationship with Renée, though friendly, was strictly business. Charmaine never confided her personal secrets or innermost feelings to the woman.

'I don't care what kind of man he is,' Charmaine said truthfully, 'as long as he pays a good price for the privilege. You don't have to worry about my safety, Renée, though it's sweet of you to care. It is clearly stipulated on the auction programme that the dinner date is to be held the following Saturday night in the By Candlelight restaurant in the Regency Hotel, which is a public place. If there's even a hint of trouble, I'll be out of there like a shot.'

Renée had no doubt she would be, too. Charmaine was one tough cookie. Much tougher than the image she projected on the catwalk and in photographs. There, she was all soft sex kitten, her looks and manner creating an unusual combination of sensuality and innocence which always fascinated men and rarely alienated women.

Renée had often tried to analyse what exactly it was about Charmaine's looks which managed this miracle. Where *did* that air of innocence come from? Perhaps from her fresh, flawless complexion or maybe her long, straight fair hair which fell in a simple curtain to her waist. Certainly not from her full, pouty mouth, almost *too* voluptuous figure or her come-to-bed blue eyes.

The contradictory nature of Charmaine's beauty was as elusive as her inner self.

Renée suspected that no one in the modelling industry knew the real Charmaine, certainly not the male models she occasionally dated. Renée knew for a fact that those particular pretty boys were just hand-bags to Charmaine, sexy accessories for public con-sumption. Real boyfriends they definitely were not.

Actually, in the time she'd known Charmaine, she'd never known her to have a real boyfriend. More than likely, the girl didn't have time for personal re-lationships these days, what with her career and her charity work. But Rico—typical testosterone-based man that he was—did not agree. He believed she'd more likely been burned by some man in the past and was going through a cynical phase. Rico had diffi-culty with the idea of any woman not really wanting a man in her life.

Maybe he was right. And maybe not. Renée was not about to risk her professional relationship with Charmaine by asking her questions about her sex life. She'd been over the moon when Australia's most suc-cessful model signed up with her agency eighteen months back.

Previously, Charmaine had employed a personal agent-manager, but he'd been fired after fiddling his expenses. If there was one thing that girl was ruthless about, it was her money. She demanded to be well paid and she didn't give an unnecessary cent away.

A good percentage of the money she earned, Renée suspected, went to Charmaine's beloved Friends of Kids with Cancer foundation, which she'd personally started up not long before she'd joined Renée's mod-elling agency. Charmaine's little sister had died of leukaemia the year before, and the tragedy had af-fected the girl greatly. After a couple of months' sab-batical from modelling to grieve the loss, she'd come out fighting to do something to help other such kids. Hence, the foundation.

When Charmaine was on the fund-raising war-path, no one was safe. She harassed everyone she met for monetary donations or their time. She'd even coerced Renée into talking Rico into being the compère at the auction on Saturday night. Renée was thankfully absolved from taking part herself because she was seven months pregnant. With twins! But she would be attending, of course.

Actually, Renée was looking forward to that evening. Charles and Dominique would be there, which meant she and Dominique could talk babies. Even Ali had promised to make an appearance, though not for the dinner, just for the auction. He hadn't been going to set his rich Arab foot in the door till Renée showed him the glossy brochure Charmaine had put together that listed all the items to be auctioned and explained where all the money raised would be going.

His change of mind had still surprised everyone at cards last Friday night; Ali kept his public appearances to a minimum because of security reasons. Perhaps the venue sold him on coming. The Regency Hotel had a reputation for keeping its famous and wealthy clientele very safe indeed.

'By the way, I managed to fill my table at last,' she told Charmaine. 'Another of my card-playing friends agreed to come. Did I mention to you I play poker with a high-rolling crowd every Friday night, in the presidential suite at the Regency Hotel no less?'

'No, you've never mentioned that. How interesting. You own racehorses as well, don't you?'

'Yes. Racing is a passion with me, I admit. So is poker. I'm a mad gambler. Anyway, you'll also be pleased to know that these other mad gamblers I play poker with are all filthy rich. Charles Brandon is one of them. You know, the brewery magnate?'

'Oh, yes, I met him at a recent première party at Fox Studios. He has a stunner of a wife, doesn't he?'

'That's the one. Dominique's her name. They're good for a few grand at the auction. Both have hearts of gold. Can't say quite the same about my number-four poker-playing partner, but he can be generous on occasion. He's—'

'Are you ready to order, ladies?' the waitress interrupted.

'Just give us a moment,' Charmaine said, and the waitress hurried off to attend to another table. The restaurant they were having lunch at was situated on one of the renovated wharves at Wooloomooloo, right on the harbour. Only a stone's throw from the city centre, it was very trendy and very popular, particularly at lunch time on a splendid spring day.

'Enough about the auction, Renée,' Charmaine said firmly. 'Back to the business at hand. *Food.* Shall we be bad and order something fattening for once?' She picked up the menu and started perusing it avidly. 'Gosh, this is all so tempting! It's been months since I had a hamburger. I hear the designer hamburgers here are out of this world. Ooh, and look, there's mango cheesecake on the dessert list. I have a penchant for cheesecake. Damn it, I'm definitely ordering that. With cream,' she finished up defiantly.

Renée laughed. She knew first-hand that models rarely ate anything really fattening, not even the naturally curvy variety like Charmaine. 'You can, if you like,' she said, 'but not me. I've already put on eight kilos with this pregnancy, and I'm told I could double that if I go full term.'

'Do you know what sex the babies are?' Charmaine asked.

Renée beamed as she always did when asked about her precious twins. 'I do indeed. A boy and a girl. Aren't I just the luckiest woman in the world?'

Till she'd married Rico, Renée had thought she'd never have children. But with her husband's love and support and the best IVF team in Australia, she was now, at the ripe old age of thirty-six, expecting not just one baby, but two! Rico was over the moon and Renée was ecstatic. Everything had gone very well so far and, other than the occasional spot of heartburn and backache, she felt as fit as a fiddle.

Charmaine smiled at her. 'I imagine you just might be. Although my mum is a pretty lucky lady. There again, she's married to my dad, so perhaps I'm biased.'

Renée absorbed this piece of information with some surprise. Charmaine never talked about her family. For some reason, Renée had assumed she was estranged from them these days. Clearly, she was mistaken. Maybe they'd just lost touch a bit. Charmaine's life was a hectic one, what with the demands on her time for her career, and now her charity work.

Renée knew from earlier Press articles about Charmaine that her parents were country folk who ran a cotton farm out west of the Great Divide, pretty well in the middle of nowhere. Their nearest town only had one garage, one hotel and one general store. From the time she was fifteen, Charmaine had used to work behind the counter of that store at the weekend, and during lulls—which was probably most of the time—

filled in her time reading magazines about models and dreaming of one day being one herself. At fifteen and a half, she'd entered her photograph into a teen magazine's cover-girl competition, and won. By sixteen she was strutting her stuff on the catwalk in Sydney during Australia's fashion week.

Renée had been a model herself back then and recalled how peeved all the other older models were when this inexperienced teenage upstart carrying far too many curves had upstaged them. But she'd been an instant hit, especially with the designers. On Charmaine's tall yet shapely figure, all clothes looked fabulous, and so sexy. When Charmaine had to go home for a while with a nasty case of glandular fever the other models had breathed a sigh of relief. But she'd returned to Sydney the following year and taken up right where she left off.

By then eighteen, a slightly slimmer but more mature-looking Charmaine had been simply stunning. Ravishing was how she was described by the fashion Press. Ravishing and ready to rule the modelling world. She hadn't quite done that, but she was soon right up there with the best of them, and Renée's agency now had a piece of that success.

'Do you take after your mother or your father?' Renée asked, her curiosity aroused.

'Both, in looks. But neither in character. Mum's a sweetie and Dad's an old softie. I might act soft and sweet, but underneath I'm a total bitch,' she said, then laughed. 'But then, you already know that, don't you?'

'Not at all,' Renée replied, astounded. 'You play hardball in business matters but that's not the same. I've met plenty of total bitches in my life and trust me, Charmaine, you are certainly not one of them. A total bitch wouldn't work so hard for charity for starters, I can tell you.'

'Aah, but that's my only Achilles heel,' Charmaine said, looking sad and wistful for a moment. 'Kids with cancer. Poor little mites. I can bear it when life is unspeakably cruel and unfair to adults. But not children. They do not deserve that fate. Not when they've done *nothing* to cause it.'

She swallowed, then gritted her teeth.

You're not going to cry, are you? Crying never achieves a thing. Crying is for babies, and the broken-hearted. You're hardly a baby, and your heart isn't broken any more, Charmaine. It's been superglued back together and nothing will ever break it again.

She reached for the complimentary glass of water that sat on the café table and sipped it till she had herself totally under control. Then she put the glass down and smiled at the woman opposite her, who had a worried frown on her lovely face.

'Sorry,' she said. 'I get emotional when I talk about kids with cancer.'

'There's no need to be sorry. I think what you feel is very admirable. I can understand it entirely.'

Charmaine refrained from laughing at this statement. How could Renée possibly understand? No one could understand who hadn't been through it themselves. Watched a child suffer and die. A sweet, innocent little child.

But she probably meant well.

How old *was* Renée? Charmaine wondered. Early thirties? Older? Must be a bit older, though she still looked marvellous. Some women glowed when they were pregnant. Others looked drawn and dreary. Renée was clearly the glowing kind.

The waitress materialised at their table again.

'Ready to order yet, ladies?' she asked chirpily.

'Absolutely,' Charmaine replied and ordered the Caribbean-style beef-burger with fries and salad, mango cheesecake with cream, and a cappuccino.

When Renée stared at her, she laughed. 'Don't worry. I won't eat any dinner tonight and I'll punish myself in the gym tomorrow.' As she always did. Every single day.

But then her whole life was now a punishment, wasn't it? For her sins, especially that one really wicked sin, the one she could never forgive herself for, the one she would never forget.

'You'll have to if you hope to fit into that dress you're planning to wear on Saturday night,' Renée pointed out. 'As it is, it looks as if you've been sewn into it.'

'Oh, darn, you're right. I'd momentarily forgotten about that.' She sighed and looked up at the patiently waiting waitress. 'Could I change my order to something less fattening, like a lettuce leaf *au naturel*?'

The waitress grinned. 'I'm so glad you have to watch what you eat, too. If I thought you could look the way you do without suffering even a little, it would kill me.'

'Then do not despair,' Charmaine said drily. 'I suffer more than a little. I suffer a lot every single day.' And then some! 'OK, give me the fish of the day, grilled, with a side salad. No dressing. No dessert. And black coffee to follow. How's that?' she asked Renée.

Renée laughed. 'Perfect. I'll have the same.'

CHAPTER TWO

THE ballroom at the Regency Hotel was a popular Sydney venue for top-drawer functions. Its spectacular Versailles-inspired walls had borne witness to many society balls, awards nights, fashion extravaganzas, product launches, company Christmas parties and, yes, quite a few charity benefits. Its ornate, high-domed ceilings and huge chandeliers had looked down upon the rich and famous on many occasions as they gathered in their finery to celebrate or support whatever cause had brought them together.

Tonight's cause was one which never failed to touch even the most hard-hearted. Kids with cancer. Charmaine knew that for a fact. And she'd exploited it shamelessly as she'd put together this, her first charity banquet and auction.

But it had been one hell of a lot of work, taking up every spare moment of her time for the last six months. Her social life—what there was of it these days—had suffered accordingly. Even her career had suffered, with her refusing any assignments that would take her overseas for more than a few days.

But it was all worth it to see the fantastic turn-out tonight. Every table filled, and all by people who could well afford the hefty thousand-dollar price tag on each ticket. For which they would get a moderately nice sit-down dinner which probably cost less than fifty dollars a head to produce.

Not that the Friends of Kids with Cancer foundation had to pay anything at all for the catering. The relatively new owner of the Regency Hotel had been persuaded to donate the three hundred dinners required, plus all the drinks and the ballroom itself. Charmaine had discovered that Max Richmond's brother had died of cancer when quite a young man, an unfortunate tragedy which she'd been quick to capitalise on.

Ah, yes, there wasn't anything she wouldn't stoop to to raise money to reach tonight's ten-million-dollar target, including going without food of any appreciable kind both yesterday and today so that she could fit into the dress she was wearing as co-host of tonight's auction, a dress that almost defied description.

Wicked was the word that sprang to mind.

How she came to be wearing this particular dress was intriguing. She'd gone to see the head of Campbell Jewels at her home, as she'd personally visited all of the CEOs of Sydney's top companies, begging and bulldozing them for donations for her auction. Most accommodated her in some way. Celeste Campbell had been very amenable, donating a lovely selection of jewellery. She'd also had that no-nonsense, straight-down-the-line manner that Charmaine admired in a woman. Charmaine had warmed to her immediately, and vice versa.

When Celeste found out the charity auction was being held in the Regency ballroom, she'd related to Charmaine the story of another auction that had been held there a decade earlier, not long before Charmaine herself had first come to Sydney. Apparently there'd been a sit-down banquet, like tonight, followed by the auction of the famed black opal called the Heart of Fire, which was now in the Australian Museum.

Charmaine had been startled to learn that during the course of the evening there'd been an attempted robbery *and* a shooting. Charmaine had been fascinated by the woman's story, then totally blown away when Celeste showed her the dress she'd worn that night. It was one of the most provocative evening gowns Charmaine had ever seen.

When Celeste proclaimed she was too old to wear such a dress these days, Charmaine had swiftly jumped in and asked if she could borrow it to wear to the charity auction. She'd known straight away that it was just the thing to get some rich fool to bid a ridiculous price for a dinner date with her. Celeste Campbell had refused—and given her the gown instead! Charmaine had been thrilled.

And now here she was, wearing it, but not feeling quite so confident, or so cocky. Her stomach was doing more somersaults than it had on her very first modelling assignment. Yet she was never nervous these days, no matter how much flesh she was flaunting.

Not that Celeste Campbell's dress showed all that much bare flesh. Its wickedness was far more subtle than that.

There was nothing at all risqué about its basic full-length strapless style, except perhaps that her breasts were having difficulty being confined in the tightly boned bodice, which was two sizes too small for her. Even that little problem was hidden to some degree by the layer of sheer chiffon stretched over the satin underdress, the chiffon reaching high up around the neck and running tightly down her arms to her wrists.

It was the skin tone of both the satin material and the chiffon, plus the selected beading on the front and back of the gown that was wicked, because it created the illusion of her wearing not a ballgown, but a very skimpy and exotic costume. From even a short distance, the skin-coloured material took on the appearance of bare flesh, with just the shimmering pattern made by the gold beads standing out.

At a glance, front-on, it looked as though the beads were stuck to her nude body in the shape of a bikini. Side-on, where there were no beads, she looked naked. Viewed from the back, the sight was possibly even more provocative, with nothing but skin-coloured chiffon to her waist, a triangular smattering of beads across her behind and a split up the middle back seam to the very top of her thighs. At least the split meant she could walk with her usual long-legged stride instead of tottering around.

Because walk she had to do, right out onto the cat-walk that had been put together for the fashion parade conducted earlier during the dinner. The long, well-lit walkway jutted out from the middle of the stage, bisecting the ballroom and giving the occupants of all the tables a top view, especially the ones seated close by. In rehearsal the other night Charmaine had told Rico she would parade out there whilst he auctioned off her dinner-date prize, an idea that hadn't seemed all that bold at the time, possibly because she'd been wearing jeans.

This outrageous dress, however, had sent her usual boldness packing. Charmaine had been bothered by it all evening. Fortunately, during the dinner she hadn't eaten, she'd been sitting down. Seated, the dress was quite modest.

But she was no longer seated. She was up on the ballroom stage, peering through the heavy, wine-coloured stage curtain at the huge crowd down below and trying to control this alien fear that she was about to make the most shameless display of herself.

What on earth was wrong with her? She wasn't usually like this. Usually, she didn't give a damn how little she wore or if people stared at her, especially the men.

A scornful anger quickly replaced these highly uncharacteristic qualms. Let them think what they liked. She really didn't care as long as one of them coughed up with a big fat cheque for her foundation.

Feeling marginally better, she glanced at her slender gold wrist-watch and was thinking it was high time for Rico to make an appearance to begin the auction when a very male whistle split the air behind her. She whirled and the man himself was standing there, smiling a wry smile.

'That is *some* dress, Charmaine. Are you sure you won't be arrested for wearing it?'

'I've worn less,' she retorted, nervous tension making her snappy.

'Yes, but in this case more is worse.'

'Do try not to leer, Rico.'

'I never leer.'

'No,' she conceded with a sigh. 'No, you don't. Sorry. Actually, you're much nicer than I thought you'd be, for someone who's so darned good-looking.' Which he was. Tall, dark and handsome. But not the kind of tall, dark and handsome that she'd once found irresistible. Big and macho were not her preference. She'd always preferred the leaner, more elegant kind of man.

'Thank you,' Rico replied. 'I think.' Straightening

his bow-tie, he scooped in a deep breath. 'So! Shall we get this show on the road?'

Again, nerves rushed in, making her want to turn tail and run. Which in turn brought forth a redeeming rush of defiance. 'Too right,' she said. 'It's time to make those poor kids some serious bucks.'

'Amen to that!' Rico agreed.

The auction started off well, at that point the target of ten million looking within easy reach. But the economic times were tough and around halfway the bids began to lag. No matter how much Rico cajoled, by the time the auction had only two prizes left, the amount raised was just under seven million. Charmaine sighed her disappointment. The island holiday Rico was about to offer might make fifty grand. But that would still leave a shortfall of nearly three million. Even if she went out onto the catwalk stark naked, no man here was going to bid that much just to have dinner with her.

'We're not even going to make *seven* million,' she groaned after Rico sold the holiday for a paltry thirty thousand.

'No, it doesn't look like it,' Rico replied quietly, having placed his hands over the microphone. 'Perhaps you should have got yourself a real auctioneer.'

'Don't be ridiculous. You've been marvellous. It's not you. It's the times. People are getting tight. We've really done quite well. My hopes were too high. Come on, let's see what we can get for my pathetic prize.'

'Now who's being ridiculous? A dinner date with you is anything but a pathetic prize, Charmaine.'

'Flatterer. Just get on with it. I want to get this

torment over and done with.' A telling comment, but
true. She'd never felt this reluctant to sell herself.

'Now, ladies and gentlemen, on to the last prize of
the evening,' Rico began again, reviving that Italian
accent which seemed to come and go at will. 'Our
lovely hostess, Charmaine, one of Australia's top supermodels, is offering a dinner date with herself right
here in the Regency's own fabulous By Candlelight
restaurant, to be taken next Saturday night. This is a
fabulous prize to end this evening with and one which
I'm sure will command a top offer.'

He flashed Charmaine an encouraging smile then
muttered, 'Off you go, sweetheart,' under his breath.
'Strut your stuff.'

Charmaine rolled her eyes at him, but off she went,
undulating her way down the catwalk, doing her best
to smile through gritted teeth, well aware that all eyes
in that ballroom were glued to her body. Not that *she*
could see much. The footlights that bathed her in light
threw the rest of the ballroom into relative darkness.
She could see silhouetted shapes but no details, no
actual eyes.

Yet she could feel them stripping her in a way that
she had never felt before. It had to be because of this
darned dress. What else *could* it be?

'Might I remind you that Charmaine was recently
voted the sexiest woman in Australia by a national
magazine?' Rico raved on. 'You can see for yourself
that that tag is no exaggeration. I would imagine having a private dinner with such a stunning creature
would be some man's dream come true. So come
along, gentlemen, make your bids for this once-in-a-
lifetime privilege!'

Charmaine almost winced with embarrassment.

Dear heavens, now she felt as though she was on the auction block of some white slaver, and that it was her body being sold, not just a few hours of her companionship.

But what the heck, she reminded herself, if the foundation ended up with a good wad of money? Still, she thanked the lord that she'd banned the Press from this do. The last thing she could stand at this moment would be being besieged with camera flashes, not to mention the prospect of seeing photographs of herself in this dress splashed all across the Sunday papers tomorrow morning, accompanied by some trashy story.

With the comfort of that last thought, she plastered a more sultry smile on her face and sashayed sexily down to the end of the catwalk, where she stood motionless for a few moments, her hands on her hips in a saucy attitude. Then slowly, seductively, she turned, the audience gasping at the sight of her back view.

Her eyes connected with Rico's and he grinned a rather lascivious grin. 'Don't be coy, now,' he urged the audience. 'If I were a single man myself, I would put my hat in the ring, I can tell you. But I'm out of the market, as my lovely wife right there will attest.'

He nodded down towards a table on Charmaine's immediate left. She automatically glanced down, then froze.

Later that night, long after this ghastly moment was well behind her, Charmaine would be grateful she hadn't been moving at the time, for she would surely have stumbled. Maybe even fallen. As it was, she still felt as if the floor had opened up under her.

At least now she knew why she'd been feeling so

aware of male eyes on her. Because *this* pair of eyes had been hiding amongst the others.

Dark, beautiful eyes. Hard eyes. Dangerous eyes.

Prince Ali of Dubar, sitting right there at Renée's table, looking dashing and debonair in a black dinner suit and gazing up at her with a coolly arrogant air.

Shock galvanised Charmaine's brain as well as her body, several blank moments passing before she regained her composure and could even *try* to put two and two together. What on earth was this man doing sitting at Renée's table? Surely they couldn't be *friends*!

This unlikely possibility had barely surfaced before things which had seemed unimportant or irrelevant at the time flashed back into her mind. The prince himself, mentioning last year that he spent every weekend in Sydney going to the races and playing cards with friends. And then Renée the other day at lunch, talking about the high-rollers she played poker with every Friday night in this very hotel, in one of the presidential suites.

Who else could afford a presidential suite but a president, or a rock-star, or an oil-rich sheikh? The worst possible scenario of that little trio, of course, was the sheikh, especially one whom she'd derided and belittled and rejected and who was here tonight for one thing and one thing only. To make her eat her words that she would never go to dinner with a man like him.

Prince Ali of Dubar was undoubtedly going to be the highest bidder for the dinner date with her. Why else would he have come? He hadn't bid for anything else so far tonight. She would have noticed if he had, a spotlight always briefly being shone on the successful bidder after an item was knocked down to them.

No, it would not be some total stranger sitting opposite her at dinner next Saturday night. It would be this man, whose pride she had severely dented last year. Now it was his turn to humiliate her, by forcing her to dine with him for several hours and endure not only his company, but also his none-too-subtle coveting of her body.

The impact of this realisation sent bile rising in Charmaine's throat. Pride demanded she would not submit herself to such a mortifying situation. But pride also demanded she conduct herself with her usual self-contained, I'm-not-afraid-of-anything-or-any-man demeanour. After all, even if the sheikh was the successful bidder—and every cell in her brain shouted to her that he would be—what could he really do to her in a public restaurant, across the table? Proposition her once more? Try to seduce her with his charm?

This last idea was laughable.

No. Let him have his pathetic little moment of triumph.

Quite deliberately, she smiled straight at him, challenging him boldly with her eyes and her mouth.

Come on, sucker. Make your bid. See if I care.

His dark eyes narrowed a little at her smile, then slowly raked over her from head to toe, as though assessing if she was worth bidding for. For a split-second, Charmaine worried that he might *not* bid. Maybe he'd come to dent her pride *that* way.

But even as she was besieged by a thousand ambivalent emotions over this possibility, his royal mouth opened.

'Five million dollars,' he said firmly, and she gasped. She couldn't help it. Neither could the rest of the people there.

Even Rico sucked in sharply. 'Wow! That is some bid. Ladies and gentlemen, Prince Ali of Dubar has bid five million dollars for the privilege of a dinner date with our lovely Charmaine. Somehow, I don't think there will be any better offers, but if there is some intrepid gentleman out there willing to top his royal highness's offer, will he speak up now or forever hold his peace?'

Charmaine winced at Rico's words, which were reminiscent of a wedding ceremony. Rather ironic, given this was as far from a romantic encounter as one could get. His royal highness just wanted the opportunity to make her eat humble pie, and he was willing to spend an exorbitant amount of money to do so.

'No more offers? In that case…*sold* to His Royal Highness, Prince Ali of Dubar!' Rico brought the gavel down on the rostrum with a loud thump that reverberated right through Charmaine.

Everyone in the ballroom started clapping, more so when the red arrow on the huge target metre displayed at the side of the stage was lifted by its attendant to twelve million dollars. Charmaine was forced to keep smiling when in fact she'd rather have been screaming, preferably at the man whose black eyes remained locked onto hers, his superior air evoking in her a burning desire to tell him that no man would *ever* own even a small piece of her, not even her time!

But, of course, that wish was to remain unrequited. No way could she turn down a five-million-dollar windfall for a cause that meant more than her silly pride. On top of that, no way in the wide world would Charmaine let this arrogant devil see how rattled and angry she was. To show anger was to show she cared. She resolved then and there to remain impeccably polite to him next Saturday night. There would be no further outbursts of temper. No rude remarks. No attempts to cut him down to size.

Given this was her intention, she really could not afford to stay standing where she was any longer. The way he kept looking at her was not conducive to ongoing politeness.

Lord knows how I'm going to control myself when I'm alone with him, Charmaine worried as she made her way—to further clapping—off the catwalk.

'I still can't believe it,' Rico said to her after he'd wrapped up the auction and clicked off the microphone. 'Good old Ali, bidding five mil just to have dinner with you. The man must have more money than sense. No offence meant, Charmaine. But even you must agree that was over-the-top.'

Charmaine frowned at Rico's familiar remarks before realising that of course *he* had to be well acquainted with the prince as well, not just Renée.

'You sound as if you're really old friends,' came her careful comment. As much as she despised herself for it, she couldn't help being curious about the man who'd just paid five million dollars to have dinner with her.

'We are,' Rico admitted. 'Been playing cards together every Friday night for nearly six years now. Been partners in a few racehorses over the years as well. Ali's a great bloke. You'll like him.'

Charmaine's top lip curled before she could stop it. But then she decided not to be a total hypocrite. There was only so far she was prepared to carry pretence, and in private was not one of them.

'The prince and I have met once before,' she confessed curtly. 'I didn't like him then and I don't like him now.'

Rico looked startled. 'You've met before? Where?'

'At the Melbourne Cup carnival last year. I was one of the fashion judges there on Ladies' Day. To put it bluntly, your royal friend hit on me.'

'*And?*'

'What do you mean, *and*? And *nothing*! I told you. I didn't like him.'

'That surprises me. Women usually do.'

'Maybe that's why I didn't like him,' she snapped. 'Look, it's immaterial whether I like him or not. He's bought my company over dinner for a few hours and I'll honour that. But if you're talking to your Arab friend, then I suggest you warn him that paying five million dollars gives him no more privileges—or rights—than he had by paying for my lunch the last time. Yes, tell him that, Rico. Oh, and tell him I will be at the By Candlelight restaurant promptly at seven next Saturday night, but he is not to attempt to contact me before that. I would be very annoyed if my private and unlisted phone number somehow found its way into his royal highness's hands. *Comprenez-vous?*'

'I get the picture. I just wonder if you do.'

'Meaning?'

'Meaning Ali is not given to flights of fancy. After what you've just told me, I suspect he came here tonight specifically to bid for that dinner with you, money being no object. Which leads me to believe that he must be somewhat smitten with you. If so, then I doubt your supposed disliking him at first sight will prove to be any more than a minor hurdle.'

Charmaine bristled. 'Is that some kind of warning?'

'I suppose so. Look, if you really don't like him, then watch yourself. Ali is not a man to be toyed with.'

'I have *never* toyed with him.'

'Come, now, Charmaine. I saw the way you were smiling down at him just now and that was not the smile of an uninterested woman.'

Heat zoomed into Charmaine's cheeks. 'You don't understand. I was just…just…'

'Taunting him?'

She shrugged irritably. 'In a way.'

'Don't,' came his sharp rebuke. 'That's not the way to behave with a man like Ali. Such behaviour could make him…dangerous.'

Her eyes widened. '*Dangerous?* In what way?'

Rico shook his head. 'Look, I'll speak to him. Make sure he understands how the land lies. I'm sure he'll respect your wishes if he believes you're genuinely not interested. You are definitely not interested?'

'Oh, please. Spare me from having to deal with a spoiled sheikh who harbours Hollywood fantasies over his irresistibility to women.'

'Maybe he has cause to harbour them.'

She could not contain a scornful laugh. 'The only thing Prince Ali of Dubar has going for him with me is the size of his wallet. And then only if he opens it for the foundation. You tell him that, Rico. Now I really must go and take off this infernal dress!'

A famous saying came to Rico's mind as he watched Charmaine flounce off, her glamorous drop earrings swinging sexily around her shoulders and her long fair hair swishing back and forth across her nearly naked back.

'The lady doth protest too much, methinks.'

CHAPTER THREE

SHORTLY before six on the following Saturday afternoon, Charmaine climbed out from behind the wheel of her nondescript white sedan, collected her overnight bag from the back seat, handed the car keys to the valet parking attendant and proceeded into the arcade-style foyer of the Regency Hotel, all without having to tolerate the harassing presence of the paparazzi.

Experience had taught the supermodel several ways to avoid them. If possible, she arrived early for publicised events, often in disguise. Unfortunately, her dinner date tonight with the sheikh was now a well-publicised event, courtesy of one pesky female journalist who'd been at the auction and written it up the following day, the main focus of her article being the astonishing amount paid by Prince Ali of Dubar for a dinner date with *our* Charmaine. Typically, the find-a-sexual-angle journo made it all sound impossibly romantic.

Charmaine had quickly regretted announcing at the auction when and where the dinner would take place. That had been a mistake. But no way was she going to contact the prince and change the arrangements. She did, however, contact the owner of the Regency again and was assured by Mr Richmond that no Press would bother either her or his most esteemed guest from Dubar over dinner. He promised heightened se-

39

curity at both the hotel entrance and complete privacy in the restaurant.

Charmaine expressed her gratitude but still booked a room in the hotel so that she could arrive early and dress there, as well as stay the night. That way she could slip out the following morning in her own good time.

Now here she was, blessedly anonymous as she walked up to the reception desk in her nondescript brown wig and wraparound sunglasses, not having had to tolerate cameras being shoved in her face and having questions shouted at her. What a relief! She might have lost her cool if there'd been reporters and photographers hanging around the hotel. It had been a very long week and her nerves were on a knife-edge today.

Charmaine glanced at her watch as she rode the lift up to the second floor. Less than an hour to go. But time enough for her to get ready. She'd washed and blow-dried her hair earlier that afternoon. *And* done her nails. All she had left to do was change her clothes and put on some make-up and earrings. None of those preparations would take much time. Charmaine had decided to dress down for this occasion.

If the sheikh thought she'd show up in something reminiscent of last Saturday night then he was in for a surprise. There would be no flesh on show tonight. Nothing for those predatory eyes to feast upon.

At precisely five minutes to seven, she was again in the lift, her stone-washed jeans now replaced by loose-fitting black crêpe evening trousers and a bronze silk Chinese-style tunic top that skimmed her figure and minimised its hourglass curves. Her hair was brushed straight back from her face and fell in a dead straight curtain to her waist. Her face had hardly any make-up at all. Just a fine layer of foundation, a touch of blue eyeshadow, a few strokes of mascara and some shiny bronze lipstick that matched the colour of her nails. Small diamond studs winked at her ear-lobes, in marked contrast to the sexy shoulder-length drops she'd worn for the auction.

The irony was that with a natural beauty like Charmaine, often less was more. But she was unaware of this fact. Being used to wearing much more make-up, especially for photo shoots and her work on the catwalk, she thought she looked as plain as she could. If only she knew how breathtakingly beautiful—and intriguingly innocent—she looked as she emerged on the mezzanine floor and made her way down the marble-floored corridor to the By Candlelight restaurant.

The *maître d'*, a tall bald-headed man with a thin moustache and intelligent grey eyes, smiled at her from behind his podium-style station.

'Mademoiselle Charmaine,' he said with a French accent, which might or might not have been genuine. The number of *maître d'*'s in Sydney restaurants with French accents seemed excessive in Charmaine's opinion. 'Such a delight to have you in our restaurant tonight. His highness has already arrived. I will take you straight to him.'

Charmaine dutifully followed in his wake as he made his way past the mostly empty tables towards the back of the restaurant. Considering the relatively early hour of their 'date', Charmaine was surprised that the prince had already arrived. She would have thought that royalty would always be a little late for engagements of the social kind.

But of course this wasn't a social occasion, she reminded herself ruefully. It was one of vengeance. Naturally, his royal highness wouldn't want to miss a moment of her humiliation.

This last realisation rescued her from any inner resentment at being here at all and sent a small smile playing around her lips. If the sheikh thought he could belittle her tonight, then he was in for more than one surprise. He had no idea what he was dealing with. No idea at all!

The alcove she was taken to was totally and utterly private, a small square-shaped room tucked away in a discreet corner. There was an open archway leading into it, but even this was flanked by huge potted palms that added to its sense of privacy. The walls of the alcove—and even the ceiling—were painted black, the darkness only minimally alleviated by several low-voltage recessed lights. There was no furniture except for the table, which was round and intimately sized, and covered with the same white linen tablecloth as the tables she'd just passed. The wine-coloured candle that graced the glass centrepiece on the table was low, perhaps because the people who normally sought to eat here wanted nothing to spoil their view of each other's face and eyes.

This area had undoubtedly been designed with lovers in mind, a real love-nest for those who wanted to keep prying eyes away whilst they banqueted on the best food and wine and whispered sweet nothings to each other. Tycoons would dine here with their mistresses, and celebrities with their latest live-in lovers.

Charmaine doubted this table would have borne witness to too many dinners like the one that would be served on its elegance surface tonight. Though possibly it was the *diners* more than the dinner who would be different.

When she'd first walked towards the dimly lit alcove, Charmaine could hardly see the sheikh sitting on the far side of the table, his dark clothes and dark colouring making him melt into the black-walled background. But, once she had passed under the archway and her eyes grew accustomed to the dimmer light, he emerged from the shadow, first his face, and then the rest of him.

Still no traditional Arab dress for him, she noted. He looked like a typical Western playboy, dressed expensively but rather casually in an exquisite black lounge suit and a black silk collarless shirt.

Did her heart beat a little faster at the sight of his handsome elegance? Or was her adrenalin surge simply the result of their next face-to-face confrontation finally being at hand?

Soldiers on the verge of going into battle would feel like this, she reasoned. There would always be a type of excitement alongside the fear.

Fear? Now, that was an odd thought. She had nothing to *fear* from this man.

Or did she?

Rico had said something about his being dangerous. And Rico was no fool. What kind of danger was he talking about? OK, so her date tonight was an Arab sheikh with perhaps more primitive ways in treating women he fancied than most men of the Western world. And yes, he still fancied her, despite what she was wearing tonight. His eyes were like hot coals on her face and body.

So much for her dressing down for the occasion, came the irritable thought. If anything, he seemed to desire her even more without her curves being on display.

But surely, that was all he could realistically do. *Desire* her. As private as this alcove was, it was hardly conducive to his ravishing her during tonight's dinner date, especially without her consent. One little scream and people would come running.

No, she had nothing to fear about this evening, except her own silly behaviour. Just keep your temper, she lectured herself. And your cool. Then, in three hours' time, you can leave and never see this infernal man ever again.

His rising from his chair as she approached the table startled her. She hadn't expected such a gentlemanly gesture from him.

'Good evening, Charmaine,' he said with a slight nod of his head of perfectly groomed black hair. Quite wavy on top, it was. And thick and clean and shining. The kind of hair that would be a joy to touch.

Charmaine was taken aback by this most alien thought. She never found joy any more in touching any part of any man. And here she was, thinking about running her fingers through *this* man's hair. The very idea!

'You look…lovely,' he added, that dark, desire-filled gaze of his never leaving her face.

Charmaine was grateful that the *maître d'* chose that moment to pull out her chair so she could occupy herself sitting down rather than answering the sheikh. He sat down also, but his eyes stayed glued to her with merciless intent.

The *maître d'* made a production of picking up her linen serviette, shaking it out of its creative folds then placing it across her lap before making his way round the table and doing the same for the sheikh.

'Your personal waiter for this evening will be along shortly, Your Highness,' he said with a deferential bow towards the prince before hurrying off, leaving them temporarily alone.

For the life of her, Charmaine could not think of a thing to say. She was still rattled by wanting to touch the sheikh's hair. A few seconds of awkward silence ticked away and she longed for their waiter to appear.

Fortunately, he did, a slim, tanned young man with graceful hands and no French accent. He handed them both a menu, ran through the chef's specials of the night, then asked them if they would like to order a pre-dinner drink, or possibly a bottle of wine from the wine list, which he placed beside the sheikh's right elbow.

'Bring me mineral water,' the prince ordered after the briefest of glances. 'Sparkling. I do not drink alcohol of any kind,' he added, for her benefit, it seemed. 'But I do not expect you to follow suit. Please…order anything that you like.' And he handed her the wine list across the table.

'I don't drink alcohol, either,' she replied, and handed it back to the waiter. 'So fizzy water would be fine for me, too.' Whereupon she threw a sweet smile over at her nemesis, satisfied that she'd just sunk any plans he had to get her sloshed and have his wicked way with her in the presidential suite afterwards.

The waiter hurried off to do their bidding, leaving them alone again.

'You never drink alcohol?' the prince asked, sounding more curious than disappointed.

'No.'

'Why is that?'

'Oh, many reasons,' she replied in an airy fashion.

He smiled a wry smile that softened the harsh lines of his mouth. 'Which you don't intend to tell me.'

'How perceptive of you.' She maintained a lightness in her voice but in her lap her hands gripped her serviette as a drowning man would a life-jacket. This man assuredly brought out the worst in her. It was definitely because of the way he looked at her. So…covetously. And at the same time so damned confidently, as though he was already picturing her in his bed. How she would have loved an excuse to slap his supercilious face, to see that polished teak cheek of his glow red with the mark of her handprint.

'You are resenting being here with me tonight.'

It was an effort not to show surprise over his being able to read her so well. Though perhaps his very correct conclusion was not evidence of any great insight on his part. It wouldn't take much brains to realise she'd be far from happy at the situation she found herself in.

'Not at all,' she said, forcing a patently false smile through her clenched jaw. 'My foundation is five million dollars richer because of tonight. How can I possibly resent that?'

'The last time we met, you vowed you'd never have dinner with me,' he reminded her, his eyes watchful.

Her shrug was supremely indifferent. 'That was then and this is now. I discovered long ago that life can throw you some unexpected curves; I find that it's far better to go with the flow rather than fight them.'

His drily amused smile annoyed her. Because she could not read its meaning.

'You are perfectly correct there, my dear Charmaine. Do you mind my calling you Charmaine? No one seemed to know your second name so I don't know what else to call you.'

'Charmaine is fine.'

She was tempted to add that he could leave out the 'my dear' bit, but she knew if she started being persnickety, she would never stop.

'You must call me Ali,' he pronounced.

Now, *that* was expecting too much. 'I don't think so, Your Highness,' she said crisply. 'That is far too intimate an address. *Everyone* calls me Charmaine, whereas I am sure not everyone calls you Ali. Probably only your relatives and your closest of friends, of which I am neither.'

His eyes blazed momentarily, giving her a glimpse of what Rico had meant by his being dangerous. The man had a right royal temper when crossed. But then, so did she.

'Why are you so determined to be rude to me?' he demanded to know.

'Actually, I am determined to be anything *but* rude this evening,' she countered. 'Sometimes, we Australians are mistakenly thought of as rude when in fact we are just trying to be honest. Calling a spade a spade, so to speak. You bought a dinner date with me tonight, Your Highness. You did not buy anything else. I told Rico to make that perfectly clear to you this week. Did he forget to relay my message?'

'No. Enrico told me exactly what you said. And I took careful note. Perhaps it was foolish of me but I hoped you might be persuaded to put aside your ir-

rational dislike. I was looking forward to the opportunity to show you that I am not... What was it you
called me last year? A spoiled and arrogant man who
had not had no said to him often enough?'

'That sounds about right,' she replied whilst thinking that it was *exactly* what she'd flung at him that
day. Clearly, each insulting word had bitten deep into
the prince's ego and he meant to exact retribution. All
that bulldust about his hoping to show her he was
really a good bloke was just that. Bulldust! The only
reason she was here tonight was because he *was*
spoiled and arrogant, and would *not* take no for an
answer.

The waiter arrived with their mineral water, at the
same time enquiring if they wanted to order their
meals yet. The prince peremptorily waved him away,
saying they had not had time to study the menu and
not to return for a good ten minutes.

The prospect of ten more minutes of this kind of
banter threatened Charmaine's resolve to remain icily
polite, so she swept up the menu and used it as a
barrier between them.

But blocking that smouldering gaze did not block
the memory of it, or the way it made her feel. As if
she was a specimen under a microscope.

Charmaine tried to focus on the food on offer, but
it was a futile activity. Her mind had other ideas, giving rise to a fanciful image of herself as a beautiful
and rare butterfly, with the prince an obsessed collector of beautiful and rare butterflies.

In her mind's eye, she could see him sitting at a
table in a lush garden somewhere and watching her
flit from flower to flower. Watching and waiting, oh,
so patiently. She did not see the net he had hidden

by his chair and when she foolishly flew too close he struck, and suddenly she was captured, unable to escape her fate—which was to be his, either dead or alive.

Charmaine came back to reality with a jolt, her heartbeat racing with alarm. Yet that was crazy, to be alarmed by a daydream, a fanciful concoction of her own imagination. And yet alarm was exactly what she was suddenly feeling.

Tightening her grip on the rather large leather-bound menu, she lowered it slowly, only to find those eyes still watching her as she'd imagined the butterfly collector had watched the butterfly.

The panic that rose in her chest made her angry.

'I have no idea what to order,' she said brusquely, and snapped the menu shut. 'Would you mind choosing something for me, Your Highness? I'm not a fussy eater so you can't really go wrong. I eat almost anything. Except prunes. I hate prunes.'

'You don't drink and you eat almost anything. A most unusual Western woman,' he muttered, but at least his eyes dropped to the menu, and away from her.

The release in tension this afforded Charmaine was amazing. She actually sighed with it and leant back into her chair.

'You sound tired,' he remarked, but thankfully without looking up.

'I've had a very busy week.'

'With your charity work, or modelling?' he asked, again without looking up.

'I've been doing a lengthy photo shoot for the Femme Fatale company. People think that being a model is glamorous work, but it's really very exhausting, getting dressed and undressed all the time and being prodded and pushed into a hundred different poses.' How much easier it was to chat away whilst those unsettling eyes were occupied elsewhere. 'Still, I suppose I shouldn't complain. At least with Femme Fatale, I get to keep all the lovely lingerie used in the shoot.'

Now those incredible eyes rose again, and once again she felt as firmly pinned as any poor butterfly on a collector's wall.

Charmaine had to concede that she'd never come across eyes so powerful, or so wickedly hypnotic. She would imagine that a normal woman would find it difficult not to fall under their spell.

Just as well she wasn't normal, then. Or the sheikh might have succeeded in his intention to seduce her. Because of course that was part of his plan tonight. Seduction. His pride wanted more from her than her company over one miserable dinner. He wanted *her* pride. He wanted her naked and willing in his bed.

Such imagery produced an almost hysterical amusement that reduced this infernal tension gripping her insides, and restored her earlier dry humour over this situation. Poor Prince Ali. He really had set his sights on a lemon this time.

'I didn't realise Femme Fatale sold lingerie,' he commented thoughtfully. 'I thought they were a perfume company. That was where I first saw you, playing Salome in one of their television advertisements.'

So that was what had first sparked his sexual interest! Charmaine wasn't surprised. The costume she'd worn as the biblical namesake of Femme Fatale's latest perfume was provocative to say the least. So was her dance of the seven veils—although for television censorship she'd had to stop at five.

'Femme Fatale has become well-known because of their highly successful perfume range, it's true,' she advised him. 'But they started out in lingerie. Very sexy lingerie,' she added naughtily. 'I'm the face of their summer range, which will shortly be advertised on their mail-order website.'

His nostrils flared. So did his eyes. 'You are to be on the internet, half-naked, for all the world to see?'

His reaction both amused and annoyed her. 'I will be by the end of next week. You look shocked, Your Highness. I suppose you think it immoral for me to be photographed wearing underwear and nightwear.'

The muscles in his jaw flexed several times, as though he was struggling with his emotions. 'I think it…beneath you.'

'Indeed! Well, that's your prerogative. It's a free country. Unlike your own, I imagine. At least where your women are concerned. I'm sure the men in Dubar have all the freedom in the world to do and think whatever they like, whilst the women are confined and controlled.'

His eyes narrowed till they were two angry slits burning under his straight black brows. 'Please do not betray your ignorance of my country, *and* my culture. Women in Dubar are respected and protected, not confined and controlled.'

Charmaine would have loved to argue with him further but the return of their waiter for their meal order brought a perhaps fortuitous halt to that topic. Her blood was getting hot, a danger signal if she meant to keep her cool. After all, the evening was still very young.

So she sat there prudently silent whilst the prince ordered all three courses of their meal in a rather abrupt tone. An oriental prawn dish as entrée. Crispy roast duckling for the main. And a decadent-sounding chocolate concoction for dessert.

Charmaine suppressed a sigh over the number of calories she would down tonight. Stress always made her hungry and tonight was proving exceptionally stressful, despite her feeling reasonably satisfied with her performance so far. Still, such sinful oral decadence would mean an added hour in the gym tomorrow.

But no matter. She had nothing else to do. There were no boyfriends in her life any more to demand her spare weekend hours. Her fund-raising work had ended for the year, thanks to his royal highness's contribution, and she had no modelling assignments tomorrow.

Sunday was not a day usually chosen for fashion parades, and rarely for photographic work. Too many people around to spoil the shoot, which often as not was done outdoors these days. She also wasn't required to fly off anywhere. Thank the lord. In fact, she had nothing coming up for a fortnight, after which she was booked solid till Christmas, with an overseas shoot in Italy for next year's Pirelli calendar. Then it was back to Melbourne for Australia's fashion week.

She really should take advantage of the next fortnight and rest. She could go visit her parents, she supposed. She hadn't seen them for ages. But her chest tightened at the thought of going home, so Charmaine decided to leave any visiting till Christmas, when it could not be avoided.

'I presume,' the prince began as soon as the waiter

departed, 'that there is nothing I can say to change your mind about the kind of man I am. You have already prejudged me because I am an Arab. You have condemned me without a hearing because of my country and my culture.'

Charmaine took a few calming sips of her mineral water before answering. 'Your being an Arab has little to do with my feelings, or *non*-feelings for you, Your Highness. Although I have to confess that I'm not impressed with the way women are treated like second-class citizens in your world. You can deny it but your history speaks for itself. And so, increasingly, are some of your women, the brave ones who risk all to speak up for themselves. What riles me about men like you, however, is not so much your country or your culture but your obscene wealth and your arrogant presumptions. Billionaires believe their money can buy them anything they desire. Planes. Palaces. Racehorses. *Me.*'

He said nothing for a moment or two. But then he leant back in his chair, removing his face from the circle of light thrown by the candle, his expressive eyes now hidden in shadow.

'You think I just *desire* you?' came his quietly delivered question.

She bristled at this ridiculous attempt to deny that his interest in her was strictly sexual. 'I *know* you just desire me, Your Highness. You made me brutally aware of your lust from the first moment we met. You watched me all that day at the races, then presumptuously expected me to say yes to whatever your royal self wanted. It knocked you for six when I turned your dinner invitation down, so much so that when you got the chance you paid five million dollars to force me to do what I told you I would never do willingly. So yes, I think you were being excessively optimistic tonight to hope that I would put aside my very *rational* dislike of you. And no, there is nothing you can say or do to make me change my mind about what kind of man you are. I already know what kind you are. I've met your kind before.'

'Oh, I doubt that, dear lady,' he said in a tone that sent shivers running up and down her spine. When he came forward again, back into the light, his face was hard and handsome and ominously determined. 'In that case,' he ground out, 'you leave me no alternative.'

Charmaine swallowed. 'What do you mean? No alternative…?'

A prickling sensation ran over her skin, breaking it out into goosebumps. Whatever he was about to say, Charmaine knew she wasn't going to like it.

'I paid five million dollars for a few short hours of your company here tonight. I will donate five *hundred* million dollars to your precious foundation…if you spend a week with me.'

CHAPTER FOUR

CHARMAINE gaped at him.

'You can't be serious!'

'I am deadly serious.'

Charmaine's hand shook as she lifted her mineral water to her lips, taking several reviving sips before she placed the glass back on the table. 'You must be mad,' she muttered.

'Possibly. But that is beside the point. The offer is genuine. What is your answer?'

Her mouth opened to tell him no. Never in a million years. But somehow the words didn't find her tongue. The sum of five hundred million dollars kept rolling round and round in her head. Five...*hundred*... million...dollars. Half a billion. An absolute fortune!

Charmaine could not hope to raise that amount in a lifetime of modelling and fund-raising. Yet it would be all hers to do immense good with...if she spent one short week in the sheikh's bed.

No use pretending he just wanted her company. The name of the game was sex this time.

'One week, you said?' she asked, and knew she'd taken her first step on the slippery slide to hell.

When his eyes glittered with a dark triumph she wanted to snatch back those telling words. But she did not. And the deal was already halfway to being sealed.

'Actually, not even a week,' he went on oh, so

coolly. 'I leave here by helicopter to return to my property every Sunday evening around six, and arrive back in Sydney each Friday afternoon around the same time. So it's really only five days. That represents one hundred million dollars a day for your time.'

'My *time*!' she scoffed. 'Now, that's one hell of an understatement. You want a lot more from me than my time, Your Highness. You want me to sleep with you.'

He did not deny a thing, his eyes remaining fixed on hers as she battled all sorts of inner demons.

'I would want the money up front,' she demanded, even as her mind reeled at the thought of actually going to bed with this man, of being at his sexual beck and call for five days and five nights.

Yet on the surface she betrayed nothing, her own gaze not wavering from his face, her own cool matching his. Was that her pride doing that? Or just practice? She'd long perfected the art of not letting any man think he'd got the better of her.

'Naturally,' he agreed. 'If you say yes, the full amount will be transferred into your foundation's account on Monday. For which I will expect you to present yourself—suitably packed—at my hotel suite on the following Sunday, no later than five o'clock.'

Next Sunday. Eight days away. Eight days to think about what she had to do with him.

'What do you mean by suitably packed?'

'You will need to bring clothes for a wide range of activities.'

Really? she thought drily. She would have thought all she'd need to bring was her birthday suit.

'Such as?'

'There is a heated pool on my property. And a tennis court. And a fully equipped gymnasium, not to mention an unparalleled stable of riding horses. Do you ride?'

'I can stay on. If the horse I'm riding isn't too wild, that is,' she added.

'I will choose a gentle mount for you,' he promised whilst the excited gleam in his eyes suggested her words had prompted thoughts of another kind of riding, and a less than gentle mount. Namely himself.

'You do that,' she snapped, her stomach twisting at the image of herself sitting astride his dark, lean body. 'What's wrong with tomorrow instead of next Sunday?' she added abruptly, deciding that if she was going to do this, then the sooner the better, a bit like getting a tooth out. Any delay would be sheer torture.

He looked startled by her suggestion. 'The money would not be in your foundation's account by then.'

'I could take your word that it would be transferred first thing on the Monday.'

'My word as an Arab?' he retorted mockingly.

'No. Your word as a gentleman. You *are* a gentleman, I hope. If not, then I would not even consider this…arrangement.' Even as she said the words, she realised how laughable they were. Would a gentleman do this—use his obscene wealth to bribe her into his bed?

His smile was wry. 'Please do not try to play me for a fool, Charmaine. You and I both know I am not a gentleman. But I have my own code of honour and I *am* a man of my word. We have mutual friends in Rico and Renée. I am sure they would both vouch for my character.'

She refrained from telling the sheikh that Rico had

actually warned her about him. Pity she'd chosen to ignore that warning.

But how could she possibly have known that he would go to such extreme limits to force her to say yes to him?

Once again, she shivered inside at what was ahead of her. How could she bear to go to bed with him? Just the thought of taking all her clothes off in front of him was making her heart thud and her stomach churn. Yet she'd posed nearly naked lots of times. Paraded herself shamelessly on the catwalk for almost a decade. Stripped down to G-strings in dressing-rooms in front of strangers without batting an eyelid.

So the undressing part shouldn't bother her unduly. Charmaine was not ashamed of her body. Or shy. She supposed it was what was to come *after* the undressing that was perturbing her.

Just think of the money, she told herself sternly. And the enormous good you can do with it. Fund research. Buy expensive medical equipment. Build new hospital wings and homes-away-from-home for families who want to be by their sick children's bedsides and can't afford expensive stays in city hotels.

Such thinking tightened her resolve to do this, no matter what the cost to her pride. She told herself that in a strictly pragmatic sense, going to bed with the sheikh should be no big deal. If he'd been revoltingly fat or ugly or crude it might have been. But he was none of these things. As she'd already noted several times, he was incredibly handsome with a fit, lean body and a graceful and elegant manner. Nothing there to repulse her.

Really, if she could only forget who he was, then it wouldn't be much different from all her other sexual encounters over the years, the ones she'd willingly endured in her futile search for normality. She hadn't enjoyed those other occasions either. Not one little bit. Of course, she had *liked* those men. That was where the difference lay, she supposed. Hard to pretend this man was similar to them. He was *not* similar at all.

Still, as the saying went, she would just have to lie back and think, not of England, but of all the poor kids with cancer. How wonderful it would be to make their lives a little easier, to help their pain and to provide some hope. With those positive thoughts in mind, she could do *anything*...except surrender her pride any more than was necessary.

'I prefer not to ask Rico and Renée about you at all,' she replied curtly. 'I do not want them to know about this. Or anyone else, for that matter. I want to keep it a secret.'

'Really? I would imagine your very sexy public image would be enhanced if people found out that our dinner date had led to our having an affair.'

'Oh, *please*. Remember what I said about calling a spade a spade? This will not be an affair. It will—'

'How do you know?' he broke in, a challenging gleam in his black eyes. 'How do you know that we will not prove to be perfectly attuned to each other? You might enjoy yourself so much in my bed that you will not want next week ever to end.'

'You *are* mad,' she muttered just as the waiter came in with their entrées.

After the waiter had left, Charmaine stared down at her plate of prawns with no interest whatsoever. Her appetite was totally gone. Not so the prince's. He picked up his fork, speared a prawn and popped it into his mouth, chewing slowly with an expression of sensual delight on his face.

'Eat up,' he said after he'd devoured two more in the same slow, almost erotic fashion.

'I'm not hungry,' she snapped.

His glance across the table showed impatience. 'I do not like women who sulk.'

'And I do not like men who force me into sleeping with them.'

'I am not forcing you, Charmaine. I never force women to sleep with me. You can still say no.'

'You know I can't. You *know* that.'

'Yes,' he agreed, his eyes glittering. 'Which only makes me want you all the more.'

She shook her head at him in utter bewilderment.

'There are many women in the world just as beautiful as I am, Your Highness, who could be had for a lot less money.'

'I am well aware of that. But it is *you* I want.'

'Why? Why *me*?'

He shrugged, but his eyes were far from casual. They locked on to hers across the candlelit table, deep, dark pools of the most amazing intensity. 'To be honest, I do not know why you. It is as much a mystery to me as it is to you. I am not normally attracted to women who flaunt themselves for all the world to see. But once I saw you, I simply had to have you. End of story.'

'Only because you had the money to buy me,' she derided. 'I would not be sitting here tonight if you'd been poor!'

His mouth pulled back into a drily amused smile. 'I beg to differ. If I had been poor, you would have looked upon me more kindly from the start. As it is, for some reason my money and my position has blinded you to the mutual attraction which sizzles between us.'

'*What?* My, but you do have a high opinion of yourself, don't you? There is no mutual attraction sizzling between us, Your Highness,' she threw at him in caustic tones. 'I told you once before and I'll tell you again, I do not like you, and I am *not* attracted to you.'

'I agree you do not seem to like me, but you lie when you say you are not attracted to me. The woman I met at the races last year could not keep her eyes off me all day. And the woman who challenged me on that stage last Saturday night was charged with so much sexual electricity, I was almost burned by it. You do want me, Charmaine, even if you will not admit it to yourself. But time will overcome that small problem,' he finished up, then returned to eating his entrée, leaving Charmaine to stare at him in sheer amazement.

The man was deluded! Couldn't keep her eyes off him last year? It had been the other way around! And what she was charged with last Saturday night hadn't been sexual electricity but fury! Same as now.

Charmaine sat there in a stunned and speechless state whilst he devoured the last of his prawns, then dabbed elegantly at his mouth with his serviette before setting his arrogant gaze upon her once more.

'I am an excellent lover,' came his next astonishing remark. 'A woman of your experience will appreciate my expertise.'

Charmaine saw that arguing with this man was futile. 'I see modesty is not one of your virtues,' she sniped.

'I am just calling a spade a spade. I know my talents, as well as my shortcomings. I am gifted with horses, cards and women. But with women most of all.'

'Is that so? Interesting. Tell me, then, have you ever had a woman, Your Highness, who did not respond to your expert lovemaking?'

'No.'

Charmaine rolled her eyes. The man was not only deluded, but was also an egomaniac. 'Has it not occurred to you that some of your lady friends might have faked it because of what you could afford to buy them?'

He smiled a roguish smile. 'But of course. And I have no doubt some of them have, in the beginning. But in the end, they were all very genuine in their pleasure and satisfaction in my bed, even those who were shy and inhibited at the start. Women are no different from horses. Some come to the saddle as if they were born to it. Others resist. But skill and patience invariably wins the day.'

'So you are claiming a one hundred per cent success rate, both with women and horses?'

'There *was* a mare once. A rogue who had been mistreated as a filly. She was the closest I ever came to failure. She would rather have died than let me ride her.'

'I see,' she said drily. Sounded familiar. 'So what happened?'

'I was advised to put her down. But I can never do that, not unless the horse in question is injured beyond repair. Besides, even if she never raced, I intended keeping her for breeding.'

'So what *did* you do?'

'I put her in a yard by herself and became her personal groom. I fed her and mucked out her stall every day. And all the while, I talked to her. In the beginning, she wouldn't let me near her. She'd back away into a corner and snort and rear up. But I could see she was only bluffing. She didn't really want to hurt me. Horses are gregarious creatures and like company. I made sure I was her only company. After a while, she started hanging over the fence, watching and waiting for me. She let me touch her a little. First her head. Then her neck. And finally, her flanks. She would actually quiver with pleasure at my rhythmic stroking.'

A quiver ran through Charmaine at the thought of his stroking *her* flanks. But not a quiver of pleasure, surely. More likely revulsion.

'Soon, I literally had her eating out of my hand,' he went on. 'After that, the breaking-in process went quickly and easily. In the end, she loved being ridden, especially by me.'

Charmaine knew that would never happen with her. Even if he had five *hundred* days, rather than five, she knew the only emotions she would experience being ridden by him would be boredom and resentment. In a perverse fashion, it was going to be interesting to see what he'd do when she didn't respond to his so-called expertise. If she could get beyond the pride factor, then going to bed with the sheikh could prove an even better act of revenge than his. How would *he* feel, this lover extraordinaire, when he failed to arouse her, never mind satisfy her?

'So how much did she cost?' she asked. 'This mare you almost failed with.'

'A couple of million.'

'That's a lot of money. I can imagine you would go to great lengths not to see it wasted. But it's not nearly as much as the half a billion dollars you paid to have sex with me.' It amused her to think he'd really wasted his money this time.

He glared at her across the table, his expression affronted. 'I do not wish to have sex with you, Charmaine. I want to make love with you.'

'Whatever.' If he wanted to play the role of romantic lover then who was she to object? In truth, she was more than happy to indulge this particular fantasy of his. At least then he wouldn't want her to do gross things in bed. Not that she would, anyway. Even five hundred million dollars wasn't enough money for her cooperation in anything other than straight sex. She would have to make that quite clear at some stage before this evening was out.

'You must agree your offer was over-the-top,' she went on. 'You probably could have had me for less.'

'I did not want you to think I thought you cheap. I wanted to offer an amount which I thought was fitting.'

'Now, don't play *me* for a fool, Your Highness,' she countered, not at all conned by his flattering words. She wondered how many women had melted with his *I don't want to have sex with you, I want to make love with you* crap?

'You have no concern over what I think, or how I feel about this,' she went on. 'The reason you offered so much was because you knew it was an amount I couldn't turn down. That's the bottom line, isn't it? You didn't want me saying no to you again.'

He smiled a coolly enigmatic smile. 'You are absolutely correct, Charmaine. That *was* the bottom line. I could not risk that happening. Not a second time.'

'Which brings us back to the main issue I have with you, Your Highness. You *are* a spoiled and arrogant man who has not had no said to him often enough.'

His gaze hardened on her again. 'Think what you will. Just be at my hotel suite on time tomorrow afternoon.'

Now was the time to put her foot down. To make her stance.

'Before I give my final word on this arrangement,' she said curtly, 'I want it understood that I will not be a party to any activity which I consider lewd, or kinky.'

He considered her thoughtfully for a few seconds, during which she had never felt more uncomfortable.

'Since I do not know what you would consider lewd or kinky, I will agree that you are perfectly free to say no to anything which makes you uncomfortable, or which you know you would not enjoy.'

She laughed. She couldn't help it. 'In that case, Your Highness, you are in for one very long, very boring and very frustrating week.'

His eyes showed both surprise and shock. 'Are you saying that you do not enjoy lovemaking?'

For a split-second, Charmaine worried that she had just ruined her chances of securing all that lovely money for her foundation. But then she remembered the sheikh's bottom line, and knew that he would not be able to resist having her, even if she said she was as frigid as an Antarctic ice-floe.

'Unfortunately, that is a fact, Your Highness. I do not enjoy sex. Not for want of trying, might I add. I have had several lovers over the years. All to no avail.

Of course, a man of your exceptional expertise,' she continued, a little wickedly, 'might have more success. I will await the moment of truth with bated breath.' The same way she awaited the moment the dentist gave her a needle.

He stared at her, his eyes assessing. 'You are mocking me,' he said.

'Think what you will, Your Highness.'

Again, his eyes searched her face. 'Is it the actual act of love that you do not enjoy, or everything that leads up to it as well? Would you object to my kissing your breasts, or other parts of your body?'

Charmaine sucked in sharply as images of those activities suddenly flooded her mind. She stared at his mouth and waited for the revulsion to kick in. Instead, an insidious heat swept over her skin at the thought of his hard, almost cruel-looking mouth roving all over her naked body, sucking on her nipples, kissing and exploring every intimate inch of her. Her stomach muscles clamped down hard and a tension such as she had never experienced before gripped all her insides. Her face flamed and her heartbeat fluttered wildly.

'I will take it by your reaction and your silence that you have no objections to foreplay,' he said. 'So I will make you this promise. I will not have actual intercourse with you till I am positive you will enjoy it. Fair enough?'

More than fair, she thought dazedly, and nodded her agreement. Impossible to talk, her tongue having cleaved to the roof of her mouth, her lips and throat as dry as the desert.

'Good,' he said. 'Now eat up.'

Ali watched her actually do as she was told for

once, well aware that something had just thrown her out of kilter. Had she finally recognised what he had known from the first moment of meeting her at the races, that he was not the only one who was smitten? Or had she been unexpectedly excited by the thought of his doing the things he had described to her?

Her blush suggested some form of arousal. When combined with the shock in her eyes he could only conclude that her sexual response to him had really surprised her.

But why would a woman this bold and this beautiful not normally enjoy making love?

Something must have happened to her in the past, something that was blocking her pleasure in sex. Some unpleasant or even traumatic personal experience.

As he'd said, women and horses had much in common. They were sensitive creatures, easily spooked, easily spoiled, especially when young. What had happened when Charmaine was young to make her like this?

Ali resolved to find out. First thing tomorrow morning, he would contact the Sydney detective agency he always used and ask them to run a more thorough background investigation into the woman sitting opposite him. They had already run a cursory security check on her this week, which had shown nothing of note to worry about regarding his own personal safety.

Now Ali would tell them to dig deeper, to go back further and find out everything that had happened to her since her birth, but to concentrate on her teenage years. There had to be something to cause a woman of her sensual nature and appearance to become frigid. He refused to believe she was born that way.

Not that she was really frigid. As he had already told her, he had *felt* her sexual response to him all along. It had been in her eyes, and her body language, sometimes subtly, sometimes flagrantly.

Her overt hostility towards him was not rational, and totally unwarranted by anything he had personally done to her. He had to find out what was causing it. He would get AIS to email a report update to him every day, and he would demand to know everything there was to know before the week was out.

Meanwhile, he would have to be patient, just as he had been with the rogue mare. As much as it would be difficult to keep his hands off Charmaine's beautiful body, he would do so to begin with…but only for a day or so. He knew he would not last any longer than that.

Ali sighed at the cold, hard reality of just how much having this woman would cost him. Was she worth it?

When she looked up from her entrée and set those incredible eyes of hers on him once more, his flesh leapt wildly and he knew it was worth every cent for him to find peace, both for his body and his mind. He had had enough of this obsession, or infatuation, or whatever it was he was suffering from. It had been going on for far too long.

Nothing during the past year—no other woman or other activity—had been able to drive this creature far from his thoughts. His desire for her was beyond desire. If fate had not put that auction in his path Ali did not know what he would have done. Kidnapped her, perhaps.

But fate had played right into his hands and now she was his. For five days; five days to seduce her to his will, to make sure that when their arrangement ran out she would still want him, even without his money.

Five days should be more than enough time. He usually had women melting for him after one night.

'You are not to worry,' he told her when she continued to look at him with fear in her eyes. 'I would never hurt you.'

Her eyes flashed and she drew herself up straight in her chair, sending him a look he had to admire. What courage she had. What spirit. What fire.

Impossible for her to be truly frigid!

'It would be *your* loss if you do, Your Highness,' she said with a proud toss of that gorgeous head of hair. 'Because if you hurt me, I will kill you.'

'You will not have to,' he returned ruefully. 'If I am stupid enough to hurt you, I will kill myself.'

CHAPTER FIVE

HIS helicopter was big and black. Ex-army, the prince told her as he guided her across the rooftop heliport towards the rather ominous-looking craft, made even more ominous perhaps by the thick black clouds gathering overhead.

The weather forecast had predicted a warm, muggy day for Sydney, followed by a late-afternoon storm. The thought of flying through rain and lightning did little for the savage knots that were already twisting in Charmaine's stomach.

'Do not worry about the weather,' he said when he saw her frown up at the sky. 'I checked the weather on the computer in my suite before you arrived. The radar map shows it is clear to the north of Sydney. The storm clouds are heading straight out to sea. If there was any danger, I would not allow the pilot to take off.'

Charmaine wasn't so sure about that. She had a feeling his royal highness would risk anything to whisk her off to the privacy of his property tonight. He'd made no attempt to hide the hunger in his eyes when she'd presented herself at the presidential suite less than fifteen minutes ago.

Yet she'd dressed down for the occasion even more than last night, choosing three-quarter-length fawn cargo trousers with a simple short-sleeved yellow shirt, not tucked in or tied at her waist to show off her toned midriff as she would normally have worn it. Flat fawn sandals covered her feet. Minimal make-up graced her face. No jewellery adorned her ears, hands, wrist or neck, and the only perfume wafting from her body was the apple scent of her shower gel and shampoo.

But nothing, it seemed, would deter this man's lust for her. It was there, in his blazing black eyes as he'd hurried her up here with telling speed, sending her luggage ahead with a lackey. Obviously, he was anxious to get things underway.

She was, too, in a perverse kind of way. The last twenty-four hours had been hell. She hadn't slept or eaten since leaving the restaurant around ten-thirty. Though, after last night's dinner, perhaps that was just as well. How *had* she got through that meal?

After she'd made her melodramatic threat about killing him if he hurt her, and he'd come back with his rather ironic-sounding reply, the rest of the evening had become somewhat surreal. All discussion of the week ahead had ceased and the prince had chatted away to her quite nonchalantly through the next two courses, and then coffee afterwards. All quite innocuous topics, mostly to do with Australia. The economy. The weather. The up-coming elections. He'd also thankfully stopped staring at her as though he was dying of thirst in the desert and she was an oasis, which had enabled her to relax enough to make some intelligible contributions to the conversation.

But once she'd left his company and returned to her hotel room, the reality of what she'd agreed to came back with a rush and all hell broke loose in her mind. What *had* she been thinking of? *No* amount of money was worth doing what she had to do.

Her stomach had churned. Her skin had crawled.

Her head had whirled. She'd paced the hotel room for ages before finally plunging herself into a long, hot shower, searching for some way to relax her tightly strung-up body.

But what she'd discovered about herself in that shower had blown her mind much more than the arrangement she'd just entered into. The memory of her rock-hard nipples, plus the telling wetness between her legs, still had the power to shock her.

Charmaine's step faltered as she became aware that her nipples were *still* like iron pokers inside her bra.

Her face flamed at the realisation that the sheikh was right. She *did* want him. At least, her body seemed to. She still disliked him intensely. How could she not? But she was attracted to him, like a moth to the flame.

There was no sensible or intelligent reason behind the attraction. It was basic and primal. Something to do with the survival of the human species, she imagined. Eons ago, cavewomen had automatically chosen to mate with the caveman who would produce the best and strongest offspring, as well as having the power to protect them.

Charmaine could understand such a choice in the primitive and untamed past. But it had no place in the civilised world of today. The qualities *she* admired and respected in a man were not size, or strength, or even wealth and power, but kindness and tenderness, honesty and decency. What a pity her body didn't agree with her, she thought agitatedly as this dark and powerful man guided her towards the ladder that led up into his huge black helicopter.

No wonder she hadn't been able to sleep last night.

But alongside her annoyance over this mortifying

situation lay the tiniest smidgeon of relief at discovering that maybe—just maybe—she was sexually normal after all. She'd just been going to bed with the wrong types. Whilst her brain had been drawn to nice guys, her traitorous body craved just the opposite.

But then, hadn't it always? she thought bitterly.

The sheikh's possessive grip on her elbow suddenly annoyed her and she threw him a savage glance over her shoulder. 'I can manage alone,' she snapped.

His deferential nod was not matched by the blaze of fire she encountered in his eyes. Clearly, she was trying his patience. Also clearly, he was eager to get her alone in his no doubt palatial residence up in the Hunter Valley so he could start seducing her.

Charmaine tried not to think about that moment, because it was fraught with so many mixed emotions. More so now because everything had changed. Last night, when she'd agreed to this liaison, she'd imagined herself lying like a log beneath him, enduring his sexual attentions with her usual lack of response, at the same time feeling triumphant that he would not have a chance in Hades of either seducing *or* satisfying her.

The new concept of his smugly discovering she *was* turned on by him appalled her, as did the prospect that she would not protest when he confidently moved from foreplay to the real thing. She hated the thought that she might actually enjoy everything he did to her.

If she told the therapist she'd consulted at one stage that she was repelled by the prospect of finally finding pleasure in sex, he would have called her truly mad. But it wasn't finding pleasure in sex itself that upset

Charmaine but finding pleasure in sex with this particular man, this…predator.

It was a most frustrating situation, but one she would have to address, come tonight. Or maybe even earlier, she realised with a jab of panic as she reached the top of the ladder and stepped into the ultraluxurious interior of the royal helicopter.

'Good lord!' she couldn't help exclaiming as her eyes darted around. No upright seats jammed together in here. The place looked like an elegant sitting-room with large armchairs and a sofa that could easily have doubled for a bed. The colour scheme befitted royalty with lots of creams and golds. The walls and ceiling were lined with a rich wooden panelling, and the cream carpet was thick and plush.

'I had it especially fitted out to my requirements,' the prince said from just behind her shoulder. 'I fly a lot so I like to be comfortable. There is a fully equipped kitchen and bathroom on board as well. And a built-in bar for my guests. You will also notice once we are underway that this area is soundproofed. The noise of a helicopter this size is bone-rattling.'

'I suppose you have drop-dead-gorgeous flight attendants as well,' she said drily, waiting for one or two to make their appearance from behind the two closed doors at the back of the aircraft.

'Not on flights this short,' he returned smoothly. 'Nor when I have a special lady-friend with me.'

She turned to stare at him, even as the large outside door was banged shut behind them.

'You mean we…we are alone back here?' Alone, and no one able to hear her scream.

'Yes,' he said simply, his eyes searching hers. 'You have some objection to that?'

'Yes. No. No, I suppose not.' But she shuddered.

'Remember what I promised. I will not do anything you do not want me to do.'

'Well, I don't want you to touch me,' she said with an hysterical edge to her voice. *'Ever!'*

'You do realise that contravenes the terms of our arrangements,' he said coolly.

'Yes.'

'I could demand you comply.'

'You could try.'

He smiled. He actually smiled. 'I could. But that is not my way. I prefer to make love, not war. Still, if you want your foundation to have five hundred million dollars placed in its account tomorrow morning, then I would suggest you reconsider your attitude between now and the time of our arrival at my home.'

Charmaine winced at this reminder of why she'd agreed to do this. Here she'd been, getting carried away with her own selfish emotions and her own foolish pride again. What did it matter if this man thought he was God's gift to women? And what did it matter if she became just another of his one hundred per cent success rate with women?

The sheikh's satisfaction and her own mortification would be even greater, she reasoned, if she made a show of resisting, only to melt when he finally took her into his arms. Better she go to him willingly. Take the initiative—and some of the triumph—away from him.

All very common-sense logic, but she just could not do it. When he walked towards her she automatically shrank back a couple of steps, her reaction bringing him to a dead halt, his eyes betraying a surprising concern.

'I am not going to touch you,' he said brusquely. 'Not in the way you think,' he added, then pried her shoulder bag away from her desperately clutching hands and placed it on a nearby table. 'Sit down in one of those chairs and rest, Charmaine. You look tired.'

'That's because I haven't slept,' she snapped, and once again his eyes searched hers.

'In that case, lie down on the sofa and have a nap.'

'How can I possibly sleep when I have tonight hanging over my head?' she threw at him. 'Not to mention this whole week. Not only do I not enjoy sex, but I have never gone to bed with a man I didn't like.'

'In that case, I had better make sure you grow to like me very quickly,' he said drily, and moved off to the side where there was a built-in wall-unit of cupboards, opening one of the large upper doors and extracting two bed-sized pillows and a blanket. She blinked in surprise when he carried them over to the sofa and arranged them into a day bed for her.

He really was an incredibly graceful mover, she conceded reluctantly as her eyes followed his every move. With a great body.

Dressed as he was that afternoon in black jeans and a wine-coloured polo top, there was no hiding his fitness, or his shape. Charmaine had never liked overly big, bulky or muscle-bound men. She preferred men who were elegantly T-shaped, with wide shoulders, slender hips, long legs and washboard stomachs. Prince Ali had all that. And more, she realised.

She flushed and looked away, but the sight of him stayed in her mind, rattling her considerably. She recalled what the sheikh had said about his knowing she wanted him because she had stared at him all day last year at the races. Which perhaps she had. And now he'd caught her staring at him again. No, lusting after him would be a better description.

Actions did speak louder than words and her actions kept contradicting her claims that she had no sexual interest in him.

'Come,' he ordered her. 'Your bed is ready.'

Her legs began to move in his direction before she could stop them, drawn by the power of his eyes and the sudden and urgent longing that swept through her like a tidal wave. She came closer and closer till she was within an arm's length of where he was standing by the sofa. What would happen, she wondered dazedly, if she just reached out to him, if she forgot everything else and just surrendered to the moment?

She almost did it. Almost lifted her hands to touch his face, and his hair. But then her pride kicked in again and her hands curled into fierce fists at her sides instead. When he saw them he scowled, whirled and stalked away from her. She watched him select the furthest armchair and ram his body into it, gripping the arm-rests angrily as he leant back. Only then did he glance back at her, his face grim.

'Lie down,' he commanded coldly.

Feeling oddly shattered and grateful at the same time, she almost fell down onto the sofa.

'Th…thank you,' she stammered as she lay back and pulled the blanket up to her suddenly shivery shoulders.

'Do not thank me yet,' he threw at her. 'Come tonight, you will not be let off so easily. You *will* let me touch you, madam. And you will do so willingly. Only then will we be able to get past all this nonsense.

Now go to sleep. That way you will be refreshed when we arrive.'

Ali was glad when she closed her eyes and did as she was told. Or appeared to. He tried to relax himself, but how could he when he was practically gnashing his teeth with frustration and irritation?

The woman was impossible, giving him mixed messages all the time. She wanted him. He *knew* she did. But nowhere near as much as he wanted her. Her claim that she never wanted him to touch her—*ever*— was patent rubbish. When she came up to him just now, she had been going to touch him. He had seen it in her eyes. But then something had happened and she had changed her mind.

A Western woman's pride, no doubt. Did she not know that women were made to touch and be touched? Women like her more than others. So soft. So exquisite. So passionate.

Oh, yes, she would be passionate in bed. She could pretend to be cold all she liked but Ali had seen the fire in her eyes when she looked at him. Besides, how could a body like hers not be responsive? Allah had made her for the delights of the flesh. Once he started kissing her, all that surface ice would melt away.

Tonight, he decided, abruptly abandoning his earlier resolve to wait a day or so before making love to her. To keep delaying the inevitable would only make her more difficult. Besides, the pain in his loins at the moment was excruciating. Frankly, he had never suffered the like, not even all those years ago when…

Ali's back and shoulders stiffened at this surprising thought. His hands curled over the arm-rests even tighter and his frown deepened. Had he really not felt like this all those years ago with Nadia? Surely his need would have been worse, given he'd been younger then and so much in love.

But, to be honest, Ali could not recall his physical frustration back then ever being this intense.

Another startling realisation came to him as he was sitting there, thinking. He had not given Nadia a single thought since first setting eyes on Charmaine on television over a year ago. Not till this moment.

Did that mean he no longer loved his brother's wife? Or had time simply dimmed his memory of her to a point where he had forgotten how Nadia had once made him feel? No doubt if he saw her again, it would all come rushing back. The passion. The all-consuming love. The willingness to sacrifice everything, just to be with her.

But he would never see her again. That was the truth of it. His family—and hers—would never allow that. Nadia was now the wife of Crown Prince Khaled and mother to Khaled's son and heir, little Faisal. One day Nadia would be Queen of Dubar. Ali had no place in her life. His life was here now, in Australia, with his horses and his...

He glanced over at the figure huddled up on the sofa, her eyes shut, the blanket pulled up around her shoulders.

He had been going to say 'hobbies' in his mind. But Charmaine could hardly be classified as a hobby. She was an obsession, a tortured and tormenting obsession. She haunted his dreams and distracted his days.

As his gaze lingered on her lovely face, Ali's flesh leapt once more and he vowed darkly to make her his. He would use every sexual skill he had acquired over the years to seduce this contrary creature into surrendering herself totally to him; to be enslaved by him; maybe even to fall in love with him.

A light flashed on in Ali's brain, brilliant and blinding in its shining truth. That was what he wanted most of all, wasn't it? For her to fall in love with him, to become as obsessed with him as he was with her.

But why? For what purpose? Revenge? Maybe it was his dark side, craving the opportunity to do to her what she had done to him. If she fell in love with him, he could have her in his bed for as long as he liked. And then, when he'd had his fill of her, he could discard and reject her as cruelly and carelessly as she had rejected him last year. *She* would be the one unable to sleep at night for wanting *him*. *She* would become the fool, driven to act without honour or pride. He could see her now, begging to see him again, crawling to him on her hands and knees and promising to do anything he wanted, if only he would let her back into his life.

Yes, he rather liked that scenario.

A glance at his gold Rolex showed they were still an hour away from their destination. Another glance at Charmaine showed the slight but steady rhythm of real sleep. She was resting. Good. She would need to be rested. She had a long night ahead of her.

CHAPTER SIX

A HAND gently shaking her shoulder had Charmaine bolting upright on the sofa, the blanket falling off her shoulders, and then onto the floor. The prince, who was leaning over her, bent to pick it up.

'We will be landing shortly,' he told her as he straightened and stepped back, the blanket in his hands. 'I thought you might like to freshen up before we do so.'

'What? Oh. Oh, yes. Yes, I would.' She pushed her hair back from her face then slowly swung her feet over the side of the sofa and stood up, amazed that she had actually fallen asleep. Maybe it had been the throbbing of the engines through the floor that had rocked her off to sleep. Or maybe just sheer exhaustion. Whatever, she did feel better than before. A little calmer. Less panicky.

'The bathroom is the door on the right.'

'Thank you,' she said and walked over to get her bag from the side-table the prince had put it on when they'd first boarded.

The feel of his black eyes burning into her back as she headed for the bathroom soon brought Charmaine right back to her earlier agitation. Not even closing the door behind her and blocking his gaze helped this time.

'Damn the man,' she told her reflection in the gold-framed vanity mirror.

By the time Charmaine emerged from the luxuriously appointed bathroom ten minutes later, the helicopter had landed and she was feeling a little more in control.

I can do this, she told herself staunchly as she headed for the exit door, which was now open. The shame is all his, not mine, and she flashed the sheikh a scathing look as she brushed past him.

He at least had the brains not to try to help her down the ladder, for which Charmaine was grateful. She suspected that she might react poorly to his finding excuses to touch her at this stage. Let him have the decency to wait, she thought viciously, till they were alone in his bedroom.

Charmaine was so consumed with her awareness of him coming down the ladder behind her that she didn't pay attention to her surroundings for a few seconds. But when she did, what she saw took her breath away. Yet she couldn't see all that much. It was almost dark, with a bank of clouds blocking any moon and stars. Most of the property remained hidden from her view. Not so the magnificent white-stuccoed residence sprawled across a hilltop, a hundred or so metres above where the helicopter had landed on a flat section of land.

Despite having expected his residence to be palatial, Charmaine gazed up in awe at the mansion's size.

'Come,' the prince said from just behind her shoulder. 'We will ride up to the house.'

'Ride?' she echoed, swinging around in astonishment. Till she saw the golf-style buggy awaiting them.

A new lackey was already putting their cases in the back. He looked Australian, not Arab, and, although probably over thirty, had a strangely childlike expression on his weatherbeaten face. Once the cases were stowed away, he jumped in behind the wheel of the buggy, being careful, Charmaine noted, not to stare too hard or too long at her.

'Thanks, Jack,' the prince said as he climbed into one of the two empty back seats. 'Coming?' he directed at Charmaine, who was still standing there.

She climbed in beside him, and the buggy immediately lurched off, Charmaine clutching the hand rail in front of her to keep her balance. The last thing she wanted was to be thrown against the man next to her, who was already too close for comfort.

The sheikh chatted away to Jack during the drive up the rather steep gravel path, mostly about the storm in Sydney and what a lucky run they'd had so far with the weather that year. Nice spring rains, et cetera.

Jack, however, didn't say much in return. Just the occasional uh-huh. Although slightly miffed that she wasn't introduced, Charmaine was grateful for the opportunity to take in more of the property. Her eyes had grown accustomed to the dusk light by then and she could make out groups of buildings in the valley below. A river too, flanked by tall trees.

On each side of the river lay huge fields covered by a crop of some kind. Oats, maybe. Or lucerne. Further away from the river the land was less flat, the gently rolling hills marked out into paddocks of various sizes by white-painted wooden fences. Horse paddocks, obviously. Enclosing the valley were two tall mountain ranges, rising moodily and magnificently into the cloud-filled sky.

Despite the enthralling panorama of the landscape, Charmaine's gaze soon returned to the prince's house, which they were rapidly approaching. It actually looked more like a convent than a house, with its cloistered verandas and myriad archways. Very Mediterranean. If she didn't know better, she would have thought she was in Spain, or Sicily.

At last they pulled up in front of several wide terracotta-tiled steps that led up onto a similarly tiled veranda and a simply huge front door, with an equally huge brass knocker. Dark wood the door was, the perfect foil for the starkly white walls of the house.

Charmaine scrambled out before the prince could stride around and gallantly take her hand, her motivation not escaping his attention, if the dry look he gave her was any indication. They walked together but apart up the steps whilst Jack bustled around with the luggage behind them.

A middle-aged woman with short spiky red hair opened the front door before anyone needed to use the brass knocker, her vivacious blue eyes sparkling with genuine welcome at Ali before widening slightly on Charmaine.

This time the prince actually deigned to introduce her.

'Cleo, this is Charmaine, whom I'm sure you'll recognise. Charmaine, this is Cleo, my housekeeper. Cleo has been with me for some years now.'

'How do you do?' Charmaine said politely.

'Delighted, I'm sure, love,' the housekeeper said breezily as she took Charmaine's hand in both of hers. 'Come in, come in.' And she drew Charmaine into the enormous, square-shaped foyer. 'Won't be a sec, love.' Patting her hand, she let it go and turned to Jack, who'd made it inside with the cases. 'Jack, you know where the cases go. The large black one in the boss's rooms. The others belong to the lady. They go in the bedroom a bit further along. I've opened the door for you so you know which one. You can go out through the side-door when you're done, OK?'

Jack nodded and took off through an archway on Charmaine's left. Cleo turned back to give Charmaine a more thorough appraisal from top to toe.

'My, you're even more beautiful than you are on all those magazine covers!' she gushed. 'You will have to keep her under lock and key, Ali, or none of the men will get any work done whilst she's here.'

Charmaine was taken aback by the woman calling her royal employer by his first name, but she supposed they did have a long relationship, and it *was* awkward calling him Your Highness all the time.

Ali laughed, startling Charmaine. He'd never laughed before in her presence. It quite transformed him from menacing predator to easy-going charmer.

'You could be right, Cleo. I dare say Norm will suddenly find all sorts of excuses to attend to the roses in the garden beds around the house.'

'I have no doubt about that. Norm's always had an eye for a pretty woman.'

'Too true, Cleo. You only have to look at who he married. Norm is my gardener and Cleo's husband of thirty years,' he explained to Charmaine, who was still amazed by his total change of manner. Suddenly, there was nothing royal or arrogant about him. He was even talking less pompously.

'Oh, go on with you,' Cleo scoffed. 'I'm fast becoming an old bag. Turned fifty the other week, love,' she told Charmaine. 'Took myself off to the hair-dresser's in a bid to turn back the clock and came home with this.' And she gesticulated to her hair. 'Come on, tell me the truth. What do you think?'

'I think it looks great. I wouldn't have taken you for a day over forty.'

Cleo beamed. 'I knew you were a girl of perfect class and taste the moment I clapped eyes on you. You can keep this one, Ali.'

'Thank you, Cleo. But I think Charmaine might have something to say about that.' And he threw her a wry smile.

Charmaine smiled back, more for Cleo's benefit than his. Charmaine liked the woman and didn't want to make her suffer for her boss's wickedness.

'I presume you have already followed through on my earlier instructions?' he asked the housekeeper.

Charmaine frowned. Earlier instructions? What earlier instructions?

'Everything is as you wanted, Ali. I will bring the food along shortly.'

'Good.'

When he turned and took her elbow, Charmaine stiffened, but the look on his face suggested she not make a fuss in front of Cleo, and she reluctantly complied, allowing him to guide her down the same dome-roofed, terracotta-tiled hallway that Jack had scuttled along earlier and which seemed to stretch into infinity.

'What earlier instructions?' she asked archly as he directed her past several shut doors on either side.

'Nothing for you to get stirred up about. I rang Cleo before leaving Sydney to tell her that I was bringing a special lady-friend home for the week and that we would be eating dinner tonight in my quarters.'

'You obviously didn't tell her my identity during this call.'

'Obviously not.'

'I dare say she's used to you bringing women home with you from your weekend sojourns to Sydney.'

'It is not an unknown situation. But you are by far the most famous and the most beautiful lady to have ever graced these halls.'

Charmaine snorted. 'I noticed she called you Ali. I'm surprised that you allow a servant to treat you with such familiarity.'

'Cleo is not a servant,' he corrected her coolly. 'She is an employee.'

'Pardon my mistake. I thought royalty always considered their employees servants.'

'I regret to say that is the case back in Dubar. But not here. Here, on this property, I am not treated like some pampered prince. Here, I have chosen to earn my respect. Admittedly, I am still the boss, but to a lot of the people who work for me I am also their friend.'

'Admirable sentiments. But I would not be too fooled if I were you, Your Highness. In my experience, the rich and famous rarely have true friends among the people who work for them.'

'That is a very cynical point of view.'

'Aah, but I am a very cynical lady.'

'Yes, I have noticed that. But cynicism, like any negative state of mind, can feed on itself and become self-destructive. I know this for a fact. When I first arrived on these shores I was a very cynical young man. But I soon discovered that if I wished to be successful and relatively content with my life here, I would have to try to adopt the Australian way of life, which is far more laid-back and informal than anything I was previously used to. Admittedly, I find I fall back into old ways when I am out in public, or in the company of my wealthy city friends, but after I come home here I am soon a different man.'

'*Relatively* content?' she echoed, picking up on the innuendo behind the word. 'That sounds as though you'll never be really happy living here in Australia. Why stay, then, if that's the case? If you miss Dubar so much, why don't you just go back?'

'Now, you surprise me, Charmaine. Or possibly you disappoint me, since you have not even been curious enough to find out the most basic facts about my past. It is quite well known, in racing circles anyway, that I did not leave Dubar voluntarily. I was exiled.'

'Exiled!' Charmaine ground to a halt, throwing a startled glance up into his face. 'But...but why?'

His smile was enigmatic. 'There are many rumours, the most common being that I was discovered in a married woman's bed chamber whilst her husband was absent.'

'And the truth?' she asked.

'The truth is the girl in question was not yet married, just betrothed. Unfortunately, her husband-to-be was my oldest brother, Crown Prince Khaled.'

'Oh! And you actually slept with her?'

'I fully intended to. But I was discovered before the joyous event, and put on the next plane out of the country. My brother was lied to over the circumstances of my hasty departure. He was told I had become dangerously infatuated with a married woman on the royal staff and that I had been exiled for my own safety.'

'I see.' Charmaine nodded, well aware that adultery in his country was one of the gravest sins. People were executed for such transgressions.

'It wasn't just a one-sided infatuation though, was it?'

'No. Nadia loved me as much as I loved her. Or I thought she did. But she married Khaled within days of my exile and has had a son by him. From what I have heard, the marriage is a happy one.'

'Are you still in love with her?' she asked.

'Do you care?' he returned, his eyes searching hers.

Charmaine blinked. *Did* she?

'I was just curious,' she insisted. 'It would perhaps explain why a man such as yourself has never married. Living as you do here on this property, surely a wife would suit your purposes better than an endless stream of female…companions.'

'Aha, so you do know a little of my reputation.'

'I was warned about you.'

'Warned? What an interesting word! Warned. But a very apt one, on this occasion. You should have taken notice of whoever warned you. I presume it was Enrico. No, do not bother to deny it, my dear Charmaine. He would be the only one who would dare. But to answer your earlier question, yes, I loved her very much. More than my life was worth. I was willing to risk anything—even death—to be with her. I am a very passionate man, as you will have an opportunity to discover tonight…first-hand,' he finished oh, so softly.

Charmaine stared at him.

He stared right back, his black eyes burning. But were they burning for her, or was there another reason for his sexual obsession with her?

'Do I...remind you in some way of Nadia?' she asked, her mouth drying as she waited for his answer.

His gaze travelled slowly down her body then up again, making her quiver inside.

'Not in the slightest.'

Charmaine heard the hard edge in his voice.

'Come,' he said abruptly, and grabbed her arm again. 'The past is the past, Charmaine. Believe me when I say it has no effect on me any more.'

In a pig's ear, she thought as he shepherded her rather roughly down the corridor. He was as affected by his past as she was by hers. Clearly, his paying an exorbitant amount of money for her was a direct result of his having once been, maybe not rejected as such, but unable to have the woman he most desperately wanted. On this occasion, Charmaine's surface beauty had inspired a savage lust in him and nothing was going to stop him satisfying that lust this time. It might not be love driving him, but it was a powerful force all the same. She could feel it, vibrating through his arm and down into hers, making her stomach tighten and her heart race.

Not before time he stopped in front of a wooden door on the right and let go of her arm. Any further and his fingers would have bruised her skin.

His facial expression was grimly determined as he reached out for the brass knob, turned it and pushed the door open, waving her inside with an impatient gesture. Her tension increased considerably as she went in, but the sight that met her eyes totally threw her.

She'd expected a bedroom, but not one quite like this.

'This will be your room during your stay,' he announced curtly, walking past her and across the expanse of pale pink carpet to where white-painted double French doors led out on to another cloistered veranda. When he opened them, a pleasant breeze wafted in, ruffling the gauzy white material that was draped around the white-painted four-poster bed.

Charmaine stared at the very pretty bed with its pink lace quilt and matching pillowcases. For the life of her she could not imagine herself and the sheikh in it together. This was a bed designed for romance and relative innocence, a room for softness and tenderness, *not* the kind of sex that was going to transpire between them during the next five days.

Charmaine already knew that their encounters weren't going to be at all romantic and innocent, let alone soft and tender.

'That door leads to your walk-in wardrobe and *en suite* bathroom,' he said, indicating a door to the left of the bedhead. 'I am sure you will find everything in there you could possibly need. And this one...' he walked over to a door in the centre of the wall opposite the bed and flung it open '...leads to my personal quarters.'

Charmaine almost laughed at her own stupidity. Of course, this wasn't the sheikh's bedroom. This was a lady's retreat, not a setting designed for sin and seduction. No doubt his room would contain an even bigger bed and other accessories to enhance the sort of erotic experiences a man of his sophistication would enjoy.

'I will expect you to join me there, suitably clothed, in half an hour,' he pronounced brusquely. And with a curt bow of his darkly handsome head he turned and disappeared into the short connecting hallway, shutting the door behind him.

Charmaine glared after him, the smidgeon of sympathy he'd evoked with his sad tale of lost love and bitter exile evaporating with his peremptory commands.

'Suitably clothed indeed,' she bit out before whirling and marching over to the door he'd said led into the walk-in wardrobe and bathroom.

Her two bags were already sitting on deep shelves in the more than adequate wardrobe. She angrily reefed them open, extracted what she needed for the night ahead then marched on through the next door.

The bathroom proved to be as pretty as the bedroom. All white tiles, with pink accessories and silver fittings. Above the white-tiled vanity bench ran a huge silver-framed mirror that slid back to reveal shelves containing an impressive assortment of toiletries.

A spa bath graced one corner of the room. A roomy shower filled another, and a toilet and bidet occupied a third. Unlike some less well-equipped bathrooms, this one had several towel rails sporting a large selection of plush pink towels. There was also a laundry basket with a sign on it saying that any clothes deposited would be cleaned, ironed and returned the same day.

Talk about spoiling one's guests!

Well, he could afford such indulgences, Charmaine supposed as she took a shower cap out of its packet then fitted it over her hair. Anyone who could afford to pay five hundred million dollars for five days' sleeping with some woman he fancied had to be obscenely rich. Still, as the saying went, you can buy sex but you can't buy love.

Not that the sheikh wanted love these days. Clearly, his heart was back in Dubar with his brother's wife. The heart that beat in his chest today was as hard as nails. You didn't have to be a genius to work that out.

What he wanted from the women he brought here had nothing to do with love.

'Suitably clothed, eh?' she repeated with a laugh as she stripped off and dropped every single item of her clothing into the laundry basket before stepping into the shower. There she lathered herself all over with the perfumed shower gel she found in the recess in the shower wall. Then she turned the water to cold and let the icy rain beat upon her body till she was shivering.

By the time she switched off the taps she figured she'd thoroughly deheated herself, although her stunningly erect nipples didn't seem to reflect that idea. Charmaine was annoyed with herself for not remembering what ice did to her nipples. She'd used that trick only recently during a lingerie photo-shoot to make herself look sexier.

As she towelled herself down, she also regretted ever telling the sheikh that she didn't like sex. How much easier this would have been if he'd thought she was a promiscuous tart right from the start. Now he looked upon her as a sexual challenge.

No way could she allow him the triumph of thinking he'd expertly seduced her with his boudoir skills. Since she was condemned to be turned on by him, whether she wanted to be or not, then she aimed to make the running here, not him!

Charmaine donned the outfit she'd brought into the

bathroom with her, then opened her make-up bag and went to work.

Finally, she was ready. Standing up straight, she inspected her reflection in the mirror.

Perfect, she decided, although a shudder did ripple down her spine at the sight she made. The negligee set she'd chosen to wear tonight was one she'd modelled recently for Femme Fatale's summer collection. The nightie was long and made of red satin, its low-cut halterneck bodice clinging like a second skin, the rest falling to the floor in slinky folds. It almost could have doubled as an evening gown, although a very provocative one, especially with the way her braless breasts and stunningly erect nipples were shamelessly displayed by the unlined satin.

The overlay was pure Hollywood. Transparent chiffon, with its hem and three-quarter-length sleeves edged in red-dyed ostrich feathers. On her feet were matching red satin high-heeled slippers that showed her toes, now painted the same scarlet as her mouth.

The whole outfit was over-the-top and in-your-face sexy. With the amount of make-up she had on, she looked like an expensive call-girl.

'Yes, perfect,' Charmaine repeated ruefully.

Squaring her slender shoulders, she whirled and left the bathroom. It was time to face the music. Time to pay the piper, but not to play the helpless victim. Oh, no. That part had been played once in her life, and would never be repeated.

CHAPTER SEVEN

CHARMAINE'S steely resolve lasted till the sheikh swept open the door to his quarters.

Did she gasp?

She hoped not. But her eyes definitely widened.

Till that moment, she hadn't given a thought to what *he* might be wearing this evening. Her focus had all been on her own appearance.

But the sheikh's bedroom attire definitely rivalled hers in the provocative department. His long black silk pyjama bottoms were slung dangerously low on his hips, the matching knee-length robe hanging so wide open she could see all of his bare, bronzed chest right down past his navel.

Clearly, he'd not long been out of the shower as his head was still shiny and wet. His feet were bare and the hair on his chest had gathered into masses of tiny damp curls.

She stared at them, her fingers itching once more to touch him, to touch all of him. Dear heaven, but he was beautiful. More beautiful than any man had a right to be. Such thick, glossy black hair. Such gorgeous olive skin. Not to mention his lean, hard, masculine body.

But most magnetic of all were still his eyes, those eyes which at this very moment were blazing with a heat and a hunger that challenged her determination to remain hard and cold in his presence.

Her own blood ignited, making the entire surface

of her skin come alive. Her brain bubbled with a feverish excitement and the most corrupting thoughts. The idea that soon she *could* be touching him, and being touched *by* him, almost tipped her into a state of meltdown.

Charmaine felt her cheeks begin to burn, which pricked her pride back into action. How could she do this? Melt for this man like some infatuated virgin. It would be the ultimate humiliation.

No. She could not do it. She would not do it. Not for all the money in the world!

With a defiant tilt of her chin, she brushed past him and took a few steps into the room, putting some physical distance between them before announcing her decision.

For a split-second she was distracted by the room itself, which was so unlike what she was expecting. Much more casual and cosy. Forest-green carpet and warm cream walls. A fireplace. Built-in bookcases and lots of comfy-looking furniture. In the big bay window sat a glass dining table, looking very inviting, with fresh flowers surrounding a candle in the middle, the perfect setting for a romantic dinner *à deux*. A stainless-steel traymobile was positioned next to the table, presumably containing their evening meal.

'Do you wish to sit down and eat dinner straight away?' he asked, and she whirled to face him once more.

'What I wish, Your Highness,' she said stiffly whilst her heart raced and her stomach churned, 'is to put a stop to this charade once and for all.'

His face darkened. 'Meaning?'

'Meaning I have changed my mind. I can't do this. I am going back to my room to get dressed and repacked. I expect you to have me flown back to Sydney tonight.'

His dark eyes glittered ominously. 'Just like that.'

'Yes. Just like that.'

He said nothing. But his body language spoke volumes.

He wasn't going to let her go. Rico had warned her. Why hadn't she listened to him?

'I'm sorry to have inconvenienced you,' she choked out, and bravely headed for the door. Unfortunately, she had to pass the prince on the way.

For a moment, she thought she was safe. But then his right hand shot out, grabbing her left wrist and yanking her back round to land hard against him.

As usual when cornered, Charmaine came out fighting. Her own right hand swung wildly and connected with his cheek. She would have hit him again if his other hand hadn't secured that wrist as well.

'Let me go,' she bit out in fury as he bent both her arms around behind her back. 'Or I'll scream the place down.'

'Scream away. This house has thick stone walls and plate-glass windows, which you will note are closed, since the air-conditioning is on. Even if some sound could escape, there is no one nearby to hear. Cleo and her husband have driven into town to go to the movies. So you are as alone with me in here as you were in my helicopter.'

His hands tightened around her wrists and dragged her arms down straight, giving her a sobering glimpse of his physical strength.

Charmaine realised that fighting him was futile. Despite all her workouts in the gym, she was no match for this man. All she had to bargain with was her brain, because she refused to involve her body, that body which even at this moment longed to submit to his.

What a traitor her flesh was! How it loved the way it was moulded to his, thigh to thigh, hip to hip, breast to chest. With him in his bare feet and her in heels, even their faces were dead level. How easy it would be to fit her mouth to his, to open her lips and accept his tongue. Just as easy to invite a far more intimate invasion.

Charmaine shuddered in shame at the excitement she experienced at the thought of doing just that.

'You…you assured me once you would never take a woman against her will,' she blurted out.

'I haven't. And I never will.'

'Then let me go.'

'You agreed to foreplay,' he reminded her.

'Is this kind of manhandling your idea of foreplay?'

'If I let you go, you will try to run away. Yet I know that is not what you want. You want me to touch you and kiss you. You want me to make love to you.'

'You're dead wrong. I *don't* want you to make love to me.' *Because I don't want you to find out that my body does!*

'Then what is it you want? To make love to me?'

'What? No! No, of course not.' Just the thought made her feel faint. 'I told you,' she protested in one last desperate gesture of defiance, 'I don't like sex. And I don't like you!'

'You will,' he promised, and actually had the gall to smile a little as his mouth descended.

She tried to keep her lips shut beneath his. Tried to resist. But her struggles defeated her even more than if she'd stayed perfectly still. Moving her head from side to side only increased the delicious friction created by their mouths being clamped together. As for wriggling her lower body…

Total disaster!

For her movements simply provided her with a perfect mental imprint of his erection, which was formidable in a way that sent her head spinning. Could he really be that long and that thick, and that hard?

He gripped her wrists tighter and pressed her hands firmly against her bottom—possibly in an attempt to still her struggles. She froze in shock, but by then the soft swell of her stomach was wrapped snugly around his swollen sex, and her mouth had gaped open a little.

His tongue immediately slid inside. Not roughly or brutally. Slowly and confidently.

He tasted of mint, and of triumph.

And why not? Despite her earlier resolve, she *was* melting. And her pride was nowhere to be seen. In its place was a powerful urge to simply sink against him and let nature take its course.

Her sigh of surrender could not be mistaken. Perhaps because it was more of a moan than a sigh, a sensual sound that echoed in her mouth and told him that she was his for the taking.

His mouth lifted and their eyes locked, hers glazed, his gleaming. But he still did not let her go.

'Kiss me,' he whispered. 'Kiss me where you hit me.'

Charmaine stared at his still reddened cheek, then deep into his eyes. If they'd been angry, or arrogant, the erotic spell he was weaving might have been broken. But they weren't. They were softly smouldering, and almost slumberous, his eyelids heavy with arousal.

His cheek felt hot under her lips. Hot and slightly bristly. His beard was beginning to grow. She liked the feel of the stubble under her already sensitised lips, rubbing her mouth across the rough surface, not once but several times. When her tongue darted forth and licked his cheek, a violent shudder rippled down her spine.

Shock had her face jerking away from his, their eyes meeting once more.

'You liked that, didn't you?' he said.

'Yes,' she agreed, though with some confusion. What was it about this man that she would even enjoy licking his stubbly skin? Was it the man himself? His masterfulness, or just the situation she found herself in?

Maybe she was secretly turned on by his having paid half a billion dollars to have sex with her. Maybe she liked the fact that she didn't have to like him. Maybe the secret to her sexual success here was that she could distance herself from any emotion which made her vulnerable.

Whatever the reason, there was no turning back. It would take a team of wild horses to drag her out of here now. She had to know what it would be like with him. *Had* to.

'Do not worry,' he murmured, and bent to brush his lips with tantalising tenderness over hers. 'You will like doing many more things before this night is over.'

His abruptly releasing her arms disorientated her for a few seconds. She even experienced a jab of disappointment at her physical freedom. The thought that she had enjoyed his holding her captive like that was a worry, as was his declaration that she would like doing many more things. Her mind boggled at the various images that came to mind. Yet alongside her shock lay a dizzying excitement and a desire to experience simply everything there was to be experienced with this man.

Such thinking really stunned her. This wasn't like her. Over the past few years she'd stopped being desperate to like sex and simply become uninterested. Bored, even.

His hands easing the red chiffon robe back off her shoulders catapulted Charmaine's mind out of her mental bewilderment and back on to the physical present. She quivered when his fingertips brushed over her collar-bones.

'You wore this outfit to provoke me,' he said as the flimsy robe fell down her arms and pooled at her feet.

She could not deny it.

'It worked,' he added before his fingers went to the straps on her nightie.

Charmaine tensed. Surely he didn't mean to strip her naked, here, in the middle of his sitting-room?

What *then*? Was she to eat dinner with him in the nude?

Was she repelled by that thought? Or turned on by it?

'It makes you look like a whore,' he ground out, and the nightie joined the negligee on the floor, leaving her standing before him in nothing but those red satin high heels.

He took a backward step, sucking in as his eyes seared over her nakedness. She stood there stiffly, stung by his saying she looked like a whore. Even though it was true.

But perhaps that was what she had become? For as he stared at her, she grew more hotly aware of her female body than she had ever been before. Her skin seemed to glow under his white-hot gaze. Her breasts grew heavier. Her nipples tightened further.

When his gaze travelled further down her body, her belly contracted. Was he looking at her recently waxed pubis and despising her for going to such lengths for her career? Or did he think she'd done it for him?

'You are far too beautiful for your own good,' he muttered angrily. 'And far too brazen.'

With that, he swept her up into his arms and carried her towards his bedroom.

CHAPTER EIGHT

His bedroom was as unexpected in décor as his sitting-room. Not an erotically designed boudoir of the Arabian-nights variety at all, but a classy, relaxing retreat.

The walls were covered in a claret-coloured, suede-style wallpaper, its rich darkness relieved by subtle gold wall lights shining down on gilt-framed photographs of racehorses. The carpet was a deep gold and the bed was larger than any bed Charmaine had ever seen, its enormous rosewood bedhead flanked by matching bedside tables on which stood brass lamps with gold shades. The bed's cream and gold brocade bedspread had been thrown back, exposing cream satin sheets and matching pillows.

'What about dinner, Your Highness?' she dared to venture as he laid her down across those cream satin sheets.

His calling her brazen had revived some of her usual boldness. Or so she told herself. More likely her attempt at conversation was a desperate ploy to delay the discovery the sheikh was about to make, which was that she *did* want him.

'Dinner can wait,' he pronounced as he straightened and ripped off his own robe. 'And you are to stop calling me Your Highness. My name is Ali.'

'Whatever. You've paid for the privilege.'

He scowled at her impertinence, plus the reminder of how she'd come to be lying naked on his bed in

103

the first place. After a savage yank at the cord on his waistband, his black silk pyjama trousers dropped to the floor.

Charmaine gulped. Now she knew why he'd always been so successful with women. Prince Ali of Dubar certainly had an unfair advantage over the other men Charmaine had been to bed with. And most others, she suspected.

But the sheikh's flagrant masculinity—and possibly promiscuous lifestyle—rang warning bells in her head. She wasn't that far gone yet that she would take stupid risks just to find out if she could enjoy sex with this lover *extraordinaire*. Fortunately she was on the Pill, so pregnancy wasn't in the equation. But pregnancy was not the only consideration in this modern world.

'One thing before you start,' she said, proud that she could still find a steady voice in the face of such a sight. 'I do hope you have protection handy, because I *will* have to go home if you're not prepared to practise safe sex.'

'There are two full boxes in there,' he said with a curt nod towards the right-hand bedside table. 'And some loose under these pillows at the ready.'

Charmaine did her best not to look stunned. Now that she had refound some spirit, she refused to revert to mindless mush. But two full *boxes*? And more under the pillows? With *this* man? Hopefully, he didn't mean to use them all tonight or she wouldn't be able to walk tomorrow, let alone go horse-riding.

'The condoms I buy are custom designed,' he continued. 'They are also one hundred per cent pregnancy proof. I, too, have a passion for protection.'

'Yes, I imagine that a man of your obscene wealth

couldn't be too careful. But you don't have to worry about me trying to trap you. I already have a good chunk of your money and the last thing I would want is your baby.'

Too late she realised he might take her remark as a personal insult. Probably had, by the flash of fury in his eyes.

The thought upset her for some reason. Silly, really. He deserved an insult or two, this man who thought he could buy her body. And had.

But she still felt compelled to apologise.

'I...I'm sorry, Ali. I didn't mean that the way it sounded. I mean...it doesn't have anything to do with you. I just don't want *any* baby.'

Ali stared down at her distressed eyes and saw that she was, indeed, sorry. He sighed and shook his head. What a complex creature she was. Ali wished he understood what made her act in so many contradictory ways. Why had she come to him tonight dressed like a whore, only to then tell him she'd changed her mind about staying the week with him?

He'd been in danger of losing it when she'd said that. Almost had, till he realised she was just afraid of sleeping with him for some reason. Afraid of sex.

All that was needed then was a little gentle persuasion to change her mind back again. For a while, she'd become the woman he knew she could be in his arms. All liquid heat and trembling passion. Now she'd reverted to that other colder, bolder creature, the one who challenged him and made him want to act like some animal with her.

But that was not his way with women. He hated the thought of being reduced to a savage beast, something she seemed capable of doing. He only had to glance down at himself to see what she had reduced him to.

Delaying his own satisfaction was going to be difficult. But not impossible.

Now, how best to proceed to win her? Because that was his goal, wasn't it? To win her. To have her coming back for more at the end of these five days, *without* any monetary bribe.

Ali bitterly regretted not having had her background thoroughly investigated right from the start. Knowledge was power, and more than anything else he wanted to have power over her. But he was in the dark where Charmaine was concerned.

One thing Ali *did* understand about the naked woman lying before him was that the main thing keeping her in this room at this moment was the half a billion dollars it would earn her foundation. In other circumstances, he might have taken more time with her, as he had with that difficult mare.

But there was no time to waste. Five days wasn't all that long…

Charmaine's whole body tensed when he stepped forward and picked up her right foot from where it had been dangling over the side of the bed.

'Relax,' he murmured, his left hand encircling her ankle whilst his right hand slid up and down her calf with the lightest of feather touches. When he bent forward slightly to caress the sensitive skin behind her knee, goose-bumps broke out over her arms.

Relax! How could she relax whilst he was doing that to her and standing before her without a stitch of clothing on? Her eyes kept going to that part of him she kept imagining inside her. *If* it would fit inside her.

Finally his hand returned to her foot, where he removed her red slipper and tossed it aside. He seemed to take longer on her left leg before removing that shoe, by which time she was trembling.

'Ali…'

She hadn't meant to speak. Hadn't meant to sound so desperate and needy.

His eyes went to hers. 'Yes?'

'Don't…don't make me wait too long.'

He nodded, then moved to scoop her up again in his arms and place her in the centre of the bed with her head on the pillows. She watched, wide-eyed, whilst he retrieved a condom from under a pillow and protected them both with a couple of well-practised moves. Her heart was thundering in her chest by the time he joined her on the bed and stretched out beside her.

'You don't want me to pleasure you with my mouth first?' he asked, his face looming over hers.

Charmaine blinked up at him. Did she?

'I…I don't know…'

He frowned at her uncertainty.

'Maybe a little,' she added breathlessly.

What was she *saying*?

But too late. He was already on his way, although not without an immediate detour to her breasts, where he suckled long and languorously on each nipple, leaving them stiff and wet and herself all twisting inside with the most excruciating need. By the time he moved on, she wanted him everywhere. On top of her. Inside her. Sucking her. Kissing her. Touching her.

'Oh,' she moaned when his tongue-tip swirled into her navel.

Who would have thought that could feel so delicious? She was so glad when he did it again. And again.

Her hands reached down to touch his hair, to run her fingers through it, luxuriating in its glossy softness. He glanced up briefly to smile at her before moving further down her body, licking over the smooth surface of her pubic bone whilst he pushed her thighs apart.

Her belly tightened in anticipation of his mouth reaching her exposed sex, and when it did she almost jackknifed off the bed.

'Sshhh,' he soothed, and reached up to press a large palm flat down on her lower stomach. 'Be still. Relax.'

More ridiculous commands. Impossible to be still, *or* to relax. His tongue was now circling her core, his fingers penetrating her. The sensations were both exhilarating and frightening, like being on a roller-coaster ride.

'Ali,' she choked out, and he immediately stopped.

She almost burst into tears, like a child whose lollipop had been snatched away.

But there was little time for ongoing dismay as he slid back up her body and started penetrating her for real. Her sharp intake of breath was a combination of pleasure and surprise. For despite his being bigger than any man she'd ever been with before—by far— she was able to accommodate him quite easily. Maybe even better if she…

When she lifted her legs and wrapped them high around him, he groaned. She did too, feeling the difference straight away. He was now very deep inside her, filling her entirely, evoking a stunning awareness of their fused flesh. Lord knew what it would feel like when he started to move.

She cried out when he started pumping back and forth, each forward movement ramming the head of his penis against her cervix.

He stopped again. 'I am in too deep,' he said.

'No, no, it's fantastic!'

'You are sure?'

'Absolutely. Don't stop.'

He laughed, then continued.

She climaxed in no time, with great, racking spasms of rapturous release, making her almost scream with pleasure. He clasped her tightly to him and came as well, his mouth opening with his own primal roar.

When she felt his flesh pulsating deep inside her, a sudden wave of decidedly primitive passion swept through Charmaine and she started kissing his shoulder, his neck and finally his gasping lips, sending her tongue deep into his mouth in an erotic echo of the way he'd penetrated her. He kissed her back and kept on moving, through his climax and her own, till astonishingly she came again. Only when she was completely done did he stop, his body collapsing on top of hers.

He was heavy but she didn't mind. She relished being enveloped by his body. She ran her hands possessively up and down his back and tried to remember why it was she didn't like him.

And then it came back to her.

He was a sexual predator who'd bullied her into

sleeping with him. Bullied and bribed and emotionally blackmailed her.

She could never tell him how grateful she was that he had. She had to find other words to explain her pleasure in his body, and to regain at least some of her pride.

'You see?' he murmured some time later as he lay beside her, one hand propping up his head whilst his other played idly with her breasts. 'You do like sex. At least you do with me.'

Charmaine, whose brain had been working overtime whilst her body had thrummed with pleasure at his tweaking her nipples, had fortunately come up with just the right reply.

'I have to confess my response to you surprised me at first. But I've since realised what turned me on so much. It's a popular female fantasy, you know, being paid a small fortune by some billionaire to have sex with them. Every woman has a secret yen to play the call-girl. And then there's the sheikh factor, of course.'

His hand stilled on her breast. 'The sheikh factor?'

'Don't act the innocent with me, Ali. I'll bet you've taken advantage of it many times. You know. The sheikh? Rudolph Valentino, sweeping the fair lady off to his desert lair to have his wicked way with her? That scenario has turned countless Western women on no end over the years. Don't pretend you don't know that.'

She finally dared to look up into his eyes, which remained annoyingly unreadable.

'And does it turn *you* on no end?' he said, plucking at her nipple once more, though not as gently as he had been doing.

Unfortunately, this seemed to excite her all the more.

'Who knows?' She shrugged, struggling to stay cool when all she wanted to do was beg him to make love to her again, to use her even more roughly this time. 'Something did. It certainly wasn't romance that got me going. Or love.'

'You don't find me romantic? Or lovable?' he added with another less than gentle tug on her other nipple.

She had to laugh. 'Oh, come, now, Ali. Paying a woman half a billion dollars to force her to be at your sexual beck and call for a week is hardly romantic, or lovable.'

'I didn't force you.'

Thank goodness he stopped with the nipple torture.

'As good as. You knew I wouldn't say no.'

'But you enjoyed yourself just now.'

'You would have demanded your pound of flesh whether I did or not.'

'No,' he said. 'I would not have.'

She stared up at him, not sure if he was telling the truth or not. Hard to believe that a man who had physically restrained her earlier tonight would have let her go if she hadn't been so easily seduced.

She shrugged. 'Whatever. It's of no consequence any more. It seems I like playing paid sex slave to your master. So, till Friday, I am yours to command. Command away, then, lover. The night, as they say, is still young.'

His eyes glittered in that way which had once made her angry but which now sent her breathing haywire. 'A sex slave does not demand her master command her,' he said in a soft, low, wickedly seductive voice.

'A sex slave remains silent and submissive and awaits his desire. A sex slave has no will of her own, surrendering it to her master's. She is nothing till he deigns to use her body. Nothing at all.'

Her mouth had grown dry as he spoke. But her heart was racing. It's just a game, she reminded herself, an erotic game. But oh, she thrilled to it.

'Sounds like fun,' she quipped.

His eyes flashed a stern rebuke at her. 'A sex slave is not concerned with her own fun. She exists just to give pleasure, not receive it.'

Charmaine pulled a face. 'Doesn't sound like a job that will catch on here in Australia. Except when the chap with the cheque-book has half a billion dollars to spare, of course. Although, if you recall, you only paid me for straight sex. So I reserve the right to object if things get too kinky. Meanwhile, would a slave really call you by your first name? I don't think so. How about just Master? That has a nicely submissive ring to it, don't you think?'

She scrambled off the bed and bowed with her hands together in front of her. 'I'll run ahead and run your bath, Master,' she said with mock-servitude.

'I *am* the master here,' he pronounced arrogantly.

'Only until I tell you the game is over,' she reminded him.

'Agreed,' came his smooth reply, but there was a devilish gleam in his black eyes. 'I must insist, however, that if you wish to quit you say so in advance, *before* the game has started in earnest. It is unfair to arouse a man, then leave him dangling.'

She laughed. 'I can't imagine you ever dangling.'

'That is just a figure of speech. So! Do you wish to continue being my sex slave?'

A quiver of nervous excitement fluttered in her stomach. Damn, but she could get addicted to this game. Dangerously addicted. Still, it was far less dangerous than the alternative—admitting that she did perhaps like Ali after all. No way was she about to do that!

'For tonight, anyway,' she said.

'Go run the bath, then,' he ordered. 'But no coloured additives or bubble bath. I wish to be able to see all of you in the water at all times.'

CHAPTER NINE

CHARMAINE often woke very early in the morning to a wave of emptiness, followed by the threat of depression. When that happened she would rise and exercise furiously till her dark mood passed, or was at least pushed aside for the moment.

That morning she woke not only very late, but also to a delicious feeling of peace, although she did experience a small knee-jerk of surprise once she realised she was back in the pretty pink bed. Ali must have carried her in there after she'd finally fallen asleep.

He hadn't stayed, however. He must have returned to his own quarters, and his own bed.

Charmaine quickly realised that waking up alone the morning after a night like last night was a definite plus. She could snuggle down under the duvet and think about all that had happened, without having to feel guilty or embarrassed, or whatever other awkward feelings might have consumed her if she'd woken still glued to Ali's naked body.

Don't think about Ali's naked body! came the immediate warning.

Too late. She was already thinking about it, and remembering. How it had looked and felt. How she'd been compelled to touch him all the time, and kiss him, and invite him back inside her, over and over and over.

Yet she didn't feel a bit sore this morning.

Obviously she'd been more than ready for him every single time.

Great sex, she finally decided after she'd wallowed for a while in her memories, had to be the best sleeping tablet in the world, plus the best anti-depressant. Once you were seriously turned on, making love was brilliantly mindless. And very morish. Once was never enough.

Fortunately, Ali was not a once-only man. He seemed to want her as much, if not more, than she wanted him. Of course, any man who'd paid five hundred million dollars for a woman had to be suffering from one huge dose of lust.

Even thinking about the money part didn't spoil Charmaine's feelings of delicious pleasure. Amazingly, she was beginning to find this whole scenario extremely satisfying indeed. All those lovely orgasms, plus all that lovely money. A girl such as herself would have to be mad not to be happy.

Or as happy as she was ever going to be. Charmaine did not delude herself into thinking that she would ever be really happy in life.

But things weren't too bad at the moment. She had five hundred million dollars to do good with. And a wickedly sexy sheikh at her disposal to be bad with.

The only problem she could foresee was Friday. Charmaine suspected that by then she might be somewhat addicted to Ali. Already she was looking forward to tonight. Would he want a rerun of the slave-girl act? She rather hoped he would. It was a good cover for her feelings, which could quite easily get out of hand if she wasn't careful. She still could not believe some of the things she'd willingly done last night.

It was obvious Ali preferred to be the boss when it came to lovemaking.

Charmaine shivered at the memory of all that he'd done to her last night. So many different positions. And so many different places, not just the bed.

Dinner in the sitting-room had been an education. Who would have thought food could be used as an aphrodisiac? Or that a dining table could become an instrument of erotic pleasure? Or was it erotic torture? The glass had felt very cold against her heated flesh.

But that had been only one of many highly imaginative interludes. Ali had come up with ways to have sex that she'd never dreamt of, but never anything she hadn't ultimately enjoyed, even if she was reduced to begging occasionally.

And didn't he like that!

Charmaine wasn't sure if Ali was a sadist at heart, or just getting even for her once having said no to him.

Saying no to him now—during sex, anyway—was no longer an option, not unless *she* was a masochist, which she wasn't. The irony of being turned on by a man like him did not elude Charmaine, but there was no point pretending. Sexually, she was putty in his hands.

Ali's boast about being an excellent lover had been an understatement. The man knew what he was doing. It was a shame that she had to give him up, come Friday.

Although, now that Charmaine came to think about it, there was no reason why she *had* to give him up after this arrangement ended. If he was willing—and she had every reason to think he would be—she could continue to see him. Ali had said he came to Sydney every weekend to play poker and to go to the races. When she was in town, she could rendezvous with him in his hotel suite on a Saturday night after he returned from the races. They could enjoy each other at their leisure and in private, without having to make their affair public.

Of course, she would have to be *very* careful that the paparazzi didn't get wind of anything. She would hate for the world to think she was Prince Ali's latest plaything, bought and paid for at an auction no less!

Charmaine shuddered at what her mother would say, and think. She'd already questioned Charmaine closely over the phone last week after reading the Sunday newspaper article about some Arab prince paying millions to have dinner with her. She'd been concerned over Charmaine falling prey to some kind of obsessed admirer. An understandable concern, under the circumstances.

Fortunately, her mother had accepted her explanation that Ali was an oil-rich sheikh who used any excuse to give millions away to charity. She had admitted that yes, she *was* going to dinner with him but no, there was *nothing* going on between them, nor would there ever be.

Charmaine sighed. Her mother would not be happy if she ever found out her darling daughter had lied to her, or that she'd been carrying on with such a man. No, the risk of continuing this affair was just too great. She'd given her parents enough angst and pain in the past. To give them more was unconscionable. Come Friday, she would have to give Ali up. But till then…till then, she aimed to enjoy what he could deliver to the full. And then some!

The bedside telephone ringing put paid to any more

planning and plotting. Charmaine rolled over and frowned at the pink instrument for a few seconds. She'd left a message on her own answering machine at home saying she was out of town and out of reach for this whole week. Then she'd bravely left her mobile phone at home as well—turned off. Instinct had warned her in advance that, whatever happened this week, it would be wise for her to be incommunicado. Since no one knew she was here, then this could only be an in-house call. Ali, perhaps?

Charmaine was irritated by the wave of girlish pleasure that suddenly swept through her at this thought. The last thing she intended to do was to start acting like some infatuated schoolgirl around him. He was still the same man who'd paid five million to force her to have dinner with him and five hundred million to sleep with him. Just because she'd enjoyed sleeping with him didn't mean she had to *become* silly.

Scooping in a gathering breath, she expelled it noisily then snatched up the pink receiver.

'Yes?' she said rather sharply.

'Cleo here. I hope I didn't wake you?'

'No, no, not at all,' she replied, relieved in a way that it was the housekeeper. Relieved yet perversely disappointed at the same time. 'I was just thinking about getting up. I know it must be horribly late. What time is it?' Her watch was still in the bathroom, and there wasn't a clock in the room. But she could see through the French doors that the sun had been up for ages.

'Going on eleven.'

'*That* late!' The last time she'd looked at the time—via Ali's Rolex—it had been just after two a.m.

She'd fallen asleep soon after that. Which meant she'd been out of it for possibly eight or nine hours. A record for her. She was usually pushed to get four hours a night.

'Ali said not to disturb you,' Cleo informed her. 'He's only been up a couple of hours himself. Had a quick breakfast and took off to do the rounds of the stud. He'll be back for a proper lunch around one so I thought you might like to join him. I'll set something extra-nice up for you both by the pool. It's a lovely day outside.'

'That sounds marvellous. Thank you. I'll get up straight away.'

'How about I bring some coffee and croissants along to your room to tide you over till lunch? Or is that too fattening?'

'No. Sounds marvellous as well.'

'My, but you're easy to please. Ali's brought a few of your modelling compatriots home to stay over the years and I always found them on the snooty side. Feeding them was an especially big problem.'

'You won't have any trouble feeding me,' Charmaine replied whilst frowning over her negative reaction to Cleo's news that Ali seemed partial to models. The thought that she was just one in a long line of the breed to grace his bed piqued more than her pride, and firmed her resolve never to see him again after Friday.

'See you soon, then,' Cleo said brightly.

Cleo was at the door in less than ten minutes, Charmaine having only managed by then to go to the toilet, brush her teeth and pull on the pink towelling robe that was hanging on the back of her bathroom door. The only nightwear she'd brought with her was

the red set and another equally tarty black outfit, neither of which seemed suitable for greeting the housekeeper in.

'You were quick,' Charmaine said as she let the
housekeeper in, trying not to look startled by the
woman's colourful clothes. Canary-yellow Bermuda
shorts, topped by a bright red and orange top that
should have clashed with Cleo's red hair but somehow didn't.

'I'm a fast worker.' Cleo carried the breakfast tray
across the room to the far corner, where two chairs
sat on either side of a good-sized corner table.

'Did you and your husband enjoy the movie last
night?' Charmaine asked as she followed her across
the room and sat down in one of the chairs.

'What?' Cleo glanced up from where she'd started
pouring the coffee. 'Oh, yes; yes, we did. Ali told
you we were going, did he?'

'He mentioned it,' she said a bit abruptly, not
happy with the reminder of Ali's threats about how
she could scream all she liked and no one would come
to help her.

But she hadn't screamed, had she? She doubted any
of the women he'd had up here ever did, except in
pleasure.

Charmaine found she didn't like thinking about
Ali's other women.

'Do—er—all Ali's female guests sleep in here?'

Cleo smiled a knowing little smile. 'There's no
need to be jealous. Ali hasn't brought any lady home
here for ages. And none have ever stayed in here.'

'I'm not jealous,' Charmaine said, but far too defensively. 'Just curious.'

'No need to be ashamed of caring for Ali, either. He's a man worth caring for.'

Charmaine thought it wasn't the right moment to mention that she didn't care for the man. Not in the way Cleo meant.

'Really,' she said noncommittally, and picked up the first of the two scrumptious-looking croissants.

'People often misjudge Ali because he can be a bit stiff at times,' Cleo said as she poured Charmaine's coffee. 'You know, *royal*. But I can honestly say he's one of the nicest men I've ever met. Genuinely kind and compassionate. Cream and sugar?'

Charmaine nodded. 'Two cubes.' She figured she'd burned up more than enough calories last night to indulge herself today. She'd hardly touched the dinner in the end. Ali had eaten most of it, some off places on her body that in the cold light of day should have shocked her. It didn't, which was telling in itself, and reminded her of the type of man she was dealing with here. A rogue and a corrupter of women.

'And how is he kind and compassionate?' she asked, scepticism in her voice.

'Oh, countless ways. Take Jack for instance.'

'Jack?'

'The fellow who carried your luggage in last night. Jack's a cousin of mine. He's got special needs. No one would give him a job, but Ali did when I asked him. Like a flash. He's often given jobs to people who were down on their luck, especially married men with kiddies. Given them free accommodation, too. There's quite a few old cottages on this place. He's very good to everyone who works for him, provided they work hard in return. But he never expects anyone to do what he isn't prepared to do himself. The men

appreciate that. There's nothing Ali won't do. Muck
out stables. Stay up all night with a mare in labour.
Plough. Paint fences. Jack thinks he's just the ant's
pants. And so does everyone else around here. You
just ask them. No, perhaps that's not a good idea,'
she added laughingly. 'I can see Ali being quite jealous if you started chatting away to the men. So just
nod and smile when he shows you around the stud
after lunch.'

'Do you think he'll do that today?' Charmaine
asked, her mind still digesting Ali's glowing character
reference. He was either a clever man, knowing how
to get the best out of his staff, or he had a good side.
Charmaine conceded no person was all black or
white. She herself was no angel but she could be kind
and generous to people less fortunate than herself.

'Oh, yes. He's terribly proud of this place. He's
done wonders since he became manager.' Cleo placed
the coffee-cup and saucer in front of Charmaine.

'Did he build this house?' Charmaine asked between mouthfuls of croissant.

'Heavens no, the manager before him did that. An
Arab sheikh too, but nothing like Ali. A big, fat, lazy
fellow. From what I've heard, he did nothing but
spend the money on himself that should have been
spent on buying decent stallions and mares. Actually,
Ali doesn't care for this house much at all. Says it's
way too large for his needs. It has twelve bedrooms,
you know. Mostly we keep a lot of them shut up with
dust covers on, but around Christmas I clean them all
out and make up the beds with fresh linen and he lets
any of the staff's relatives who want to visit stay here.
It's bedlam, really, but wonderful. I love it.'

Surprise had stopped Charmaine's coffee-cup halfway to her lips. 'But...but Muslims don't celebrate Christmas!'

'Ali lives by the credo of when in Rome do as the Romans do. I suppose one might call him a lapsed Muslim, in some ways. A lapsed prince when he's home here as well. Not that you can blame him. That lot over in Dubar never contact him for anything other than business. I throw him a birthday party every year and not once has he received a present, or a card, or even a phone call. Miserable lot! Who needs enemies when you have family like that? But I'd better not gossip about them,' she muttered. 'Ali wouldn't like it. He likes *you*, though, love. More than likes, I'd say. Have you known him long?'

Charmaine wondered what to say to this question. Clearly, Cleo didn't know anything about the auction or the dinner date Ali had won with her. She couldn't have read that article in the Sunday paper last week.

'We met at the Melbourne Cup carnival last year.'

'Goodness, *that* long ago. And he's only just brought you up here? Been playing hard to get, have you, love?' she said cheekily. 'Well, whatever, it's working. Never known a man so hyped up as he was last week. Then when he rang on Sunday to say he was bringing home a special guest and I was to get this particular room ready, I said to Norm that our Ali must have met someone really special, and when you turned up I knew I was right.'

'I'm not so very special,' Charmaine refuted, embarrassed by the housekeeper's compliments, plus her mistaken notion that Ali had been smitten by a once-in-a-lifetime love. 'People think fame makes you special but it doesn't.'

'Oh, I know that, love. I wasn't talking about your

fame. Or even about your beauty. I was talking about
you. You're a real sweetie. And wonderfully down-
to-earth. Just the sort of girl Ali needs to bring him
out of that shell he goes into occasionally. Been extra
bad this past year. But he was bright-eyed and bushy-
tailed at breakfast this morning, I can tell you,' she
said with a wickedly knowing gleam in her eye.

Charmaine was hard-pushed not to blush. The
woman was incorrigible, but lovable at the same time.

'That's nice to hear,' she said.

Cleo laughed. 'You play your cards close to your
chest, don't you, love? Smart girl. Look, I'll get Ali
to come and collect you when he gets back. He's sure
to want to shower and change before lunch.'

'No, I'd really rather not do that,' Charmaine said
swiftly. 'I'd rather come and help you with the lunch.
It won't take me more than half an hour to get ready,
which means I'd just be sitting around in here, doing
nothing.'

Cleo blinked in surprise. 'You really are a most
unusual girl. But I won't say no to some help. Righto,
when you're ready, just make your way to the
kitchen.'

'You'd better give me directions. This house is
huge. I'll probably get lost.'

'No, you won't. The house *is* big, but the floor plan
is simple. It's shaped like a T. Go back along the
corridor you came along last night till you get to the
foyer, then turn left and go down that corridor. The
kitchen is the second door on the right.'

'Well, that's straightforward.'

'One thing before I go. Please don't go making
your bed. I have a girl who works for me who does
that. She does all the washing and ironing as well.

She'll do your room and be along to empty your clothes basket whilst you're at lunch. She couldn't do it earlier because you were asleep.'

After Cleo left, Charmaine bolted down her coffee and croissants then set about getting herself ready in record time. Having declared she wasn't one of those vain pusses who spent hours on their appearance, she had to live up to the claim. But even the most minimal of self-care took time, especially when you had hair that fell to your waist. In the end, she plaited it whilst still wet then dressed in white stretch jeans and a simple white vest top that had no sleeves and a not-too-low V-neckline. In light of a possible tour around the stud after lunch, she chose comfy flat fawn loafers and kept her make-up to a dusting of blusher and coral lipstick. No perfume, either. She would save that for tonight.

Her trip to the kitchen was as direct and simple as Cleo had indicated. Once again, Charmaine spied little of the house on the way, although this time she took more note of the artwork that hung on the walls. No doubt original oils, they ranged from very modern to more traditional landscapes. Charmaine had an eye for art and was well-aware each one would have cost a small fortune.

The kitchen itself proved to be as large and well-equipped as one would expect in the home of royalty. It also had lovely large windows that overlooked a terracotta-tiled terrace and a huge swimming pool with water as blue as the sky above. At the far end of the pool stood a pavilion-style structure with three-hundred-and-sixty-degree views of the property, and it was in there, Cleo informed Charmaine, that lunch was to be set up on a marble table fit for a prince and his lady-love.

Once again, Charmaine didn't bother denying that she was Ali's lady-love. No point. Cleo wouldn't believe her.

In the end, Charmaine didn't do very much of the food preparations, with Cleo only allowing her to do minimal fetching and carrying. Somehow—possibly by the sound of water running through pipes—Cleo knew the exact moment Ali arrived back, announcing that he would be along shortly, and she—Charmaine—should await him out by the pool. Cleo seemed to think he wouldn't be too thrilled with her playing maid.

Charmaine chose to wait for him at the table inside the pavilion rather than at one of the outdoor settings by the pool itself. When Ali made his appearance through the kitchen door a couple of minutes later, she was glad she'd made that choice.

Charmaine had often scorned women who said some man took their breath away. But as Ali stepped out onto the sun-drenched terrace, her own heartbeat stopped for a few drama-filled seconds.

The shadowed privacy—plus the distance from the house that the pavilion afforded her—gave Charmaine sufficient time to recover from the shock of her reaction. But her eyes continued to follow him slavishly as he made his way along the side of the pool, her mind revolving as it sought the reasons behind this most uncharacteristic response.

It couldn't be his handsome elegance which had sent her into temporary cardiac arrest. Ali had always been excessively good-looking. And a cool dresser. The denim shorts he was wearing looked great on him, as did the sky-blue polo top. And, whilst some men looked ridiculous in sandals, he did not, perhaps because his feet were as brown as the rest of him.

She swallowed as she recalled again how magnificent his body looked naked. That had to be it, she decided with something like relief. It was lust which had made her heart stop, and more lust now making it pound.

She'd never been in lust before. Not really. That long-ago sexual attraction which had made her act so foolishly—and so disastrously—was nothing like this. This was on a different level entirely.

Thank goodness she now had the maturity and the character to handle her feelings, however primal and powerful they were. Charmaine wasn't ashamed of the way she'd acted last night, but she valued her composure at moments like this. She had no patience with females who ogled and drooled.

Of course, it would help if Ali didn't keep looking at her as if he'd prefer to have *her* for lunch, instead of the food on the table. Those hot black eyes of his seared over her face and body as he approached, telling her in no uncertain terms that any tour of the stud this afternoon was going to be brief.

Charmaine swallowed again.

'You slept well, I hear,' he said as he dragged a chair out at the table in the place opposite her.

'Very. And you?'

'The best I have in a year.'

His meaning did not escape her. He meant since he'd first set eyes on her. Charmaine tried not to let his flattery—or her own rapidly increasing lust—undermine her intention to have done with this affair, come Friday.

'So what would you like to do after lunch?' he asked as he selected one of the warm, crunchy bread rolls from the basket on the centre of the table and tore it in two.

Charmaine fought temptation with every shred of will-power she owned. As bold as she'd been last night, today was another day. And the situation was entirely different, especially now that she realised how weak she could be around him. She had to exercise some control over herself, or she might be in serious trouble. Men like Ali were fine to have a fling with, but not to become obsessed with, or, heaven help her, fall in love with.

As Rico had said, he could be dangerous.

'Cleo said you would like to take me for a tour of the stud,' she commented lightly, and occupied herself pouring a glass of mineral water from one of the chilled bottles on the table.

He smiled, a smile that carried a sip of cynicism and a large dose of devilry. 'And do you think that is how I would like to spend this afternoon with you?'

Her gaze met his squarely and coolly. 'I am certainly hoping you do,' she returned. 'Your insatiability last night has left me just a little...tender in places. I need a few more hours to recover before this evening.'

He laughed. '*My* insatiability. I seem to recall it was you who kept begging for more.'

She feigned a nonchalance she far from felt. 'Possibly I did. Once or twice. I have to admit you are very good in bed, Ali. You've certainly set a benchmark for the performances of my future lovers. I almost regret that this arrangement has to end.' She noted the tightening in his facial muscles when she said this, but deliberately ignored it.

'Oh, and speaking of this arrangement,' she went on matter-of-factly, 'have you checked to see if the money was properly transferred to the foundation's account this morning?'

CHAPTER TEN

IN HINDSIGHT, Ali didn't know how he managed to hide his feelings at that moment.

Dismay was his first reaction to her monetary reminder. Followed by a crushing sense of his own stupidity.

Had he honestly begun to believe she felt something for him; that by the time he'd carried her back to her bed in the wee hours of the morning, she'd surrendered to more than the sexual chemistry that had always sizzled between them?

What a fool he was. A besotted fool. A *bewitched* fool. Yes, that was what he was. Bewitched. She had bewitched him from the first moment he laid eyes on her in that television commercial, then bewitched him further last night with her astonishingly sensual abandonment. When he thought of the way she'd moaned beneath his mouth, and trembled at his touch, and clung to him as she came…

But there was no glaze of desire in her eyes today. They were clear and cool and very much in control.

His gaze raked over her, taking in the virginal white clothes and schoolgirl plait which only emphasised the air of innocence that had always intrigued him and which this morning seemed to be especially mocking.

His dismay finally gave way to anger, his male ego smarting under the realisation that, regardless of how much delight she experienced in his arms, her priority with him was always going to be that five hundred million dollars.

'It is all there,' he ground out, vowing to make her pay tonight for every single dollar.

Charmaine regretted her words the moment they were out of her mouth. She hadn't meant to sound so mercenary, or to make him angry. But for pity's sake, what did he expect? That she would *forget* that he'd virtually forced her to come here with him? Did he think she was going to let bygones be bygones and start playing the role of romantic lady-love for him?

OK, so they'd shared some amazing sex last night. And yes, he was one fabulous lover. But she had no intention of pretending that they shared anything more. For Cleo she might, yes, but not for him.

At the same time, she didn't want to spend the next four days in an atmosphere of open hostility. Ali in a bad mood was not fit for human consumption, let alone lovemaking. The one thing bound to turn her off was a lover whose passion was overlaid with anger. What she'd liked about last night was that, in the end, it had been such fun. Clearly, some compromise was called for.

'Look, I'm sorry,' she said, realising ruefully that there would be no smoothing over of things from Prince Ali of Dubar. She could tell by the set of his jaw and the cold fury in his black eyes that he'd just declared war on her again. 'I didn't mean to upset you, but I can't pretend that the foundation doesn't come first with me. That doesn't mean I didn't enjoy last night, or even that I'm not looking forward to a repeat performance. I'm even growing to like you…a little bit,' she added swiftly when his highly expressive eyes gleamed with satisfaction. 'Cleo has said such nice things about you this morning that I can't continue to hold to the view that you're totally arrogant and spoiled. You do seem to have some redeeming qualities. Although the way you react to the word no is not one of your virtues. How many men do you think would go to the lengths you have to get a woman into your bed?'

'Not any woman,' he retorted. 'Just you, Charmaine.'

'Flattery won't get you anywhere with me, Your Highness. I think I told you that once before.'

'Ali,' he reminded her curtly.

'Ali,' she repeated with a sigh. 'See what I mean? You still must have things all your way.'

'We all like our own way. You do, too, Charmaine. But you might be surprised to discover that in my dealings with you I have not always given in to my desires. If I had been totally selfish, I would have had you during our helicopter ride here. I would not have waited. And if I was to yield to my dark side right now, it would not be this roll I would continue eating. I would sweep this table clear and spread you across its marble surface and feast myself on a far less dry food.'

The scenario he described brought a wave of heat washing through her body, burning its way up her neck and into her face.

'Would you let me, I wonder?' he asked her, his smouldering eyes locked to hers.

'No,' came her surprisingly firm reply.

'No...'

He smiled, then shrugged. 'See? I *can* take no for an answer. It will be the grand tour instead, in that case, followed by a swim, if you would like. Would you like?'

'I…I can't really afford to be out in the sun long on days like this,' she said by way of an excuse, though privately thinking she wouldn't be able to keep her hands off him once he was half-naked. 'I might burn. Or tan unevenly, which doesn't look good either on the catwalk or in photographs.'

'I see. I had better use the golf-cart to show you around the property in that case. It has a roof. I was thinking of riding, but under the circumstances that can keep for another time. The swim as well. After the tour, I would suggest you lie down till dinner or have a long, leisurely bath. Speaking of dinner, I have decided we will dine in the main dining-room tonight. It will give you a little more time to be less…tender.'

'How kind of you,' she murmured, thinking what a wicked devil he was. But an entertaining one. 'Cleo tells me you're often kind. I heard what you did for Jack.'

He seemed embarrassed by this revelation, which endeared him to her more than anything else he had done so far. She respected people who did good work without wanting praise or publicity for it. A large number of the wealthy businessmen she canvassed for donations often wanted their so-called philanthropy to be widely known.

'It was little enough to do for someone less fortunate than myself,' he muttered. 'So what are *you* going to do with my five hundred million dollars? I hope you do not waste it on paying the exorbitant salaries of financial consultants. You should spend the money as *you* see fit. I am confident that you have your char-

ity's—and the children's—best interests at heart.
Others might have more selfish and greedy agendas.'

'Don't worry. The money will be spent wisely and
well. I won't fall into that trap. But I will take some
advice from a few people whose business acumen I
respect, then I'll get to work setting several projects
in motion without delay. Time is of the essence when
it comes to research, and in providing the right equipment and facilities to treat the poor little mites already
afflicted. Trust me, I won't be letting grass grow under my feet. I'll be getting right on to things when I
get back to Sydney. Fortunately, I have next week
free of work, so I should be able to make some solid
inroads during that time. I would also like to…'

Charmaine broke off her chatter and smiled. 'Sorry.
Get me started on that subject and I never stop.'

'I really do not mind,' he said. 'I like to listen to
a woman with passion in her voice.'

Charmaine swallowed, thinking he'd heard more
than passion in the sounds she'd made last night. Each
had had its own special message, from her gasps of
startled pleasure to her groans of frustration, but the
most obvious had been her cries of ecstatic release
followed by her sighs of satisfaction.

'We should eat some of this delicious food Cleo's
prepared,' she said, abruptly changing the subject
from sex. 'Which reminds me—I really like your
housekeeper, Ali. She's a lovely woman.'

'Yes. She is. I have become somewhat of a substitute son to her. She and Norman cannot have children.'

'Oh. Oh, how sad. She would have made a wonderful mother.'

'I agree.'

Charmaine didn't want to dwell on the subject of being a wonderful mother, either, so she started asking him about the stud. Being country born and bred, she wasn't totally ignorant of horses and surprised him, she thought, with her knowledge.

The lunch went well after that, and the tour of the stud afterwards even better. Charmaine couldn't help being impressed, both by the magnificent horses Ali owned and the amazingly modern amenities he'd had built to accommodate them. The breeding barn was something to behold, a huge structure with countless stalls, a very high insulated ceiling and a lovely wide breezeway through the middle to keep the inside at a pleasant temperature, even on the hottest summer's day.

The stud currently had six stallions on its books, Ali informed her, ranging from hopeful beginners to established top liners. One of these—a black named Ebony Boy—was breathtakingly beautiful, and an incorrigible show-off. When he was let out into his private yard for a spot of exercise, the stallion put on a real show, galloping around and kicking up his heels, as well as rearing up several times before pounding down onto all fours again and shaking his glorious mane.

'He's very spirited,' she commented. 'I'll bet he's hard to handle.'

'Not during the breeding season. But his book is winding down for this year and he is beginning to feel his oats once more. He is one of those stallions who is only content when he is covering several mares a day.'

Charmaine was taken aback. 'That seems excessive. Doesn't he ever get tired?'

'Of mating? Never.' And his eyes met hers, sending the same message to her about himself. If last night was anything to go by, then it was not an idle boast.

And yet…

'Cleo says I am the first female you have had up here for ages,' she remarked.

Ali scowled. 'Cleo's one flaw is that she is inclined to gossip.'

'Maybe, but she doesn't strike me as a liar.'

'I do go to Sydney every weekend, Charmaine,' he pointed out curtly. 'Trust me when I say that my carnal needs have always been well catered for. Do not imagine that I have been waiting for you to fall into my arms.'

Why did his remark hurt? It should not matter to her if he'd been sleeping with every second woman in Sydney. But strangely, she did feel hurt. And jealous. And downright snaky.

'If you had,' she snapped, 'you would have been waiting a long time.'

'I am well aware of that. Why do you think I took the extreme measures I did to achieve my goal?'

She turned to eye him rather coldly, as was her usual attitude when angry. 'And did you get your money's worth last night?'

His dark brows lifted in an attitude of total arrogance and nonchalance, both of which made her seethe. 'It was a reasonable return on my investment. But I aim to capitalise further tonight. And the next two nights. I would think that by Friday I will be well satisfied. But if not, I will make sure that the helicopter trip back to Sydney is much more eventful than the one up here.'

It was back. The hostility between them. And the tension. He claimed he liked to make love, not war, but with them there would never be one without the other.

'And that will be it?' she asked tartly.

'Are you saying you want an extension?'

'Never in a million years. Five days is what you paid for and that's all you'll be getting.'

He did not say a word in response to this. Just gave her one long, thoughtful look before turning to tell the groom to take the stallion inside again, leaving Charmaine with the awful feeling that she'd betrayed far too much. If this was war between them again, then she'd just made a tactical error.

Things said in anger—or fear—were always a mistake. She should have kept her cool, not jumped down his throat like that. No doubt he suspected now that he was getting to her; that underneath, she wanted more than Friday.

But suspicion was only suspicion, not fact. She would just have to pull herself together before tonight and show him that she wasn't total putty in his hands.

And just how are you going to do that? came the taunting question. How is this miracle going to be achieved? The man can turn you on with a look. If he touched you—even now, when you're as mad as a hatter—lord knows what you would still allow him to do.

You're trapped!

'Trapped' was not a state of mind to bring out the best in Charmaine. No man was ever going to trap her. She had vowed long ago to stay in total control of her life, and that included her sex life. That was why she'd sought out men she liked to go to bed with.

Because she refused to let one rotten, depraved bastard totally spoil that part of her life.

So stop waffling about *this* man, she lectured herself. You want him as your lover. You know you do. If you don't say as much then it will look as if he has won. You *will* fall into his arms whenever he wants. Is that what *you* want, to look a silly, weak fool in his eyes, to say one thing then do another?

Her small laugh got his attention.

'What is it that you find so amusing?' he ground out.

'You,' she answered. 'And me. We are both being silly here. But me especially. You are right, Ali. I do not want our affair to end, come Friday. That was my pride talking a moment ago. Plus some lingering anger over your bully-boy tactics. Oh, do not bother to open your royal mouth and deny it. You ruthlessly used your obscene wealth to come up with an offer you *knew* I could not refuse.'

'Sometimes a man has to do what a man has to do.'

Again, she laughed. 'Only a man like you. But that is water under the bridge now and it would be crazy of me to cling to my pride when you are as good in bed as you said you would be. Frankly, having discovered the delights of the flesh, I do not want to give them up yet. It worries me that I might not find another man who can meet my—er—special needs as well as you do. Clearly, I am not a girl who responds well to normal romancing. I seem to require a certain type of partner to turn me on. Someone very… masterful. If nothing else, you are that, Ali. Very… masterful.'

'Why is it, my dear Charmaine, that you can make a compliment sound like an insult?'

'Because beneath my sweet exterior, Ali, darling, I am a total bitch. Surely you must know that by now?'

He just stared at her.

'But back to the issue at hand. I am happy to continue being your lover after Friday, till one or both of us tires of the arrangement, that is. Not mistress, mind. Lover. I do not want a single thing more from you. No money. No gifts. Nothing, except that gorgeous body of yours, plus your titillating technique. *Comprenez-vous?*'

Again he did not speak a word, although his eyes spoke volumes. Dislike and desire darted across the distance between them like hot daggers.

'I thought I could come to you at your hotel suite each Saturday night,' she continued, determined to be pragmatic and not romantic. 'Except when I am overseas, of course. We could spend the night together, and Sunday, if you like. Are you happy with that arrangement?'

'Happy?' he echoed with a dry laugh. 'What is happy where you are concerned?'

'Oh, please, do not pretend I am the love of your life. We both know I'm not. I am an itch to be scratched. I am giving you the opportunity to scratch it. And before you ask, no, I will not be seen in public with you. That is my one firm rule. No dinner dates. No accompanying you to the races. Nothing but a sexual liaison. Agreed?'

For one awful moment, she thought he was going to reject her. Pay-back for what she'd done to him.

'And am I expected to be faithful to you?' he

asked, his voice as cold as his eyes had suddenly become.

What to say? *If you touch another woman, I will kill you* seemed over-the-top and very telling. But it was what she wanted to scream at him, what had burst forth from somewhere deep in her heart.

She had a ghastly feeling she had just made the biggest mistake of her life. But it was done now.

'That is your business,' she said offhandedly. 'I have no right to demand anything of you, as you have no right to demand anything of me.'

She could see that he didn't like her saying that. But that was too bad. He could damned well like it or lump it. The infernal man should have left her alone. But no, he had to have her, didn't he? Well, he could have her body but not her heart. Not to his knowledge, anyway.

'But if we promise exclusivity to each other,' he said whilst his eyes continued to shower her with fire and ice together, 'you could go on the Pill and we could enjoy each other more fully and more spontaneously without having to stop all the time to use protection.'

Little did he know but she was already on the Pill. One method of protection was never enough for Charmaine.

'Nature did not intend there to be anything between a man and a woman during the act of love,' he continued. 'Sensitivity is greatly enhanced by the feel of flesh sliding against flesh. The pleasure is far greater.'

Charmaine's head whirled at the promise of experiencing even greater pleasure than she had last night.

'Some women automatically come when they feel a man's seed flood their womb,' he murmured. 'They say this type of orgasm is not only physically more intense but emotionally highly satisfying.'

If he'd thought that the image of his seed flooding her womb would make her melt, then he was sadly mistaken. It served to snap her out of her silly, almost-surrendered self and see him once again for what he was. A male predator who would use any weapon at his disposal to have what he'd always wanted, which was her as his sexual plaything, to be used without thought or care till he grew tired of her.

'I won't be going on the Pill,' she stated brusquely. 'And if you ever fail to use protection, Ali, I will *never* see you again.'

Shock flared in his face, followed by a studied thoughtfulness.

'I will do whatever you want,' he said at last.

'Good,' she snapped. 'In that case, I want to go back to the house now. I have a headache coming on.'

His eyes narrowed upon her. 'Is that the truth or an excuse to exit my company?'

'The absolute truth.' Little did he know it but he'd stirred up more than her hormones just now. He'd stirred up memories that were best forgotten, but which when remembered always made her blood pressure rise rapidly, resulting in the worst kind of headache. 'I suffer from migraines,' she told him, already seeing swirling flashes of light at the corners of her eyes, the precursor of the dreadful throbbing and nausea that would soon follow. 'I need to get to my pills quickly and lie down or tonight will be a non-event.'

'Come, then,' he said, and took her arm.

Charmaine wasn't sure if his solicitousness over the

next half-hour was out of kindness, or fear that she would not grace his bed again that night. Whatever, he whisked her back to the house and took her straight to her room, where he himself pulled the curtains, turned back her bed, fetched her a glass of water to wash down her pills with, then saw her comfortably settled before telling her that if the headache hadn't totally gone by seven this evening he would cancel dinner in the dining-room for that night. She could have a tray in her room, or in his, if she felt well enough. She only had to let him know. He would be in his quarters next door. She only had to knock. Or she could pick up the phone and ring Cleo if she preferred.

'Just dial zero,' he told her on his way out, then softly closed the door behind him.

Charmaine lay there underneath the pink sheet, staring up at the canopy for ages, waiting for the discomfort to start. But the throbbing in her head did not eventuate. Neither did the nausea. It seemed the pills had worked their magic in time. They also forced her to relax, and with that relaxation came tears. Not tears for what had happened in the past this time, but tears for what was happening now, in the present.

What a mess!

But then she was always a mess, she accepted, deep inside where all the bitter truths lay. Ali had asked if her headache was an excuse to exit his company. She hadn't thought so at the time but maybe it was, because as much as she pretended a non-emotional involvement with him to his face she knew, in her heart, that she *was* becoming involved. So involved that it scared her silly.

Of all the men to start falling in love with!

'Oh, God,' she sobbed, and turned her head into the pillow, clutching it for dear life. Tears rolled down her cheeks and dripped from her nose, wetting the pillowcase through. But nothing could stop them. They rolled on and on till exhaustion finally overcame her and tipped her into the blessed oblivion of sleep.

In his quarters next door, Ali was sitting at his desk and frowning at the email from AIS. It was not a progress report but a request that he call the office personally. When he did, he was put straight through to the head of security, a man named Ryan Harris, whom he'd dealt with many times before.

'Glad you called, Your Highness,' Ryan said. 'I wanted to have a private chat with you concerning the in-depth background check we're conducting on your behalf on a certain lady. Pardon my being circumspect, but I think it best I not say her name. Phone lines are not always as secure as we would like, and e-mails, of course, are notoriously insecure.'

'I appreciate your care, Mr Harris,' Ali said. 'Having anyone investigated is always a sensitive issue. So what is it that you have found out?'

'A certain rumour has come to light during the past day, which, in view of the lady's high public profile, might present a problem if pursued further. Just asking questions, no matter how discreetly, can create a steamrolling effect where the rich and famous are concerned. I wanted to make sure you want us to continue.'

'What rumour are you referring to?' Ali asked with an instant tightening in his chest.

'One person in the lady's home town seems to

think that her younger sister—the one who died from cancer—was not, in fact, her sister, but her daughter.'

Shock at this news had Ali's hand gripping the receiver with white fingertips.

'How this has been kept secret is beyond me, given the fame of the person in question,' Harris went on. 'But I gather the community is close-knit, and my operative only gleaned this information via an off-the-cuff crack by a barmaid who works in the hotel there and who went to school with the lady in question. She might have been speaking out of jealousy or spite, but to dig further would be to give credence to the rumour and the gutter Press might get wind of it. They seem to have ears everywhere these days. I thought you might not want that, Your Highness, given your interest in the lady.'

'You are perfectly correct, Mr Harris. That is the last thing I would want. Please cancel the investigation immediately. And destroy the files in question. Naturally, the agreed fee still stands, as well as the bonus promised. I am most grateful for your discretion.'

Ali hung up and leant back into his desk chair, running his hands through his hair in agitation. Was it true? And, if so, when had the child been born and why had Charmaine denied her own daughter?

Shame?

She didn't seem like the type to be ashamed of being a single mother.

Ambition?

If she'd been that ambitious, why have the child in the first place? There were alternatives at her disposal.

A broken heart?

Now, that had the ring of truth about it. Being seduced, then later abandoned by a lover, explained Charmaine's actions and attitude to sex and men best of all. Love-turned-to-hatred-of-the-father could have resulted in her rejecting the child, although it did not condone such an action. Only the most hard-hearted or bitter woman, in Ali's opinion, would deny her own baby.

Of course, Charmaine *was* pretty tough. Tough *and* cynical.

Ali scowled and swivelled round in his office chair to face the window behind and the view beyond, a view that usually had the power to distract and soothe, especially when the sun was going down and the rolling hills took on that wonderfully warm glow. But his eyes did not see the glorious sunset at that moment. Or the splendid scenery. They were turned relentlessly inward, to his troubled thoughts and feelings.

How *could* he be in love with such a creature?

'Perverse,' he growled aloud, then grimaced.

Yes, such a love was perverse. He had imagined that knowing about her past would give him power over her. Instead, all it had done was make him sure he had no future with her, not the one he wanted, anyway.

She was good for one thing and one thing only. Foolish to fantasise anything else. She thought so too, having spelt out her intentions where he was concerned. The only role she wanted for him in her life was that of lover. Till she grew tired of him. She didn't even care if he was unfaithful to her. In fact, she *expected* him to be.

The realisation that she had such little regard and respect for him upset Ali more than anything else. She thought him a conscienceless womaniser, a man who took women to his bed all the time without affection or caring.

The trouble was...she was right. That was exactly what he had become over the past decade. A cold-blooded user of women.

But his blood was not cold when dealing with this woman. It was hot. Hotter than it had ever been before.

As for caring and affection...

Ali groaned. He did not *want* to be in love with her. Given the circumstances, he would much rather his feelings be confined to lust. Lust always passed. But Ali knew he was already way beyond lust.

What to do to get her to at least agree to live with him? He needed more of her than the occasional Saturday night. What *could* he do to persuade her?

She would laugh at a declaration of love. Charm and flattery had little to no effect. More bribing was out of the question. He really had only one weapon to use to get her to do what he wanted.

Ali's teeth clenched down hard in his jaw. It went against the grain to use such tactics but she left him no option. No option at all.

CHAPTER ELEVEN

'ARE you not glad that your headache is gone?' Ali murmured as he pushed aside her hair and bent his lips to her neck.

Charmaine shivered then turned her head to one side to give him better access. 'Mmm,' was all she could manage at the moment.

She was lying face down in the middle of his huge bed, dazed and dizzy with his lovemaking. His lips were working their way down her spine, licking and kissing her skin, his hands stroking her at the same time. His mouth lingered in the small of her back, whilst those oh, so wonderful hands slid between her legs.

She moaned, then whimpered with her rapidly escalating need to have him back where he had been just a few minutes before.

'Ali,' she choked out.

'What, my darling?'

She tensed at the endearment, or was it because his fingers had moved on to that spot which could not be ignored, or denied?

'Oh, yes. *Yes.*'

'Patience,' he exhorted softly. 'The time has not yet come.'

But she *was* going to come. Very soon. Her second climax since she'd presented herself at the connecting door to his suite an amazingly short time ago.

She'd woken from her sleep to find her room in

147

darkness and her head at peace. Not so her body. Within seconds, it was craving him. She'd tried a cold shower but that hadn't worked. The urgency of her need had driven her to don the pink towelling guest robe over her naked body and present herself at his door with not a scrap of make-up on, but her cheeks pink with desire. Or had it been shame?

One look into her eyes was all it had taken for him to know what she had come for.

He hadn't said a word, just swept her up into his arms and carried her into his bedroom once more. His eyes never left her as he'd laid her across the bed, parted the robe and then her legs, leaving her sprea-deagled like that, ordering her not to move whilst he stripped off and reached for protection. By the time he was ready, she'd been beyond ready.

She'd come within thirty seconds of his entering her. But he hadn't. He'd withdrawn then joined her on the bed, kissing and caressing her all the while. Now she was on the verge of coming again, trembling with need whilst he remained very much in control.

How did he do that? she wondered in bewilderment. Ignore his own arousal whilst she was off the planet?

He'd reached her behind by now and was rubbing his stubbly cheeks over her softly rounded ones. She moaned, her bottom automatically lifting off the mattress for more. When he stuffed a pillow under her stomach and pushed her thighs apart, she tensed in anticipation of his entering her. But no, he started rubbing his stubble over the soft skin of her inner thighs, at the same time blowing his hot breath against her wetness.

She whimpered in frustration and wriggled her bottom. But still he did not give her what she desperately wanted. Instead, his mouth zeroed in, and her belly tightened further. His tongue swept down the valley of her desire and danced around her core. She squirmed and tried to hold on, squeezing everything tight to stop herself splintering apart. The waiting was cruel as he continued to tease and torment her. But then suddenly, blessedly, he was there, filling her, making her shudder with relief.

When he pulled her up onto all fours and cupped her breasts, she gasped with pleasure. He'd introduced her to this way of making love last night on the green carpet in the sitting-room. She had loved it then and she welcomed it even more now, partly because he couldn't see her eyes. He seemed to like to watch her face when she came and it worried her that he might see the increasingly emotional feelings that consumed her now each time his body joined her.

When he started pumping into her, she closed her eyes and tried to think of themselves as just two animals mating in the jungle somewhere. This wasn't about love. Just sex. Especially on his part. She had to keep remembering that.

His rhythm was punishing, his penetration deep, the grip on her both powerful and possessive. Gradually, she put aside all thought and let him take her to that brilliantly mindless place where she was reduced to primitive woman, free of all civilised concepts, free to mate like some wild animal in heat.

They made loud noises together, he grunting and she groaning. When she tensed then cried out in climax, Ali roared in reply. He arched backwards, pulling her upright and hard against him, his hands clamped over her breasts. Her mouth fell wide open and she dragged in much-needed air, her mind whirling with the wildness of it all, her flesh squeezing then releasing him during seemingly endless contractions.

It felt an eternity before their mutual spasms ended and they fell back onto the bed, Ali rolling her onto her side, keeping her body moulded to his in the spoon position.

'Incredible,' he said softly into her ear. 'We are magic together, my darling. Magic.'

Charmaine was extra-glad that she couldn't look into his face at that moment, especially with tears suddenly stinging her eyes.

The telephone beside his bed ringing was not a welcome sound. Ali muttered something under his breath and Charmaine blinked madly in anticipation of his withdrawing. Terrified that he might roll her over and see her tears, she began to pull away from him herself.

'Do not move,' he barked, and, keeping one arm firmly around her waist, he reached over her and picked up the receiver.

With the phone only centimetres from her own ear, Charmaine could hear every word that was said. The trouble was the person on the other end was speaking in a foreign language, probably Arabic. Nevertheless, nothing could disguise the fact that the caller was a woman. When Ali exclaimed, 'Nadia?' in a shocked voice, Charmaine knew exactly who he was talking to. It was her, his brother's wife, the woman he loved, the married woman he'd been exiled over.

Dismay claimed Charmaine as she lay there, still fused with Ali's body and forced to listen to every emotion in his expressive voice. His surprise at hearing from this Nadia. His concern over something. His soft words of comfort and caring.

The intimate-sounding chat went on and on, with Charmaine becoming increasingly distressed. How dared he make lovey-dovey small talk with this woman whilst he was inside *her*? How dared he?

When she made a further move to disengage their bodies, his arm clamped even more tightly around her, reminding her how strong he was. Too strong for her. Better she just lie quietly here till he was done. To struggle and to carry on would be very telling.

But the black jealousy that began to seethe through her was even more telling. To her.

She was not just *becoming* emotionally involved with Ali, she realised. She *was* involved. Hopelessly. Deeply. That was why she'd felt like crying just now. Because she knew that no matter how much Ali enjoyed making love to her, he did not love her; would *never* love her.

At last he was finished with the call. But it seemed he wasn't finished with *her*.

Not a word of explanation after he'd hung up. Nothing but a short, sharp silence before his attention snapped back to Charmaine's appalled body. Appalled, because she knew she still wanted him to continue, despite knowing his heart lay elsewhere and always would.

'Now, where was I?' he muttered, his hands stroking rather roughly up and down the front of her body. When they grazed over her bullet-tipped breasts, she shuddered convulsively.

Her disgusting vulnerability to him made her angry. And when Charmaine was angry she became very snaky, and stubborn.

'I thought I told you not to move,' he ground out.

'Go to hell,' she snapped. 'I'll move if I want to, whenever I want to. I am sick of you telling me not to move all the time.'

He sighed. 'You will never become really good in bed, my darling Charmaine, if you are not prepared to learn, or to practise control.'

'I am not, nor ever will be, your darling Charmaine.' She knew who his precious darling was. 'And maybe I'm not into control. Unlike yourself,' she added tartly.

'You think I want to control you?'

'Don't you?'

'I do not think any man could control you. Not totally. But it seems that the more control a woman practises over her public life, the more pleasure she often finds in abandoning all such control in the privacy of her bedroom. Is it not liberating to do as I say? To be mindless for once? To let someone else take responsibility for your pleasure, and your satisfaction? I am well equipped to give you both. But then, you know that is so. That is why you came to me tonight, and why you will continue to come to me from now on, whenever and wherever I want.'

'You wish,' she said, and laughed. But her laughter soon faded under the onslaught of sensation his hands began to create. The man must have sold his soul to the devil to know how to touch her like that, to make her crave like this.

She was desperate to move but refused to give in. She would show him that she could control herself, *and* resist him.

I will not move, she vowed frantically. I will not wriggle and writhe. I will not!

'You may move now,' he whispered after a few tortuous minutes. And with a tortured sob, she did.

CHAPTER TWELVE

ALI could not believe it when, shortly after the helicopter landed on the Regency rooftop that Friday, Charmaine refused to accompany him to his suite, telling him that she had wasted enough time that week. She said she had much to do with her foundation's new finances and would be in touch. She did not even leave him with her phone numbers or address, although he already knew both. She lived alone in a security-conscious apartment near Chatswood Station and had an unlisted number.

Pride, he decided after his anger had receded. Her damned pride. His pride then came into play too, because as much as he wanted her all that weekend he made no move to contact her, or force her hand in any way. He would wait for her to come to him.

And she would. He *knew* she would. No woman who had experienced what she had all week could indefinitely turn her back on such pleasure. Her body would eventually crave him again, as his craved hers. Sooner or later she would give in to that craving. He just had to be patient.

One week. One week since she'd seen him. One week of sheer hell, of sleepless nights and mental torment. She'd kept herself busy, working extremely long hours, having meetings with the people who could help put the foundation's incredible new bank balance

154

to work. Bank managers. Hospital administrators. Cancer specialists. Construction-company bosses.

By Friday, decisions had been made and put into action. There was to be a brand-new cancer wing at the children's hospital with a top-flight research unit included. The latest medical equipment was put on order from overseas and a real-estate agent had been commissioned to buy more homes near the hospital to provide accommodation for the families of the sick children, especially those who had to travel to Sydney from the country. Several new cars had also been bought and presented to the parents of patients who did not have a reliable vehicle for the extensive travelling often required with a sick child.

But by that same Friday, Charmaine found herself at breaking point where Ali was concerned. She had to go to him, even though she knew the time spent away from his corrupting presence was not nearly long enough. The sexual hold he had over her was even worse than she'd realised. Love made it worse. But denying herself his company, especially his love-making, had become unbearable.

So Charmaine booked a room at the Regency on the Friday morning for that night, a place in which to dress and to escape to if she needed a bolt-hole. Ali had mentioned to her the previous week during the helicopter ride back to Sydney that his friends arrived to play poker just before eight and didn't leave till after midnight. At the time, he'd obviously been expecting her to stay with him that night, a reasonable expectation, given she seemed to have lost all her will-power that week. She'd not only been at his sexual beck and call during the rest of her stay at the stud, but had continued with her role of besotted bed-mate during the trip back to Sydney.

But the thought of his playing cards with Rico and Renée whilst she hid in his bedroom, waiting up for his return like some genuine sex slave, was beyond the pale. She could not do that to herself. And she hadn't.

She would not do it tonight, either. Hence her own room. But neither could she wait till after midnight. She needed to be with him, and soon!

Charmaine's telephone call, shortly after his arrival at his hotel suite, brought Ali great emotional relief, although nothing short of her presence in his bed would do anything for his physical frustration. Her abrupt announcement that she was actually in the hotel and would like to come up and see him for a short while before he settled down for his card-playing evening both excited and worried him. Did she mean what he thought she meant? He dared not ask. He might not like the answer. Just to see her was enough for the moment.

'I will have James organise a pass-key to be delivered to you,' he said.

'James?'

'The in-house butler.'

'Yes, do that,' she remarked drily. 'Then perhaps it would be wise to dispense with his services for a while. I wish to see you alone.'

Alone.

Was that good news or bad news? Ali's body hoped it would be good, since it had already leapt at the prospect of being with her again.

'I will dismiss him immediately.'

'I suspected you might.'

Cynicism in her voice. Naturally, she thought all he wanted from her was sex. He had to make her see this time that this was not so. He had missed her terribly, and not just her body.

She had garnered great respect from him when she'd actually left him last Friday. More so because he knew how hard it had been for her to do that. He had been merciless in his quest to bond her to him sexually that week, to programme her to do his bidding. He had used every seduction technique he knew. Every way of making her surrender herself totally to him.

But in the end she had still remained her own person. What courage she had. What character. What wonderful pride.

This last thought brought a moment of panic. Was she coming to see him to tell him to his face she did not want anything more to do with him?

Ali could not imagine what he might do if that was the case. Life, he had realised this last week, would not be worth living without her.

His mission impossible now was not to get her just to live with him, but to marry him.

By the time the doorbell rang ten minutes later, he was in a right royal state. It was an effort to relax his hands from the fierce fists they had become. The act of walking to the door and opening it was one of the hardest things he had ever done.

His breath exited his lungs in a slow stream of ill-concealed desire at the sight of her.

She looked breathtakingly beautiful, and wickedly sexy. There again, she *always* looked breathtakingly beautiful and wickedly sexy. But more so in what she was wearing that evening, a pale blue silk slip-dress with tiny shoulder straps and a swishy skirt. Her legs, he noted, were bare of stockings and her feet were shod in silver sandals with heels high enough to bring her to eye level with him. Her hair was brushed back from her face but down, as he preferred it. Her face was quite heavily made up, her eyes surrounded by black eye-liner and smoky blue shadows, her full mouth made to look even fuller with a dark pink lipstick. Silver drops hung from her ear-lobes. That perfume, which always drove him insane, wafted in merciless waves from her cleavage.

Impossible not to notice that she was bra-less, especially considering the erect state of her nipples. Impossible not to notice as well that *she* was looking at *him* with an almost shocking hunger, her eyes glittering as they raked over him from top to toe.

'Is he gone?' she demanded huskily. 'The butler—is he gone?'

He nodded. Difficult to speak. Her hunger had instantly become his hunger, bringing with it a fierce erection.

She stepped inside the foyer and shut the door behind her, her breathing shallow and rapid as she reached forward and pressed her right hand over his groin.

'Cruel,' she bit out.

He understood what she meant. It *was* cruel, the way they felt around each other.

Her fingers worked quickly on his clothes, freeing him to the suddenly cloying air in the foyer. Heat seemed to come from her in waves. Or was it him in danger of spontaneous combustion? For a split-second, Ali thought she was going to kneel and take him into her mouth.

But she didn't. She just held his eyes whilst she pleated her skirt upwards with her hands, watching his stunned reaction to her nakedness underneath. When her dress was bunched at her waist she leant back against the door, bracing herself with her bottom and shoulders as she moved her legs apart.

'Do it to me,' she commanded, her breathing quickening further. 'No fancy foreplay. Just hard and fast sex.'

As brutally aroused as he was, Ali still recalled what she'd said if he ever made love to her without protection. Was this some kind of trap, a test, some twisted excuse for her to leave him?

'But what about pro—'

'I'm on the Pill,' she broke in brusquely. 'I have been all along. Don't look at me like that!' she snapped. 'It's what you always wanted, isn't it? To show me how incredible it is without anything between us? Do it, then. But do it quickly before I change my mind.'

He did it. Quickly. Roughly. Surging up into her again and again, glorying in her violent trembling, triumphant when her body came apart in his arms.

Now she was truly his, he thought with savage satisfaction as he came too, crying out his own raw release, unaware of the great gut-wrenching sobs which had overtaken her at some stage. It wasn't till his own cataclysmic orgasm began to pass that Ali realised something was wrong. Very, very wrong.

'Charmaine? Charmaine, darling, what is it?' He cupped her face with his hands but she just continued to weep hysterically. When her knees began to buckle, he hoisted her up onto his hips and carried her into the bedroom.

His distress was as great as his confusion as he gently disengaged her from his body and laid her still shaking body on top of the blue quilt. When he pulled down her dress to a semblance of modesty, she sobbed and rolled away to curl into a foetal ball, her hands pressed under her neck, her eyes tightly shut. But even so, she kept on crying.

Ali didn't know what to do or to say to comfort her. Why was she weeping like this, as though her heart and soul were disintegrating? Hadn't he done what she wanted? Hadn't she enjoyed their mating?

Clearly not. Possibly, it *had* been a test and he had just failed it miserably. Whatever, he *felt* a failure. There he'd been, only minutes before, saying to himself that just seeing her would be enough. And what had he done? Taken her like some savage up against a door.

Self-disgust overtook him when he looked down at his own far from sated flesh. Stuffing it angrily back out of sight, he zipped up his trousers and climbed onto the bed behind her distressed figure.

'Hush, my love,' he murmured, and started to stroke her hair. 'You will make yourself ill.'

'You don't understand,' she choked out. 'I am be-ing…punished.'

'Punished! How are you being punished? And for what?'

'The greatest sin of all.'

'Which is?'

'Being a bad mother. Oh, God, I didn't mean to tell you that. Now you'll despise me even more than you already do.'

'*Despise* you? Charmaine, darling, I *love* you. Surely you must know that by now.'

She froze, then slowly rolled over to glower up at him through soggy lashes. 'How dare you say that to me when you know I know it's not true? I was there, remember, when you took that phone-call from your true love? I *heard* you talking to Nadia. So warm and so loving.'

Ali winced in regret that he had not explained Nadia's call earlier. But he had been so angry with Charmaine at the time. And he honestly had not thought she cared. But now he saw how it must have looked to her and he was very sorry indeed. On the bright side, however, Charmaine's jealousy pointed to her having feelings for him that encompassed more than just lust.

He leant over her and pressed her back onto the pillow with a gentle kiss. 'Nadia is not my true love any more. I'm not sure she ever was. I did love her once. But it was the love of a spoiled young man who had always been given everything he wanted. I think not being able to have Nadia made my feelings for her seem stronger than they were. It wasn't till I fell in love with you that I realised what true love is all about. What you heard that night weren't words of love. Just caring and concern. Nadia called to tell me she had had cancer.'

'Cancer!'

'Yes. Cancer of the cervix. The doctors have cleared her, but facing the possibility of death, it seemed, made her see how much she really loved her husband, and vice versa. They talked together honestly for perhaps the first time in their marriage, telling each other of their true feelings. When she confessed to Khaled about me, she was shocked to discover that he already knew about our forbidden romance and had been afraid all this time that she still loved me. When she reassured him that he was the only man she loved, he suggested she call me and clear the air. They were both worried that the reason I had not married was because of her. I was happy to tell her that I had met someone else, someone whom I loved and wanted to marry.'

'You want to *marry* me?'

'More than anything.'

'But...but you can't possibly. You don't really know me. I told you. I'm a bitch.'

'You mean because of this child you had? The one you were a bad mother to?' He had to be very careful not to betray his knowledge, to let her tell him everything in her own words and her own good time.

She nodded, tears filling her eyes again. 'Becky,' she said huskily. 'She...she died. Of leukaemia. She was only six and she...she never knew I was her mother. She thought I was her sister.'

At this she broke down again. Ali took her in his arms and just held her, till she finally stopped weeping.

'Sorry,' she muttered, drawing back to wipe her eyes with her hands. 'I...I don't like to talk about it. I get upset.'

'I think you should tell me about it, Charmaine. If we are going to be married there should not be any secrets between us.'

She stared at him again. 'You really mean it, about loving me and wanting to marry me? It...it isn't just a devious ploy to keep me sweet for some more sex?'

Ali had to smile. 'My dear Charmaine, do you

think after the way you acted when you came to see me tonight that I would have to lie to you to get more sex?'

She flushed. 'I…I don't know what's got into me. I've never been like this before. But then…I…I've never been in love before.'

Ali could hardly believe what he had just heard. He had hoped she might have fallen in love with him. But to hear the words…

'Not even with the father of your child?' he asked softly.

'With John? God, no. *No,*' she repeated with a shudder. 'I *was* very attracted to him, I admit. He was a little like you, actually. Very rich. Very handsome. Very suave. I met him when I first came to Sydney to do modelling. He was a good deal older than me. About thirty, I think. When he asked me out to dinner, I was flattered and excited. When he asked me to go back to his apartment for a nightcap afterwards, I foolishly went. I…I'd already had quite a bit to drink, and then I stupidly had another glass when I got to his place.'

Aha, so now he had some of the answers as to why she had been hostile to him to begin with. And why she no longer drank alcohol. He reminded her of this rich playboy who had seduced her, then abandoned her. 'The bastard took advantage of you whilst you were intoxicated.'

'No. Nothing as civilised as that,' she said with a cold little laugh, and his own blood ran to ice.

'He *raped* you?'

She nodded.

Ali sucked in sharply. 'I hope he is rotting in some

jail somewhere. Because if he is not, I will have to kill him.'

'He is already dead,' she said flatly. 'He died of a drug overdose a few years back.'

'Allah is just.'

'I actually don't remember the rape,' she said. 'He put something in the drink I had when I first arrived at his apartment. I remember feeling woozy and lying down on the sofa, then nothing till the next day. When I woke up, I was naked in his bed and I just knew he…he'd done things while I was unconscious. The trouble was I had no evidence of any assault. I wasn't bruised or bleeding in any way. I wasn't a virgin, you see. There'd been a boy at home. A…a neighbour's son whom I'd fooled around with the previous summer.'

Ali was taken aback by this admission. As much as he had always enjoyed the refreshing lack of sexual inhibition in Western women, he was sometimes still shocked by them. 'You were in love with this boy?' he asked carefully, trying to find some excuse for such behaviour.

'No,' she returned without a shred of guilt, or shame. 'We were just curious kids experimenting with each other. Things like that happen in the country, Ali. You have to be brought up there to understand. But it meant John had no trouble having sex with me. When I accused him of doing it to me whilst I was asleep, he freely admitted it. Then he told me not to bother to go to the police, that his father was a very important man and nothing would come of it. But I went anyway, more fool me.'

'What happened?'

'Oh, all the usual things. An embarrassing trip to

the hospital for tests and an internal examination. No evidence of rape there, unfortunately. Only lots of semen. And the blood test didn't show any drugs. By then whatever he'd given me was out of my system. When the police questioned him, he admitted having sex with me several times but claimed it was consensual. It didn't look good that I had gone to his apartment willingly, quite late at night. But his *coup de grâce* was the Polaroid photographs of me he'd taken.'

'Photographs,' Ali repeated, feeling sick to his stomach.

'Yes, he'd taken photographs of me, naked. In all sorts of lewd poses. Unfortunately, in some of them my eyes were half-open. I thought I definitely looked drugged and out of it. But the police said they looked like the glazed eyes of a turned-on girl during and after sex.'

Ali smothered a groan. As much as this whole scenario sickened him, he had to remember that she had had to live through it, then live with the consequences. His admiration of her courage grew, as did his sympathy for her plight.

'He told the police that I was an ambitious young model who had posed for the photos quite happily, but that I had turned nasty when he wanted to leave things at a one-night stand. His father called in some top lawyer to defend him and it wasn't long before all charges were dropped and I was left holding the baby, so to speak.'

'I do not wish to be insensitive here, Charmaine, but under the circumstances, why did you not consider a termination?'

'I went into denial. Refused to believe I was even

pregnant. It wasn't till I lost a modelling assignment because I was putting on so much weight that I was forced to face reality. I told my agent I was sick and went home to my parents. By then I was almost five months gone. I...I had some kind of nervous breakdown and demanded the baby be adopted.'

'You poor darling,' Ali said, and reached to touch her. But she shrank back from his hand, her eyes focusing blankly on some spot on the ceiling.

'Mum could see that I couldn't cope at that time but she thought that eventually I would regret having given up my baby. She came up with the plan to tell everyone it was *her* baby. We lived on an isolated farm, so it was easy for me to have the baby there at home without anyone knowing. No one even knew I was at home at that stage. All the locals thought I was still in Sydney. Mum just started putting some padding under her dresses and telling everyone she was expecting. I slept in my room most of the time, only too happy to have someone else solve my problem.'

Her eyes lifted at last to look at him. Such sad eyes.

'I know you must be thinking it was wicked of me to reject my own child,' she said brokenly, 'but I just couldn't look at the baby and not think about what John had done to me. After the birth, I...I couldn't get away quickly enough. By then I'd changed into a cynical, cold-blooded, truly ambitious bitch, determined not to let what one man had done spoil my life. I was still young and I vowed to be a success, not just as a model but in every area of my life. So I took a lover. He was a very sweet boy, but perhaps a little too sweet. Or too inexperienced. I rapidly moved on from one boyfriend to another, desperate to prove I wasn't frigid. But nothing seemed to work.

In the end I gave up men and sex, and just concentrated on my career.'

'So when did you begin to regret giving up your child, and motherhood?'

'It happened gradually, I suppose. Every time I went home, I would see Becky growing into such a lovely child. So outgoing and intelligent. It was worrying at first the way she gravitated towards me, the way she ran to me whenever I visited. But after a while, I thrilled to her open affection. I guess I also spoiled her, especially on her birthday and at Christmas. I bought her outrageously expensive presents. Compensating, I guess. Mum and Dad adored her and I kept telling myself I had done the right thing by Becky.'

Her sigh carried enormous regret and sadness. 'I didn't realise just how much I loved Becky, and what I had missed out on, till she was diagnosed with leukaemia. I'll never forget that phone call when Mum told me the news. It was like...'

She broke off and closed her eyes for a second before opening them and throwing Ali the most heart-rending look.

'I...I can't describe it. Anyway, we tried everything but nothing worked,' she went on in an artificially matter-of-fact voice. 'She had some rare form of the disease which didn't respond to a bone-marrow transplant. Chemotherapy put her into remission for a short while but then it came back, stronger than ever.'

Again she broke off, and just lay there, silent and sad for a few moments.

'It almost killed me to watch her die like that,' she resumed softly. 'It almost killed Mum, too. But at least she had the joy of being called Mum by my little girl. Those last days…when we knew there was no hope, I…I wanted to tell Becky. I wanted to hold her and say, I am your mummy, darling, not your sister. But that seemed cruel and selfish. So I kept my silence. I kept my silence and she died in my mother's arms, not mine, and I… Oh, God, Ali…' Her eyes flooded as she turned them despairingly to his. 'Hold me. Just hold me.'

He held her and she just cried and cried. Ali vowed then and there that somehow he would make things right for this beautiful woman he loved. Somehow, he would make her happy again. Somehow…

CHAPTER THIRTEEN

CHARMAINE lay back in the deep bath Ali had run for her, still amazed at how wonderful he had been. Not shocked by her confessions, or in any way judgemental. Just sympathetic and kind and so very understanding.

Maybe he does truly love you.

Charmaine smiled to herself at the maybe. What did it take to convince her, for pity's sake? The man had paid five million dollars to have dinner with her and five hundred million to sleep with her. Lust alone did not explain such extraordinary extravagances.

But possibly the most loving thing Ali had done for her so far was what he was doing at that moment. He was out there cancelling his Friday-night poker game so that he could spend the evening with her. How romantic was that!

Rico turned to Renée after putting down his phone.

'Ali just cancelled cards for tonight,' he said, his tone amazed.

Renée blinked. 'Good lord. That's a first. Why?'

'You know Ali. He didn't really explain. A personal emergency, he said.'

'Some woman, probably,' Renée surmised.

'He's never cancelled before.'

'Maybe he's finally met a woman who's made him forget that one back in Dubar you told me about.'

'I wonder...'

'Rico, what are you thinking?'

'Remember how you mentioned you couldn't contact Charmaine the week before last, that she'd gone out of town you knew not where? And when she came back and finally answered her phone, she was evasive over where she'd been.'

'You don't think…'

'*Sì*. I *do* think.'

'No!'

'Ali is not a man who recognises that word,' Rico said drily.

'Ali is also not Charmaine's type. He's far too macho a man. She'd run a mile.'

'Shall we bet on it?'

Renée smiled. 'You'll lose.'

'I bet he shows up at the races with her tomorrow.'

'Wow, that's some crazy bet! What stakes are we betting for?'

'The right to name our babies.' They had been arguing over that for days. Renée wanted Australian names whilst he wanted traditionally Italian.

'Done!' Renée said, supremely confident in winning.

Rico smiled, whereupon Renée looked worried.

'Is there anything you know that I don't know?'

'Absolutely not.' But Rico had not forgotten the way Charmaine had talked about Ali the night of the auction. If you simply disliked someone, you didn't bother with that kind of passion.

'One small problem, though,' Renée said with a sigh. 'I'm not sure I'll be making the races myself tomorrow. I'm feeling a bit funny in the tummy.'

'That's just the pickles and pizza you ate today. You know, if you keep giving in to all these cravings, darling, you're going to be as big as a bus by the time you have those babies. You've still got a month to go.'

'I know. I've really ballooned out over the last couple of weeks. I look disgusting. I don't think I've even got a dress big enough to wear tomorrow.'

'You'll find something. I know you. You won't want to miss both cards *and* the races in one weekend.'

'You could be right. We are all slaves to our passions, aren't we?'

Rico didn't think she could have said a truer word.

When Charmaine emerged from the bathroom, the master bedroom was empty. Sashing the thick white hotel robe tightly around her, she went in search of Ali, and found him wheeling an elegant traymobile across the sitting-room. He stopped on seeing her, his black eyes looking her up and down.

'I am relieved that you did not put that blue dress back on again,' he said. 'That robe is much better for what I had in mind.'

Charmaine's eyebrows arched. 'And what exactly, Your Highness, did you have in mind?'

He smiled a wry smile. 'Not that.'

'Oh.' Was she surprised or disappointed?

'I would like us to start over and get to know each other a bit better before we make love again. It is very easy to be distracted by matters of the flesh. So I thought that for this evening we would sit out on the terrace and just eat and talk.'

Although knowing she would probably be frustrated as hell by the time the evening was out,

Charmaine had to agree with him. 'Good idea. Oh, and Ali…'

'Yes?'

'I know I said I loved you and I do. But please… don't try to rush me into marriage. I'm not at all sure that marriage between us would ever work.'

Ali refused to panic. It was only natural that she would be cautious.

'I think I know you well enough, Charmaine, to realise you would not be rushed into anything against your will. But I also want you to know that I believe marriage between us would work wonderfully.'

'But…but what about children?'

'What about children?'

'I…I'm not sure I want to have any.'

Ali's heart sank but he kept his cool. 'And why is that, my love?' he asked gently. 'Is it because of your past, or your career, perhaps?'

'My career! I don't give a damn about my career. Modelling has become just a means to an end for me over the last couple of years. It was the money I wanted, not the attention or the fame. I couldn't care less if I never set foot on a catwalk again.'

Ali was very pleased to hear that. 'When you marry me, you won't have to,' he told her. 'You will have all the money you need.'

'I would still want to be hands-on with my foundation.'

'Of course.'

'Would you marry me even if I said I would never have children?'

'Yes.'

'Just like that. Yes.'

'Yes.'

'Oh, Ali...' She came forward and reached out to lay a tender hand against his cheek. 'What a wonderful fool you are. But I do so love you. *Too* much.'

'There is no such thing as too much love,' Ali said, struggling not to forget his plans for a platonic evening and just sweep her into his arms once more.

'You do realise we won't last even one night,' Charmaine murmured, gazing deep into his eyes.

'Yes,' he said with a resigned sigh.

'But we can try,' she added, and dropped her hand away from his face.

Ali actually trembled with relief.

'Do you want me to help you with the food?' she asked.

'No. I want you to go out onto the terrace, sit down and keep your hands to yourself.'

Her laughter carried delight. 'I was getting to you, was I?'

He scowled. 'You will be made to suffer for your many transgressions.'

'Aah, promises, promises,' she countered saucily and sashayed out onto the terrace.

Ali followed in her wake, pushing the traymobile with white-knuckled hands whilst his dark side plotted all sorts of erotic revenge.

CHAPTER FOURTEEN

'WELL, you were right,' Renée sighed, still not totally recovered from the shock of seeing Ali arrive at the races with a glowing Charmaine on his arm.

'Of course I was right,' Rico replied smugly. 'Now I can name my daughter Angelina, and my son Alphonso.'

Renée shrugged. 'OK. Angie and Alfie it is.'

Rico looked appalled. 'Their names are not to be shortened like that. What is the point of giving proud Italian names if you turn them into English nick-names?'

'Rico, might I remind you that no one calls you Enrico except Ali. This is Australia. If your name is more than two syllables you haven't got a chance of keeping it once you hit school. So get used to having your children called Angie and Alfie. Or Ange and Alf.'

'Even worse!'

'Well, you could always let me have my way and give them good Aussie names to begin with like Lisa and Luke. No shortening to be done there!'

Rico growled under his breath. '*You* lost the bet. *I* get to name the children.'

'Whilst I get to go to the loo again,' Renée said with another sigh, levering herself up out of her seat in the stand. 'How long is it till the next race?'

'Four minutes. Maybe you'd better wait till after-wards.'

'Can't. I'm desperate.'

When Rico stood up and took his wife's elbow she told him, 'No, don't worry. I can go on my own.'

'Are you sure?'

'I'll get Charmaine to come with me. If I can pry her away from lover-boy, that is,' she added under her breath. 'Do you see the way she's looking at him, Rico?'

'Mmm. Sure do. I'd like to be a fly on the wall in *their* bedroom.'

'You might get your wings singed.'

'More likely burnt right off, I'd say. Not that we can talk. We've made a few fires in our day, haven't we, darling?' And he gave Renée a loving squeeze. 'I dare say we'll make a few more, once you pop those babies out.'

'I dare say, Casanova. Meanwhile, I really must... Oh. Oh, my God!' And she stared down in horror at the floor between her legs.

Rico thought she'd wet herself for a moment, but then he realised what had happened. Only last night, he'd been reading one of the several books on childbirth he'd bought and which listed all the ways labour started.

Rico had wanted to be well prepared for every eventuality. After all, with Renée expecting twins, it was highly likely the babies might want to arrive before full term.

He'd been so calm reading about it. Now, staring down at the puddle of water, panic was only a heartbeat away.

'We...we have to get you to the hospital as soon as possible,' he gabbled. 'That's what the book said.

Even if you haven't got any contractions. Have you got any contractions?'

'No. I mean…I have had this sort of backache on and off all day.'

'Why didn't you tell me? Backache is often the first sign of labour.'

'Rico,' she said wearily, 'I have had an aching back on and off for weeks. How would I have known the difference? Please let's not argue. Let's just go call a taxi.'

'Yes, yes, a taxi. I don't think I should drive. I feel a bit rattled.'

'How could you drive, anyway, when we didn't bring a car? We caught a taxi here, remember? But I will still have to go home first and collect my bag.'

'What's wrong?'

They both whirled to find Ali standing there, Charmaine with him, both of them looking anxiously at the puddle on the floor.

'My waters have broken,' Renée explained, holding on to her swollen belly for dear life.

'She has to get to hospital as soon as possible,' Rico jumped in, feeling more nauseous by the minute.

'We came in a limousine,' Ali informed them. 'I will instruct my security man to call the chauffeur and have him bring the car round to the main gate immediately. Can you walk that far, Renée?'

'Yes. I'm only leaking, Ali, not dying.'

'I'll carry her,' Rico said, which brought an exasperated glance from Renée.

'Don't be ridiculous, Rico. I weigh a ton. Just hold my arm and let's go.'

'She's still got a month to go,' Charmaine whispered to Ali as they followed Rico and Renée through the crowd. 'I hope the babies will be all right. Renée'll die if anything goes wrong.'

'She will be fine,' Ali replied reassuringly. 'The babies will be fine.'

Charmaine wished she could be so confident. Life was not always fine, or fair. Just because Renée desperately wanted these babies didn't mean everything had to go right.

Fortunately, the limousine was there waiting when they reached the gate and the exclusive private hospital Renée was booked into was only a short drive away. Once they reached the hospital, Renée was popped into a wheelchair and whisked away with Rico to the maternity ward whilst Ali and Charmaine were given the job of driving further into the city to their penthouse and returning with the bag Renée had already packed and which was sitting in the foyer coat cupboard.

By the time they returned to the hospital and found the right wing and the right sister to make suitable enquiries to, Charmaine was amazed to be briskly told that, 'Mrs Mandretti's labour has progressed rapidly, she is fully dilated, the doctor has been called and all is ready for an imminent birth.'

'But what about the babies?' Charmaine asked worriedly. 'Will they be all right? They're early.'

'All their vital signs are good. Look, they have the best doctor, the best midwifery nurses and the best medical equipment money can buy,' the sister said briskly. 'They will be fine.'

'I told you so,' Ali said as he led Charmaine away to the waiting-room. 'Stop worrying. You will make yourself ill.'

Charmaine *felt* ill. Her heart was racing madly and

her head had a vice around it which was gradually being tightened by some unseen torturer.

'I could never do this,' she muttered. 'Never.'

Ali knew what she meant. She could never have a baby. Never have *his* baby. His heart ached with the loss of what would have been a great joy to him. But nothing would change his mind about marrying this woman.

He sat down on an empty chair and watched her anxiously pace the room, her eyes continuously darting towards the wall clock. Ali wished there was something he could do to ease her anxiety, but he knew nothing but good news would achieve this goal. Time passed with agonising slowness, his own eyes checking the time every once in a while. About forty-five minutes after they had arrived, the sister they'd been talking to earlier suddenly popped her head round the door, all smiles.

'The babies have arrived. Both healthy and quite large for thirty-two weeks. The boy weighed just under three kilos and the girl two and half. They don't even need humidicribs. Both parents survived the ordeal, although I'm told the father had a few sticky moments. He's fine now, though. Proud as a peacock. The mother said to ask you to come in, and to bring her bag. She said she wants to have a shower and wash her hair. I'll show you the way...'

Tears flooded Charmaine's eyes as a smiling Ali took her arm. 'I told you everything would be fine.'

'Yes, you did,' she said, dabbing at her eyes with a tissue from her handbag. 'I'll take notice of you next time.'

Charmaine thought Renée looked remarkably well for a woman who'd just given birth. And blindingly happy. Rico wasn't far behind in the happiness stakes, beaming like a Cheshire cat as he called his mother on his cellphone to tell her their good news. Charmaine could hear the Italian woman's excitement from across the room.

But it was the babies Charmaine could not take her eyes off, both wrapped up tightly and sleeping in their cribs beside Renée's bed. They had masses of black hair and weren't all red and wrinkly as Charmaine imagined even slightly premature babies would look.

'Oh, Renée,' she said as she walked over and stared admiringly down at them. 'They're so beautiful.'

'Indeed,' Ali agreed, having come over for a look as well.

'Would you like to nurse them?' Renée suggested generously. 'Charmaine, you take Lisa there. And Ali, you can pick up Luke.'

Ali didn't hesitate, scooping up the boy baby with surprisingly confident hands and rocking him back and forth like an old hand at it. Charmaine froze, suddenly stricken with the memory that not once had she held her own baby girl at this age. She'd refused to set eyes on Becky till she was six months old.

'I don't think I can,' she said, consumed with regret and guilt, but at the same time the most terrible yearning. 'I...I might drop her.'

'No,' Ali said, 'you won't.' And, handing Luke to his mother, he scooped up the baby in the pink bunny blanket and placed her in Charmaine's arms.

Little Lisa woke, and started to cry, her hands finding their way free and flapping around.

For a second, Charmaine froze further. But then automatically—no, *instinctively*—she took both of the tiny hands within her own firm grasp and held them still as she settled the baby girl into the crook of her arm, then rocked and sang to her till she drifted off to sleep again.

'You're really good at that,' Renée praised. 'I might have to hire you as chief babysitter.'

'Any time,' Charmaine said huskily, then glanced up through shimmering eyes to smile at Ali.

His heart caught. Did she mean what he thought she meant? Was it possible?

Not a word did he dare say on the matter either during their visit at the hospital, or on the rather silent drive back to the hotel. If she had changed her mind about having a baby, then it had to come from her own lips. He would not try to pressure. Or persuade.

She didn't say much about anything, actually, not till after they'd made love that night and she was wrapped tightly in his arms.

'Ali,' she began.

'Mmm.'

'You know I have to go to Italy next week for a photo shoot. I've signed a contract so I really can't get out of it without the possibility of being sued.'

'Yes, I understand.'

'Then I have a few more modelling commitments I have to honour before the end of the year. There's fashion week in Melbourne, and after that I have to do another perfume ad for Femme Fatale.'

'You must do what you must do.'

'Yes, I must. I'd like to cut down on my modelling come the new year, however, and move in with you. Is that all right?'

'I would prefer us to be married.'

He felt her smile. 'I knew you were going to say that. In that case, a New Year wedding it will be. We could have it at your property. An outdoor ceremony. Either around the pool or in the pavilion. But nothing too grand. And please, not too many guests. Just close family and friends. Cleo could do the catering for the reception.'

'Sounds perfect. But for a lady who did not want to be rushed, that does seem a little quick.'

'I want to make sure I don't look fat in the photos.'

'What do you mean? You would never look fat.'

'I will when I'm pregnant.'

Ali stopped breathing.

'I'm going to stop taking the Pill tomorrow, if it's all right with you.'

He began breathing again. 'Perfectly all right.'

'I realised tonight that I *do* want a baby, Ali. And this time, I think I might make a pretty good mother.'

'You will make the best mother.'

'I don't know about that. But I'd like to give it a try.'

Ali's arms closed more tightly around her, his lips in her hair. 'You have made me the happiest man in the world.'

'Happier than Rico?'

'Enrico is a very lucky man. But I am luckier. I have you.'

'Oh, Ali...I think I am the lucky one to have you.'

'We are both lucky.'

'Yes,' she said, and sighed with happiness. 'Yes, we certainly are.'

EPILOGUE

Christmas Day the following year

'WHOSE idea was it,' Charmaine said to Ali as she dashed into the bathroom to do her hair, 'to have absolutely everyone come to our place for Christmas this year?'

'Yours,' Ali said to her reflection in the mirror, and calmly continued shaving.

Charmaine picked up a hairbrush. 'You could have said no.'

'I never say no to you, my darling. You know that. But what is worrying you? Everything is organised. Cleo told me less than half an hour ago that all the women had helped her get the food ready and there was nothing left to do except get cleaned up and dressed.'

'Yes, Renée and Dominique have been marvellous all morning. And Rico and Charles have been doing their childminding bit. I guess I'm just in a bit of a tizz because Mum and Dad are here. They make me nervous after the way they reacted to our marriage. I mean…they weren't exactly thrilled, were they?'

'It is understandable that they were wary of me at first. But by the time Amanda was born, they believed my intentions towards their daughter were honourable.'

'Yes. You're right. They adore you now. And they

182

adore Amanda. But then, she is just so adorable. Only five months old and already a heartbreaker in the looks department.'

'Must take after her mother,' Ali murmured as he tipped his head back to shave under his chin.

Charmaine laughed. 'You know very well, you arrogant devil, that there's hardly a scrap of me in her. She's you through and through. It seems you're one of those pre-potent sires.'

Ali stopped shaving, his eyes whipping round to stare at her with surprise. 'You have been reading my books on breeding horses.'

Her shrug was light. But inside, she was far from nonchalant. It wasn't her parents' presence so much making her nervous, but the news she had to tell him.

'I—er—I thought if I was going to be a stay-at-home mum, I would have to get interested in something. So I've decided to educate myself on the main topic of conversation around this place. On top of that, Cleo promised to teach me loads of card games for us to play together.'

'But that is wonderful!' Ali exclaimed.

'I'm glad you're pleased. Hopefully, you'll also be pleased with my other Christmas present.'

His dark brows drew together. 'Another Christmas present? But you have already given me a digital camera and the lovely clothes I will be wearing today. What else have you bought me?'

'It is not a present that can be bought, Ali.'

'Really? What, then?'

'I...I'm pretty sure I'm pregnant again. We're going to have another baby.'

'But I thought you could not conceive whilst you were breastfeeding.'

'It's not a sure-fire method of contraception. And Amanda's not having as much breast milk now that she's on solids. I haven't been to the doctor yet but my period is over a week late and the three home tests I used this week all turned blue.'

Ali put down his razor and reached out to take her into his arms. 'Another child,' he said. 'Now, that is the best Christmas present of all.'

'Maybe we will have a boy this time.'

'It does not matter. I would be just as happy with another girl.'

'But I thought…'

'You think too much sometimes.'

Charmaine sighed her relief. She'd been a bit worried that Ali might think it was too soon for her to have another baby. Or that he was set on having a boy. She wasn't all that keen on men—or cultures—who valued boy babies over girl babies.

'I would like a dozen children,' he said. 'And it would not matter if they were all girls. We are living in Australia, Charmaine, not Arabia.'

'But what about in your heart? Is a baby girl as important as a boy there?'

'How can you ask such a thing when my heart has already been captivated by the most beautiful girl in the world?'

'Oh…'

He took her chin with his fingers and gave it an affectionate squeeze. 'Come, do not cry.'

'I am crying with happiness.'

'Is that the truth? You are really, truly happy?'

'I never knew you could be this happy.'

Ali almost cried himself. 'I am going to kiss you

now. But only once. You know what happens if I kiss you twice.'

He kissed her. Then he kissed her again.

They were only a little late for dinner.